# Fortune's Hand

## R.N. MORRIS

# CONTENTS

My lost delights, now clean from sight of land,
Have left me all alone in unknown ways,
My mind to woe, my life in fortune's hand;
Of all which pass'd, the sorrow only stays.

Walter Raleigh, *Farewell to the Court*


Sir Walter Raleigh's head was separated from the rest of his body on the 29th of October, 1618.

Wikipedia tells us that Raleigh is 'well known as the populariser of tobacco'.

It also tells us that his last words, after he lay his neck upon the block, were: 'Strike, man, strike!'

And that his embalmed head was given to his wife Bess, who kept it in a velvet bag until her death.

Wikipedia does not tell us what was going through Walter's head as the blade struck.

# Oakfast

I see the acorn falling to the ground, full of energy and intent. The stippled cup splits. A tiny tongue licks out.

I see it. I see it all. Now.

This tongue, a shoot, parts the sodden ground, probing it with its insinuating tip. Taking root.

It is Nature's business to be questing.

I see this. Though it happens within the closed darkness of the soil.

The speed of it would take your breath away.

And above, another shoot hurtles upwards, a fine jet of living matter fired towards the Sun.

The stem writhes as it grows, whipping the air. It is almost too fast for itself, has not the strength to support its vaunting height. Quick, quick, quickening, it girds itself with growth, thickening into a sapling's adolescent tremor.

I see the parting and spreading of the roots, the restless subterranean colonisation. It is the nature of all life, the urge to encroach.

I see the orb of the heavens wheel about. I see the Sun on its ceaseless course, a bouncing ball across the horizon. The waxing and waning of countless moons. The slow strophes of an eternal dance sped up into a frantic jig.

I see the sapling's tremor steady as it takes on girth. The Sun warms its coarsening skin. It is lashed by downpours. Bent by winds. Pert and unbowed, it springs back, the stamp of its future stalwart nature already showing. It laps up the rain.

A fountain of tendrils shoots out from the stem, lightning thrown back at the sky: the young plant's first branches. No sooner have they waved themselves into rude existence, than a rash of green bursts over them. The leaves are lips that kiss the sky.

The elastic vigour quickly slackens. Autumn's golden cloak crackles like a benign fire over the branches.

Boughs thicken, effortlessly bearing their swaying burden. Acorns!

I see this.

I see the secret accretions building within. Each summer's growth encircling the last.

The tree stands its ground, chests itself out like a warrior, staking its claim for a corner of the forest. But is never still. Its thrusting energy strains ever outwards and upwards.

I see the acorn falling to the ground. I see a host of acorns falling. I see forests shooting up. I see the Earth colonised by the Empire of Oak.

And then I see them come into the forests. The men.

I see men differently now. The oak is more my brother.

The men are kindred with the mites that flit in the sunshine. With the spiders that weave between the leaves. With the woodlice and maggots that scuttle and twitch in the forest's darkest places.

They seek out the finest, grandest oak. I see them survey it with proprietary pride, abrogating its creation to their own account. It is theirs already. Its monumental steadfastness a challenge to their quicksilver wits.

They wield their axes with a sidelong swoop. Two men planting alternate blows, digging the future out of the tree's flesh with remorseless precision. The blows lack reverberation, empty dead clacks hushed up by the surrounding forest, as if in shame.

A pulpy wound deepens. The men's shoulders grow as their work progresses. I see the sweat on their brow, the crook of their wrist as they wipe it away.

A thunderclap cracks within the stricken tree. The men step back, their final blow a sharp nod of twin satisfaction. The forest quakes. The leaves shiver on the outspread tremble of branches. The tree topples into timber.

A horse as big as a dromedary drags it over to the saw pit. The men fall on it like locusts. It doesn't stand a chance against their savage rip saws and adzes. Their hearty muscular swinging of blades. Their oaths and earthy songs. Their cunning wielding of the unwieldy. I see the long flexing metal snap into shape, biting when bidden.

I see this happening all over the forest. Other men bringing low other trees. And in other forests, the same thing.

The forests are converted into open ground, piled high with massive logs.

But it is not over yet. The hurtling of the oak.

The stripped logs are rolled and loaded onto wagons, which hurtle and rattle along country lanes. Or they float in solid torrent towards a new becoming.

The Empire of Oak has been conquered, enslaved, transported. Now it will serve the Empire of Man.

It hurtles into the sawmill, eager for its reformation.

I see the fine, unrelenting teeth of enormous saws.

Water turns the wheel that drives the gang saw, a swinging chisel-toothed pendulum that measures the tree's end and the ship's beginning. It is somehow appropriate that water powers this transition.

I see the saw's teeth sink into the timber. Sawdust fills my eyes. I do not blink.

Sawing and hewing and rasping and shaping. A focused bustle of activity.

The men throw themselves at it, all hands to the latent decks.

I see the swift, smooth glide of the plane, as rough logs are tamed. The men peel off planks and beams and masts, the timbers of a preordained fleet.

Fleet! One word expresses the hastening destiny of the oak.

The raw wood hurtles on, to the shipyards now.

Here I see the timbers bent and beckoned into shape. The workmen stand sweating over pits of humid ash. Steam seeps into the grain, loosening the fibres of the wood, making malleable that unyielding matter. It is slow, aching, patient work. But to my eyes, it happens in an instant. The great wood beams curl like furled paper.

The hefting and hammering begins. The shaped timbers offered up and butted, joints mallet-slammed together. A skeleton of oak forms. The boards fly onto it, as fast as the ruffling of a hawk's feathers. I see the nails fly into the boards, the neat carvel hull complete in the unblinking of my eyes. This is not industry, it is conjuring. The wood of six-hundred trees flies together to form one ship.

Miles of rigging, the ropes from Muscovy, the cordage wound and bound into dense bundles, all are hauled on board and stowed. The folded sails are borne with reverence and ceremony, sacraments on a vast scale.

I see the towering masts rise up. And hear the cheer that rises with them. I smell the tar that caulks the keel.

The quarters are subdivided and fitted, before the mainmast for the men, behind the mainmast for the gentlemen and officers. Chisels snout out details. Abrasive blocks wear away the wood's last coarseness. Under the master carpenter's overseeing eye, beneath the touch of his fine, critical fingers, a perfect surface emerges. He blows away the flecks that mar it.

And now a carnival, a riotous assembly. Exultant colour splashes onto primed and burnished ornamenting. The brushes dance in the artisans' hands. But the music that accompanies this is a solemn death march. The sonorous rumble of the guns manoeuvred into place.

This is what it has all been about, so far, the placing of the guns. For what is this vessel but a courier of cannon fire? The cargo it will trade in: death.

The ovens are built, deep in the ship's belly. In a universe of wood, the fire must be held in brick prisons.

I see the barrels of supplies, the salted meat and fish, the hard tack, the casks of pickled and dried produce, the butts of drinking water, beer and brandy. And the livestock too. The capons and chickens. The goats. Sustenance for the men who will set the course, steer the ship, climb the rigging, swab the decks, for those who will drink and swear and brawl, who will man the watch, who will sicken and die, who will live to tell the tale. But above all, for the men who will load and aim and fire the cannon, for that is what they are all about.

I see them now, the crew, filing on. They bring with them a couple of cats and a dog, platters and tankards and backgammon boards, playing cards, knives – for cutting food, whittling wood and settling arguments – fiddles, whistles, bass viol and drum, even a portative organ for the captain's company of musicians. One or two may bring a Bible or some other, more dangerous tract.

I see them teem over the decks, a flood of life, raucous and unruly. There is a whetted edge to them, sharp enough to kill. They have that glint in their eyes, a keen hunger: they are avid for movement and action and plunder. They see the prize already. They look into the empty hold and see its expected cargo manifest. The plate, the coins, the gold.

I have looked through eyes like theirs.

And now I see the floodgates open. I see the inundation. The dry dock is no more. The ship at last is in her element.

Another cheer, as the men feel the kick of buoyancy enter their legs, the sudden, giddy instability that can reduce even the saltiest dog to sickness. They know there is no going back. The water will bear them to their destiny.

The hurtling continues. The onrush of oak.

The first commands go out. The sails are raised. The cries of the men are lusty and eager. They are pulling together, with a common purpose. The river widens into estuary. The tide, the wind, the gulls concur. The ocean opens up before them.

But it is not just this one ship I see. I see others too. Setting sail from other shipyards. On other days. (The links of time have been unchained for me now. The minutes, hours and days do not connect. It is one of the ways I see things differently.)

A great hurtling from the forest to the sea.

The energy and intent of the acorn.

All this I see.

## Seedburst

I see my own begetting.

The burst of seed from my father's cock, buried in the seedbed of my mother's cunt. I hear her gasps of rapture. His half angry grunt of release. Be assured, these are things no man wishes to witness. I am no different in that. But my unblinking eyes…

I see it. The especial delight my father takes in his cavorting beneath the canopy he had cut from a clerical cope. You must have heard talk of that legendary cope, purloined from a rebellious church that once dared to detain him. That will teach those damned Papist swine.

I see the ruby darkness within my mother's womb. I see the formation of my own limbs. My tiny grasping fingers flex and reach and practise pointing. The eternally replicated genesis. It is Nature's way, Nature's reach. My beginning is merely Nature's continuation. My greed, Nature's greed.

My mother's matter rushes into me with the throb and pulse of her great heart. I am dwarfed and drowned and deafened by her heart. It is my sun. I am warmed by it. Nourished by it.

These are not memories, these visions. It is simply that I see everything now. And my ever-open eyes admit more than vision. All sense, all feeling, all understanding, comes to me through my eyes.

I test my limbs, kicking out like a submerged frog. But there is nowhere for my leg to go. The soft membrane that nurtured me is now my prison.

And all the time, the tiny hurtling of my cells continues. A second pulse beats counterpoint to my mother's heart, my own. The thunder of my becoming.

My frog's legs kick out with intent now, not testing but manoeuvring. I know what is expected of me. I am ripe. I have come to fruition. The term is up. I will tear apart this prison of flesh, I will show no mercy, if that is what it takes. Again, this is Nature's way. I am part of Nature. My purpose is Her purpose.

I feel the universe quake. But I am not afraid. I know that my will and the will of the universe are one.

I am propelled. The dark soft prison splits asunder. I feel the first shock of air in my lungs! My eyes are there inside my neonatal lungs to see the vaporous inrush, to witness that first expansion, my lungs filled, like a sail catching the wind, I am on my way, I am launched!

I see my mother's tears of relief and joy. She sees – and hears! – that I am alive, I am healthy. I am a boy. Suddenly it strikes her, she is alive too. Her tears turn to laughter. Her pain is forgotten. She holds out her arms to take me from the midwife. I am bloody and screaming and never still. A sudden new intractable knot of being, another someone to be grappled with and appeased. And I see that she is as amazed by me as I am amazed by me. I am in the world.

My hands are still grasping, will always be grasping.

My eyes swivel wildly, my gaze is cast out to swim and float and bait and catch.

And the hunger. I feel the hunger from the first.

My mother's scent is home to me, I nuzzle into it and find a teat. My smacking lips, my hard hungry gums latch on.

I am trussed up like an Aegyptian mummy, a biggin on my baby noggin. I cannot even tread water in the air. I am held by firm but loving arms.

I am pulled in two directions. This is my nature. I am tidal.

I cut my teeth on coral, a foretaste of my life to come.

I see things hidden to the greatest doctors of our age, an occult universe beyond their wit to understand, or their dreams to encompass.

I see the first eager contractions of my gullet as my mother's milk rushes into me. Its warmth floods me. I feel its strength become mine. My tiny fingers grip more tightly.

I am even able to see the closing of my fontanelle. What eyes are these!

I see that I am part of the ceaseless motion of the world. Even as I sleep, the world hurtles, and I with it.

I am a cannonball of flesh fired into the world. I hurtle from my mother's fragrant lap, between my brothers' and my half brothers' legs, towards my father's arms, I'm quaking with giggles as I evade his bearded leer and bony fingers at the last. He lets me go. I see that now. It's all in the game, the terrorising and the threat of tickles. When I think I'm safe, *away!*, his hand snaps out and catches me and pulls me back and throws me up and turns me round and shakes and spins me till I throw up giddy happy sick.

'Oh, now look what you've made him do!' says mother.

Father laughs and lets me go, with a hefty wallop on the rear to send me on my way.

I run through a forest of uncles, aunts, the numberless cousins of varying degrees of removal. There is a common something to their eyes as they condescend to regard me, a wry, teasing mockery: fundamentally benign. If they affect contempt it is only to arm me for the contempt of the world. For they are my family. And whether they will or not, they must love me. The Raleghs, Champernownes, Gilberts, and even the distant elevated Dennys and Carews... I am bound to them all with fine silken hawsers.

The men have muscled calves in brightly coloured hose. The women, mountainous skirts. If anything can distract me from my breakneck course, it is the skirts. Or rather, the sumptuous materials from which they are sewn. They have the power to turn my head, to entrance me, the damasks, silks and satin weaves, the golden threads, the gossamer lace, the silver embroidery on cream-coloured linen.

The most splendid dress of all stops me in my tracks. I look up to see what fabulous creature is so bedecked. Pearls like tiny blind eyes sewn along the seams. My Aunt Kat smiles down at me.

'He'll go far, this one!'

I have caught the eye of the family's star, governess to the princess royal.

I giggle, store it up, and take her at her word.

I run. And keep running, gathering strength and speed as my legs grow beneath me: they bear me taller with each lengthening step.

Out of the house I run. Through the kitchen garden: borage, basil, rosemary and sage, for now a mere blur of nameless scents. Past the lettuce and the lovage. Past the startled pigs and the disapproving hens. Past the coriander and thyme. Their scents are hooks cast into my memory.

The sun bursts between the shimmering leaves, filling the spaces with a gentle pearly fire. And yet, with what breathtaking carelessness, I run past it.

Out of the garden gate, I bolt.

There is a forest there, at the end of our garden path. It lies between our cob-built house and the sea.

One swift backward glance, but I do not falter or tarry. My course is set. Onwards, into the forest, towards the sea. Away from the homely glint in an upstairs window, the twist of woodsmoke above the chimney.

I run along the path worn in the red earth, the same red earth from which our house was stitched.

I hear a voice, a distant voice, distinctly call my name. The shock of it perturbs my heart into a still more frantic pounding. I stand afeared. Some sprite beckons me. Or the forest has found voice... but no, the voice comes from beyond the forest. I look back. The cob house is nowhere to be seen. I am alone in the forest. I find my legs again and run towards the dying echo.

I burst out of the forest, and the land vanishes beneath me. My legs wheel in the air. But I land on my feet on the sand below. The sea applauds my dashing entrance, as if the beach is the world's stage. Waves rush up, falling over themselves to greet me. I do not stop running.

My stride spans lines of latitude in a single bound. My reach can plumb the ocean's depths, or pull up gleaming nuggets from the earth's dark bowels. I feel such capacity within me. I see the golden aura that surrounds me and sustains me. But I see too – these eyes will not be blind to anything! – I see the plump, wriggling worm of doubt that nibbles away from within, like a moth folded away in a fabulous suit of clothes.

I see it inside me as I vault over my fear, leaping into the unknown, coming down heavy on a transport.

This is the point at which my destiny meets the destiny of the acorn. The thud of my boot as it hits the deck.

## Crossing

The ship bucks like an untamed stallion beneath my feet. An armoured fist of nausea pummels me from within, resentful and sour and unforgiving. The slop of vomit over the side brings no relief.

With lurching step I circle the deck. But movement is no remedy, nor is throwing myself down to hunch against the gunwales.

I am tossed heavenward. A grim, pewter-dark heaven today, devoid of angels. They're all off dancing on a pinhead somewhere. An atheist's heaven. My bony boy's backside parts company with the unyielding wood. My guts remain suspended as the rest of me plummets.

Salt water spray stings my eyes to tears. I'm drenched and shivering. And can see no end to this torture.

There are pale lumpy pools of vomit all over the decks. The times I venture to flee my misery, I slip in someone else's.

Beneath us, the frightened horses in the hold shit themselves prodigiously. The stink of that is not helping.

My company is divided: between the surly and dejected (I count myself one of this number); and the strange, mad breed who seem to take delight in all of this. They stand at the bow and taunt the waves as they crash around them. They laugh like devils at each gut-mangling roll of the ship, as if they are at the tilts and this is some courtly tourney, not the last listing of a frail bark on a death-fraught sea. One degree deeper on the starboard side and we are sunk, I swear.

The leering devils raise cheers as the ship tips us over. The further we roll, the louder their hurrahs.

They dance around the mizzenmast, like maids around the maypole.

I know these men. They are men of the West. Men born facing the sea, as was I. I know the cut of their jib, even if I do not know their names. I have seen that selfsame covetous, exultant leer in my brothers and my half-brothers, and in my father too, in his more piratical moods. For them, Death is just another magistrate at whom to cock a snook.

'Are we not having a merry time of it!' cries one.

We are brothers in arms, united in our endeavour, and in our Religion. Of one company and one heart. But the man who cries that out, the moment he cries it out, I swear I hate him with a keener passion than I have ever hated a Papist. And if I had strength to move, I would happily kill the wretch. Upon my oath, I would.

'What's that, young Wat?'

Ah, it is my cousin, Henry. One of the Champernownes. That is to say, a cousin on my mother's side.

He is one of the exultant crew, the most exultant of them all. For we are his men. His words have brought us this far. The gleam in his eye has fired up us all. He has fought the Turk in Hungary. It shows in his eye: the glamour of Death is in his eye.

It is *that* we follow, *that* we trust, that cold, clear acquaintance with Death. It is the source of his authority, for he carries no commission from our Queen. And if we are in any doubt, he marches under a black banner, and every man of us looks up to it.

He stands now, as tall as a mast, to rally the spirits of the weak-bellied in his troop. His voice booms out from a plated chest. His words hush the crashing sea.

'Friends, countrymen, true believers, be not in any doubt: today the faithless Papist pigs are bent on the destruction of our Huguenot cousins. If we do nothing, if we stand back and allow this slaughter, then tomorrow they will come after us. They will come after our mothers, our wives, our daughters and our sisters. Will you allow *that*? A pox-ridden French Papist to force his suppurating crosier between your mother's legs? You will allow it? They will burn our homes and starve our children. You will allow it? Like thieves in the night, they will cut our throats while we sleep. You will allow it? For tell me this, who will come to our aid in our hour of need? Not our French cousins, the Huguenots, for they will all be dead. Believe me, the Papist will not rest until every last true believer is slaughtered. This small stretch of water will not stand in his way. He will lap up these waves, believing them no doubt to be the blood of Christ. A storm? This? This is nothing to a Papist! He will not be deterred by a roiling sea. He will not hang his head and cower, praying to be back home, tucked up in his bed. I see him now, this Papist dog, looking out from the prow of his ship for the first sight of England. He is already thinking of the Devonshire virgins he will deflower. And you will allow it? Stand up, step forward! Find your legs! Be men! Be *English* men! Remember your faith. Hold true to your faith. Heed not the buffeting of the waves. This is a trial sent to test your mettle. Soon, soon, it will pass. Soon, we will put ashore. And I promise you French doxies to cavort upon! What buffetings will you see then! And I promise you Papist churches to despoil! What treasures there for you to strip away!'

We are borne up and along by his words, into the port of La Rochelle at last.

The hooves of the horses clip crisply on the boards of the pier. I spit the sour taste of the crossing into the water.

The clouds part at our arrival, pierced by the sky-blue cones of the harbour turrets. The beaming sun seems suddenly pleased to see us. We are met by the glance of bold corsairs as they supervise the barefaced unburdening of their racing galleons. The indiscriminate sun shines on their endeavours too. The swaying masts nod connivance. Sumptuous bolts of Dutch cloth, no doubt once intended for a Cardinal's vestry, are now coveted by the harbour whores. With these clairvoyant eyes, I even see inside the padlocked chests, at the plundered bullion within. I see the sweet Canary sack inside the great butts stacked upon the dockside. And my gaze is stung as it plunges into the dense-packed dark interiors of spice casks.

We grin back at the corsairs, delighting in their prizes and their plunder. We know whence it has come and who has been injured in its taking. A merry game's afoot. We are eager now to join the fray. All sickness and fear forgotten, we sit tall in the saddle and take the sun's benediction in our horses' stride.

Onwards, my will is always to go onwards. But war has a will of its own and there is always delay. The town is fortified and tense, the enemy expected daily. We cannot simply march out; we must first receive our marching orders.

We kick our heels and spend the time as waiting soldiers are wont to do. One of those Canary butts has somehow found its way into our keeping, a gift from a grateful Huguenot no doubt. It does not keep long in our company. And now we lurch around the city as once we lurched around the ship, vomiting as liberally too.

I have fallen in with the leering, exultant rabble, the devils.

They seem to accept me. I am only fourteen, but tall for my age. Taller than many men. And I am gifted with a quick wit and a cutting tongue that belies my youthfulness. I can proffer an occasional pun upon provocation, and an oath upon another; such trifles seem to pass for wit among them. Do they know that I am Henry Champernowne's cousin? Or is there something of my own, some distinct quality in me, that wins them over?

They call me their golden talisman, believing that I will bring them luck. It suits me to encourage them in this belief, although I do not, quite, believe it myself.

In matters of gaming, they are the makers of their own luck. To begin with, I am their dupe. I wonder at the speed with which they empty my purse. My wonder wins them over. It pleases them to recruit me to their roguery and initiate me in the secrets of their conveyances. They teach me how to chop a card. They train me in the part of Barnacle when they employ Barnard's Law. That is to say, now I play the false dupe in duping others.

And as we rampage through the cowering town, I perceive that somehow it has come about that I am no longer led but am their leader. *They look to me!* And I a mere boy who has never set foot in this place before.

'This way! My cunning nose smells French queans!'

We are drawn by music to a tavern. And it is held as my great accomplishment to have led us there.

The smell of tallow dips and table slops, a sudden blast of noise, the door thrown open on a secret, dimly flickering world. I am carried across the threshold by my fellows. Their cheer is absorbed by the angry clamour of a place that is at once foreign and familiar to them.

The music comes from a viol de gamba and a set of bagpipes, played with demonic fixity by two furious-looking musicians. Indeed, the general mood of the tavern is easily mistaken for hostility and our roistering entrance seems out of place. The paltry French I have does not equip me to understand what is being said around us. I am not afraid though, for I have my own devils about me.

I soon see that what I took for hostility is nothing other than despair. But when the locals there learn that we are English volunteers come over to fight their cause against the Papist foe, we are handed flagons and black jacks, filled to the top with a sharp strong cider. The wenches of the house are put at our disposal.

The comeliest of them (I swear she is!) lifts her skirts for me. With a smile I find quite irresistible. My father's words of warning against French whores and their pox are ringing in my ears. But her smile, I told you it was irresistible. And I cannot back out of this. My fellows are at my back, slapping me into her, the nameless girl, so willing and ready for me.

How can I describe that first encompassing? In one moment, I am opened up, my questing soul embodied, it is in the nature of things, this questing, thrusting, this going out of ourselves into something else. And all of me, all the sensation that I am capable of, is contained in this clenched ache of flesh, this question asked of a stranger's body. Then I am all encompassed. She is all about me. Her warmth. Her merry, wet, enfolding warmth. And a memory of a time before memory, of a state before grace and its loss, rushes over me and completes me.

I hurtle into her and out of myself. There is another cheer at my coming. I am slapped on the back. A belt whips across my buttocks for good measure.

## War

Bursting out of La Rochelle with a clatter of eager hooves. We send our voices out before us. Flinging English songs into the whistling French wind, with a derry down, down hey, derry down.

Before long the eagerness goes out of our step. The wind sets our teeth clashing so fitfully we can barely force the d-d-d-derry downs out. Churned mud sucks at our onset. What quagmire is this that we have stumbled into?

We shiver in our saddles, benumbed beneath clouds as black as our banner, as doom-laden as our motto: *Let valour end my life.* Then out of the clouds hurtle hailstones the size of cannon shot. The heavy weather rattles off our armour. It is fruitless to check at the blows. One strikes me squarely in the face.

The hail abates. Our relief is short-lived. A league from Jazeneuil, on the road to Poitiers, word spreads down the line: the hated enemy is at last in sight. It is to be our first chance of engagement, and likely our last before winter sets in. I grind my spurs into my horse's flanks to goad her on. I have no fear that I will die. Life has me in its grip; I am too dear to it, too precious a jewel to be tossed aside. Life, I believe, will guard me jealously.

I stand in my stirrups and lean forward into the Future's blast. This is my Destiny. It is the reason I was born. Proof I am alive.

But the chaos and confusion of the action appals me. We, the horse, leap blindly over the ditches within which our infantry are entrenched. Contingents of our army are separated, only drawn together by the sound of field artillery. We cannot see the forces towards which we charge. The Papist commander has filled the plain with smoke, out of which the lethal lead whips and whistles.

All around me I hear the chiming of countless dainty bells, a pleasant metal trilling.

It is the stinging smoke, I swear, that provokes the tears. Not the explosion of pain and nausea as I land heavy in the saddle after a badly judged jump. It goes through my head that I have most surely burst my bollocks. But it is the smoke, not that, that brings the tears.

The smoke dissipates. I am surrounded by empty horses. Suddenly I understand what betokened the chiming of those dainty bells: twas the ringing of armour as it is pierced by lead shot.

History records the encounter as a mere skirmish. By the sound of the word, a skittish, merry, trivial thing. It is over as soon as it began. Our enemy is gone with the drifting smoke. And our ranks are somewhat thinned. We leave the field. Our horses lift their hooves fastidiously as we pick our way between the fallen. It is a mistake to look down. But a mistake to which we all succumb. I see a man with his face blasted off and another with a shredded bloody stump at the end of his arm. Absurdly, my gaze scurries about the field searching out his missing hand.

The leader of the Huguenot forces, the prince of Condé, Louis de Bourbon, is pointed out to me. He has the reputation of a fearless soldier. And yet I am shocked by the figure he cuts.

'What? That shrunken hunchback?'

The prince glares in my direction as if he has heard me. And in that glance I understand;: what has spurred him into action has been the sting of such remarks. He perches high on a massive charger, its size in some way compensating for his own diminished person. Despite the curvature of his spine, he holds his head tilted upwards, away from the men with their faces blasted off, and the limbs strewn on the ground as if they are seeds for another army.

And suddenly I feel sicker than ever I did on the crossing over. We have braved all this for such a man? I will later learn that in his time he has professed both the Roman superstition and the true faith, as great a turncoat in religion as he is in other matters.

We gather and face the enemy again, but this time there is no hurtling on either side. Each has tasted what the other may do. And so we stand off, and wait for winter to release us from the obligation to slaughter.

As if by some secret agreement, both sides back away from the fight at the same moment on the third day. I hope that it will never be said that I am a coward, whatever else is alleged against me. I have seen death now. I accept it is a possibility, even for a gilded youth such as I am. But I own it rankles with me to imagine the prince of Condé refusing to look down at my fallen body.

We ride into a snow storm. We cannot see the man in front of us. Can barely see our own mount's neck. We trust to the shouts of our fellows to keep formation.

When the storm blows over, the sky is stark and bereft. The way has vanished beneath unfathomed depths of white. We have become separated from the rest of the army. Our horses high-step through virgin drifts. All we can do is continue in the direction we are facing. We pray God keep us on the hidden road. But the featureless land tests our blind faith.

There are days of this.

We grow hungry, as well as saddle-sore and rawly cold. The only relief is to sleep as we ride. One man falls from his horse. Icicles colonise his beard. We leave him where he lies, the ground too hard for grave-digging. Nor is there any foraging to be had in this frozen vastness. Not even kindling for a campfire.

We descry a black ant toiling across the middle distance and hie towards it. The ant is discovered to be a bundled peasant who hurries his step at our approach. He ignores our cries of Hold! So that we reckon him to be either deaf or witless or worse…

My cousin addresses him in courteous French but receives no reply. Not even upon the drawing of his sword. The man keeps on with head bowed and dogged step. Clearly he has nothing that we may take from him. His death would serve no purpose other than to relieve the white tedium with a splash of crimson. And so my cousin sheaths his sword again.

We fall into sullen step behind our unwitting guide. He walks us back to a trodden road, where we part company with him. Soon we encounter a troop of German rheiters and hear from them the latest news of battles and bloodlettings. The slaughter to a man of a whole company of their compatriots has left them vengeful.

The snow is packed to a sleek glass. We rejoin the line, marching with foot soldiers who regularly lose their footing. In truth, I doubt the wretches can feel their feet, which skid wildly beneath them. It is not unusual to see a man fall and pull his fellows down on top of him. The first time this happens, it is met with mirth. By the third, fourth, and tenth, all good humour has evaporated. Each man blames the other and they fall to squabbling and blows. Their commander restores order with a pistolet shot over their heads. He swears that the next man to fall will be shot dead. We make no progress at all now, the men too fearful to set one frozen toe in front of another.

The horses fare little better, though they have the advantage in being quadrupedal.

Let valour end my life? Vain hope: we are more likely to fall from our saddles and crack our skulls open. Or famine will take us, or the cold.

By some means, we reach the main camp. The supplies that were meant to see the army through the winter are all but spent and we have hardly tasted of them. The foraging sorties take longer every day and produce daily diminishing returns. It is a close run thing whether winter or warfare will carry off more of our number. We huddle around meagre fires.

The thaw begins. Mounds of snow dwindle into pools of standing water, which a constant drizzle replenishes. My frozen bones are the last of me to feel the warmth. How old am I now? Old enough to have seen death in diverse forms. Old enough to have prayed for it to come bring an end to my sufferings.

I have a past now, something I am propelled away from, as likewise I have a future towards which I hurtle.

And that death-informed gleam in my cousin Champernowne's eye, it no longer strikes me as exceptional.

We are on the road again, though the road is just another long quagmire to trudge through. I feel the pull of my twofold nature, ebb and flood. I long for onrush but think often of that cob-built house in Devon.

The Prince of Condé races on ahead of us, chasing his reputation, not waiting for reinforcements, carelessly leading four hundred horsemen to their death at Jarnac. The fearless soldier himself surrenders, no doubt reckoning to switch back to the Papist side. But some Papist pistolier has other ideas and shoots him in the eye at close range. And now it is the Prince of Condé who lies with his face blasted off.

The Papists raise a cheer. The murmured rumour of his death reaches us like a swarm of buzzing flies departing his corpse. It surprises me how sadly dejected are the Huguenots by this loss. I little liked what little I saw of the man. There are those who will say he died a hero's death. I say rather that he died the death of a vain fool. Those men that died with him were the heroes.

My gaze is a sheet of vengeful flame that shoots out across the countryside, burning crops and razing villages, smoking Papists out of their hiding places. My gaze is the flash of a sword at a child's throat. My gaze is the fist that bruises a French wench's cheek. My gaze, the hands that force apart her legs. My gaze shoots inside her with an angry thrust. My gaze is the outspread palm that pushes back her screams of protest.

This is how we fight back. I make weapons of my eyes.

## A damask sea

My foot stamps on English soil once more. And the sound, unsentimental land kicks back, a blunt walloping welcome home. I feel it in my bones.

I hurtle eastward, shedding my smoke-scented, blood-spattered soldier's garb along the way, exchanging it briefly for a scholar's gown in Oxford. But Oxford does not detain me. I have no patience for its particular species of learning. In truth, I learnt more at my mother's lap. To see her deft hands fillet a book, to hear the words form on her lips, to discover the worlds of meaning within: the adventures that may be undertaken, the treasures that may be unearthed, the heavens scaled, all without stirring from the hearth. This becomes a part of me, another of her mother's gifts: my ever-roaming mind, the swinging compass of my restless body.

Into London I burst. To my dismay London hurtles back at me heedless and undaunted, my manifest excellence set at naught. It is almost as if London believes it has seen the like of me before!

I am swallowed into a tide of bustling busybodies. We are each the pattern of the other. Young men all of vaunting ambition, but of various means and accomplishments. We rush along the teeming muddy streets, one hand on our sword, kicking our pattens through puddles, skipping the shit heaps where we can, our nether hoses hourly more spotted and mired, sniffing out our prospects among the divers stews, stinks and savours of the City, listening for the rumour of advancement between the cries of costermongers and the rabble's riotous carousing (to which, on occasion, we add voice). My ears are attuned to the West Country lilt, the indolent caressing rhythm, words slipping like kisses from a curling lip. I can pick it out at a hundred paces. I follow its murmur to Lyon's Inn and thence to Middle Temple. The places where my cousins congregate. I linger there too, hoping for some of their understanding to rub off on me. It might profit a man of fortune to have a smattering of the Law. And the Inns have served many as a conduit to Court.

But then I see that there is something that will profit me more than moots.

The thing is, you see, the crux, the rub, the nub of it, one must stand out from one's fellows. Lawyers are ten a penny in this City. A lawyer's gown, a dreary uniform. To play the part, one must first look the part. And I have set my heart on a part to play.

I hurry to a house by the well in Aldgate, where Leadenhall meets Fenchurch Street. There a tailor keeps his workshop, at the sign of the Golden Shears.

We settle on the details of my outfit, taking Leicester's image for a model. Naturally I would have more buttons, and pearls sewn into the seams, and a further set of tabbed embroidered wings at the shoulders. The trunkhose paned as Leicester's are, though perhaps a touch more swollen. And a cloak, of course. The latter to be lined in gold silk. We fix a date a week hence for my fitting. And agree a fee for the clothes.

The fee presents some difficulties as it exceeds the sum of my worldly wealth. I betray no qualms to the tailor, affecting a lordly bow as I depart his workshop.

I pass the days pacing the Temple, circulating the church where petitioners and patrons gather. I do not wish to be taken for a demander, so I cultivate the air of a man by no means in need of funds. All around me, men dissemble and dissimulate. It is ever thus. I remember the Prince of Condé putting on the mask of religion to further his ambition. And so I strut and swagger like a duke. Scattering coins to the canting beggars, the upright men, the Abram men and cripples alike.

 It is too demeaning to offer one's self for hire like a servant. (Besides, I have two servants of my own to support, the brothers Pansfurthe.) But I find ways to be of service to my friends. Alas, man cannot live on favours owed. For not all of my friends have the means to show their appreciation in a manner I can use to pay my tailor. And even those that have, affect not to understand my pressing need. Such friends a man can ill afford.

Round and round that ancient monument I revolve, like the hand of a giant clock face, marking time but going nowhere. With these all-seeing eyes of mine, I picture the tailor's great shears cutting through the blue damask, like a ship holding its course on the high sea. I must reach the means to pay for the suit before his shears reach the edge of the cloth.

### Cozening

Tiny tongues of light lap the gloom.

I look up at a dizzying cascade of beams and rafters. The great oak ceiling is like the inside of an upturned ship. The thought brings a wave of queasy seasick giddiness at the world turned topsy-turvy. My gaze falls upwards. My imagination sails away, seeking some Northwest Passage of the sky, buoyed up on the dreams and discourse of my friends.

I even hear the shriek of a parrot and see it swoop between the hammerbeams.

The voices of the Middle Temple benchers bring me back to earth. They are at their supper, already in their cups, a rowdier crowd than any I rubbed shoulders with at Oxford. I dare say they could even give the La Rochelle rabble a run for their money. Faces garish in the candlelight, their shouts drown out the haughty lutenists in the gallery.

Sullen clerks, obliged to serve at table to make ends meet, look down on the slobbering law students as they pass between them. They run along the length of the table, topping up goblets, clattering down platters, tripping over slumbering dogs. And what a length of table it is. A gift from the Queen, its planks were hewn from one immense Windsor oak and floated down the Thames.

I see the slow, clanking journey of the patient wood, clogging the bends of the river with unyielding length.

I see the table pieced together and the hall built around it.

Cards dance in my hands. The Queen of Hearts trips a merry galliard with the King of Spades. And now executes a volte with the Knave of Diamonds. Sinkapace, sinkapace, where's the Ace?

I have not forgotten the conveyances taught me by my comrades in La Rochelle.

I have sought out my cousin Richard Carew and his crew in order to cheat them out of a pretty penny for a handsome suit of clothes. If my kinsmen will not voluntarily surrender the purse for me to pursue my career, I must find a way to take it from them. So I cozen my cousins and fleece my friends. Have I no shame? Not so's you'd notice. Never had much use for it.

I am abetted by the dim, unsteady light of the hall, and by my opponents' sack-dimmed wits. I have a fondness for the loosening pleasures of sack myself. But if you would know the one secret of card-sharping, it is simply this: always drink less than those you play against. I have prepared the ground too, having deliberately lost, in a small way, the last time I gamed with Carew. To his mind, I am the gull. More than that, he thinks me a good fellow well met. For my own quick wit and merry tongue also come into play. I have often found that the better a man likes me, the easier it is to con him.

All sides get something out of it. They have the enjoyment of my company. They laugh and slap their thighs as they hand over their money. Once again, as in La Rochelle, I am pet, mascot, talisman. So entertained are they by my jests and teases, they seem not to see that I am robbing them blind.

The real trick is to know when to quit. I make to rise from table. Carew reaches out a hand to stay me.

'No, no, Ralegh, you cannot leave us now. You must give us a chance to win it back.'

'Have I not already taken you for all you have?'

'We will write promissory notes.'

'And if you lose, you will be in my debt. It would be ungentle of me to lead you to the Clink.'

'Our luck is set to change. You cannot win all night.'

'Which is why I choose to leave the table now. Adieu.'

'But whither are you?'

'I wish to speak with Richard Hakluyt.'

'You are planning a voyage?'

My cousin's grip tightens. He uses me to hoist himself to his feet. The rest of his crew follow his lead. This is vexing. My business with Hakluyt is my business alone. But to make a secret of it would be to pique their interest further.

'You may come if you wish.'

I catch a flash of gaudy wings flapping overhead and follow the swooping parrot to the shoulder of Richard Hakluyt. He keeps the bird as his pet and has trained it to come for tidbits. This Hakluyt is about twenty years my senior, and a barrister. He is a silver-bearded, skull-capped wizard of a man. He is in the company of his cousin and ward, another Richard Hakluyt, a friend of mine from my Oxford days.

He was but a boy when first he fell under his cosmographic cousin's spell. Their imaginations have travelled further than any one of us men of seafaring families. They are forever poring over maps and globes, charting voyages which they will never undertake. Indeed Richard Hakluyt the elder has made a map of his dinner. One slice of mutton serves as the coast of America. Another he has roughly shaped to represent Europe. Between them stands an Atlantic Ocean of meaty juice, across which he navigates a bark of gristle. He steers the ship northwards and westwards with his dagger blade.

At our approach, he spears the American land mass and hurriedly bites off a portion. He hunches conspiratorially over his geographic dinner, protecting it from predatory gaze, and eyes my entourage warily.

'Greetings, Ralegh. You have in your wake a fleet of followers, I see.'

'Empty vessels. I have taken everything from them.'

Richard Carew takes my jibe in good part:

'Is there any hope for us, Master Hakluyt? We would happily recapture what we have lost. Can you chart us a route to riches?'

'If you want my advice, exchange your playing cards for a pack of navigator's cards.'

'We need no persuading of that. We are all West-countrymen, born within a spit of the sea's spray. But whither set our course? And how to navigate through the Scylla and Charybdis of Spanish hegemony and Barbary pirates?'

'There is a way.'

The younger Richard Hakluyt is fired by the desire to command attention. To hold the room in his thrall by some thrilling revelation.

The elder intervenes, his eyes flashing a wary warning: 'Not here.'

I scan the room with a quick, sceptical interest.

'There are spies here, in Middle Temple hall?'

'There is a surfeit here of over-educated and under-remunerated youth. The pinch of poverty makes men unscrupulous. And a lack of prospects may force an otherwise upright fellow to bend his principles in order to fill his purse. Any here may turn intelligencer for a foreign cause. Or they may seek to turn our intelligence to their advantage. In short, to beat us to it.'

Richard Hakluyt the elder rises to his feet. The parrot squawks and takes wing. The lawyer spreads his gown, as if he would fly after it.

## Drunk on geography

Every surface is strewn with maps and charts; even the walls have windows to distant worlds pinned upon them. Cartographical and cosmographical treatises lie open.

The eye is entranced by the array of mechanical contrivances and models: a working orrery, several quadrants, a collection of astrolabes and globes. It seems as if the whole room is a machine whose function is to ravage the imagination and enflame enthusiasm.

The elder Richard Hakluyt stands amidst it all, a wand in one hand to conjure up the known world, naming each feature as he points it out to us: first the Old World, the territories and terrains of Europe, Africa and Asia. He takes us on detours along meandering rivers, we traverse vast deserts in a trice, scale towering mountain ranges, penetrate dense forests. He guides us east through the towns of the Hanseatic League, into Muscovy and Cathay, the alien place names rolling off his tongue with native ease although he has never ventured farther east than Kent.

Oh, the alchemy of trade! It is the means by which we may transmute Cornish lead to gold.

But the bloated empire of the Spaniard squats across our way, and the rapacious Turk lies in wait to unburden us of our cargo.

In two taps of the wand's tip we have crossed an ocean to the New World. The very land spews forth gold. Its every rock is seamed with ore. Cast nets for salmon and you will catch nuggets. This rarest, most precious of metals is so prevalent there that the native Indians value it at naught. They eat their dinners off of it! In such abundance is it that one of their princes suffers himself to be regularly covered head to toe in gold dust, which he then washes off in a lake. The lake is silted with gold from the frequent bathings of this Golden Man. If any of us would find this lake and dredge it, we would make Golden Men of ourselves, and earn the fervent gratitude of our sovereign.

We are quickly drunk on geography. A bust of Ptolemy looks out from a niche and winks in silent approval.

But my cousin Carew is a melancholy drunk: 'The Spanish have already conquered that continent. There will be nothing left for us.'

Says the elder Hakluyt: 'They are as gnats upon the hide of an elephant. We may easily find some other part of the beast to settle upon. Even now, our friend Martin Frobisher is making ready an exploratory expedition that will lay the seeds for future colonies.'

He turns to me.

'Your brother, Sir Humphrey, has been most energetic in the endeavour. The funds are very nearly in place. The Queen has let it be known she will not stand in the way, and Captain Frobisher has received instruction, compass and maps from the eminent scientist, Dr John Dee of Mortlake. I have in my possession the copy of a map drawn by an Italian cartographer which clearly shows the existence of the Straits of Anián. This irrefutable passage not only opens up the possibility of trade with China, unmolested by Imperial galleons, it also gives us a means to attack the Spanish interests in America on two fronts.'

'But isn't it too cold to go over the top of America? By all accounts, the sea is frozen there.'

'Not so, friend Carew. You are forgetting that the sea is salt water. As Dr Dee teaches us all, science will be the navigator's friend.'

Happily enlightened, we nod for him to go on.

'Emboldened by our successes, we will wrest from the Spaniard control of his vital island assets of Cuba and Hispaniola. In a few bold decisive manoeuvres, America is ours.'

Now the younger Richard Hakluyt unrolls a scroll: 'The first step in all this is the establishment of a colony on the north eastern seaboard of America. My cousin and I have already drawn up a prospectus.'

He meets the gaze of each one of us in turn.

'All that we lack is a consortium of bold and willing men. God will bless the venture.'

I study the prospectus and scan the maps. I trace my finger along the Atlantic trade route. And tickle the serrated coast of America.

### The new Aphrodite

I hurtle out of Middle Temple pausing only to pick up my fabulous suit of clothes from the tailor in Aldgate. I don the cloak and wrap myself in that damask sea. I am the manifestation of my own destiny. I hold the hem and spread my arms. You can sail a galleon across my back.

There are scrapes. Sack and swords do not mix well.

We hurtle through the night, our hands never far from the hilts of our swords. Beards are pulled. Noses are tweaked. Faces are slapped. But we are like tomcats hissing. We arch our backs and fluff our fur to make ourselves bigger. Occasionally we lash out: our daggers drawn draw blood.

In a tavern near St Paul's, my half-brother Humphrey Gilbert bangs the table. Our blackjacks jump.

'Do you see it? Ships laden to the gunwales with ore and precious rocks? The beams creaking under the strain of so much riches? You'll see. The world will see.'

He speaks as if he already has it. His tensile hand clutches at the air, raking fingers through an imagined barrel of coin.

'The Earth is tilting on her axis. Feel it? The old continents are shifting, making way for their new sister, who has arisen like Aphrodite out of the waves. And she, the new Aphrodite, reclines for us, for England, with her legs wide open and a great torrent of gold shooting out from her vast glistening cunt.'

We pause to give this striking figure the full contemplation that it warrants.

'This time, when Frobisher returns, sailing in from the East, having set sail from the West, he will have accomplished more than a simple circumnavigation of the globe.'

He makes this tremendous feat sound like a child skipping over a puddle.

'He will have secured the salvation of our sovereign, whose precarious security unsettles all her subjects. She is under attack on all sides. She lacks even the bulwark of a husband to protect her from hostile advances. When Frobisher forges through the Northwest Passage, raping the virgin land's maidenhead, the whole world will be forced to yield to England. He will herald in a new era of Empire. The Spaniards and the Portingales will be powerless to stop us. And it's all down to me! Haven't I always argued for it? Only to be refuted by fools.'

My other half-brother, Adrian Gilbert, breaks wind. 'There's a fair wind from my Northwest Passage for you.'

His glistening florid face is momentarily anxious as he awaits the reception of his merry blast.

But the choler does not predominate in Humphrey tonight. He rewards his brother with a short indulgent snort before returning to his theme.

'We must follow the example of Marcellus. Strike first! It is irrefutably the best defence. Attack the Spaniard's interests in America. Distract him from his intention to attack us. We must take the initiative. Be more feared than fearing.'

His gaze goes to a distant place. I do not need to be told where. I see it in his eyes. Ireland. My dear brother Humphrey knew how to make himself feared in Ireland. No man was ever more feared there than he. And no man imposed his will on that wild wilful place with more success.

All know the story. An avenue of severed heads leading to his tent. It is more than a story to me. It is a lesson.

I cannot look at him without seeing an image of those twin lines of heads, so vividly is the memory of it writ in his face. I see them as a strange crop sprouting in the ground, two rows of bloody cabbages. Sometimes the heads turn and look at me. Their unblinking eyes confront me with a blankness so complete it sucks at my heart. The blankness of their eyes is a question to which there can never be an answer. Sometimes too their mouths open and incomprehensible oaths escape their morbid Irish lips.

### The savage tongue

The savage child peeps out from behind his mother's head. She carries him on her back inside her hooded coat of skin.

The savage man takes to his little boat. The woman looks on. Her face is blank, impassive. Her eyes seem to look in opposite directions at once. A divided gaze that refuses to fix on any object, as if every prospect is anathema to her.

Dr John Dee is making a study of their tongue. Certain words have been divulged to him by Frobisher's mariners.

Dr Dee points to his eye. 'Arered? Ar-*ar*-red? *Arr*-er-ed? Arrowred?'

His Welsh tongue mangles their already outlandish vowels.

Her eyes refuse to see him. The child, however, is fascinated by the doctor's finger, his little mouth circled in wonder.

'Arrow-*red*?… eye. Is that it?'

The savage child stretches out a delicate finger towards the learned philosopher. And giggles.

Dee is dressed all in black with his doctor's robe and skull cap. The point of his grey triangular beard extends far below the ruff. He presents an imposing figure. His eyes project a beam of fearless inquiry. One senses that there is nothing he would not gaze upon in the pursuit of knowledge, no question he would not dare to ask, no door he would shrink from opening. His face is wrinkled and strained, as if the arcane knowledge he has garnered has taken a terrible toll on his mortality.

For all that, his smile is not unkindly.

The woman's face does not soften. Her eyes show no more tendency to align. Her refusal to look upon the world she has been brought to seems a wilful act of revolt, the only rebellion open to her.

We have hurried here, to Bristol, Humphrey, Dee, the two Hakluyts and I, to see Frobisher's savages before they die. We are not sanguine that they will live long. The last one, the one brought back on his first voyage, survived only days in England.

We are come to talk with Frobisher too, newly returned from his latest voyage, ships weighted down below the waterline with strange black rocks.

Martin Frobisher preens and struts on the Bristol harbour side. He shifts his weight from foot to foot in demonstration of the great impatience that comes with great importance. For all that, I cannot but notice that his step is tentative. He seems to be trying to shake off a limp. When he thinks no eyes are on him, he even stoops a little.

But my eyes miss nothing now.

When he feels the glare of public scrutiny he affects a face of studied affront. Let his critics command a fleet through the crashing ice, let them sail blind into thick black mists, and navigate the narrow straits of the frozen

25

North! Let them be buffeted by biting winds, battered by dense storms of hail! Let them brave the arrows of savage, godless tribes!

Most of all he is affronted by the scepticism of those who would count his prize worthless without the courtesy of assaying it.

He scowls down at the man plashing softly through the English water in his little boat.

'And have you spoke to him of *gold*?' It is ever Humphrey's preoccupation now.

Frobisher is tetchy on the subject: 'God's wounds! There is *gawld* there! I tell ye. Hasn't Agnello proven it?'

Giovanni Agnello is the Italian alchemist who extracted gold from the rock that Frobisher brought back from his first voyage. Though many others who tested the same rock were unable to discover anything more precious than tin.

Frobisher's north country vowels still have the power to shock my senses. A Yorkshire sea captain? He is a stranger prodigy than the savages he has brought back.

'Are they… I mean to ask, are they husband and wife? Is he the child's father?'

Frobisher shakes his head. 'Nay. We took man near Mount Warwick.' He winces at some memory of the occasion. 'Woman and babe, on Bloody Point. They were strangers to one another till we brought 'em together.'

'She does not seem to like him much.'

'She scolds him bitterly, from morn 'til night. And though they bed together, she will not let him anywhere near her.'

'You have spied on them?'

'In the interests of scientific enquiry, you understand…'

I look closely into the woman's face. She has the features of her race, unmistakably Oriental.

'You would think, being of the same race, thrown together in a strange land, they would seek and offer mutual comfort.'

'Aye, tis queer. They got along well enough at first. All singing and chattering away to each other in that savage tongue of theirs. As well as he was able, all things considering.'

I wonder at his meaning. What things are to be considered?

'God knows what they found to talk about. But then, after a day of their ungodly noise, a sullen silence settled on them. Next, she fell to wailing and lamenting. Then her lamentation turned to a vicious ungrateful railing. She revealed a fiery tempestuous nature and would rain blows on any who approached her, him most of all. It just goes to show, there are shrews in their land as well as ours.'

I notice that the child has switched his gaze from Dr Dee's finger to my own face. I stick out my tongue at him. He stares at it gravely.

I find that I want to catch his mother's eye. I am drawn to the savage eastern strangeness of her features. The dark hue of her skin is made darker still by the azure marks etched into it. (How unlike the chalk white faces of our English ladies!) These mysterious lines and symbols make of her face a secret text that piques my curiosity. I would fain decipher it. And yet… her strange and filthy attire, her mean estate, of which she is unconscious, being so lowly placed in the Kingdom of Creation: all ought to be a source of disgust to me.

Why do I feel it so provoking that she refuses to look at me? Does she not know how much I spent on this suit? Let her sneer at her stunted, sallow-skinned fellow in his dun and dowdy furs. But this trunk hose is made of damask silk!

The man on the water quickens the strokes of his oar. But her divergent eyes still refuse to settle on the busy spectacle of him. Even when he takes up his bow and lets fly an arrow. The arrow flies straight and true, piercing a duck on the wing that plops into the channel.

The watching Englishmen, myself included, raise cheers and applaud. Only Frobisher does not acknowledge the masterly display. He snarls and grumbles under his breath.

The younger Richard Hakluyt leans in to confidentially explain: 'He took an arrow in the arse out there.'

The savage man retrieves the dead water fowl, with a sullen look towards the woman on the quayside. A look she does not return.

'Shall we have your cook roast it for him later?'

Frobisher shakes his head glumly at my question. 'Yon fellow would not thank us fer it. Tis their custom to eat all flesh raw, whether fish, fowl or…' He contracts his lips disapprovingly.

'Or?'

'I believe they are not averse to eating human flesh. Some of the things I have seen them sink their teeth into. Human flesh would be the lesser evil.'

'There is a greater evil than anthropophagy?' It is Dr Dee who wonders this. His bristling eyebrows quiver with an alert, eager curiosity.

'Why, yon fellow even ate his own tongue.'

The startled worthies view the savage on the water with renewed curiosity. They are dumbstruck. So, if no one else will, then I must ask: 'I beg you, why on earth did he do that?'

'What goes on in their heads is a mystery to me.

'He truly ate his own tongue?'

'It is truer to say he bit it off and spat it out. T'taste presumably was not to his liking.'

'Are you sure he meant to eat it?'

Frobisher gives every sign of finding my questions impertinent. His hand twitches towards his dagger. He glares his disapproval at Humphrey. Humphrey nods for Frobisher to go on.

'Devil knows what he meant to do! He is an unchristian heathen, born into a state of depravity and damnation.'

The others nod solemnly. But Frobisher's argument *e religione* does not quite satisfy me: 'But when did he do this? Was it when you sat down to sup?'

'What does it matter when it was!'

The colour is high in Frobisher's face, which blazes with a copper blush, the alloy of sunburn and indignation. He fidgets on his sailor's legs. I am made to understand that he considers me a greater pain in the arse than the arrow wound he bears.

'I wish I had never mentioned his bloody tongue! What matters his tongue? It is gone now. The seabirds picked over it.'

Dr Dee cannot conceal his dismay: 'You did not preserve it?'

'Why in Heaven's name should we preserve it?'

The good doctor looks somewhat abashed, but prefers not to answer the question. I cannot exclude the possibility that he has in mind the necromantic potency of the severed object. He is, after all, a man of science.

Frobisher strains towards a degree of placidity as he explains: 'When we first took yon brute aboard our ship, suffice it to say that he was not entirely delighted to accept our hospitality. Such is t'extent of his barbarism. Twas then he bit his tongue off. I dare say he did it to spite us.'

'You were supposed to treat the naturals with civility…' My brother is quite as quick to choler as Frobisher. His rising tone warns of the welling of his wrath.

'As indeed I did, Sir Humphrey.'

Richard Hakluyt the younger returns to the question of cannibalism: 'Did you see them eat human flesh? With your own eyes?'

Frobisher shakes his head impatiently. 'Nay. For they were well fed on voyage.'

Perhaps he senses our collective disappointment. We want so much for the savages to be cannibals. He offers this: 'At any rate, cooked meat is too refined for them. It makes them vomit copiously.'

We watch as the savage plucks the dead duck from his arrow.

The man tosses the bird towards the female. It lies at her feet, bedraggled with blood. Another object that she refuses to see.

Richard Hakluyt the elder murmurs confidentially to Frobisher, as if there is a danger of his words being overheard by the savages: 'Perhaps she can be encouraged to eat it now? So that we may witness her barbarism.'

'She will not accept a gift from him. She hates him, I tell you.'

The two Hakluyts confer: 'The poor fellow is quite in love with her.'

'A pretty little drama has been played out here.'

'Verily. In their savage way, they evince a marvellous refinement of feeling.'

I turn to Frobisher: 'What of your men? Did they enjoy her favours on the voyage back?'

He flicks his hand carelessly, swatting away an invisible fly. The question need not be asked, his gesture signifies.

The ambiguity does not satisfy me. I must know for sure. 'I beg you tell me.'

'They are not beasts. Or savages.'

I cannot say why it is so important to me to have this question settled. But it is. 'They are men, however.'

His refutation does not amount to a denial: 'Aye, Christian men!'

'Even Christians sin. And is it not considered one of the entitlements of conquest?'

I again approach the savage woman, her face veiled by those fine blue markings. They make of her humanity a palimpsest.

Only her eyes are unwritten upon, and they in their divided gaze are as indecipherable as the rest of her. One cannot even look into them. She is all unknowable. And would be even without the lines imprinted into her skin.

Her infant child twitches and squeals at my approach. Then hides behind his mother's head. I can still hear him whimpering out of sight.

'What is her name?'

'Egnock.'

I repeat the strange name: 'Egnock.'

As I raise a hand to touch a finger on her inscribed face.

R.N. MORRIS


**Solar alchemy**


It is a cabinet of curiosities, a library, a laboratorium, a forge, a chapel, a sanctuary, a treasure house, a school. It is a ramshackle labyrinth of rooms, each containing a dusty mystery. It is a universe. A microcosm. It floats in a dark abyss of infinitude, entire unto itself, containing everything. It is a storehouse of Platonic ideals.

The air is musty and sulphurous.

We have stepped into the mind of Dr John Dee.

The walls are hidden by piles of arcane parchments and books. We are surrounded by dim shapes dipped in gloom. The candle Dr Dee holds high in front of him casts fleet and flickering illumination. A mummified crocodilus leaps out. Globes turn. Astrolabes swivel. Orreries orbit. Oil swirls in obscure glasses. The tools of the good doctor's trade are set in motion by our passing.

Dr Dee leads us to a lectern where a book lies open at its title page. An engraving shows the Queen enthroned aboard a ship. The ship is moored by a headland and called Europa. Above a fortress, a beckoning figure rests one foot on the apex of a pyramid.

The motto *MORE LIES HIDDEN THAN IS APPARENT* frames the title of Dee's book, *General and rare memorials pertayning to the Perfect Arte of Navigation.*

'There is no need, I think, for me to explain the allegory to you gentlemen.'

At this school-masterly prompt, Humphrey ventures an interpretation: 'The New World is our fortress. In its exploration lies our salvation.'

Dr Dee nods approvingly. 'This island of ours is uniquely placed. Who can doubt that we have been put here by God for the very purpose of sailing the seas, of discovering new lands, and bringing the souls of the savages we encounter from darkness into light? God's will too that we be enriched in return for the pains we must necessarily take. The portents are clear on this. First there was the new star that appeared in the constellation Cassiopeia five years since. It portends the discovery of some great treasure, perhaps the greatest treasure of all, the Philosopher's Stone. And now a comet has appeared in the sky, its tail pointing towards the Low Countries. We must take it as an omen of great good fortune. The comet shows its arse to the *Spanish* Netherlands. It is a glorious nativity. Britain's Empire is being born. It is our divine destiny, and it is your great privilege, Sir Humphrey, to be the agent of it.'

Dr Dee turns the pages of his book.

'Your voyage is to be understood in this way. It is a transmutation, an alchemical operation. The storms and vicissitudes of the vessel in the furnace, the nigredo, the dark night... all this precedes the alchemist's reward. His discovery of the Philosopher's Stone, his emergence as the golden man, the celestial one. Out of the darkness, is born the light. It is not simply a question of the gold you will carry back from your expedition. Your inmost hidden virtues will come forth. You will yourselves be transmuted. You will become the golden ones.'

We bask in the projected glow of his words.

Humphrey gestures towards the book. 'We have come to you for instruction, Master Dee. It is my earnest wish to set our intended expedition on a scientific footing.'

Dr Dee begins pulling volumes down from his shelves. 'You would do well therefore to study the stars. Know you that scientific geography has its basis in astronomy? Geometry too shall come to your aid. For as you know, the earth is nothing more than a geometric sphere. It may be divided into sections, laterally and longitudinally. To calculate your position at sea, you must know how to calculate the sections and segments of a sphere. An invention of my own devising... The Paradoxal Compass, will aid you greatly in this.'

'What manner of device is it? Mechanical?'

'I would say, Sir Humphrey, that it is more a Philosophical Device. Or rather, Intellectual. And yet its usages are eminently Practical. It will serve you well, and your pilots also.'

Humphrey nods. I detect impatience rather than enthusiasm in the brisk vigour of his agreement. 'I have heard talk of a map...'

'You are referring to my map of Atlantis?'

'By Atlantis, you mean...'

'What you call America. Though he gave his name to the land he alighted upon, Amerigo Vespucci was by no means the first European to reach there. A late interloper, we might even call him. Englishmen, Robert Thorne the elder and Hugh Eliot, merchants of Bristol, were discoverers of the new found land before him. And even John Cabot, who came after Masters Thorne and Eliot, preceded Amerigo. Cabot too, though a Venetian, was sailing under English flag, on behalf of King Henry.'

'What about Columbus?'

Dr Dee dismisses my question with an impatient shake of the head, vigorous enough to set his long beard swaying. I expect disturbed owls to scatter from it.

'My researches have shown that England's claim to this supposed New World in fact goes back to ancient times. As far back as King Arthur, and before him even to Brutus, the first king of Britain. A manuscript has recently come into my possession which relates the voyage of the Welsh prince Madoc. He founded a colony in the New World when Henry the Second was on the throne of England, in the year of our Lord 1170. Columbus himself describes the Welsh-speaking Indian tribes he encountered when he arrived in America. There can be no doubt: the British claim to this continent precedes that of the Spaniard or the Portingale. You, gentlemen, will be continuing in a long and venerable tradition. England's destiny has been working itself out over the centuries and will at last come to fruition in your voyage.'

Here in his Mortlake house, it is easy to believe in the inevitability of the future that Dr Dee promises us.

31

Every word he utters, in his rich Welch voice, is an incantation that binds us to his golden vision.

Humphrey is impatient to be away: 'Have you shared the fruit of your researches with her Majesty?'

'I have so.'

'And is she persuaded of the case you make?'

'How can she not be?'

'I wonder then, why she has not yet approved the letters patent that will authorise our venture.'

'Trust to the rightfulness of your cause, Sir Humphrey.'

'I intend to introduce young Wat at court.'

Dr Dee tilts his head as if hearing a distant voice call his name. Or angels conversing perhaps. Some sound inaudible to us lesser mortals. A shiver passes through me. I am a boy again, running through the forest at the end of our garden.

The great man turns to face me with a frown of concentration. He speaks quietly, his voice dry like the snapping of a twig: 'Walter.'

It comes to me from a point more westerly than the West. The same voice that called to me that day in my childhood. The voice of my future then. The voice of my Destiny now.

## The Great Comet

I am an arrow fired into the sky. I shoot past the thatched roofs of houses, past church spires, cutting through the tops of the tallest trees, leaving the Empires of Oak and of Men quivering behind me. I startle the lark and stir the mountain-dwelling eagle from her nest.

I cut through clouds. The high winds whistle through me, howling malice as they strive to tear me asunder.

Behind me the rivers, mountains, forests, towns and shorelines of the earth are like the features on Mercator's great map.

And now, ahead of me, I see a vast void of blackness. I have never felt such utter empty loneliness. Not even the howling winds have kept company with me.

The blackness is leavened by tiny twinkling pinpoints of light. Stars!

I feel myself spin. The points of light become swirling streaks. All at once a great disc of luminescence comes into sight. I am so close to the moon that I can see the pockmarks of its face.

In a trice, I have left the moon behind me. It dwindles like a punctured bladder.

Another twist in my trajectory and there in the distance is the fiery ball of the Sun. I find that I am able to look directly into it. The flames lick out in bursts of raging fury.

Yet another turn. Ahead of me now lies a curve of sparkling substance streaking through the studded vault. I take it to be the much-bruited Great Comet.

Its head I see to be a spinning rock of unimaginable scale. The speed of its progress through the airless wastes causes sparks of combustion to erupt continuously. A burning halo surrounds it.

Clouds of debris break forth from its surface and scatter outwards in all directions. The greatest of these streams is the tail it leaves in its wake. At first, these remnant trails appear like the discarded dregs of a human city: soil, dust, the broken and the dead. But in the fire, this refuse is ignited and – yes, there is no other word for it – transmuted. It becomes gold.

I know then that what I am seeing is none other than the fabled Philosopher's Stone.

My arrow-fast gaze flies on and at last hits its target. I strike the surface of the comet and burrow deep within its dense and obdurate material. My gaze is sharper than any diamond.

As I am cast out into the incandescent aura that surrounds the comet's head, I am filled with light. The divine fire of the Universe enters me. I feel it deep within me: I am become gold. Incorruptible gold.

I feel an unspeakable harmony, an alignment of my inner being with the light and motive power of God.

There is no question of loneliness now. I have travelled beyond self.

The arrowshot of my vision has reached its apex and now must begin its fall. I feel the weight of the world inside me.

The Great Comet moves away.

On my descent, I pass through layers of being, arranged in concentric spheres.

The most notable of these spheres is the vaporous barrier that surrounds the Earth. As I plummet into it, I am again ignited. This second burning drives out any remaining impurities from my being and seals me in a burnished carapace.

I am still on fire as I fall through the air. The Earth shifts beneath me, as if she is trying to turn away from the impact of my landfall. An ocean rolls away from me. I can no longer see the towns and villages of England. A strange and savage land has taken its place, a land of wilderness and woods. I sense the presence of winding rivers and creeks hidden beneath impenetrable canopies of green. I see Nature forced into unnatural shapes and hues. Birds no bigger than dragonflies. Plants that feed on flesh. Lurid blooms of gargantuan size, the fevered dreams of a disordered mind.

The alien Earth comes up to meet me. The expected cataclysm does not come. I am plunged into a lake of cooling water. A secret lake that lies atop a mountain, deep within a boundless forest.

I continue to sink until I settle into the mud at the bottom of the lake. I move now at a different speed. The speed at which a continent shrugs a mountain range into existence.

It is dark here, in the clay beneath the secret lake. But I bring with me my own fierce glow, a beam plucked from the Sun, forged in the comet's halo. This is my nature now. And it is this in me that the Earth loves.

I feel her suck at me, the pressure of her immense embrace on every side of me. She squeezes me tight and draws me out into a seam of mineral glimmer.

I feel the malleable mud petrify around me. The jealous Earth's grip on me tightens into a vice.

## Lunar alchemy

We cross the night, that portion of it that lies between Aldersgate and Islington, following the road through Wenloxbarne. In the daytime, the washerwomen come here to the fields to stretch out their linen for drying. At night, it is a wild place, given over to owls and robbers. The wildness suits our tempers. We are young, impatient of the city's confining topography. We like to feel the boundless sky above us, indeed to feel unbounded on every side. And we believe ourselves to be more than a match for the gangs of cut-throat ruffians reputed to roam here.

Ebb and flood, I surge and roar. The sea cannot match me for surging and roaring.

We are aerial spirits, armoured in weightless silver. Denizens of an unearthly realm, capable of anything. If we so wish, we can soar to the maternal moon, responding to her mute attractive force. We hold that up our silver sleeves. We run and laugh and throw ourselves into the future. And at each other. A rollicking, rambunctious, roistering rabble.

'Arse!'

Tis one of my fellows cannoning into me. He knocks me to the ground, and the wind out of me, before bounding off with a high-pitched animal screech. I spring to my feet, after him, chasing the wake of his yell.

We are like lion cubs play-fighting, cuffing with claws and testing our teeth. The bruises that we blithely dispense are the badges of our band. Each punch is landed with love and laughter. Just that it is rough love and brutal laughter. And of course, our sack-numbed bodies do not feel the blows so heavily.

We are practising to be fearless. We are the gilded youth (or at the very least, moon-silvered), enchanted by the charm of our own existence.

It has been decided. I am on my way. America! I will command one of Humphrey's ships, as soon as he has drawn a fleet together. But first I will go to court and make my name and bolster his faction. My other brother will stand the requisite fee. Good old Adrian. Let no man ever say a word against him, or he will have me to answer to.

I spread my arms and run. I feel the night fill and billow in the damask cloak behind me. I am irresistible. I am *perpetuum mobile*.

And then it comes, just as we attain Mount Mill. A cry in the night that is not from our company.

'You there! Halt. In the name of Queen Elizabeth.'

We had not expected this.

'Curfew!'

The officers of the Watch ply their petty complaint.

I calculate that there are more of us. We can divide and scatter, and some of us at least will escape their arrest. Or we can stand and fight.

I remember my brother's words. *Be more feared than fearing.*

It will not take much to see them off. A simple show of force. I do not doubt they will turn tail before the flourish of our noble swords.

We are no band of rogues. Even these dolts will see that. They have no business with us.

I urge my fellows, and hear my steely hushed voice as if another speaks my words: 'Stand to.'

I thrust out the point of my steel into the night. I mean no more by it than a gesture of defiance. But this fool of a constable, a bloated, broken-winded booby, runs straight onto my blade. Perhaps he cannot stop himself. It has cost him so much effort to reach this speed that he cannot think of stopping. At any rate, I do not retract. I hold steady. I feel the weight of his error in my wrist. I feel the sinking of steel into something softly resistant. His sodden punctured cry of surprise and pain confirms the message of his mass. He totters. And when I at last reclaim my sword, he falls away from me.

There is a moment when we are all in awe of what has happened. No one moves. We stand and watch as he shivers out his lifeblood. My fellows and I, rooted to the spot. The other Watchmen make no move to avenge their fallen comrade.

It is left to me to signal the ending of that moment. My throat fills with a flesh-throbbing scream. My fellows and I turn and run. We can hear from their shouts that some of the Watch have given chase. The others, I must presume, tend the fallen man.

## The Presence Chamber

Red and white Tudor roses sprout and bloom in the ceiling. Golden tendrils curl along the walls, shooting out to entwine themselves around marble columns. Golden leaves unfurl. Fabulous beasts frolic among the foliage. Greyhounds, bears, lions, unicorns, perfect in every miniature detail. We are walking through the very idea of heraldry.

We approach an open arch cut into the wall, through which can be glimpsed a throng of courtiers.

Humphrey waits for me to draw level. Before cuffing me about the ear.

'What's that for?'

'Fool. You young fool. You risk destroying everything.'

'Pray, what have I done?'

'Do you think if the Queen sees you making eyes at one of her ladies-in-waiting she would tolerate your presence here at Court?'

'I swear I was not.'

My lie draws a second cuff.

'I heard the whore's laughter.'

'I did nothing to provoke it.'

'I did not bring you here for whoring. Greater men than you have been sent to the Tower for less. Promise me you will conduct yourself in a seemly manner.'

'I promise you, brother.'

He seems content at this. But cannot resist pressing his point:

'The Queen insists on the probity of her gentlemen courtiers and the purity of her ladies.'

'The court then is a more moral place than I have heard it bruited.'

'The court is what the Queen wishes it to be. We must all strive to ensure she is not disappointed in her wishes.'

'It is not my intent to disappoint Her Majesty.'

'Remember what we discussed. Kneel as soon as you hear the trumpets announcing Her Majesty's entrance to the Presence Chamber. Her Majesty's head must always be the highest in any room. Therefore, for a tall man such as you, the surest way to avoid giving offence is to kneel. You do not speak unless you are first spoken to. When and if she does address you, you may look up and let her see your face. Your conversation will be at all times decorous and witty.'

'At *all* times witty?'

'You have but one chance to make a first impression.'

'But what if my wit deserts me?'

'You must see to it that it does not. Imagine that your life depends on it. As one day it may.'

With that he leads me through the arch.

The room shimmers and shifts. Taffeta bulbs bulge and baffle even my all-seeing eyes. It is a moment before I realise they are not undulations in the lustrous hangings, but the gold-threaded clothes of the assembled courtiers: trunk hoses, doublets, and skirts like vast swaying bells silently tolling. Heads float in a molten tide. Never has a congregation of humanity been more at one with its surroundings.

The floating heads turn in my direction, tilting to size me up. I am reminded that I am grown to be that much taller than other men. That Humphrey and I are both fine examples of manhood and together constitute an imposing spectacle. In the court of an unmarried Queen, this is an enviable advantage for any faction.

The room adjusts to make sense of my intrusion. The silken shiver of one hundred accommodations. Am I to be ally or enemy? Threat or opportunity?

Certainly they cannot ignore me. I am wearing turquoise, my suit of turquoise damask, when all around me are wearing gold. I sense the outrage at this act of sartorial boldness. It delights me more than I can say to so disconcert the noble assembly by a simple suit of clothes.

A silken stir presages by half a heartbeat the clarion trumpets' blast, so finely attuned to the approach of the sovereign are the court's senses. A discreet cuff from Humphrey has me on my knees.

I know immediately where she is without having to look for her. Even as she moves about the chamber. It is not that I hear her step or the whispering of her clothes. It is simply that she pulls me to her.

I am tidal. She is lunar.

I smell her proximity. A complex, spicy odour. I discern cloves and cumin, over-laden with the sweet, deep scent of ambergris. And something else that all these masking perfumes cannot conceal: the sour, sickly breath of decay. It is that odour more than any other that makes me want to look at her. Because it is the true smell of her. And it is her mortal essence, that part of her that I must understand and overmaster.

'Who have we here?'

Her voice strikes my ears as shrill.

Her words are my licence to look up.

Her face, as white as the moon. I know it is a mask, constructed daily out of white lead and vinegar by her ladies of the bedchamber. And yet it stirs my heart to skipping. For this is the very idea of her, that she has chosen and perfected and presented. It shimmers with a disarming frailty.

Her gaze is bold. In any other woman, you would call it brazen. But she is our Queen. And yet I see the flicker that betrays an inner conflict. Between doubt and decision. Between what the world expects of her and what she feels herself capable of.

Hers are the loneliest eyes I have ever seen.

As I feared, my wits have deserted me. And so it is left to Humphrey to speak up for me: 'Your Majesty, may I present Walter Ralegh, nephew of your late and much-beloved lady, Kat Ashley.'

Humphrey is like a hunter who has studied well the habits and anatomy of his prey. He knows precisely where to strike.

Her gaze softens towards me. 'You are Kat Ashley's kin?'

The harshness that I earlier discerned is gone from her voice. It is not her. It never was her. It is something she has practised and put on to keep her Privy Councillors in their place.

'Aye, your Majesty.'

A snigger passes round the assembly at what I cannot imagine, until I hear one of the courtiers: *Ay-yerrrr Majesty!* Others pipe in with a chorus of *Ahoy! Avarrrst! A-harr!*

The Queen silences their amusement with a sharp, birdlike cocking of her head. She frowns before softening her gaze again for my benefit.

'Your aunt was very dear to us.'

She knows that she has revealed herself to me. It is a moment fraught with privilege and peril. Perhaps a door has opened. Perhaps many other doors have closed.

Upon the dark bed of her dress, fabulous silver birds and butterflies weave between neatly tangled vines. Lines of golden thread are hung with clusters of pearls.

The Queen smiles indulgently at my unconcealed wonder. 'You are bold, sir, in your admiration of the Queen's person.'

'Majesty, I cannot help but marvel at the wondrous riches of your dress.'

'Ah, so it is my seamstress's skill and not the perfection of my womanly form that earns your approbation?'

Half-brother Humphrey grimaces tensely.

It is left to me to extricate myself from this dilemma. 'I am like one of the birds on your dress, your Majesty, who has just found himself caught in a trap.'

'How so?'

'I cannot turn, neither this way nor that. My feet are limed to the floor. I beat my wings but to no avail.'

'Your wings?'

'My wit. The wings stand for my wit. By my wit I would soar.'

'But your wit is wanting?'

'I want for nothing while I am in your presence, Majesty.'

'But you cannot fly?'

'Forsooth, I do not wish to. I am happily entrapped.'

'And I? What am I in this figure? The fowler?'

'Nay, you are the forest, in whose branches we birds do roost. You are the sustenance and support of every winged creature. You are our world. More… you are the entire world, your Majesty. And if I may be so bold…'

'What? Bolder still?'

'What first entranced me when I saw your dress was that I read in it the story of our nation's future. I bethought myself already in America. Your Highness is clothed in Terra Incognita. I saw you as the embodiment of all our destinies.'

'It is your wish to go with Sir Humphrey Gilbert on his venture to the New World?'

'Verily, it is my most earnest wish. But more than that, I would consider it my duty.'

'It is only your duty if we command you to do it. As yet we have not commanded.'

'That is all I want…'

'And yet you said you wanted nothing while in my presence? Have you been caught in a lie?'

'No lie, your Majesty. My Queen's command is no different from my own heart's desire. And so when I say I want your command, I mean I wish it.'

'You want for nothing then? My command is nothing?'

'On the contrary, your command is all.'

'I would not stand in your way. If you would go to America, I bid you go.'

Humphrey cries out: 'And we shall have the letters patent? Without further delay?'

What he has laboured for all these months, I have achieved in one audience. In his excitement, my brother stands to his full height, raising his head above the Queen's. A hiss of disapproval wildfires around the chamber.

'You forget yourself, Sir Humphrey.'

The Queen gestures for him to lower himself. He bows in eager abasement.

The Queen gives him no definite answer and turns her attention again to me instead: 'And you… What is your name again?'

'Aye, your Majesty. That's right. Wat is my name. Wat Ralegh.'

'Too droll.' She makes the observation critically, meaning it. 'Tell me this, young Wat. If I am clothed in Terra Incognita, what is the meaning of your own suit of clothes?'

I lift my arms, spreading my turquoise cloak. 'I am the Ocean. I am your passage to the future, Majesty, the means by which all our destinies will be met.'

Her red-painted lips contract in prim approval. She nods once regally and moves on.

The speed of her passage leaves me breathless in admiration. Contrary to the reports I have heard, when she puts her mind to it, she is capable of swift action.

## Gallows fly

He stands as still as a spider, dressed in a robe as black as a shadow.

A black felt skullcap encloses his head, as if to guard his thoughts from eavesdroppers. Set deep in dark-dusted sockets, two eyes glisten like the sunken surface water of bottomless wells. For all their recessed retirement, they are eyes that miss nothing.

'I wish you God's speed, Sir Humphrey.'

Strange though it is to relate, I have never heard anything so chilling as the Principal Secretary's good wishes.

Even brother Humphrey, who takes Walsingham's support as given, is thrown into confusion. 'God's speed? I am not yet aboard my ship.'

'But all is set for our adventure now. You have the Queen's consent, do you not?'

'I would be more content to have the letters patent in my hand.'

'The letters patent will be forthcoming. You may look to me for that.'

'I thank you, my Lord Secretary.'

'You must repose all your trust in me.'

'I most surely do.'

'Prepare your fleet.'

'My fleet is ready.'

'And the men to sail in it?'

'There is no shortage of good men eager for such a bold adventure as this, both gentlemen and mariners.'

Sir Francis lowers his voice to a murmur. There is something irrefutably compelling about the whisper of great men. 'Concerning the matter you raised with me…If I may offer you my advice…'

He draws my half-brother away from me. I note, however, that he keeps his eyes fixed on me throughout their fervent conversing. Once or twice, Humphrey looks up in my direction, nodding in agreement with Sir Francis. I am prey to the uncomfortable sensation that the advice he is offering pertains to me.

At last their private colloquy concludes. Sir Francis's head declines one final time sharply in my direction. His nod is like the pronouncement of sentence. He turns and sweeps his flow of shadow away with him.

'What did he say?'

Humphrey does not meet my eye. 'He merely wished to remind me of our duty.'

'I do not need reminding of my duty. I trust that what profits me will profit my Queen too.'

'No doubt. His argument was merely this: we must not overlook the opportunity to hurt our enemies, should it present itself.'

'He means to have us harry the Spanish?'

'You would not scruple at such a policy?'

'That is a question that need not be asked.' I look wonderingly after Walsingham's vanished shadow. 'That is all?'

'He has in his patronage men who may be useful to us in our endeavour. However, there were certain difficulties attaching to these men.'

'Difficulties?'

'Legal difficulties. One of these men, I believe, was under sentence of death. Indeed, I believe he had already ascended the scaffold and felt the halter around his neck, when Sir Francis made his intervention.'

'How very interesting.'

'The truth is no one knows the coast of America as well as this fellow.'

'I can believe it.'

'Fortunately for us, Sir Francis has secured his release. As a consequence, he is bound to him. And has therefore consented to his request to serve us on the voyage as pilot. And other men too, of similar ilk, have been commissioned to our service. Seasoned seafarers to a man. If a little…'

'Piratical?'

Humphrey makes a qualifying gesture but does not contradict the thrust of my answer.

I set him at his ease: 'It will not go amiss. If we do not find gold in the American ground, we may count on retrieving it from the Atlantic sea.'

'There may be danger in it.'

'I do not baulk at a little skirmishing. To set sail across the broad Ocean, in search of prizes and praise. It is a game played for high stakes. And I am weary of gambling groats to pay my tailor's bill.'

'This fellow, the individual I spoke of…'

'The gallows fly?'

'He is to sail with you, aboard the *Falcon*. As pilot. Sir Francis thinks it for the best.'

'Splendid.'

'He is a Portingale. A renegade. One of the conditions of his release was that he denounced the Catholic profession and converted to the true faith. Sir Francis insisted upon it.'

I look around the Presence Chamber, as if I fear there are spies behind the arrases. I drop my voice in conscious emulation of Walsinghman's whisper: 'Can he be trusted?'

'It is said he hates the King of Spain with a passion.'

'Then we will get along very well.'

The hall is nigh on empty now, the Queen's absence as fully felt as her presence. I imagine the chamber choked with courtiers as it was moments before. They are waiting for me. At last, I stride in, laden with unicorn horns and plate, surrounded by the savages I have brought back with me, and captive Spanish nobles in my train.

My fantasy fails me at that point. For there is nothing beyond that imagined moment that interests me. As if the purpose of our mission is to convert the jealous contempt of the court creatures to joyous admiration.

### A very pirate

And so our destinies are finally entwined, the oak's and mine.

I walk the red-painted boards of the *Falcon* as the stores are loaded on. I am trying to walk myself into the role that I am called upon to play. As if the boards of the ship's deck are the boards of a playhouse stage. I want to stand tall, but am forced to stoop as I enter my cabin. I wear the ship like a costume. It is a little on the rigid side. And heavy. Tucked away in the pockets of the costume: the culverins and the demi-culverins, the port pieces and the top pieces. Their iron and their fire is mine to wield. I draw comfort and command from their potent presence.

I have come to the stern of the ship, where the captain's cabin is housed. It is at the highest part of the hull, its roof providing the poop deck. The bulk of the ship will sit before and beneath me as we cut through the waves. My demesne, for me to lord over and survey.

I touch the wainscotting of my cabin. I am reassured enough to believe she is a good vessel, well-made. Owned by the Queen herself. Humphrey urges me to consider it a signal honour. I must confess such preferment unnerves me. It is my first command.

I stand tall, only to crack my skull on the ceiling of the cabin.

The ship is moored on the Thames at Greenwich. Larboard side to the harbour. It shifts uneasily, though tethered with hawsers as thick as a cabin boy's arm.

The river's tang. The seagull's bleat. The ship's dip and roll. I am reminded of the discomforts of my last sea crossings. My guts are already rendered to a bilge water swill.

There is a lurch away to starboard. A restive cry from the crew breaks the low overlapping rhythm of their chants. I have lived enough of my life among seafaring folk to know the cause of it. They take the ship's movement as a bad omen, according to which we will have a difficult voyage and meagre rewards. There are times when I think mariners are more superstitious than Papists.

From what I have seen of my crew, they are a rough and surly lot. But their sunburnt scowls trouble me less than the pale contemptuous sniggers of the courtiers I have left behind. These men understand as well as I that I am their commander. I will brook no nonsense from them. I intend to be firm but fair. Sparing with the lash. And generous with the rations. Not too generous, of course. The men will not thank me if we exhaust our supplies before we have opportunity to reprovision.

I have studied the logs and records of divers maritime voyages, as well as books on the theory of statecraft and command. My friends the Richard Hakluyts have been most obliging to me in this respect, giving me the run of their considerable collection of navigational texts. The library of Dr Dee at Mortlake has been open to me also. His recent publication pertaining to the

*Perfect Art Of Navigation* has been my Vademecum (though I have yet to navigate my way through the intricacies of his Paradoxal Compass).

These gentlemen each have a deep and profound interest in the success of our enterprise. They have much invested in it, more than mere finance. Dr Dee has staked his vision and his dreams; the Richard Hakluyts the sum of their inestimable learning.

Such is their combined commitment to the voyage that they have consented for me to pack a number of their precious volumes in the trunk which my servants, the Pansfurthe brothers, even now let slip to the deck with a weighty thud.

'Careful with that!'

I must keep my eye on the Pansfurthes, William especially, after I obliged him to stand for me before the magistrate Jasper Fisher over the fracas with the Watch. Naturally, I could not allow the stabbing of a constable to stand in the way of my destiny. And it was not as if the man died. It was only a matter of breach of the peace, not murder, after all. A trivial matter. With the help of some friends, I was able to secure William's release from judicial constraints. Though it cost a pretty penny. That Jasper Fisher is more grasping than any Jew. He took one look at my suit of clothes and made his calculations.

William's brief spell in gaol seems to have done nothing to improve his docility. He has expressed no gratitude for the pains I took on his behalf. And seems determined to vent his dissatisfaction in little acts of insubordination and rebellion.

I will have no jetting on my command. No riotous and unruly rampaging, such as was the source and cause of all their troubles. I cannot indulge my own servants or it will set a bad example to the other men. The whole society of our ship depends on the due observance of the hierarchy between masters and servants.

A quick cuff around the face with the back of my hand and the point is made. There is no need to belabour it.

If I can only quell my unruly stomach so easily, all will be well on the voyage.

A further stir among the crew alerts me to some new disruption. A singular voice raised above the rabble's raucous chorus. Its edges are harsh and jagged, like the rough stones thrown out to aid a boarding party. And though the accent is thick and foreign, the oaths are understandable enough. The men are scurvy dogs. Their mothers are mangy bitches. With whom the speaker claims to have had the most intimate relations. (He blames one individual's mother for a recent dose of the burning that has plagued his *membrum virile*.) All these revelations are met with ribald laughter. It seems the crew delights in being so lewdly abused.

I venture forth from my cabin to greet the man who is to pilot my ship, and indeed our fleet.

I step between the shrouds of rigging on the mizzenmast. From my high vantage point, I have a good view of the activity on the lower deck. The hold lies open, but the lines of lading are at a standstill, and fall to loose array. The men down their loads and lean upon the nearest tun to give ear to the performance of the Portuguese pilot. For it can only be he.

If there are dried fruit in those tuns, they are no more wrinkled than this man's skin, nor darker than his eyes. If it be rum they contain, it will not shine more than those that black tresses that fall across his shoulders, nor flow more fluidly.

His ears are ringed with gold. I see it flash, brandished by the broad summer day, as it hones its brilliance. Here is his self-advertisement for the role he is to play. Gold. I have gold. I can take you to gold. Put down those barrels. I have gold. There is even a ring through one nostril. As if to say he has a nose for it. A great sundial of a nose pointing to the treasures he will truffle out for us. I would follow a man with such a nose to the ends of the earth and I suspect I am not the only one aboard who thinks as much.

He spins and dances rings around his audience, drawing his cutlass to drive home his arguments. I see my man William has joined the congregation and stands gawping at the spectacle. He never can resist a flashing steel.

Our pilot is like a travelling player. A gypsy bandolier, with a cutlass instead of a fiddle. He is dressed all in black, a black tunic and black hose. Another self-advertisement I suspect. Of his black heart. A black sash of silk is bound around his head, a bandage to a wound not yet inflicted.

He tells a garbled tale in mangled English, of the whores he has tupped and the men he has killed.

It is easy to paint him as a crude and ludicrous figure. A cutthroat and a roguish knave. A shameless turncoat, a gallows cheat, a blasphemer and an atheist. A braggart and a cynic. Which is to say, a dog-hearted man.

A very pirate.

And yet he is also a man whose usefulness cannot be overestimated. A man whose qualities brought him to the attention of the Principal Secretary, Sir Francis Walsingham. He is Walsingham's man, in bond to him for his life. But it is also true that Walsingham is now his. For in redeeming this indisputable scoundrel, it may be argued that Sir Francis has perforce demeaned himself.

I have to confess, there is something irrefutable about the man in person. He is like a swirling vortex in the high seas that draws ships into it.

He pretends that he has not seen me, although it is clear that this whole performance is for my benefit.

I descend to the lower deck. Into the thick of his salty tirade. Imagine the following words fired at you through an arquebus of utterance. Imagine them singed, malformed and molten by the blast. Imagine them chewed and spat between corrupted teeth.

'Seven whoreson dayvils, I tell ye. They cunting curs come at me hall at once. Harméd up to they harmpits, they sheetspitting harsey-holes. Daggarz in they teeth. Peestols drawn and trained upon me precious noggin. One false move and I'm a dead un. Well, I tell ye, me blood fair boiled. No gang of poxy buggarez is going to make a mincemeat of Simone Fernandez without he fight. I see what must be done. I see it. And I do it. They biggest of them. A mountain of man. He broad as he tall. And he tall as a Godfucking church. He is they one. They one I must keel first. I must keel him with my hands. I must rip his Popesucking head off his neck with my bare hands. And I must sheet in his neck. That is what I must do. And I must waste my seed in his dead mouth. I scream they scream of a man who is going to do these things. They hear of my scream and they sheet themselves. It is no word of a lie. They soil they hose with they sheet and they piss of they fear. It make my blood boil, I tell ye. I do not like they smell of they sheet. I come at heem. I bite his fucking hear off. You do not fuck with me, you fucking hearless cunt. I laugh. He has no hear, you see. He cannot hear me. The fucking deaf hearless cunt.'

I judge it the opportune moment to end the charade of his feigned ignorance of me.

'Master Simon Fernandez, if I am not mistaken.'

The pilot's extravagant show of surprise inclines me to think that he too feels himself to be a player on the stage, as did I earlier when alone in my cabin. I draw myself up to my full height. However animated and impressive his presence, it has to be said he cannot match me for sheer length of body. Few men can.

'Hand you must be Captain Ha-r-r-rowawlayee.'

Of all the many possible pronunciations of my name, I have never heard it said quite like that before.

'I have heard a lot about you, Master Fernandez. It may be fairly said that your reputation precedes you. Due in large part to your own efforts, I see.'

Fernandez fixes me for a long moment as he shifts his jaw from side to side ruminatively. At last he hawks up a loose mouthful of phlegmy gob. It lands on the deck between us with a heavy splatter. Fernandez regards the globule forlornly for a moment, as if he regrets parting with it, before returning his gaze impudently to my own.

I consider a pretty little speech, but no matter what words I try to piece together in my mind, I cannot escape the feeling that I will sound to myself too like Humphrey.

I feel the rocking of the boat in the queasy pit of my treacherous stomach.

My mouth fills with the flood of salty saliva, the lubricant that presages a greater purging. There is nothing for it. I fire the brimming mouthful towards Fernandez's own product.

I know I have not long before my body follows through and expels the lumpy contents of my stomach. I manage to get out the words: 'You will find me in my cabin, studying the charts. When you have finished your duties here, Master Fernandez, I trust you will do me the honour of waiting upon me.'

I hurry back up the steps, making the cabin just in time. I slam the door at the precise same moment as I release the stinking slops of my vomit.

## Poor John

The insect is the colour of Poor John, the ship's biscuits that it feasts upon. Its body is lined and bristling with fine hairs. If you could shine a light on it, you would see it glisten with the sticky mucus that it secretes as it eats its way through the hard tack. Grinding its mandibles. Excreting the grey mulch that one day will be all that is left for the ship's crew to feed upon.

It began as one of countless eggs laid deep in a store of biscuits. What weevil heaven is this! To find yourself born inside a banquet and to eat your way into existence! My crew may find Poor John poor fare, but it is manna to this weevil.

And now it stretches its fine limbs out from its bulbous body and flexes its restless antennae, feeling itself into its full grown form.

It has no use for eyes inside the densely packed barrel. So mine will serve for it.

Vibrations set its antennae quivering. Its whole being fills with percussive blasts. Incomprehensible gratings and scrapings and throbbings. Obscure intimations of an existence outside the dark universe of its barrel.

Do I have Dr Dee to thank for this? Dee the great imaginer. He has dreamt up the British Empire. It would be an easy thing for him to dream me inside a barrel of Poor John.

Is this my escape? Has he conjured me here from beyond the grave? He always was a cunning man. I would not put it past him.

If so, the refuge he has magicked for me is worse than the fate I flee.

He has made of me a weevil!

Take me out of this barrel! I would rather face the axeman's fell blade, than the inhuman determination of that weevil.

The horror multiplies. A second shifting in the musty, dusty darkness. I scry another weevil. Then another. Then another. Then another. They are all about me. And not just weevils. But weevil grubs and wriggling maggots and all manner of creatures too small and repulsive to be named. Mere writhing spots of living matter. Life's most basic manifestation, in which the base horror of all life is manifested.

I am not this! I am better than this. I am a man. I can write villanelles and dance a galliard. I am long of limb. And can carry off a silk suit with effortless aplomb.

I am a man, I say. Not a weevil! I have the power to dream. And that of which I dream, I have the will to bring about. Wit and will. You have me in a nutshell.

Can a weevil dream?

If his dream is to live in a barrel of ship's biscuit, then, aye, we must own that he has ordered the world to conform to that dream. How content he must be.

Perchance that is the meaning I am to take from the presentation of this image. The humble weevil is to be my exemplum. A symbol not of degradation but of triumph.

The degradation lies all outside the barrel.

The degradation lies in the eight weeks it takes for us to sail from Dartmouth to Plymouth. Eight weeks at sea, and still off the Devon coast. We are surprised and scattered by the winds. We had not counted on the winds.

The degradation lies in the sweats of fever, the convulsions of sickness, the slop of vomit. The long nights shivering in my cabin at the chills I cannot shake off.

And all this before we have made Plymouth.

The degradation lies in the grim fare, and the meagre supplies. The cheap salted meat rotting even before it reaches the hold. The watered down beer and the adulterated wine, both tasting of the whale oil once kept in the casks.

The degradation lies in the the sudden seeming severing of my legs, as a blast of wind throws me against a capstan bar. The degradation lies in the mocking howl of the wind, in the rattling of the timbers, the fearful quaking of the masts, the uncontrollable whipping of the sails, the wild flailing ropes that lash out against their coilers, the inescapable taste of salt, the spray of saline needles in our eyes. The terror inherent in all of this, in the careless power of the wind, the utter black vastness of the sea and the pitiable insignificance of a man who pits himself against it. A man who may be plucked from the rigging and cast to the decks. His brains voided from his cracked skull like a mollusc teased from its shell. The strength of the strongest amongst us is nothing next to the high raging might of a rolling breaker.

And dear God, I am meant to be in command of all this!

The degradation lies in the folly of it all. How did we dare to...?

The degradation lies in the smouldering resentment at my half-brother Humphrey who has led me into this. But who, it soon becomes apparent, has no conception of how to equip or lead a fleet of ten armed ships and five hundred souls. His laughable commands. His elaborate, insane, impractical secrecy.

We are given orders (sealed with yellow wax) which we are to break open when we depart from Land's End. But will we ever reach Land's End?

Eight weeks to sail from Dartmouth to Plymouth, I tell you! Eight weeks in which our meagre stores are eaten up. Those that are not putrified or turned to weevil excreta.

The men, of course, whether gentleman, mariner or soldier, are grown fractious to the point of mutiny. We have used up our fresh water supplies and the beer is undrinkable. To make matters worse, one of our supply ships is stolen. The degradation lies now in hearing Humphrey openly mocked, and the vilest rumours about him spread. I see the men regard me as if wondering do I share his vices as well as his blood.

And when at last we reach Plymouth, we find Knollys, who had broken rank and sailed alone, already there. His men have run riot through the town. I hear the reverberations of their rough deeds vibrate through the barrel. Mayhem and murder. Rape and robbery. All manner of ill-mannered behaviour. Whatever secret orders Humphrey may have drawn up, our mission was never this. To openly terrorize an *English* town. Even Simon Fernandez is somewhat daunted.

The weevils continue to twitch and chomp and secrete. As the bitter arguments of distant gods rumble over them.

But still the real degradation lies outside the barrel. The bruited rumour reaches me that Knollys is openly defying Humphrey. He will not deliver the murderers in his company. But shields them from justice and so condones their wrongdoing. You may imagine my own dudgeon at his conduct. It cost me much to give up William Pansfourthe to justice, but I knew it was my duty. The law is the law, after all. Discipline must be maintained. It is always up to the gentleman to set the example.

But Knollys proves himself a rascal surrounded by villains. Worse still, he will not even consent to sit down with his admiral.

He makes a public bonfire of his orders and sails off, taking near half the fleet with him. I cannot look at Humphrey. I shun his company, keeping to my cabin, losing myself in my books.

We seek to put it all behind us, and England too, choosing our own day to set sail on our own account, our fleet now reduced to six. But we had not reckoned on those winds again. The winds conspire with our enemies and blow us back into Plymouth harbour. I hear the shriek of a gull that labours on the wing. Like us, the poor bird makes no headway, flying backwards, for all its showy flapping.

The barrel's motion tells me that we have set sail again. The regular roll and rise of the ship is strangely soothing. I realise that I do not feel seasick here in the barrel. Around me the weevils and the maggots and the other too-small-to-be-named creatures carry on their toil. The biscuits sink and settle as their unpalatable hardness is converted to inedible porridge. There is a smell. It is akin to the smell of fermentation but it is also reminiscent of the taste of a dyspeptic belch. At first it is every bit as unpleasant as you imagine it will be. But as with most things, one becomes inured to it.

The barrel is a goodly well made thing, though its contents be shoddy. A fine example of the cooper's craft. The degradation lies not there. It lies in the creaking timbers of the *Falcon*. Can this leaking bucket really be owned by Her Majesty? The wainscotting that was once so solid to my touch now hangs loose off my gaping cabin wall. At night, I hear it rattling in the wind, the bones of a shivering skeleton. In places, you can force your finger into the rotten wood. Daylight shows between boards. Below the water line constant rivulets trickle through the straining planks. The hold fills with brine and doom. Living fish flash and dart in the ballast. The stores, what is left of them, are sodden and ruined. *All hands to the pumps!* Is the refrain to every sailor's chant. But there are nary enough pumps nor bailing buckets to stem the swelling seas.

By now it is winter. The winds that have beset us thus far are nothing to the winds that now come howling out of the West to drive us back.

The ship sits lower in the water every day. As the waves loom ever higher over her. Will we make it to America? Twill be a miracle if we make it as far west as Ireland. More likely we will follow the example of my brother Carew Ralegh's ship. Forced to turn back into Plymouth for repairs, the *Hope of Greenaway* gives up all hope.

The agitation of the weevils increases. It is as if they sense the extremity of our condition and want no part of it. They sense the coming of the end.

And now it comes. Their dark universe is ripped apart. An explosion of light sends them scuttling deep into the ravaged pulp that they have made of the hard tack.

I see the starved and haggard face of a man. He is little more than a skeleton with skin, his eyes deep sunk in dark caves.

### Aboard the admiral

We put in for repairs on the sullen, southern coast of Ireland. Our ship the *Falcon* is careened and caulked. She lies like the corpse of a boat, somewhat bloated, slick and glistening with an unhealthy necrotic slime. Strange growths and festering encrustations are revealed. We men thought we were her crew, but now we see a submerged world of limpet-limbed stowaways, and I cannot but wonder if the ship does not belong more to them than us.

Visiting Humphrey aboard the admiral ship, I suspect he will not meet my eye, so I do not go seeking his.

He is in his cups. Smells vinegary. As always when he is sodden, the melancholia predominates.

'My enemies have thwarted me.'

Humphrey hides his face in his hands. I see his shoulders begin to quake. His weeping is silent, and all the more pathetic for that. At last he takes another sup from his cup of sack and is somewhat fortified. Though his face be red and slicked with despair.

He braves a broken smile for my benefit. I feel my heart breaking at its shadowed ruin.

'The things we might have accomplished, Wat! This was to have been a glorious enterprise. The dawning of a new Golden Age.'

'Was to have been?'

'It's over, Wat. I have received a new commission from Walsingham. He has lost faith in us. The Queen has lost faith in us.'

'Us?'

'Aye.'

*Nay!* I wish to say. *They have lost faith in you!*

'I am to stay here, in Ireland.' Humphrey shakes his head as he says this. As if he would so easily shake me off. *Him* shake *me* off?

And so he is returned to the scene of his greatest triumph, though he seems morose enough about it. I warrant the Irish will be no happier to have him returned to them.

'What shall *I* do?'

'Go back to London, Wat. Our brothers Adrian and John Gilbert will aid you in furthering your career at court. And I will write letters of recommendation to certain lords and gentlemen of my acquaintance.'

How do I tell him that a recommendation from Sir Humphrey Gilbert, at this present moment, would be as favourably looked upon as a plague sore?

I leave him to his cask of sack, without a 'by your leave'.

At last our repairs are completed, or so we are told. The ship is righted and the crew rooted out of whatever dens they have fallen into. Stores are laden, though with no profit to the voyage as yet, I needs must exercise a spirit of parsimony, or be forced to turn a blind eye to a spot of enterprising larceny.

The ship feels alien beneath my feet, as if another vessel has been put in her place. I did not wholly trust her before. I trust her less now.

I find Simon Fernandez astride a culverin, the barrel of the ordinance protruding like an exaggerated advertisement of his virility.

'You have see your brother?'

'He is my half-brother.'

'He is weak man.'

It is an invitation to defend Humphrey. I do not take it. 'We must set our course for London.'

'I did no hexscape they angman's noose to sail haround they Irish Sea.'

'What do you propose?'

'We have a vessel, we have a crew, we have soldiers, we have cannon. You are not like your brother, I see this. You are a man. You stand tall. They men, they look up to you. They will go to they end of they earth for you. They will die for you. You have this. I see it.'

He tells me something I have sometimes sensed, and sometimes even dared to whisper to myself. I do not understand it. And if I think too much about why this should be, I begin to feel it desert me.

'The King of Spain is my sworn enemy. I will not rest until every last Spanish ship his blown from they sea. I will fuck they Spaniard's mothers hand his children too.'

Fernandez spits into the palm of his right hand and holds it out to me. 'Hharr you with me?'

I take the proffered hand. 'Set a course for the Canaries, Mister Fernandez.'

## Tar

The ship bounds and bounces like a dog let off the leash. Snouting the sea. It has caught the scent. The hunt is on, the chase begun.

The sails clatter like a chorus of clacking devils. *Dayvils*, as Simon Fernandez has it.

The storms weigh the heavier on us as the equinox approaches. We smell the hurricanoes before we feel their rage, just as you can smell an enemy's anger as he rushes at you. There are moments when the *Falcon* appears to be on the verge of shaking asunder. It takes all of Simon Fernandez's experience and profanities to keep her on course.

There are moments too when I might wish that I had ordered more fresh supplies to be laden on when we had the chance. Water especially. Or beer that did not taste of blubber. But the crew, I think, understand the economics of seafaring. Until we have secured a prize, we cannot raise a toast.

We ride the storms. The ship's hull holds, and keeps the icy depths at bay. And the men's thirst serves only to spur them on to greater effort, those of them that do not keel over. They put their backs into it because they know they are hurrying themselves towards a quenching of one sort or another.

Fernandez struts the decks, barking orders and obscenities. He employs gentler means to coax back to their feet the men who have collapsed, bending over them and whispering intently until they bestir themselves and resume their labour. I know not what he says. Could it be he promises riches beyond imagining? Or teases them with the more piquant prospect of a ladle of fresh water. Mayhap he shares some ribald pleasantry, beguiling them with the image of a whore's moist quim. Undoubtedly there is something lascivious about his confiding demeanour, as if he is welcoming them into a bawdyhouse rather than coaxing them back to life. But perhaps it is the same thing.

I note only that in most cases they come around smiling. And more eager than ever to get to it. Of course, some men prove to be beyond even Fernandez's sweet enticements. It is not long, I fear, before their dead weight must be bailed over the bulwarks.

To have the moaning sick and the stinking dead mounting on the decks would further no one's interests. And the example may keep others on their feet who might otherwise feign to faint.

From time to time, Simon Fernandez treats me to a lavish wink.

I do confess, I like the man. Undoubtedly he is rough, and not just about the edges. But in rough seas, one needs rough men.

Aye, they all are rough men, but they are Christians too. You may take it that I call the crew to the mainmast three times daily to hear prayers and sermons delivered by our parson, Maddox. This Maddox is a good enough fellow, with a stronger sense of duty than imagination. It is impossible for him to conceive of the full wickedness of sailors. Therefore he is not dismayed to preach to them every day. And for all their sins, the men prefer to serve on a ship that has a parson aboard, especially on such a voyage as this, across a torrid Ocean, to an unknown land. They are content enough to be preached at, even if they are little inclined to mend their ways.

I believe he is some kind of talisman for them. His prayers will keep the death they fear at bay. They carry their religion like a shield, or wield it like a weapon against the hated Papist foe.

We are surrounded by ocean. Those who doubt the spherical formation of the Earth would do well to place themselves in the midst of a vast expanse of empty sea. In every direction one turns, one sees the low curved horizon where the water meets the sky.

Like Simon Fernandez, who is its creature, the ocean never ceases movement. On calmer days, its twinkling surface is deceiving. One is almost lulled into thinking it means us well. But, as Simon Fernandez explains it to me, the Canary Current that carries us south constantly churns the waters. The frigid depths are forever brought to the top. The seeming warmth that so enticingly beckons the eye belies the cold and fatal truth: to plunge in would mean almost instant death.

As the sun sets, the sky is mired with smears of gold. Master Maddox's God hangs over us a blazing vision of the future that we chase. Deep beneath us, the holds of sunken wrecks open and give up their lost treasures of plate. The phantom bullion floats to the surface and catches fire. In that burnished moment, I can almost believe the ocean is God's mirror.

At night, I invite Maddox and the other gentlemen of my company into my cabin to sup with me. If his duties allow, Simon Fernandez joins us. We are a snug assembly, huddled around the flickering light of my gimbal lantern. The ship's musicians whip up a medley of merry English songs to keep the rumbling darkness at bay. The pilot regales us with lively tales of past adventures. It is the greatest of God's miracles that even now, after so many months at sea with the Portingale, Maddox still affects to be shocked by these recounted exploits. Every night, I must assure him that it is all only so much bragging. He must not pay it any heed. He prefers to believe me than countenance there may be one grain of truth in Fernandez's outrageous boasts.

Through the night, the bell tolls the hours, drawing me from dreams I am only too ready to relinquish. I hear the muted voices as the watch is changed and allow myself to drift off for another hour. It is part of the rhythm of the sea, this nightly pattern of snatched and broken sleep.

My dreams are of the deep. Of dark, slow-moving creatures drifting ponderously. Leviathans. They smash the ship to splinters with a swish of their immense tails. I see myself plummet through the water, my scream silenced by the inrush of brine, an icy punch ripping through my throat deep into my lungs. One of the monsters turns its lugubrious eye towards me. Its vast maw opens, revealing row upon row of ragged teeth. Another flick of its tail propels the creature towards me. Powerless to resist the onrushing weight of the ocean, I am borne inside the gaping circle of teeth. The roof of the monstrous mouth looms over me. My arms flail to steer me away from the massive tongue, of which I have conceived a great horror. I fear it more, even, than the deadly teeth. It is not simply that it has the mass to crush me. There is something viscerally repulsive about the very idea of that immense organ and its proximity to me.

The mouth begins to close. I thrash and writhe uselessly against the inevitable, my lungs on the verge of exploding. Darkness and the end engulfs me. To my surprise, given that I am underwater, and in the mouth of a sea monster, my screams are audible to me. This shock, more than any other, is what wakes me. I can still hear my screams as I open my eyes. But with a strange admixture of relief and foreboding, I realise they are not mine.

They are raw and wretched sounds, like the bleats of a wounded animal rather than a man. But we have slaughtered all our livestock long ago. One of the crew has captured a rat mayhap and is torturing it for sport? If so, it must indeed be a colossus of a rat, and he the Devil's own torturer.

I pull on my doublet and hose.

By some mysterious premonition, I feel that I know what sight will meet my eyes before I see it.

I step out of my cabin to see the bosun wrestle a sailor to the blood-red deck. A harsh and eager shout goes through the handful of rabble watching. On their faces is writ a vengeful ire. The bosun pins the man there with his knee in the middle of his back. Still the bleating screams continue. And now that I can see their source, this scrawny wreck of a man pinioned on the deck, it strikes me that, pitiable as they are, there is something impressive in these sounds.

The bosun can bear it no longer. He pushes the man's face into the deck to silence him. But he will not be silenced. His cries now reach us through the muffling wood. They have lost none of their power to appal.

'Fetch an axe!'

At this fierce command, the trapped man's cries reach a new frenzy of terror. One of the sailors hurries off to the carpenter's workshop. The rest cry out their approval. Nay, it is more than approval. Their blood is up. They demand retribution. The Parson's sermons have turned each man of them into a wrathful Old Testament God.

The bosun must see some soft glow of pity in my eyes. 'I caught him stealing tack, cap'n.'

I know full well what parlous state the ship's biscuits are in by now. What's left of them. It is hard to conceive what drove him to this crime, though the observation escapes me: 'He is hungry.'

'We are all hungry, cap'n. Tis no excuse for thievery.'

'Show me his face.'

Somehow it is important to me to look into his eyes before I assent to his punishment. The bosun wrests his head around. Released from the hard gag of the deck, the screams fill the air with fresh misery and fear.

The sailor's face is grey and haggard. His eyes deep sunk in dark pits. I see no remorse in them. Only an insatiable criminality. It is clear that if the bosun were to release him, he would run straight back to the galley to steal again. No doubt some derangement has so disordered his mind. It will necessitate a mighty shock to shake him out of his error.

I give my approval with a terse nod just as Simon Fernandez joins us. I inform him of the essentials of the case: 'He stole hard tack.'

Simon Fernandez looks down at the bleating thief. For a moment, I think that he is about to question my command. Instead, he merely shrugs, before returning to his cabin. I confess I am surprised he does not remain to see justice done.

The axe is fetched. It is an impressive tool, weighty and long-handled. Its broad, whetted blade gleams with a pristine eagerness. It is so sharp it cuts the very day as it is handed through the crowd.

It is given to the ship's carpenter, for he is the most skilled wielder of axes among the company. But he receives it with a clumsy fumbling, as if he has never handled an axe before. Or as if it were far heavier than sense suggests it can be. The man seems to have forgotten his calling and his craft, so I must remind him of it: 'See to it that it is a clean blow.'

Justice must always be tempered with mercy.

The bosun grapples with the captive, extending his right arm along the line of a board. Two other men put themselves forward to aid with the arrangement of the culprit. However, it is as well that I am there to oversee the affair: 'May we not cut off the left? Cut off the right and he will be no use to us at all.'

Now the right arm is pulled back in and pinioned abaft the man. The left extended. The bosun raises a practical issue: 'We will need tar!'

There is a further delay while a burning brazier and a cauldron of tar is fetched. The smell of the dark matter adds a pungency to the moment. The brazier's heat spreads a deceptive warmth. The tar is stirred and teased until it glistens and flows. The choking smoke brings tears to the hardened sailors' eyes.

At last, all is ready. The carpenter stumbles towards his duty, impelled by the crew members around him.

The thief's bleats quicken and rise in pitch. His face is once again driven into the deck, averted from the culmination of the act he has set in play by his larceny.

His left arm is held steady by the bosun's two helpers. He is so emaciated it is like a yardarm protruding from a mast. The arm is immobilised. But all the constrained motion of that limb is transmitted into the hand at the end of it. The hand claws the air restlessly. It circles on the pivot of its wrist. Its fingers splay and wriggle. It writhes and squirms. As I watch it, I entertain the notion that it is itself a living creature, possessing an animus of its own. Given half the chance, it would break free and bolt for it. So firmly entrenched is this fancy, that I am convinced we shall soon see it scuttle across the deck on the tips of its digits.

I am shaken from this daydream by the bosun's curses as he strives to goad the reluctant carpenter to his task. I add my voice to the admonishments: 'Your dallying only prolongs this wretch's suffering. The swifter the blow, the sooner ends the agony for us all.'

'Everybody knows poor John is not right in the head. Who else but a madman would pilfer the weevil's leavings?'

'Good order on-board a ship, as in the ship of state, depends upon the swift and ruthless prosecution of wrongdoing. To show too much leniency may encourage others to follow his example, in the expectation that they may hide behind the mask of seeming madness. And for all we know, the shock of this punishment will shake his wits back to order.'

I had not thought it possible, but the thief's cries reach a new pitch of frenzied despair. The hand convulses and vibrates with unnatural animation. Not a man there can take his eyes off it. It is the horror of this sight, I think, that decides the carpenter. For the hand at that moment seems possessed. Even I, who am not given to superstition, can believe a devil has got into it. Perhaps the carpenter reasons that it is this devil that is responsible for John's thieving.

We feel rather than see the swift blur of metal as the axehead is swung back. And feel too the weight of its falling in the pit of our stomachs. The axehead lands with a crisp and strangely satisfying thump. The hand jumps a little away from the blow. Then lies inert. There is no scuttling after all.

The blood is pooling now, red on the red-painted deck.

John's cries have fallen to a babbling whimper. He is lifted to his feet and dragged over to the brazier, blood spraying from his abrupt arm. The bosun knows his business. Speed is of the essence. The open stump is plunged into the cauldron of thickly-bubbling tar.

The screams that woke me are nothing to the screams I hear now.

### Cannonshot

Early one mist-morn'd day, a spring in our keel, we make good headway on an even sea, running before a light wind. The cry goes up, from the lookout up top. *Ship ahoy! Port side! Three leagues distant!* Simon Fernandez stands atop the forecastle. Shields his eyes against the flaring sun. Leans out over the bulwarks, in the direction of the cry.

'Spanish. Merchantman.' This muttered under his breath. He cracks a sly one-sided grin. Then shouts the order: 'Ready about! Hard starb'rd.'

I see the steersman put his shoulder into the whipstaff.

The *Falcon* creaks and leans as she begins her laborious turn to port. The straining sails swing on the masts, holding their angle with the wind. Then the wind dies and the sails slacken. I hold my breath and on my oath I swear my heart stops beating.

Since John's punishment the crew have displayed a curious admixture of restive agitation and sullen torpor. I had hoped the incident would prove a crisis in the men's passions. That they might draw a lesson from their fellow's fate. And as the victims of John's crime, were not the men themselves the most enthusiastic advocates of his judicial maiming?

Be that as it may, I confess the mood on board took a dark turn after the carpenter fell overboard. To batten down their loyalty, I must deliver them a prize soon, and a prize that contains fresh water and sound provisions. Gold would be welcome too.

The snap of the canvas as it bellies out is the signal for my heart to start again. It beats our advance so loudly I fear it can be heard above the whip of the wind.

Sailing cross beam now (or holding as close to it as we can in our stiff-keeled vessel) we move steadily towards the other. Simon Fernandez keeps up a restless prowl around our prow.

'Man they GUNS!' He screams the last word as if it is a cannonball discharged. His fierce eye is on me, a challenge and a rebuke.

I haul myself alongside and add my command to his: 'BATTLE STATIONS!'

A cheer goes up. This is what they have been waiting for. The crossbow archers clamber into the rigging. Simon Fernandez smiles his approval.

The other ship continues on her course towards us. Her crew must be half asleep. By the time she descries our hostile intent, it is too late. She tries to swing around but Simon Fernandez reads her well and cuts across her trajectory.

We hold a broad circle that draws us closer to her. Close enough now to confirm her Spanish flag, and for her to see our colours too. She is a small, two-masted caravel, low in the water. The one hundred-ton *Falcon* looms over her.

He Spanish crew keep within the sterncastle.

Simon Fernandez again reminds me of my duty. 'You must give they command to fire into her rigging.'

I feel an iron hammer pounding at my wrists. I think of the men, of the desperate hunger in their eyes. It started as hunger for glory and gold. But is now just hunger.

'Starboard guns. FIRE!'

The cannon and the demi-cannon, the culverins and demi-culverins. The falconets and sakers. I can see each gun's charging and discharging: the black powder packed and pounded in; the shot loaded; the fuse lit; the gunners' fleet retreat before the moment of explosion and recoil.

One side of our ship erupts in a ragged sequence of booming flashes. Smoke fills the space between the two vessels. I see the chain-shot fly, the two linked balls whirling around each other in a wild, shrieking dance of destruction.

The throaty clamour of the crew savages the acrid air.

A cheer goes up as the smoke clears upon the destruction we have wrought. The masts shattered. The sails hanging in tattered disarray. The rigging ripped to ribbons.

We drift ever closer to our target. The first man hurls himself from the *Falcon*'s rigging, but falls between the two vessels. A moment later, the yard arm of the *Falcon*'s main mast overhangs the other ship's deck. Now is the time. Dripping with swords, axes and arquebuses, our boarding soldiers scamper out and dangle from the rigging, before dropping onto the foreign deck below. Ropes are thrown across, caught and tautened, binding prize to prize-taker.

I watch as her sterncastle is breached. A cluster of my men hew at the door and burst in. Nature's questing, invasive impulse in action. They are like ants clambering one over another to be at the beetle cadaver.

The Spaniards offer no resistance. They huddle in the corners of their cabins. I see the fear in their eyes. They hold up their hands in abject surrender. But the bloodlust is up in my men. They are blind to the signals of submission. Deaf to all pleas and protestations. They see only the hated enemy. Hear only the roaring of blood in their ears, and their own goading screams. There is more hewing, this time of human flesh and bone. Arquebuses crackle and splutter. The Spanish mariners drop, too startled to fight or even cry out in protest. The slaughter is over in the blinking of an eye, although my all-seeing eyes do not blink.

The rage does not abate in my men. They search the quarters, drag out the cabin boy, a quivering, pretty youth of no more than twelve, with long girlish hair. He is made to bare his arse and submit to corporate buggery. But soon his incessant weeping annoys my men, and so his throat is slit.

It gives me no satisfaction to say that my crew is comprised of the very dregs of society. Even the gentlemen in my company are the second sons of second sons, and want no hard driving to resort to desperate measures. And you may warrant it that by this stage of the voyage, the desperation of all has reached its nadir.

On the deck of the *Falcon*, Simon Fernandez somehow divines the run of my troubled thoughts. 'You owe them this, my captain. They have waited for it. It is theirs.'

Casks of water and wine are transferred, together with supplies of dates, fish, and salted meat. There are even live guinea fowl to be handed up. The caravel cannot have been long out of port. She is found to have a hold full of hides. But no gold. The hides will have to do.

Before they can be hauled up, however, we hear a low boom from the belly of the Spanish vessel.

One last surviving crewman has thrown a spark into a powder keg. One last act of defiance to deprive his enemies of the pleasure of killing him. It blows a hole below the waterline and throws a spreading blanket of flame in every direction. The first to be engulfed by it is the Spanish sailor. His screams are lively but short-lived.

The scuttled caravel begins to list. My men scramble up the swiftly tilting deck, fighting each other for handholds on the hanging ropes. To save ourselves we must cut loose the cables that bind us to the burning ship, giving up all claim on her cargo.

I see the men. The men who do not find a handhold. I see them fall into the bubbling water. I see their arms fail hopelessly as the oceanic undercurrent pulls them down.

I see the lugubrious eye of a Leviathan move steadily towards them out of the depths.

## The Paradoxal Compass

It is a paradox that to approach something, first one may have to travel away from it.

To understand a paradox fully, one must immerse one's self in it. That becomes my sole occupation over the remainder of the voyage. I largely confine myself to my cabin. There I open up my trunk of books. I am drawn to the accounts of other voyages that the Richard Hakluyts have compiled for me. I voyage with Octher to the lands beyond Norway. With Ingulphus, from Croyland, where he was abbot, into Jerusalem. I accompany Macham as he discovers Madeira. And venture to Candia and Chios with Roger Bodenham. I am there in Muscovy, with George Killingworth. And reach as far as Bokhara in Bactria with Anthony Jenkinson.

How easy it is to accomplish these far-ranging journeyings in the turning of a few pages.

Along the way what prodigies I encounter. Men with no heads, but faces in the midst of their breasts. Men who stand, and somehow ambulate, on one enormous foot, at the end of their singular leg. Horned men, men with tails, others with fur-covered pelts. Skins of every hue, from yellow to inky black. Giants, pygmies, and men of middling size, who have some limb or member grotesquely elongated, a neck, for example, that extends as far as a giraffe's, or a nose that emulates that of the elephant. Tribe after tribe of cannibals. And that most fearsome tribe of Amazons, those warlike women whose martial inclination is so great that they do hew off their own right breasts the more easily to accommodate the drawing of their bowstrings.

I put in at spice-scented harbours, am met by inquisitive but amicable savages. I am favoured by Tsars, captured by Turks, I dine on monkeys' brains and camel meat. I sup wine fermented from mares' milk.

And all the while, my ship continues on her paradoxical way: we approach our destination by holding a course perpendicular to it.

The Paradoxal Compass is indeed a strange device: every time that I take it out of my trunk, it appears to be a different object to that which it was the last time I handled it. I cannot even tell you from what material it is fashioned. Only that it must necessarily be constructed from something highly mutable. This should not surprise you. Its maker is none other than the Philosopher of Mutability.

As I hold it now in my hands, it appears to be a small wooden panel, into which are set a series of rotatable rings of brass. Each is etched with the motif of an arrowhead and surrounds the design of a compass rose, which is carved into the wood and painted. As far as I am able to ascertain by my own experimentation, I must rotate the first ring so that the arrowhead is aligned with the direction, as the crow flies, of my ultimate destination. The second ring I move to indicate the direction from which the wind reaches us. The third ring I set to indicate the tidal direction. The hidden mechanism of the contraption turns the fourth ring to indicate the bearing at which I must hold my course. There is a fifth ring, the purpose of which I have not yet been able to fathom.

Yesterday it was a sheaf of thin translucent sheets filled with charts and tables of figures. I deduced that the papers were to be placed in a specific manner (aligning certain marks depending upon the time of day, the direction of our intended bearing, our time out of port, et cetera, et cetera) one on top of the other. It then transpired that when I held them up to the light, I saw a map of the world with my corrected course depicted in red. So that I may not be in any doubt, letters from each page came together to confirm that I was indeed holding the PARADOXAL COMPASS.

You may be sure that the workings of the Paradoxal Compass occupy me more than any of the other contents of my trunk. More too than the progress of the very voyage upon which I am embarked. What vistas have passed by me outside my cabin porte, what shorelines we have shadowed, what schools of porpoises have accompanied us, what native embassies have parlayed with us, what prizes taken, what enemies repelled, where, if and how we re-victualled along the way – of all of this I have no inkling. Nor of how many more men we have lost.

Simon Fernandez scorns to consult the Paradoxal Compass. I fear that he is afraid of it. Like all mariners, he is deeply superstitious, even if he has recanted his erstwhile Papism. He mistakes the scientific wonder of it for some species of the Devil's work.

Instead, he taps the side of his formidable nose with a grubby forefinger. And sniffs prodigiously, doubtless scenting out the breeze to bear us home.

## Tennis

The ball trips along the penthouse roof with a pert jounce, dwindling into a trickle before dropping into the receiver's court. The player mistimes his swing and misses his shot entirely. He had too long to prepare for it, I think.

The ball dies in the sixth chase.

Watching from the gallery, I add my voice to the chorus of jeers. I confess I have not the patience for playing, and little interest in watching, unless I have a wager at stake. I am assured that the vigorous action has a beneficial effect on a man's digestion. I prefer the stimulation of hard coin easily won.

I am back at court, which now resides at Greenwich, in the Pleasant Palace. I will not say I returned with my tail between my legs, but neither were my arms full of unicorn horns. I boldly faced the contemptuous sneers of the sniggering creatures, and let it be known that I have sailed across the Atlantic Ocean with Simon Fernandez, fought the Spanish and taken rich prizes. My puffed chest asks the question: *And what have you done all the while?*

More than once, the answer has resulted in a brawl. Some have seen fit to remind me of the government order now confining me by name to land. And I have seen fit to box their ears and stuff their mouths with wax.

Upon my return, I found myself propelled into the Earl of Oxford's circle. In truth, I cannot remember whether I am spying on Oxford for Walsingham, or reporting back on Walsingham to Oxford. Either way, I serve myself the best I can. Certainly, the disaffection of that faction suits my own mood of sullen resentment. I draw from them a dark energy that consoles me for my failures.

Rebellion is never openly talked about. The Earl is not such a fool as that. But we are all drunk with the anticipation that he is the man to shake things up somewhat. And that when he does, things will fall out well for us.

No doubt this is why Walsingham wants him watched.

The world has turned topsy-turvy since I took off on my voyage. The French are at court now, courting our Queen for their Duc d'Anjou et Alençon. (Some of them stand near us in the gallery. I resent their laughter. It is one thing for an Englishman to mock another Englishman, quite another for a foreigner.) Oxford, who favours the marriage, is in the ascendant. Even as he makes vile, treasonable jokes about Her Majesty's person.

In truth I find his remarks too tiresome to be alarming. They are meant, I believe, to amuse. It is that grim, intoxicating amusement that comes from wilful wrong-doing. I force myself to laugh with the others. Men usually laugh when they are merry, or mayhap to make themselves merry. I laugh when I am soul-sick and despairing.

One day, soon, he will make an Oxfordian Utopia for us. In the meantime, it is his pleasure simply to make trouble.

As now. With one eye on our French visitors, he loudly proclaims: 'This game is tedious. These leaden-footed oafs are a disgrace. They bring shame upon all Englishmen.'

One of the players looks up towards the gallery, the sting of Oxford's rebuke showing in the deep flush of his pock-marked face. It is Sidney. As well favoured in his diverse talents as he is ill-favoured in his person. It is said the Queen admires him greatly, but likes him little. Perhaps his disfigurement reminds Her Majesty too much of his mother, whose own ravaged face was her sole reward for nursing the Queen through a bout of smallpox.

If the truth be told, we are all a little in awe of him. He does not seem to seek the Queen's favour, but merely expects it. Nor does he betray his principles in order to attach himself to a dubious faction. There is nothing so hateful in a man of talent as integrity, especially for those who have prostituted their own.

Hence our pleasure in his recent, unwonted mistake on the tennis court. We all know he is a better tennis player than that. But we are pleased to see him fall below his own standards.

Oxford, who came to the courts prepared for a game, thrashes the air with his own racket. He fixes Sidney with a cold stare, to indicate the pleasure it would give him to inflict such a thrashing on the man himself.

Of all of us, it is Oxford who hates Sidney the most. He has more reason than any other. For one thing, Sidney has had the effrontery to speak out against the proposed marriage. For another, he promises to be by far the better poet. In all he does, he emanates a fixed commitment to the truth, an unwavering honesty and precision, an unalloyed purity of intellect. The poets among us recognise in him the spirit of the natural poet.

And was not Sidney engaged to Anne Cecil, only to be rejected by her father on account of his family's lowly status and poverty? That cannot but rankle with the man. But it may also be a seed of envy in Oxford. For whereas Anne Cecil was given to him to be his wife, her heart already belonged to Sidney.

Oxford mutters beneath his breath: 'I'll wager a sovereign that I will have them yield their court to me.'

I hold out my hand and nod, accepting the bet. Even if I lose, the entertainment that it promises will be sufficient compensation.

'Come then, Howard. Let us teach them a lesson in tennis.'

And so Oxford draws Henry Howard into his quarrel. As he draws us all in, eventually.

In truth, this Henry Howard, Earl of Northampton, needs less drawing than most, being a most choleric and quarrelsome man by nature. He is as quick to ignite as phosphorus. I care little for him, and I daresay he cares even less for me. I am not earl of anywhere, nor even a lord, nor even a mere knight. I am only one more ambitious gentleman, whom the Queen has seen fit to notice. As he would have it, as much for my long body and keen wit, as for any evident talent. I cannot count the ways in which Henry Howard contrives to make manifest his dislike for me. A frown of incomprehension creases his brow whenever I come into the same room as he. He looks to Oxford indignantly, as though expecting his idol to order my eviction. Such an order never comes. It seems to afford my Lord Oxford a perverse pleasure to have us thrown together, as if he somehow feeds off the energy of our antipathy.

Sensing the approach of a scandal, spectators from other games rush to swell the crowd over Sidney's court. The murmur of expectancy waxes into a clamour. There are many of Oxford's French friends in the gallery with us. Their alien language sharpens the edge of dark excitement that cuts the air.

Sidney and his opponent have resumed their play by the time Oxford bursts in on them.

'Come now, it is time for you to cede the court to better players.'

Sidney lobs a shot in Oxford's direction. The Earl is able to avoid injury by executing a nimble dance step and returning the ball with a firm stab of his racket. His timing is as impeccable as Sidney's was amiss. He doffs his Italianate hat to the cheering French in the gallery.

Sidney's patience is tested by this piece of foolery. 'Look to your manners, sir. I have hired the court for the day. I shall cede it to no one. Now kindly leave us to continue our play. Before you are hurt indeed. For if you remain I cannot vouch for your safety.'

'You dare threaten me?'

'I mean only that you place yourself in danger of receiving a blow from the ball. We will not stop our game. I have paid good money for the court, which I have no desire to squander.'

'Thus speaks a poor man and a poor player.'

'I do not know who you think you are…'

'I do not *think* I am anyone. I know that I am the Earl of Oxford. And you are…?'

Of course, Oxford knows well the answer to the question he asks. I think he would know the identity of his wife's erstwhile lover.

'I am Philip Sidney.'

'Philip Sidney? Philip Sidney. Philip. *Sidney*.'

Unaccountably, Oxford's blank repetition of his enemy's name, for all the world as if he had never heard it before, reduces his supporters in the gallery to fits of helpless hilarity. He contrives to charge the expression of it with a degree of contempt that ought to be devastating to the recipient.

Sidney, however, fails to be devastated. 'Is this what passes for wit in your witless cabal?'

'Careful, Philip Sidney. You insult my friends. And he who insults my friends insults me.'

'They insult themselves by their association.'

'Why, you young puppy!'

'Will you repeat that? Repeat it or retract it. I wish to be sure that I heard you aright.'

'I said, puppy. You young puppy.'

'Puppy? Nay, sir. I am not a puppy. A puppy is the offspring of a dog. Children are born of women.'

'Pup.'

'You lie, sir.'

'You dare give me the lie, puppy?'

'You are a liar. And you persist in your lie, I see.'

'No one gives me the lie!'

Oxford's voice rises to an ugly piping treble. His face is contorted with red wrath. It is at this supreme moment that Sidney turns his back on him, with infinite disregard.

'I give you the lie and leave you to consider your honour.'

And so Sidney cedes the court after all, not before glancing with satisfaction up at the now hushed throng in the gallery.

Oxford wins his wager, it is true. But the prevailing sense is that it is a hollow victory. It cost him his temper and his dignity. He does not look up at us. His face is very dark now. No doubt with rage, though the inclination of his body I would say is rather more cowed than anything. Somehow the young puppy got the better of him and he knows it.

Sidney knows it too, for his stride is buoyant. He faces the gallery with a defiant stare.

Oxford strikes the ball as if he is striking his enemy's head. His shot is snagged by the net. The hangdog ball falls short into his own court. And the earl must face the ignominy of walking to retrieve it.

The jeers now are at his expense. The French contingent drift away, to other games that promise a more entertaining spectacle.

### Making ink

The night defers, the dawn decides. The earl
Delays the day by lying long abed.
While Sidney rises early, seeking out
His foe to lay before him his neglect
Of honour's duty clear. *How can the earl*
*Allow insult to go without redress?*
Thus goads he Oxford's friends, who hie in haste
from Sidney's slurs to urge the earl to stir
From out his bed for shame to boot himself.
Each passing hour, his name more tarnish'd grows.
But Oxford's deaf to honour's urging. And blind
To friends' dismay. He claims the puppy's yaps
So far beneath him are, t'would shame him more
To stoop to meet them, yea, than them ignore.
But Henry Howard who was there with him
On court when first the lie was cast, and so
Partakes in equal portion of his shame;
He will not let it lie, oh no. He will,
He swears, have Oxford's honour satisfied.
A message swift is sent to Sidney straight.
Two men the bearers, Arundell and I.
Forsooth, I wish no part in this charade,
Which more befits rude boys than gentle men.
Alas, the game begun must now be play'd.
What started on the tennis court must end
In one or other's death.
                              Unlike the earl,
We find young Sidney calm, and occupied
In making ink. He has no truck, he says,
With scrivener's nor apothecary's wares,
But much prefers to make his own. I own
It strikes me as an affectatión.
But I am curious to see it done.
He grinds five ounce of gall of oak into
A quart of wine. To this he adds the flower
Of copper, copperas so called. To this
He adds gum arabic and lasting salt.
And last, to match his black design, he grinds
To powder lampblack in a mortar's bowl.
'Such labour just to fill your inkhorn up!'
'Not for my inkhorn, Master Ralegh, no,
But for my poetry I take these pains.

67

And I would spill my blood into the horn
If such libation should my Muse suborn.'
'Let's hope you have a gentler Muse than that.'
'Speaking of blood.'

(Tis he who brings it up.)

'Speaking of blood.'

(Again.)
'I do accept.'

'Accept?'

'Your    master's    tardy    gauntlet
thrown.'
'We bring no gauntlet. You anticipate.'
'Then bear my gauntlet with you back to him.'
'Is't true? A game of tennis has brought us here,
My friend, to talk of gauntlets, duels and death?'
'You're wrong again. Twas not tennis that brought
Us to this pass. But honour.'

'If I may…'

(Says Arundell.) 'Ralegh too rashly speaks.
Lord Oxford's as honour-bound as any man.'
'So do you bear his challenge here to me?'
'We do.'
'We don't.'

(The metre meets, the meaning not.)

'Make up your minds.'

He takes a quill and frowns,

Then opens up his knife to sharpen it.
'Mayhap I rashly speak, if it be rash
To wish for men's blood to stay in men's veins.
I have seen war, in France. I saw enough
Of blood on both sides shed for no good cause.
I fought the Huguenot's fight and it was right.
The men I fought beside were goodly men.
But, oh, their leader, Condé, false was he.
The men, they lived by honour but were led
By lies to die, their honour all betrayed.
This honour that you now invoke is false
And like the lies that led good men to death.
Be good, I pray! Take back your heated words.
Retract, forgive, and be forgiven, live!
The nobler heart moves first to reconcile.
Come, show yourself a better man than he.
And so more noble than an earl you'll be.
Let's not turn words to wounds and, worse, to worms.'
'You speak not rashly, Ralegh, but… your words
I can't commend. I too saw Huguenots die.

68

I was in Paris on St Bartholomew's Night.'
'You mean to say Saint Bartholomew's *Day*?'
'So dark the deeds, they turned the Day to Night.
The sun did hide his bloodied face in shame
To see the streets beneath him run with blood.
While in the Seine the fish fed on the dead,
Its waters swelled with strange and swollen food.
Along the banks the bodies mounted up.
Thousands heaped on thousands. The city's rank
Detritus was too much for men to clear.
Why, Hercules would balk at such a task!
These crimes though grave were nothing next the crime
That mothered them all: the first murther done
Against the noble soldier Coligny,
Already wounded from assassin's gun.
They promised justice and sanctuary safe.
Then dragged him fighting from his bed and drove
A dagger through his heart and tipped him out
A window high. And for good measure then
Lopped off his head and left him dead.
It was the worst because in cold blood done.
What crimes ensued were all blind frenzy's work.
The King's mother, the bold dowager Queen,
Caterina de' Medici, twas she
Who birthed this treacherous deed, and so begat
A breeding ground of criminality.
And who was suckled on the same sow's teat?
On Caterina de' Medici's dug?
But Duc d'Anjou, who's here to seek our Queen's
Dear hand for matrimony's solemn vow.
Whose cause is furthered by your noble friend.
Th'ignoble Earl of Oxford, sodomite,
Blasphemer, traitor, liar, coward, cheat.
Retract? I'll not retract. Will he? That cur
Who called my dame a dog when first he tried
To make a pup of me.'
And so he speaks.

## A dozen devils

The noble Oxford's answer to all this?

He summons us to meet with him at Greenwich, close to Philip Sidney's dwelling place. We find him at the riverbank, dismissing a dozen dark-clad devils. We do not see their faces. They turn and swish their cloaks at us before we are upon them. And are gone. Scattering themselves to the breathless winds.

Arundell informs him of the issue of our yesterday's interview with Sidney. ''Tis as well.'

'Honour will be satisfied,' says Arundell.

Oxford doesn't see it so. 'I cannot fight that puppy. He has no title. I will be dishonoured if I kill him.'

I cannot help myself: 'You killed a servant once.'

Oxford does not take my intervention well: 'Your memory's faulty, Ralegh. I did not kill him. He killed himself by running on my sword. So found the Coroner's Jury, who gave a verdict of suicide. But shall we walk a little?'

Thus he wishes to walk away from his past. It is a natural enough urging.

Henry Howard is perplexed by Oxford's disinclination to a contest. 'But did you not issue a challenge to him?'

'I think not. I would not so demean myself.'

'But has he not issued a challenge to you?'

'It is not his place so to do.'

Arundell shakes his head uneasily. 'This will not end well.'

''Twill end very well, I vouch you. Those men, they are brave fellows, and biddable too. I have bid them visit Sidney in his chamber this night. Why, I even pointed out the very place to them. They are twelve men, with twelve guns, who will leave twelve holes in Sidney's sorry corpse.'

The scandal of what he is proposing hits me: 'You would have him murdered?'

'Yes, Ralegh. I will have him murdered.'

'But what of honour?'

Oxford smiles as he sniffs his scented cuff, as if to remind himself of pleasanter things: ''Tis well this way. It will not touch upon my honour.'

'You will turn England into a race of assassins?'

'What, Ralegh? You think it is not that already? Beneath the trappings of civility, are we not all murderers and rapists? Strip away the courtier's manners, the churchman's morals. Beneath it all, we are savage, bestial and ravening. Remember that. Exult in it.'

Arundell, for all that he is a boon friend to Oxford, is no craven murderer. He ventures to suggest: 'There may yet be a way out of this. The Queen…'

'The Queen! Ah yes, the Queen. God save the Queen. God save her black and rotted teeth, her stinking breath, her grating voice, her graceless form, her withered paps, her dry and rancid cunt. The filthiest fishwife ne'er smelled so foul as the Queen's quim. If I were not paid to tickle it, I would not go near it. You may be sure, gentlemen, that I was obliged to close my eyes and hold my nose and do my duty for England. I cannot be blamed if I go elsewhere for my pleasure.'

If he aims to amuse, he is wide of the mark. His remarks dumbfound us, stun us to utter silence. My mouth gapes and trembles, is suddenly as dry as my palms are drenched. I feel my heart knock out a pattern of revolt.

Oxford tests us to the limit, teasing out the limits of our love. Are we loyal to him, to the true, false, empty, hate-filled, blackened core of him, to the nothing that is all he is, and all he offers? Or will we abandon him to his treacherous bile, that leaks from him like the poisonous pus from a rash of suppurating pores?

Henry Howard sniggers like a school boy. A blast of putrid breath strikes my nostrils. I cannot check myself.

'By Christ, what foul stink is that! A dead corpse exudes a fairer air than comes from your mouth, sir! Can you not cover it? For pity's sake!'

The Earl of Northampton looks for a moment as if he will draw his sword and cut me down. He looks to Oxford for permission. But Oxford only laughs, as if I had essayed the most amusing witticism.

His sword stays in its sheath. And he must content himself with much curling of the lip.

I am aware that I have attacked the Fool because I may not strike the King of our little circle. I cannot doubt that Oxford recognises himself as the true target of my wrath.

He means to try me further, I think: 'But what of the Queen's cunt, Ralegh? Does that not have a fouler stench than even Henry's breath? What say you, as one who has deep knowledge of the matter?'

Arundell quietly comments: 'You go too far, Oxford.'

And I… I do not answer. I feel his arm around my shoulder, pulling me to him as we walk beside the river's side. Does he presume complicity from my taciturnity? Or is this another test? If so, it is one I fear I must fail, for I shiver at his touch. The man is all at once loathsome to me. How can he not see that?

He whispers further vile insults against the Queen's dear person, for my ears only.

I writhe to wrest myself away from him but he tightens his grip on me.

He means to know, am I with him or against him?

'I know you do not mean it. Any of it,' I say, at last.

This seems to disappoint him. 'Do not ever doubt me at my word. To doubt me at my word, why, that is tantamount to giving me the lie, is't not?'

'Let us not go down this avenue again,' I wearily reply.

I feel his grip loosen on my shoulder. I sense the turning of a catastrophe. Irrevocable, final, tragic. My fate, I feel, has been sealed.

I make my excuses. An appointment remembered. My brother. I don't say which one. Desirous to talk with me concerning some future project. I don't say what. I hurry away from him, chasing along the riverfront towards the palace.

Sweat breaks out beneath my silk and linen layers. Oxford's eye, as I turned away from it, was as cold and devouring as any leviathan's.

### For a suit of clothes

My finest suit donned – indeed my only suitable suit – and my cloak drawn against the nip and spit in the March air, sword swaying against my leg, I stride beneath the Cockpit Gate onto the Street. Whatever trepidation or disappointment shadows you, it is important as a courtier to enter the palace at a brisk, confident step. You must not be seen to hesitate. For you never know who may be watching. The Queen herself is said to be in the habit of observing the comings and goings along this thoroughfare from the window of her Privy Gallery. And so, you must put your best foot forward and stride.

But you must also skip and dance over puddles and mud, as well as keep an eye out for the sudden lurches of carts and carriages. The drivers care not if they mow down a courtier or two. A raucous chorus explodes from a wagon of caged poultry. Beady-eyed capons and chickens regard each other with startled indignation. For a moment I am conveyed back to the old cob-house garden where disapproving hens looked up from pecking grains to watch me on my way.

Between the carts, a drove of pushy geese competes with human wayfarers for precedence. Though their wings are clipped, they cede to none, not to lords upon their mounts, ladies in their litters, servants sent on errands, or those like me who go about our own business on our own account. It pleases me to think how little do these conceited fowl know that they are strutting towards kitchens where their necks will be twisted and snapped, and their luxuriant feathers plucked from their cold dead gooseflesh.

This squalid traffic passes through the heart of Whitehall Palace, like a motion passed through the gut.

The geese cry out in angry alarm. A cow is being led against them, coming from the King Street Gate end, and they must navigate their way around her, or give battle. She stops and lows, then lowers and sways her heavy head, to regard the agitated geese from an eye of calm and singular beauty. (Not without reason did Homer describe Hera, the Queen of the Gods, as having bovine eyes.)

For some reason my own eye is drawn by this trivial farmyard incident. The cow's tail rises as she discharges a healthy jet of shit, no respecter she of the majesty of a royal palace.

I keep close to the wall that screens the palace gardens from public view, as far from the press and pollution of the traffic as is possible. It is at that moment, as I am distracted by the need to maintain the perfection of my hosiery, that I begin to sense the presence of an observer other than the Queen.

I see him almost as soon as I sense him. He is daggers drawn. Or rather, has dagger in one hand, sword in the other. Bearing down on me, like a charging bullock. He roars, or almost roars. It is rather that his throat produces a gurgling sound that seems to startle him more than it terrorises me. I wager that he wishes he had practised that.

73

I am backed against the garden wall. If I run to either side, he will hack me down. So it is better to draw and stand and fight. My hand is never far from my hilt at any time.

My rapier whips out with a steely satisfying whisper.

I look into the man's eyes, expecting to see there some explanation of his murderous charge. Hatred, perhaps. I think I know what hatred looks like. But no. I see not hatred there. Not the real thing at least. He has buckled up a belt of borrowed hate.

His eyes are wild in the sense that he does not seem to have control over them. They roll about like drunks. For, yes, the fellow is deep in his cups. Three sheets to the wind. As he gets closer, I can smell it on him. Not just on his breath. It's sweating out of him. The alehouse stench. He has bought his courage in a tavern.

Paradoxically, it makes him more dangerous, because harder to predict. He is not so far gone that he will fall over at the slightest push. His feet stagger somewhat, but they are weighted firmly to the ground, and it is this weightiness that renders them unmanageable. He seems to sense his own limitations and this enrages him the more. It makes him absurd. But also capable of anything. He stumbles and thrashes like a baited bear. It is not difficult to imagine him rousing himself to one mad, desperate lunge.

All too easy to underestimate him. That sheen of grease upon his forehead. His thinning hair. The frayed cuffs and grubby lace. I find myself distracted by these details. And so, before I know it, he is upon me.

The gurgle in his throat solidifies into a fleshy yell.

His steel clashes with mine. It is a sobering moment for both of us. I see his eyes swivel to the front and meet mine. His head begins to quake with a minute vibration of… what? It could be denial. Or regret. Apology. Or fear. Or perhaps it is simply the sobering shock of realising himself to be on the brink of his destiny. Either he will kill a man. Or he will die in the attempt. If ever there is a time when he must concentrate, it is now.

I weigh the strength of the arm holding the sword in its resistance to my parry. But I also sense its inherent weakness too. Not a physical weakness. He is a brutish, muscular, physical man. And he pushes hard against my defence. No, his arm's weakness is a moral one. I am fighting for my life. There can be no greater, juster cause. He, I suspect, has initiated the attack for something less.

I read the assassin's intent without too much difficulty, ducking and dodging his heavy-handed thrusts. It is almost as if he loses heart as we tussle. I feel the fight go out of him. He can only grunt and groan now.

The balance of the battle tips. Now it is I pushing forward against him, and he on the back foot.

The difference is, whereas I was backed against a wall, he can simply back away. He swipes a wild blow, his Parthian shot, designed to beat me back while he takes flight. It glances off my guard to nick my arm. His sword's edge cuts through my sleeve, adding a slash where my tailor never intended one.

This unrequested amendment to my apparel outrages me more than the drawing of my blood that ensues upon it.

Rage propels my body at him. Though he is squarer in build than I, I tower head and shoulders over him.

I hilt him in the face. There is something strangely apposite in that particular blow, which for all its bluntness will, I think, hurt him. I daresay I consider him beneath a clean, gentlemanly sword cut. I want only to thrash him, as one would thrash a careless or disobedient servant.

My assailant appears momentarily dazed. At last he gathers his wits enough to turn tail, or at least to attempt to do so. But he trips over his feet and falls headlong on the cobbles of the Street. His weapons fly from his hands, cutting the fingers of his dagger hand in the process.

I am aware now of the braying crowd that has gathered around us. And as the other man lies sprawled, it seems to me the mood of the spectators changes.

A moment ago they were, I realise, cheering the would-be assassin on. Now that the advantage lies with me, a sullen discontent has descended over them. And so it comes home to me, how little I am liked here.

The crowd's humour worsens as I take a step towards my fallen foe. A restive, warning grumble builds into a threatening growl. But I am no cold-blooded murderer. I fought only to defend myself. He lies defenceless now. I have overcome him. I have taught him a lesson with the hilt of my sword.

I must understand one thing, however: 'Who sent you? Oxford?'

He rolls onto his back to look up at me standing over him. He squints and blinks as if he is gazing directly into the sun.

He closes his eyes and moves his head in a minimal nod of confirmation.

'How much is he paying you?'

I own I am curious to have this question settled. The answer will act as a measure of the Earl of Oxford's enmity. How troublesome he warrants me. The extent of threat I represent to him. It is all in the price that he puts on my life.

'A suit of clothes.'

I can make no sense of his answer.

'What?'

'He promised a suit of clothes to any who would rid him of the upstart Ralegh.'

The mood of the crowd is somewhat restored by this. It would not be too much to say a certain hilarity now prevails. If I had no inclination to kill him a moment before, I certainly feel a strong compulsion in that direction now. Why, I would take out the whole scurvy gang of them.

But the arrival of the palace guard urges restraint.

## Conjuring enemies

This west-most, wild-most tilt of the land into the sea. A yearning place. The fingers of the coast reaching out towards the distant West. A wistful greeting, gestured towards the rumoured New World. A way station of a place. A place for riding along the scrubby shoreline and looking out over the ocean with a possessing gaze.

Here where sea mists meet the choking smoke of burning peat.

Somewhere out there: Greenland, Groecland, Estotiland, Friseland, Baffin Island. And turn your head towards the South for Cape Verde and the Caribbean. The Spaniard's possessions. While those lying to the frozen, forgotten North are ours by right, or so argues Dr Dee. He has the papers to prove it.

I crane my neck and squint my eyes to penetrate the swirling fog with my imagination.

Also out there: Leviathans and Utopias. Sunken galleons, the bones of drowned sailors, floating islands and buried riches. Flotillas of treasure, golden chains stretched across the Atlantic, there for the gathering.

And beyond it all: America. The point towards which all this yearning leans. The focus of my dreams and fears. The shape of my ambition.

Between the shore I stand upon and the land I look towards, the irresistible ebb and flow of the vast Atlantic. I know what it is like to voyage upon those mighty waves. I have felt the kick and collapse of the sea beneath me. To be raised to the stars and hurled down into the depths. To taste the sea's salt rising in my throat. To hurl a stomach's worth of sickness across the deck. The endless, unrelieved misery comes back to me. My legs tremble. My throat convulses. And here I am standing on solid ground, only thinking of the sea, imagining it through a shroud of mist.

I know too well the cost that will be demanded of me should I venture out upon the restless waves again.

But at my back, impelling me westward, out towards my ambition, into my fear, into the inescapable sickness of sea transit, stand the ranks of troublous Irishmen. And behind them, my own more troubling past. That is to say, the braying courtiers gathered to gloat at my downfall.

Behind me too, a string of small disgraces and bigger disappointments. (Hauled before the Privy Council for the debacle in the Street. A spell in gaol, in Southwark's Marshalsea.)

And Humphrey, poor Humphrey, I left him mocked and maligned. Fortune's discarded toy, trampled into the mud. I confess I fled the ignomy of his association as much as the threat of Oxford's murderous plots. And yet, by some circuitous alignment of our destinies, I find myself here. Close to the locus of his greatest triumph.

Perhaps I can redeem us both, reminding all of his great deeds by equalling them.

For here I am. In Ireland.

More than anything, I long for action. I must be up and doing. At court, that instinct could only ever result in quarrels and brawls.

This opportunity then, is one at which I throw myself in desperate abandon. He who manoeuvred to secure me the commission (as well my speedy release from Marshalsea) made sure I understood. I was nothing but trouble. This move was as much to get me out of the way as to allow me the means to further my ambition.

*He* being my Lord Dudley, the Earl of Leicester, now my reluctant patron. I will not say friend. What brought us together was Oxford's enmity, which we both share. But to be hated by the same man is an uneasy basis for an alliance. It is no guarantee of warm feelings on either side.

I can almost hear him say, in some sitting of the Privy Council, (to which, of course, I was never privy): 'Send him to Ireland. It will either make him or destroy him.'

My mount shifts beneath me and snorts jets of mist from her nostrils. Two immense black apostrophes in shape, a horse's nostrils are perfect and monstrous at the same time. The steam that billows out from hers is added to the fog that creeps upon us from the sea. Indeed, it is as if she alone is producing all the restless, rolling obscurity that surrounds us.

She is impatient. And nervous. A far from skittish animal generally, yet she senses the enemies at our back. To say nothing of the enemies out there, concealed within the mists she has exhaled. The Papist forces that we daily expect.

Let them come.

I for one am eager to prove my loyalty to my Queen by killing a few Catholics. It will suffice to undo the suspicions that were aroused by my late association with the Earl of Oxford.

I have the command of a hundred men, my own pick of the Munster muster. What do you look for in a man you wish to take to slaughter Irish rebels? To say you want them lean and hungry would not be discriminating enough, for it goes without saying that none but the lean and hungry would be standing in Finsbury Fields waiting to be shipped to Ireland to fight. Hunger and indigence are the greatest spurs to action, the only true spurs I believe in. No man fights for a cause, he fights for himself. The greater his need, the greater his fight. If you can persuade him that your cause meets his need, then he will fight well for you.

You may disregard the crooked and the scabrous, or any who have a listless air. You want to see focused desperation in their eyes. They must have no hope but you. Without hope, they are without mercy, which is a good quality in a soldier. If your first thought is *These be dogs!*, it is not a bad first thought to have. The fierce, ravening hunger of dogs straining at the leash is precisely what you are looking for. A dog will do the bidding of the man who throws him scraps. There will be troublemakers among them. Again, all to the good. Your very purpose is to make trouble. If you keep them busy, they will not turn against you. Pay them well, and always hold out the promise of even greater reward. (The letters I write back to Lord Burghley, demanding payment of the arrears due to me, are not the product of greed or idleness. I must pay my men, or they will not be my men much longer.)

It is not hard to find a hundred such human dogs in London.

So, yes. Let them come, the Papist hordes. We are ready for them.

I do not count myself a diehard Protestant. But when I think about the Pope, I tell you in all honesty that my blood runs cold. That damnable anti-Christ, who dared to pass a death sentence upon our own dear sovereign, and call upon all Catholics to kill Her, giving them not only licence but encouragement… I sit here, astride my broad-beamed mount, shivering in my saddle. So much so that I might wish to have a woollen brat about me (had not the wearing of such overtly Gaelic garb been outlawed by a previous lord deputy).

England's enemies will always strike her at her weakest point: these fragile, easily broken fingers of land tickling the Atlantic's edge.

The mist rises off Smerwick Bay, like an advance party of ghosts landing. It is almost too much even for my all-seeing eyes. I must rely on other senses. We scouts cannot even see one another. We only hear the stir of our comrades' horses.

I must learn to sniff out the fear-infested sweat of foreign mercenaries as they hunker beneath the bulwarks. I ought to recognise the stench of their vomit.

I must strain to listen for the intimate lap of water against wood, as the hulls of the invaders' ships cut the waves.

The narrowing of eyes and pricking of ears and the twitching of other senses conjures up the stealthy image that I'm straining for. This is a kind of magic. I could serve as scryer to Dr Dee.

But it is not real. Or I cannot be sure it is. For the troop ships are no sooner sighted than they are vanished again. Utterly vanished.

Did I see them, or imagine them? I cannot be sure.

In truth, I cannot be sure I am even here on this promontory looking out over the shrouded sea, or where I imagine that sea to be. Sometimes my all-seeing eyes deceive me. Their strange omniscience persuades me I am present at more occurrences than can be.

I know I am somewhere, but it is hard for me to say where exactly.

### The Golden Fort

It enters you.

Fear is one part of it. But it is only one of its constituents. Perhaps the first part, the motive part. But it is not simple fear. It is fear and hate and rage. Short simple syllables that each bear a massive burden of meaning. The fear activates the hate. The hate, the rage. The rage, the Thing. The Thing that enters you. The Thing you become.

It is bigger than any of the words there are for it.

I set my eyes upon it, this Thing.

They see a cold black rock. Utterly unmoving, with diamond sharp edges. Its surface is so black it glistens in places. It is hard to gauge the scale of the rock. It could be small enough to wield in the hand and dash out the brains of a single enemy. Or large enough to squat in the road and block the passage of an entire army.

It is as hard as adamantine. And weighs as much as the world.

My eyes have shown me the image of my own Will. The Thing that enters me, the Thing that I become, is what I will myself to be.

And fear is not the prime mover.

I can see now that the Thing is composed more of desire than fear. More of self-love than hate of other. More of fierce, dark glee than rage.

And, I might add, more of greed than hunger. It is the fiercest kind of greed, the darkest lust.

My eyes pierce the dark rock, only to discover that it is not a rock at all, but a dense knot of gristle. Black blood pulses through it.

It is more than my mere Will that I behold. It is my very heart.

It is the kernel of animal nature that resides within us all.

*Be more feared than fearing.*

Such were my brother Humphrey's words to me. From the very moment I first heard it, I felt my heart vibrate in sympathy with the sentiment. His words were not advice, but licence.

And so, this Thing that enters me, this Thing that I become, this one grain of fear surrounded by a carapace of rock-hard sinew: I discover that it was there all along. That it is the core of me, the truest part of me.

Reports have reached us. Sightings have been confirmed. Eight troop ships full of Papal forces have at last touched the tip of a westward promontory of this western isle. I watched for them and waited for them and now they have come. I wanted them. They answer something in me.

We have allowed the invaders to be ensconced in the fort of Dún an Óir. I am told the name means 'Golden Fort' in the local language. As we march towards it, through the cold damp air and the clouds of biting gnats, I imagine a palace built from bricks of gold bullion, gleaming spectacularly between the two tips of the Smerwick promontory, as if it were a pearl held in the pincer grip of a crab.

Since we first left London some months ago, my mustered men have marched nigh on three hundred miles all told. They are footsore and hungry. It is a daily struggle to feed an army in this blasted country. There are few farms. The locals disappear into the woods and bogs, so we are denied the satisfaction even of a pitched battle. And so our hunger for blood must go unsated too, though at every moment we expect to be ambushed.

The woodlands are the worst. At every rustle of leaves or crack of twig, we cringe and hold our breath, our clammy hands clenched upon our weapons. The men stay silent and tense, the prickle of unease on the back of their necks, like the breath of an assassin about to slit their throats from behind.

In truth, we have lost more of them to disease than to the rebels' slingshots. The island's damp air conspires with its fractious natives to bring us low.

Our pace is set by the trundle of heavy artillery over soft ground. Our enemy has no big guns. The Irish kerns fight for the most part without armour, or even helmets on their heads. But by a strange paradox, that which gives us our greatest advantage also makes us most vulnerable. We are slow and exposed in manoeuvre; they are quick and agile in attack. They come out of the mists and woods and melt back into them. Whereas we…

We must stand by and watch as yet another of our cannons sinks slowly into the sodden earth. It is a magnificent piece, its bronze barrel over ten feet long and ringed along its length with mouldings, astragals and fillets. The gun sits low on its carriage, and is tilted forwards on its trunnions so that the muzzle seems directed against the bog that holds it, as if the gunners intend to blast their way out of their predicament. The entire lower half of each carriage wheel has disappeared, and the rest of it is thoroughly caked in claggy mud. This land repels us by drawing us into it.

The dray horses bridle and stamp. They dip their massive heads to cast an impatient eye sidelong at the waiting men. Perhaps they sense the danger every delay places us in as much as their human masters. They too must feel themselves sinking ever lower.

The gun crew shovel out channels and wedge planks and spread burlap sacks in front of the wheels. A company of volunteers surround the sinking bombard, like ants clustering around a discarded morsel of sweetmeat. On the cry of *Heave!,* they put their shoulders against whatever part of the gun they can find purchase on. They push in concert with the renewed pulling of the horses. Slowly the wheels begin to turn, and the belly of the cannon rises with a bubbling crackle out of its peaty bed. A moment later it is fully free, and its sudden release takes all by surprise. The weight of the cannon runs away from the men and pushes the horses into a panicked canter.

And so we progress in staggering lurches. All the time, fearing attack from the phantom army of the rebel Desmonds.

At last we reach the mountains of Slieve Mish, which guard the entrance to the Dingle promontory. Slanting light pierces the cloud-filled sky, spreading a milky film over flimsy mountains. Not rocks, but fairy stuff that may be blown away with a breath.

But again we are held back by the weight of our cannon, which resists the inclination to ascend. It seems fitting, somehow: that one must struggle to convey these grave engines of destruction to the place of their deployment. Death is not a light thing. But by the strenuous haulage, we earn the right to marshall it.

I see no gleam of gold ahead as we crest the mountain range. Rather, the sea in the bay is leaden, beneath a sky of hammered tin.

We press on, descending the unnamed mountainside. (Is it named in the Irish tongue? To us, it has no name.) The hard task now is to hold our artillery pieces back, so that they do not roll into our horses and knock them down like skittles. This long drawn Death has grown no more wieldy for all our handling of it.

And so we continue, heaving ourselves up and over each successive undulation until we stand on the crest of the land's last mountain.

I spy the fort now. It squats down in the bay like a turd deposited in a privy pit. A strangely geometric turd, with sheer straight sides, and sharp-angled corners. No, it is not made of gold bricks, I see now. Its walls are banks of soggy Irish turf. The same sucking earth that swallowed the wheels of our cannon carriages.

Perchance there is alchemical significance in the naming of the fort. Just as the Philosopher's Stone (which some sages aver to be nothing other than excrement) is capable of transmuting base metal to precious, so the earthwork of Dún an Óir may transform a man's fortune in a similar manner.

Seagulls circle, riding the raw salty wind, casting their wild caws into its howl.

### Very well

I am not an astrologer. I cannot deny, however, that the stars do exert their influence on the lives of men. And at certain times in a man's life, circumstances conspire so completely that one can feel the action of the stars at work.

I feel it now.

I feel a sense of universal harmony. I feel the power of the cosmos – *of the entire cosmos!* – enter my blood. I feel it articulate my bones and move my sinews.

Everything has come together for this moment. This is my destiny. It has entered me. And I have entered it.

The universe is in concordance. And it is directing me.

It is no longer a question of policy or polity.

I take my orders from the planets and the stars.

We have moved our guns up to within range of the fort. And so those in the fort can see their doom more clearly now. They are staring down the barrel of it.

Wilton has returned with the fleet, and keeps up a steady bombardment from the sea. There are no enemy ships left in the bay. Our scouts inform us that the Spanish bishop, who had come to claim Ireland for the Pope, has sailed them all away, abandoning the remnant forces in the fortress to their fate. Thus our fleet has it all its own way. One ship after another sails up to fire off broadsides. The Golden Fort is a great sitting duck.

We hammer them too from our emplacements on land. While they shelter from the hail of cannonshot, we send a band of English brave hearts to attack them with spades, digging away beneath their earthworks.

Our unmolested transit here turns out to have been an omen. The Desmond forces that the invaders were counting on for relief are nowhere to be seen. The kerns and gallowglass companies have melted away.

For two days we keep up the bombardment. The boom of our cannonades is unrelenting. We have taken thunder from the heavens and thrown it at our enemies.

Once I conjured enemies out of the Irish mist. Now we create a thick fog of our own and fill the Smerwick bay with it. The Golden Fort is greyed and vanished. My eyes pierce the swirling smoke, and see what is contained in it. The hardening of intent that screams as it whips and rends the nitrous cloud. Spheres of black stone, heavy harbingers of our malamour.

We have it all our way and lose, in fact, only one man. To a bullet fired blindly into the deafening obscurity? Perhaps. Or perhaps the sniper's eyes are as clairvoyant as my own? But if so, why this man? John Cheke, it is, a gentle youth who served Leicester as equerry. I only know that he was as hated by the Earl of Oxford as I. And so perhaps it is not a Spanish bullet that blows apart his head, but one paid for by Oxford?

On the third day, we allow the air to clear. I swear I can hear the coughs and groans of the huddled troops within the fort. Through the thinning shifts of smoke, we see the black flag lowered.

And the white flag raised, seeking parlay. We fill the air with cheers.

We line up behind Lord Grey. A small party of trusted officers, sitting high and straight in our saddles. I feel the propitious alignment of planets and stars in every step our horses take. We are moving towards a destiny.

The Golden Fort opens its studded gates to us. The enemy soldiers stand in squalid disarray, their faces grimed with the soot of our assaults. When courage departs an army, so too does discipline: the men lose faith in their commander as much as in themselves. These have about them the look of dogs caught stealing sausages, who know they are in for a whipping. I dare say in their hearts they want to stare us down defiantly, but know that it will avail them naught. They are already defeated, so it little behoves them to swagger. They must know that it would serve them better to appease us, and some of them indeed send out mild beseeching glances, like shy maids a-wooing. The majority though give themselves up to an abject, sullen churlishness. They cannot bear to look us in the eye.

Only the Irish among them retain their open hostility. If the beams shooting from their eyes were given physical form, they would be steel lances to knock us from our mounts. Instead, the boldest of them, a surly faced scoundrel, must content himself with spitting on the ground at our passing.

We are greeted by the colonel of the garrison, an Italian by the name of di San Giuseppe. An obsequious and contemptible individual, he does not baulk at throwing himself on the ground to beg my Lord Grey's mercy. He even grips his lordship's knees as he cries: 'Misericordia! Misericordia!'

This is understandably distasteful to Lord Grey. He gestures for the man to get to his feet and demands to know if he will surrender the fort and give up all claim to Ireland on behalf of the Pope.

The Italian lets it be known that he surrenders unconditionally. He is most emphatic: '*Nullis praeconditionibus*.'

'Very well. Very well. *Ita wero. Ita wero*.'

His Lordship rubs his hands in quiet satisfaction. All those of us of his party look about us at our sorry prize. It will take some application, or alchemy, to extract anything precious from this unpropitious mine. The Golden Fort, now that we are inside it, appears singularly lacking in gilded trappings. The seeping walls of mud infect everything within them with a dank mildewed filth.

But fear not, if there is gold to be found in there, I will find it.

The Italian craves one more night in the fort to prepare his troops for their surrender.

Lord Grey is magnanimous: 'Very well. Very well.'

In these exchanges, each man understands most definitely what he means to say, though it is another matter whether he says it. So too, each hears what he wants to hear, whether or not it is in fact said. And one thing that is said may imply another that is not. So too, the manner, or bearing, of a speaker may lead the auditor into certain assumptions. You may take it that Lord Grey, being the very model of a chivalrous knight, conducts himself with restraint and dignity. No strutting Tarquin he, nor Marcellus even.

But a man may pity with his whole heart and yet be governed by something other than his heart. By policy, for example. Or a man may be like the courtiers in London, who are content to enjoy the fruits of others' enterprise without questioning what that enterprise necessitates. He prefers not to imagine what duty may one day call upon him to do. (Or others to do in his name, which is the same.)

And so he says: 'Very well. Very well.'

We, who are not called upon to say anything, say nothing.

The Italian abases himself again and pours out a stream of gratitude to his lordship's shoes. But to thank someone for a gift not yet given, or even promised, does not secure its granting.

In thus dishonouring himself he brings dishonour on all soldiery. It shames us simply to witness his grovelling. Lord Grey brings the parlay to an abrupt end. It is decided and agreed: they will surrender the fort on the morrow. Nothing more need be said.

Victor leaves the vanquished to one last night. Let him lick his wounds and ready himself for whatever the dawn may bring.

But what a roistering celebration there is in the English camp. The men's chants have a harsh and greedy rhythm to them. I will admit to a certain apprehension. I have seen what booty the fort has to offer. I cannot imagine that it will sate the fierce appetite on display tonight.

I allow my gaze to drift upwards with the sparks from the camp fires. The cold November night absorbs the orange splinters of light into its vast black belly. The golden sparks become silver stars, high overhead.

In the communion of sparks and stars, our destinies are written.

Gold falls from the Heavens to be seeded on Earth. Gold rises from the Earth, through the intermediacy of Fire, to join the stars.

I feel the concordance of the Cosmos in my blood. What will happen on the morrow is decided not by the parlaying of men, but by the alignment of stars and planets.

I sleep fitfully under canvas. The men are rowdy through the watches. Their leering shouts are with me in my tent.

At some point, the cries of drunken soldiers give way to the clamour of raucous birds. I rise to see the land shoulder itself into existence as the sun breaks over the top of Mount Brandon.

Soon after dawn, the fort gates open and, still under white flag, di San Giuseppe and a dozen or so of his capitanos parade out. They affect the air of tragic heroes, holding their heads high, not realising it is too late for holding your head high. They do not see how absurd they appear: to seek to cling onto their dignity even as they hand over their swords. You cannot have the former without the latter about your person.

They carry their ensigns rolled up and tucked beneath their arms. Di San Giuseppe bows to Lord Grey with such studied solemnity that I cannot doubt he practised the look in front of a glass. Has he forgotten his grovelling self-abasement of yesterday? Once you have clung onto the knees of another man, you cannot then look him in the eye as if you are his equal.

Lord Grey condescends to bestow the briefest of glances on the surrendered ensigns. He seems to indicate that he regards them as rather an inconvenience, as if he has nowhere suitable to put them.

The surrendered officers must now consider themselves his prisoners. Undoubtedly, his lordship is chivalrous and polite. His captives are of elevated rank and so he insists that they are handled with due respect as they are led off to the English camp. But such consideration should not deceive anyone.

The Golden Fort is now my Lord Grey's to do with as he wishes.

He looks over at the mounded earth construction with unconcealed disgust. It is certainly beneath his dignity to set foot inside it.

'Ralegh, you and Captain Macworth will see to the removal of all enemy arms from the fort. Secure the safeguarding of such munitions and stores as you find in there. You must keep your men under a tight rein. I want no spoliation. We must conduct ourselves with decorum.'

'What are your orders regarding the enemy combatants, and their whores and followers?'

'Do as you see fit.'

The wind from the bay blows cold and hard into his face, streaking a tear from his right eye. But I do not believe he is weeping for anyone in the fort (or for anyone in the world, for that matter). It is true that he quickly turns his back on the place. But it is done to take his face out of the wind, I would say, and because there is nothing here to detain him any longer.

## This

Our men make piles of ironmongery and wood in front of the fort. It is like the harvesting of a strange martial orchard. The tangled curves of long bows and crossbows, the criss-crossed barrels of harquebuses, in mingled melée with pikes and arrows and unsheathed blades of every length. There for all to see, the weapons that they meant to use against us, the sum of their ill-will made manifest. A goading sight.

When the gathering is done, I and Macworth walk among our men. Whenever I see a fiercer hunger in one man's sunken cheeks, or a colder glint of hate in his eye, when I see a man I think would not hesitate to cut my throat if I withheld his bread, that man I touch upon the shoulder. And so, in this wise, we choose our bands for the next commission. These men, the most desperate, sullen and depraved of our army, are perhaps surprised to find themselves so favoured. They frown as they try to imagine what possible task would call for their singular qualities.

Then it dawns on them, and the same slow twisted smile creeps into place on every face.

I confide to Macworth: 'If it is to be done, it must be done quickly.'

It is not my will that decides this. It is not my recommendation that calls for such action. All has been decided by the alignments of stars and planets. We know that the Moon pulls the oceans of the Earth, thus dictating the ebb and flood of their tides. We must therefore agree that the great congregation of heavenly bodies operates a similar influence on the tides of blood and humours that circulate within the human body. And so, it is my contention that when we feel ourselves impelled to act in a certain way, it is because at that moment we are peculiarly sensitive to the occult forces that direct our lives at all times. We are only obeying the hidden bidding of the universe.

There can be no pause for pity. For pity lies only in the speed of commission.

The men, you see. I know the men. I was there at their mustering. If it is not done quickly, I will not answer for the men. This will be our gift to them. This will be how we appease them. This will be how we keep them on our side.

Our chosen men stalk and separate, spreading out from my swift nod of licence, like spilled malice pooling; like dogs unleashed; like demons let loose from Hell; like Englishmen given the run of a Papist fort in Ireland.

Aye, it is a mean, dirty and forsaken place. It stinks like a cesspit. I had not noticed the smell before, and soon it will smell worse than ever.

We have men guarding the entrance, so that none may escape. Because it is soon evident what we are about. As soon as the first blade slices through the first throat, the element of surprise is lost. The screams begin.

I will not look away from that which I have begun. Besides, it is compelling. One must always confront the inevitable.

This is the will of the universe enacted. This doing is ordained by constellations. For that reason, it has about it a certain… I will not say *beauty*. I accept that is a strange word to use of such deeds.

But this spectacle possesses a power to compel the eye that it shares with beauty. As if the very beautiful and the utterly appalling are two sides of the same coin.

Like beauty, it is a force that squeezes my heart in a cold, steel-strong grip. Like beauty, it tightens its violent grip upon my rawest place and lifts me. Like beauty, it tears me apart and turns me inside out.

The slick choreography of arms, the manly bracing, the stalwart, unflinching regard. Precision and control imposing itself in swift decisive steps upon the unwieldy disorder of the inconvenient living. The grim-set lips, concealing a secret dark delight. The sheer remorseless intervention of a weapon's edge into a tender palpitating throat. The appeal of the straight and brutal steel. The polish and the absoluteness of it. The surrender of the flesh. The hopeless, abandoned agony of it. The sudden spray of hot blood. The liquid gurgle in the flooded wound. The second mouth gaping, sagging, spewing forth the fluid red. The stiffening of last resistance. The hopeless flapping and bothering of death-weakened limbs. A flattened palm batting ineffectually against the fluttering away of life. The fluttering away of life. The last spasms. The spasms that come after the last. The swivel of unseeing eyes away from the centrality of life. The unexpected blinding of the dead. They are blind as well as dead, occurs to me.

How long it takes to do this. How long it takes to pin down every last man of them, every last man, woman, child, and do this.

This. A thousand times this. Not quite a thousand. Closer to six hundred. But still.

This. Here. And again. Over here. And here. And here. And again. Here. This. Six hundred times this.

There are more of them in here than we thought. To see the Golden Fort from outside, you would not think it could contain so many throats. Six hundred throats. And each one must be opened.

They try to run away from it. From this. But there is nowhere for them to run to. There is no space for running at all. They are like apples in a barrel. Tightly packed into the corners of the huts within the fort. The scratching of their fingernails against the walls. I wish they would not scratch their fingernails against the walls. It will not help them. And the sound is unpleasant.

I can hear nothing but the scratching of their fingernails against the walls. It even drowns out their screams.

They try to run from this. But this is everywhere about them. So wherever they run to, they run to this. It is on the ground, now. It has made the ground slick and treacherous. They slip and slide in puddles of this.

My office, my function, my duty I might almost say, is to fix my gaze upon the doing of this. Whatever else I do, I may not flinch.

I must bear witness to the product of my own bidding. Lord Grey will not. He has already sought to distance himself from this. He has turned his back on the Golden Fort and walked away from it, back to the English camp. He will talk symbolism and husbandry with his secretary Spenser. (I am told the man is a poet, the author of a book of Georgics, in the manner of Vergil.) Perchance in the course of the day Lord Grey will for no good reason lose his temper with a servant, and afterwards feel a pang of remorse for hasty words spoken in anger. He will consider that he has fallen below the mark of civility and justice that he sets for himself. He will confront this aspect of his imperfect nature and swear to mend his conduct in future. The servant may only be a servant, but he is still a man, his Christian brother. And so he deserves to be dealt with fairly by his master. Lord Grey will see this as his duty, just as it is the duty of a sovereign to rule benignly over his subjects, and not to play the dictator. Lord Grey will turn to his volumes of humanist philosophy for guidance and consolation, and to his prayer books too.

He will examine his conscience and confront the lapse, the fault in him, that led him to intemperate words.

But he will not confront this, what we are about.

This is something that must take place out of sight of lords and princes.

I will not turn from it. I cannot. My eyes would see this, even if I would not. My eyes that have privileged me such visions and wonders as the light within my own mother's womb, the fire of a gold-seeding comet, the darkness within a barrel of hard tack. My eyes would not deny me this, even if I were not here in person. But I am here. And I do not desire to be anywhere else.

I want to see that it is done. I want to see that it is done well. And I want to see how the world looks when it is done. I am a soldier. And a poet. I must look upon such things as this.

I send my eyes in with the swift-despatching daggers, I send my eyes into the flesh of my enemies. The beam of my eyes is edged with the blade of a surgeon-barber's razor. I have stropped the beam of my eyes on a leather strip until the very glance of it is keen enough to draw blood from everything it brushes. The beam of my eyes is doing this. The beam of my eyes is the weapon I wield. It fells my enemies and floods the ground with their blood.

I have only to look upon an enemy and he falls.

There are women here too. The soldiers' whores. As soon as I see them, as soon as the beam of my eyes falls upon them, they are dead. I cannot be blamed for this. It is their presence here that kills them. If they were not here, I would not see them.

This is a place of death. If you are in a place of death, you will die.

Even the screams of the women, even of the pregnant women, and of the mothers with babes in arms, even their screams do not have the power to deflect the beam of my eyes. On the contrary. Their screams, because they are of a different timbre and pitch to the screams of the men, draw my gaze. As novelty always must attract attention.

I and my fellow captains, Macworth, Denny and Zouch, do our best to keep the men from rifling the dead. There must be a line drawn, I think. So much we will permit, but no more. It is not out of respect, nor is it because we wish to deny them the privilege of spoil. There will be spoil. But it will be fairly distributed, or as fairly as we may arrange it. We turn a blind eye to baubles ripped from earlobes, or fingers severed for a ring. And even gold crucifixes and their chains yanked off. But we cannot permit the men's larcenous fingers to probe the pockets of the dead. In those dark recesses there may be greater treasures than these honest brutes can imagine.

And so it is left to me and my fellow captains, Macworth, Denny and Zouch to investigate such soft enfolded mines of secrecy. We squeeze our hands between the press of body upon body. Elongating our fingers into fine threads that weave between the warp of cadavers. As yet, we have discovered nothing of value. Unless you count the heat that hastens from murdered flesh, at which we vainly catch.

## Letters

It is a damnably hard business. I would it were over. But we are not done yet. Even some relief from it would be welcome. The workers in a slaughterhouse are granted leave now and then to look up from their task, to straighten their backs and stretch their arms. But I cannot allow the men a moment's respite. It must be done quickly, if it is to be done at all.

And yet the sudden piping up of an English voice provides an unwanted interlude: 'Mercy! Mercy! I am English! An Englishman, your countryman! Mercy! For mercy's sake.'

Our man who has the dagger at the fellow's throat looks to me. I gesture for him to hold.

'An Englishman, you say?'

I see quicksilver hope dash into his eyes. Sweat glistens on his brow. He nods vehement affirmation. His mouth is stretched into a tense, desperate grin. It is the effect you might see if you wound his innards on a screw.

I see the crucifix hung from a chain of beads about his neck. 'Who do you obey? The Pope or the Queen?'

'The Queen! I' faith, the Queen!'

'Did the Queen bid you invite these Papist murderers into her sovereign territory? 'Tis the first I have heard of it.'

'I confess! I confess I was in error. In error, I joined with these men. In error.'

'Do not mistake me for your confessor. I can give you no Hail Marys to exculpate your error. Indeed it is a signal error. A grave error. A loathsome error. 'Tis the error of treason.'

'If you charge me with treason, then you must try me for the offence. You must allow me that. I am an Englishman, I say. And these gentlemen here…'

He indicates a priest in his cassock, and a man of seeming genteel rank.

'These men are Irish. They are subjects of your Queen too.'

'*My* Queen?'

'The Queen. Our Queen, I meant to say. Her Majesty.'

'And so… what of it? They are still Catholic curs, I think.'

'Y-you cannot summarily execute them, no more than me.'

'You would tell me what I can and cannot do?'

'No, I simply seek to remind you of our legal standing.'

'I will see to it that you are treated in accordance with your standing. You did invite these men, these foreign soldiers, into our land?'

'I was in error! I have confessed to that. We were in error! We have surrendered! To your mercy… to your commander's mercy.'

'These are the Pope's men?'

'Aye! I can tell you of the Pope's plan – of all that he means to do. I can tell you of plots and conspiracies. Against the Queen. If you only spare me.'

'Would you have shown our Queen mercy, had you a dagger at her throat?'

'I never wished for that.'

'You meddled! And for your meddling, I would have you justly treated.'

'Justly! Aye, justly! Have us justly treated. We will submit to that.'

'Very well. Escort these men hence. Have them bound and restrained in a place of safety until we are able to treat them justly.'

The priest kisses his crucifix, believing himself saved.

Our soldier gives me the look of a dog whose bone I have wrested from his jaws. For a moment I fear that he will turn upon me for robbing him of the pleasure of a few more throats to cut.

And now I think our English captive must see what's writ in my face. He begins to thrash and scream, shaking his head in violent denial. His body leans at an acute angle away from the direction I would have him led.

'Peace, man. This will not help you.'

You push a man to a point beyond the extreme of despair and he will break.

'I tell you, there are letters. Evidence. They disclose the Pope's entire purpose.'

He leads me to a dwelling house at the rear of the fort. We must pick our way through the fallen. The business of adding to their number goes on everywhere about us. The screams that are rendered up grow tedious as well as fruitless.

The door to the house is a flimsy board that groans as I push against it. The building itself is a rude timber hut. The darkness of the interior has an absorbent quality to it.

The air in that wooden box is choking-thick with the metallic tang of spilled blood. My foot kicks against an obstacle on the floor. I look down at a soft dark heavy mound. My adjusting eyes see now that it is a body. The first of them.

It is like a storeroom of the dead.

I step over the first obstacle and find a space to plant my foot, then totter like a drunk to bring my other foot down next to it. This is a heady place, an intoxicating place.

I look for the Pope's Englishman. He stumbles into the room, no doubt impelled by a rough thrust from one of our men. He is forced to trample on his comrades to remain upright. He holds his head angled upwards, as if he is drowning and must keep his nose above the water. It is just, I think, that he cannot bear to look down at the stock of bodies on the floor.

He points, without looking, at the far corner.

'This one here?'

He nods, one hand clasped tightly over his mouth, as if there are words he might say but must not.

I tread over corpses to reach the one that he has indicated. A lean unlikely fellow, a look of startled disappointment on his face. The kind of man, it strikes me, who would always be taken by surprise by events. But I cannot discount the possibility that his sodden red-stained ruff has drained the qualities that qualified him for the role of intelligencer. No doubt once he was a prospector of fortune, living on his wits, and ever giddy with bombastic hope. Now he is all that remains of any man after death: a witless, hopeless husk.

I pat and peel apart the dead man's clothing. His bones come out to meet me, the flesh already sinking back from living touch. The stiffening of death has not yet come upon him. He seems a light and loosely held together thing. As life is: it takes only one swift severing to undo it.

At last my fingertips alight on what I commissioned them to find. I feel it and know it at once for what it is: a bundle of folded papers. In the tightness of their binding, the flimsiness of each single sheet is compacted into something firmer, steelier. Such is the way conspiracies work. For this is a paper conspiracy.

I lift the cache out of its hiding place and open it up. Remember, it is dark in this dwelling house of the dead. I must move over to the doorway to discern what is written; but even with that advantage, I can make neither head nor tail of the contents. The writers have employed some kind of cypher. Meaningless chains of letters executed in a tidy enough hand are strung across each page. The letters are grouped in blocks that resemble words, but are no words in any language that I know. I understand enough to know that there is something dark afoot here. This is matter for such as Dr Dee to ponder over.

Mayhap they are demonic spells, fashioned to bring ruin and destruction on our Queen and country. If so, he will discover that too.

Who will be undone by these letters is for others to decipher and decide. It is for me to ensure they prove the making of their discoverer.

The Pope's Englishman is anxious to claim his share of the credit: 'It is as I said? As I promised. These letters are of value?'

I am only a hair's breadth away from giving the nod to his immediate execution.

But the day's work has played havoc with my humours. I do not think I can endure the screaming of another Catholic.

### Groans

The noise of our doing has at last abated. The air still rings: the echo of the last scream lingers. As that echo dies I hear a peculiar gurgling sound, as of water draining from a trough. From somewhere, groans. I do not think they are the groans of the dying, for everyone is dead now. And they cannot be the groans of the dead. It occurs to me that they may perhaps be my own. As soon as I think it, they cease.

Now all that I can hear is the scratching of fingernails against the walls, but I know this cannot be. There is, here and there, some movement in amongst the heaps of bodies. But everyone is dead now. They are all dead. My men have seen to that. The movement can only be the reflex twitching that sometimes occurs after death.

I have seen the same phenomenon in executed men, whose heads are completely severed from their shoulders.

It is animation, but it is not life.

## Further examples

Any English carpenter worth his salt should be able to knock you up a half decent gibbet. And it is a merry sound, the assembling. Your English carpenter will whistle as cheerily at a gallows-raising, or a coffin-framing, as at any barn-topping. The happy tapping of the hammerhead as it drives home the nails is nearly enough to dispel the gloom even of the condemned. All honest labour naturally elevates the spirits. As does the waft of sawdust from a fresh-hewn timber.

But our three prisoners are a morose lot, irredeemably so. It is beyond me to imagine that they can have entertained any great expectation of an outcome other than this. Any man who sets himself against his own Sovereign and State, such a man deserves all that befalls him. There can be no question of mercy in these circumstances.

'I was in error!' So pleads the Pope's Englishman.

Well, now is the time to discover where your error has led you.

To the blacksmith's.

Two soldiers drag him up to the anvil. One to hold him from behind. The other to grapple his hand into place. He is told to spread his fingers out. He does not want to spread his fingers out, no more than he wishes to open his tight compressed lips. It will be worse for you if you do not spread your fingers out, he is told. It is hard to imagine how it could be any worse for him. But the blacksmith raising in his tongs a red hot rod from the smithy furnace suggests possibilities. The Pope's Englishman screams. Spread your fingers out, he is told. It will be better for you if we do this quickly. He cannot take his eyes off the red-hot rod. You do not want this up your arse, do you? He is asked. No, no, please God no. Then spread your fingers out. There is weariness now in the voice of the one who tells him this. Is it really necessary to repeat such a simple command? He spreads his fingers out, his hand shaking all the time with tensely splayed anticipation.

The blacksmith returns the red-hot rod to the fire and takes up his hammer. Who can fail to be impressed by the thick, blunt head of the blacksmith's hammer, black and round-edged after a lifetime of pounding? We have all seen such a hammerhead bounce sprightly and sonorously up after striking the metal. We have even felt the tensioned kick of the blow on the blacksmith's behalf. Imagining our own hands as deft and capable as his. We feel it, though we are only observers: strike, stricken and striker as one, in the elated moment of percussion. Such a weight of volition handled with so lissom a precision. We have all watched with wonder as a finely wrought blade, utterly straight and true, is hammered out of a thick, unpromising rod such as that with which the priest's arse was threatened. The blade of a weapon that will be wielded against our enemies perhaps. In just such a manner are we fashioning a weapon today. For there are different kinds of weapons. And a man may be turned into a weapon, if first you make of him an example.

There is no buoyant bounce in the hammer now. No pleasing chime of metal on metal. It crashes with a damp and deadened crunch, a quick and muted catastrophe, its motion absorbed by the cushion of its aftermath. Four more stifled blows befall. All eyes, my own included, are keen to see what product has been made by the blacksmith's work .

The Pope's Englishman holds up a bundle of misshapen chitterlings, ruptured and raw and glistening. At first they appear squashed and wilted. Before the onlookers' eyes, they wax and swell like bloated bladders. Tis the stiffening blood rushing in. Livid colours bloom and spread across his devastated skin.

His body is in convulsion. Throwing itself away from that compressed, exploded wreckage of a hand.

This is something your coddled courtier will never understand. He who holds his nose, and blocks his ears and closes his eyes to all that is necessary to keep him in silk frills and scented pomades and gilded brocades. He fills his leisure with tennis games and humanist philosophy and garlands of lyric poetry. With fine sentiments and sport. He oils his beard and pens billets-doux which he smuggles into his mistress's pocket. But there are others, while he attends to all that, who must keep the enemy at bay. The enemy who cares nought for his silk frills and pomades. The enemy who will take not the trouble to pen a billet-doux before raping the courtier's very mistress. The enemy who would turn the tennis court into a slaughterhouse, flooded with the courtier's blood and his mistress's blood and the blood of the unborn child in her womb.

No, it is not enough simply to kill them. We kill our foreign foes, but these men are traitors. We must make their deaths mean more than mere death. We must send out a message. We must make examples of them.

We must pay them back for their meddling, but we must also deter further meddlers.

And we must delight in it. How else would you have us do it?

We are naturally delighted that it is not our hand stretched out on some Spanish anvil. Or our neck that feels the touch of Toledo steel. I will not begrudge my men that delight. I will even do my best to share in it. It is beneath my dignity to add my voice to their cheers. But I will nod approvingly at them. And I will reward the blacksmith handsomely for each Papist finger flattened: sixpence per bloody battered chitterling.

Three men, thirty meddling digits that must be hammered. You might imagine that the enjoyment of such work would soon pall, and it would become as tedious as any other task. But the blacksmith is a patient craftsman, who takes pride in a job well done. And there is fifteen shillings in it for him if he sees it through.

For the observers, the spectacle has enough variation and drama to retain the interest. Each finger wrecked provokes a different reaction from the man it is attached to. A gamut of squeals and wailings to be run through. We become tutored in the divers degrees and qualities of panic, pain and terror. There are the whimpers of the man who is nursing his already broken fingers. There are the screams of the man who is at that moment suffering the hammer blows. And there are the anticipatory sobs of the man who watches the treatment of his fellow, knowing that he is soon to suffer the same fate himself.

No tragedy upon the stage has as much power to compel the gaze and stir the heart as this. Do not believe we are without pity. But it is the pity of those who have no power to intervene. The pity of the audience at the theatre. Our pity is an indulgence, a pretence. It cannot change anything.

It cannot take down the gibbets that await the three traitors.

For we have not done with them yet.

A man does not so much swing on the gibbet as kick and writhe and wriggle. Only when he is done kicking and writhing and wriggling, can he at all be said to swing. It is a satisfying moment when the ungainly thrashing about settles into a rhythmic to-and-fro. His eyes bulge from his head. His cock stands out in a last, miraculous lusting after death. And gradually, his neck stretches to twice its wonted length or more.

It is diverting for the men to take potshots at the three swinging weights upon the scaffold, like sacks of discarded humanity. When the shot strikes, the body is set spinning on its halter, another shot sets it spinning in the counter direction, and each shot rips away a little more of the traitor. The men are drunk, of course. So their shots do not hit home every time. It is as well to stand behind the line of fire.

## Wintergreen

The Palace of Whitehall is all decked out in green, hung with sprigs of holly, ivy, spruce and pine. A resinous scent conjures forth the forest in its wintergreen glory. As if the forest has brought itself inside for us. And the hunting scenes depicted on the hanging tapestries are in the process of coming to life.

I move among the boughs of an enchanted woodland, towards the music. Conifer needles crunch beneath my tread, strewn over the reed mats. In the candlelit flicker, dim presences flit in and out of my vision. I almost believe I can hear the clip of cloven hooves. The conviction takes root that there is a stag wandering the palace corridors. Its antlers throw tangled shapes onto the walls. At least that is how I interpret the eerie shadows I see there. My heart beats in time with the heavy tambour rhythm.

I imagine myself armed with a crossbow, hunting down the stag. But the image is not entirely apt. I am no longer the hunter in search of a target. I have shot my bolt and killed the finest beast in the forest. My task now is merely to gather up my fallen prey, to claim my reward.

But if I have killed the prey, why do I still hear its hoof steps echo?

I must hold my head angled upwards to see my way, and fully turn my head if I wish to look to the left or the right. Otherwise the fabric of my mask obscures my vision. It turns the floor into a black void into which I fear to tread.

Strange sounds come to me out of the encompassing blackness, sounds other than the clip of the phantom buck and the pulse of the music. Whispered insults, hissed slurs, the click of disapproving tongues.

'Butcher!'

'Shame on you!'

'Monster!'

So, despite my mask for the revels, they know me for who I am. It does not surprise me. There are few at court who can match me for length of leg and stature of frame. My brother Humphrey Gilbert, perhaps, but these days, his figure is somewhat reduced by a regrettable stoop, his step slowed by a faltering reticence. And that is to say nothing of his grey head and beard.

They know me. And they have the temerity to despise me.

As soon as I turn to face an accuser, he vanishes into the darkness of the internal woodland. My face flushes hot inside the close press of the mask.

I want to rip it off and face them openly, unashamed, unafraid, but most of all, unapologetic.

I will save my arguments for my sovereign. It is for her that I did what I did. And so it is her approval only that I seek. I will consent to be condemned by her alone.

But there has been no word yet of official condemnation. No summons to explain myself before the Privy Council. No guards hammering on my door at midnight.

It is a calculation, always a calculation. If you would be a man of action, you must act. And if you will act, you must calculate.

Her Majesty is no great lover of Catholics. Why should she be when this Pope has reaffirmed the edict that she must be overthrown? Once deciphered, the letters I have in my possession will, I think, confirm his ill intent, if any further confirmation be needed.

At such a time as this, it is as well to dispel any lingering suspicions of Catholic sympathies. I will not deny that this was a factor in my calculation too. The desire to distance myself still further from the Oxfordian rump. Most of all, I wished to serve my sovereign. I gave no thought either to pleasing or displeasing her courtiers.

So I will hold my head high, and not only because that is how I am obliged to hold it in order to see.

I hear the hawk and whistle of spittle gobbed in my direction. I feel its phlegmy mass hit my shoulder.

I draw my sword and brandish it towards the dancing shadows from whence the gobbet emanated.

There is a silken rustle behind the screen of greenery. Methinks I detect the whiff of certain scented gloves.

'I thank ye for this… badge of honour.'

My railing provokes predictable jeers from the unseen detractors.

I content myself with some loose slicing of the air. My blade clatters through holly boughs, dispersing leaves and fragments of twig. As if in festive liberality.

## Revels

The choirs sing of the rivalry between the holly and the ivy. The men's voices taking the part of the holly, the women's of the ivy.

There is a spicy smell in the Presence Chamber. Of wine warmed through with cloves and fruit. Of sweetmeats and cakes and honeyed treats. I detect other smells too. The burning of the beeswax candles arranged all around the chamber, their flames forming a flickering constellation. The logs hissing in the grates, exhaling thick clouds of damp and heady smoke. The scented clothes of the courtiers. The vinegary waft in the carolling breaths.

And beneath it all, a sharp and musky undertone. The hint of something animal. The bestial wildness in the human heart. I feel its feral thump within my own. Or mayhap it is the beast methought I glimpsed before. The horned and hunted hart that stalks the green-decked palace with a faltering clip.

The Queen's mask is of silk sewn with pearls, so that it appears that a pox of milky splendour has burst out over the upper part of her face. I see in her eyes as she approaches me – she approaches *me!* – a strength of purpose that I once mistook for loneliness. *Hers are the loneliest eyes I have ever seen*, I remember thinking. The truth is, they are the strongest, the most forthright and frank. Her gaze looks upon everything, even upon that from which her woman's nature ought to shrink. But she does not shrink from anything. Least of all from me.

There can be no doubt. She knows me who I am. I have been pointed out to her. She approaches me with stately, unwavering step; with hand held out to greet me; with eyes fixed firmly on mine.

The procession falls apart. The music of revelry starts up again. The tabor's beat speaks for my heart.

She is the moon. And I am the tide drawn towards her.

I sink to my knees as I take her hand. She bids me rise. I am allowed to stand to my full height, my head above hers. She leads me away to a corner of the room, signalling as she goes for the revelling to resume.

She invites me to kneel once more before her. I am aware of huddle of masked presences forming around us, screening our conversation from prying ears.

'I hear there is a gentleman, recently returned from Munster, who has done the Queen great service. If you know such a one, kindly pass on the Queen's thanks to him.'

'Majesty…'

Her lips pulse out in disapproval. Am I to pretend that I do not recognise my Queen?

'I know the gentleman. And if I may speak on his behalf, I know that he will be gratified his actions have met with the Queen's approval.'

I give my answer as quietly as she made her opening observation. I think at first that she has not heard, for it is a moment before she replies. A long moment in which she holds me with those clear, fearless eyes. She leans her head down towards me and now her voice is even softer than before, so that I am obliged to lift my own head up towards her too.

'More than her approval.'

I had not expected this. I wish to make sure that I have understood her: 'There are those who condemn… the gentleman's commanding officer for exercising too much severity. They say he betrayed those who surrendered to him.'

'They surrendered to him. What can they expect? Those who condemn my Lord Grey should consult the meaning of the word surrender. You understand the word, do you not?'

'To surrender is to place one's self entirely at another's mercy.'

'Just so. One is not entitled to set terms upon that mercy. It is either given or it is withheld.'

'And so, your M…'

A swift shake of her head cuts me short.

'Madam…?'

She nods approval.

'And so, may I presume that the Queen finds no fault in what was done?'

'The Queen has only one complaint. That those who did it were too lenient.'

'Too lenient?'

'They spared the ringleaders.'

'My Lord Grey…'

My protest is cut curtly short. 'Yes, yes, Lord Grey. It is all Lord Grey's fault. It was not for him to spare their lives. That gift was ours alone to grant.' She corrects herself: 'I mean to say, the Queen's alone.'

'And the Queen would not have granted it?'

'She would not.'

'I'faith, nor would I.'

Her mouth tenses into a thin smile, before her eyes become suddenly solemn again. 'I am surrounded by men…'

Her voice has lowered itself to a barely audible whisper. My heart thrums at the intimacy of it. I am astonished to realise that she is no longer pretending to be anyone other than who she is. She has even dropped the majestic plural. She is no longer a sovereign. She is a woman. And my body responds to the thrilling throb of her voice as to a woman's.

'…who think me weak.'

I shake my head in violent contradiction of her words. I want to seize her hands so that I may smother them in reassuring kisses. More, to take her in my arms. My very cock, harbinger of my adoration, springs up urgently to worship her, prepared to make the ultimate sacrifice in her honour. (And I needs must adjust my body to conceal the sudden tent made of my netherhose.)

She is good enough to continue as if she has not noticed. 'Here, at court. In the Privy Council. In the kingdom at large. Beyond the bounds of the

Kingdom. My enemies abroad. My friends abroad. Even those who profess to love me.'

There is regret in her voice as she casts a glance in the direction of a tall, shapely-legged man standing nearby.

'All deem me weak, because I am a woman. There is no denying it, I am a woman. I do manifestly possess the attributes of womanliness. And women are inarguably the weaker sex. Even we women must agree to that. It would be folly not to. To say nothing of going against God's law and Nature's too. There is no manly strength in these my arms. I may gird myself in armour, but I will never cut the figure that my father did upon a horse. To say nothing of entering the tilts as he did. You laugh? You are right to. It is an absurd idea. So I must have men about me who will do the things I am too weak to do myself. For though my arm be weak and womanly, my heart is a man's. My stomach too. You need not fear. I have the stomach for such deeds as yours. And the will. How could I not? I am attacked from all sides. My enemies are all about me. Even now the seditious Jesuit Campion goes about my Kingdom seeking to turn my subjects against me. It was not enough for the Pope to send an army against me. He must send meddling priests.'

She curls one hand into a fist and pounds her breast.

'I am attacked! On all sides! It is because I am a woman they do this. But I have shown them. Through you.'

And so, there is to be no more talk of 'a gentleman'. This breach in the etiquette of a masque causes a flurry of consternation around us. I feel it too in my quickening heart.

'You have been the instrument of my strength.'

I am conscious of the agitation of the tall masked man watching us. But I do not look in his direction. The act of consciously ignoring a rival is curiously exhilarating.

## She gives

The tables are brought out and laid. We take our places. Mine is on the High table. There are those who cannot conceal their resentment, even though they wear masks. Do they not see how the sour set of their mouths must be taken as censure of Her Majesty's judgement and favour? It amuses me to see them wrestle with themselves to bring to bay their own jealous passions.

Seated next the Queen is that tall fellow whose jealousy I remarked earlier. Even with his mask I recognise him. Sir Christopher Hatton. It is clear he places great store in his proximity to the Queen. His preening self-regard is no doubt intended for my benefit, for I am equally sure that he knows who I am. He is at pains to signal that he considers his position nothing more or less than his prerogative. In truth, it matters little to me where I am seated at a masked banquet. But I do confess that it gratifies me to see that it matters to him.

My gaze is fixed upon her lips as they part and the smallest sweetmeat is placed between her rotten teeth. I do not see her chew, or not at least with any great enthusiasm. I get the impression it is painful to her. She partakes in the main of sweets and confections, which it seems she sucks until they disintegrate. Of the savoury dishes, she leaves the fleshy meats wholly untouched. I do believe I spied her devour a portion of roe. A soft enough mouthful to mash with her tongue. Her eagerness for the dish perhaps reflecting its ease of mastication.

After the banquet is cleared away, a platform is raised and we take our places for the performance of a play. The Queen deigns to acknowledge me again in passing, and in passing, reveals her talent to astonish.

'Your mask is slipping, sir.'

I fumble to adjust it. The mask is perfectly in place.

'It would do you well, I think, to mask your pleasure at another's pain.'

'I hope I was not gloating. But if it pains him to see me in your Majesty's favour…'

'Hold! You cannot speak of any Majesty's favour.'

'Her Majesty does not grant me favour?'

'I cannot speak for Her Majesty.'

'You might ask her if she knows a man called Walter Ralegh. And if she deigns to look favourably upon him.'

'Walter Ralegh?'

'Aye, your… Madam.'

'His aunt was very dear to the Queen, I believe.'

The pretence is tiresome to me now: 'And she did love you greatly, Majesty. No greater love did ever governess have for her ward.'

The Queen smiles, an unguarded smile that seems to take her by surprise. She blinks her eyes on some unwonted emotion.

She condescends at last to speak as herself, even though she maintains the majestic plural: 'Her friendship was our rock.'

'She will always be an example to me. I hope that I may be of so great service to you as she was.'

'You wish to be the Queen's governess?'

'Rather, I wish to be governed in all by the Queen.'

'In that you would be no different from any other of our loyal subjects.'

'I have no ambition other than to prove my loyalty to the Crown.'

'Sir Christopher will be pleased to hear that. Though we doubt he will believe it.'

'Sir Christopher may be assured, your Majesty, I do not dare compete with him. I have no talent for the galliard.'

She makes a small attempt to conceal her mirth, pursing her lips in a public chiding. But her eyes avow her private approval of my wit. 'Then you must find our revels very tiresome, Mr Ralegh?'

'Please, your Majesty, will you not call me Walter?'

I detect a distancing flicker and know immediately that I have overstepped the mark. I do what I can to retrieve her good favour: 'As you did once call my aunt Kat?'

'*Warrrter*?'

Oh, she is quick to mock me. Quick and cruel. To use my own West Country burr against me, dragging my name out into a ludicrous travesty. Her harsh teasing draws harsher laughter from the surrounding courtiers. You may count on it that they have been hanging on our every word. I feel the throb of their accumulated envy in their gleeful braying. Sir Christopher Hatton laughs loudest of them all.

I would like to think that Her Majesty is somewhat penitent as she takes in their appreciation of her jest. But they are her wonted audience, and she cannot resist playing to them. 'Yes, you will be our Water!'

I bow my head in meek acceptance of her mockery. 'And you, Majesty, will be my Moon.'

I do not know if she hears my response as she sweeps by.

But I am not dismayed. She means not to mock me but to make me. The name is an exhortation. And a challenge.

The play is a drama made out of the life of Pompey, presented by the Children of Paul's. You'll find me, as the prologue begins, no great *aficionado* of boy players. Or rather, of child companies. I take no exception to the odd boy playing a part in a company of men. How else are you to have the female roles acted? But to have entire companies made up of children seems to me aberrant. Tis a freakish spectacle, to see those piping boys take on the parts of strapping men. And yet, this once, I am unmindful of my wonted objections. Perhaps it is because I see how much delight is occasioned to the Queen by the strutting entrance of the little gentlemen. By their earnest assumption of manly postures. By their impeccable, if high-pitched, enunciation of the playwright's lines. By the marvellous range of their expressions, from stately gravity to martial ferocity. Even, simply, by the way their little tailored suits fit perfectly around their diminutive limbs. I find that I am as charmed by all this as is she.

I soon forget that I am watching a company of boy actors and become immersed in the drama presented. It occurs to me that the employment of boy actors transforms a dull piece into something quite enthralling. The boys become central to the drama's meaning. It is not that they are boys pretending to be great generals. It is that all great generals are revealed to be but boys.

The tender age of the actor playing Pompey is most effective when his character is at his most brutal. His merciless slaughter of his enemies while still so young earned him the epithet of *adolescens carnifex*. And yet, by the casting of an adolescent to play him, we see that Pompey remained such for the whole of his life.

The Queen is not among those who feign to be offended by this scene. Indeed, she murmurs her approval.

The play plays out. And after the boards and trestles are borne away, the Queen retires to her privy chambers in company with her Ladies of the Bedchamber. Am I alone in discerning that these chaste and chosen Maids of Honour do cast longing glances back at the continuing revels?

As the doors close behind the Queen's departing party, Sir Christopher takes his place to stand jealous guard. He struts a little, while his wary, warning eye glares out from behind his mask. He reminds me of the boys whose performance we have just watched. Does he truly expect me to rush the door and so force myself into the Queen's bedchamber? Perhaps my bluff West Country speaking encourages in him such a low opinion of my manners. He only makes himself more absurd by his posturing.

Besides, I have reason to believe that such privileged admittance as he fears will one day be granted to me. I draw myself up, shoulders sharply back, as I thrust my groin in his direction.

After Her Majesty's departure, some new spirit of licence is released among the revellers. The men lay hands upon the women more greedily, and lift them higher, and spin them faster. And in the women's eyes, the glint of promise and desire gleams brighter. I would say it is the harlot's glint, but these are all highborn ladies here. Far be it from me to suggest that every lady is, at heart, a harlot. But these are the revels. And they are masked. And a mask is a kind of licence. All is allowed.

Each bright adoring eye that meets mine canvasses my desire. This maid I fain would choose because she has the prettiest chin. This one because she is the most elegant dancer. This one has the sweetest lips. This one, the daintiest hands. From this one's mouth escapes the sauciest laughter. This maid's eyes are the darkest. This one's skin the fairest. This one has a slender waist. This one a buxom breast. These two sisters with their flaxen hair and identical smiles – how to choose between them? Must I choose between them? If I am not mistaken, they do both comply to give themselves to me? A brace of comely noble strumpets.

This one is another man's wife, and yet she is no less eager for my attention. Does the licence of the revel go so far, I wonder? And this one here, I am certain she is my enemy's mistress. I would know her delicate jaw and fine, white, enticing neck anywhere. Sweet Anne Vavasour. I confess she tempts me more than any of the others. But to have my way with her just to have one over Oxford? Truly, dare I?

They go around again, the Chain of Beauties, giving me more time to make my choice.

As they revolve, their qualities merge. Truth be told, I would have them all. I cannot conceive of any objection that the fair maids could honestly raise. For once one consents to play the wanton, why put bounds upon one's wantonness?

Whomever I choose tonight will earn the envy of her companions. It is not unreasonable to conjecture that, in some future turn of the dance, another will step forward to offer herself, if only to supplant her favoured sister. I may not have them all this night, but I am sanguine that I may have most of them in time. A good number even before the New Year revels are over, I am encouraged to hope.

But choose one I must. All my conquests in Ireland count for naught next to the conquest of one of Her Majesty's Ladies. For in the conquest of one, I conquer all. I conquer the entire court.

The circuit of the dance comes round again, like the slow stirring of a great cauldron. Fires blaze upon the several grates that are set into the walls of the chamber. To their heat may be added the press and exertion of bodies, together with the quantity of sack and other wines that you may take it the company has consumed.

I see beads of sweat glisten on foreheads and breasts. I feel my own face begin to melt inside my mask. The room grows dizzy and uncertain in the flickering candlelight. A swarm of inky shadows conducts its own shifting dance in tandem with that of the courtiers. To my eyes' constrained vision, it increasingly appears as if there is not a Chain of Beauties processing about the room, but a tumble of disparate limbs and body parts. A head suddenly manifests itself out of darkness. A hand belonging to no one gestures to no one. The flesh of two plump disembodied breasts flashes in front of me.

Unaccountably I am put in mind of the last writhings we saw in the mounds of bodies at Smerwick.

The music stops and all are taken by surprise. I, not the least. My decision is made for me. I do not choose. I am chosen. The hand belonging to no one grasps mine. I pull it to me and hook a plump enough breast, a fine enough neck, a pretty enough chin, a pert enough mouth, beneath a promisingly simple mask of black velvet. My tongue finds the gratifying moistness of her mouth.

The first kiss is brief. She pulls away and smiles, but does not release my hand. Instead she turns and draws me into a darkened recess at one corner of the room.

We sink onto a couch. I find her lips again. My hands plunge into the dark mysteries of her attire. She is my helpmate in the task of her undoing. Her own hands come to my aid to unbutton and unbuckle the taut layers in which she is enfolded. The night continues in its unloosening. She shifts and parts and welcomes me. Into the heart of a deeper warmth.

She gives.

She gives.

She gives.

## The old cob house

I live now every day with her bounty. In time, so many gifts do come to me that to enumerate them all would be a greater labour than the winning of them.

Look here, at this. This length of tawny cloth, this collar of fur. The trappings of my office as Captain of the Yeomen of the Guard. And look at this. Here. The bitter glitter in Sir Christopher Hatton's eye, he who once held the very same post. Not so long ago – remember? – he was the trusted guardian at the door to her bedchamber. No more. I think I would surrender all my other gifts from her for this. The lands I now possess in Ireland, all 12,000 bleak acres of them. The cold, wind-blown castle in Youghal that is my home when I am there. The Irish wench who serves me in the night's alchemical works. The baby daughter she has borne me. The transformation that has thus been wrought in me. For all that the child is born in bastardy, I do confess: her fine-wrought fingers clutching out for life's harsh prizes, or pointing heavenward like a tiny saint, her wondrous mewling, so frail and yet so indefatigable, the perfect neatness of her milk-skinned limbs, all stir in me the manful and unmastered throb of paternal pride. I see myself in her. Suckling at her mother's breast, she takes me back to unremembered memories of my own mother's pap. For, no, I was not wet-nursed. That was not the way in our family then. Through her eyes I see the world renewed. It is inconceivable that I should disown her.

Through her eyes, I glimpse again the flickering firelight by which once my father's broad grasping hands took me up and hauled me in to his great tickling beard and spun me till I was happy giddy sick. It happened just one blink of these all-seeing eyes ago.

And I am to her what he once was to me. And his way of tickling me and teasing me and blowing blasts in my delighted face is my way of tickling and teasing her now. And his way of being suddenly gone about his business must be my way too. There can be no other way.

She, my Queen, gives me this, this remembering, for all gifts come through her. And it is a sad, sweet happiness, a pang that fills me and yet leaves me emptied, a feeling very like the flames in the cob house hearth; there is warmth and brilliance in it, but it cannot last and is ever swallowed by a quick and hungry darkness.

For the news has reached me of his death. The man who was my father is no more. He has gone about his business elsewhere, and for the last time. The old cob house is no longer in the family. 'Twas only ever rented, and is returned now to its owner.

Of all the gifts Her Majesty has given me, if she could give me that, I would be forever grateful. I would value it even above Sir Christopher's jealousy.

I ask her for it. Mayhap it is one request too far. Rather than admit it is not within her gift, she complains of me, loudly, for all attendant upon her to hear: 'When will you cease to be a beggar?'

My face burns as if slapped with her displeasure. I bow my head and mumble some reply, attempting wit in the face of insult.

But if she could just give me this one gift, the old cob house in Hayes Barton, methinks I would never ask her for anything else.

## I am Water

I am Water. My eyes are the eyes of the sea. Not merely the eyes of fishes swimming in the sea. But the very Ocean's eyes. My vision is everywhere that the Ocean is, borne along on a floodtide of unstoppable sensation. The tiny bubbles fomented by the vast ceaseless swirling of the waters – these are my eyes.

I am the Ocean! I am all the Earth's Oceans conjoined. Flooding one into the other, one great macrocosmic system of mutual sustenance and devouring. I am all the Rivers of the World too. I am every cascading cataract. I am every subterranean torrent bubbling through the porous heart of the land. I am the slow frigid drips that wear away vast caverns. I am the tides that gently lap and wash the shingled shores. The waves that crash with a mighty unheard roar over solitary crags. I am the old, cold, ink-black presence at the bottom of a deep well. The artesian torrent surging through a bore hole for release. I am the spray of fountains in Vitruvian pleasure gardens, my multitudinous eyes contained inside each particle of water cast up into the air. My vision is a joyous explosion. But so too it bears within itself the weight of my whole being. And the utter, impenetrable darkness of my fathomless depths. I am not blind here, in these lightless places. I need no luminescent sphere, as the lantern fish does, to show my way. My vision is not curtailed by the darkness. It absorbs it. It accommodates it. It transforms it. And is in turn itself transformed.

I come eye to eye with murky bottom feeders. I rush into the nooks and crannies of rocky outcrops, discovering the strange and startled monsters that lurk within. All of my many mysteries are revealed to me.

My energy is the ceaseless turbulent energy of the floodtide. I am irresistible.

I bear life within me. Great leviathans flex their mighty tails to propel themselves through me. Their immense eyes swivel to take in the immeasurable vastness of me. No doubt, they feel themselves dwarfed by my profound infinitude. Tiny spores of invisible life teem in the spume that rises to my restless, ruffled surface. Quicksilver salmon, eager to spawn, speed along my rushing courses. Fullgrown eels spring into writhing spontaneous life, the miraculous fruit of my fertile currents.

I am drawn through the gills of every fish that inhabits me. I am absorbed into their icy blood and feel the beating of their aqueous hearts as if they were my own. So many hearts do I possess. Though their number is nothing compared to the number of my eyes.

The sun blazes down on me. I bear its glints along like a flotsam of celestial bullion. Here, where I broach the sky, where my jettisoned spray bursts in elemental coition, the force and intensity of my being is almost unbearable. I break apart. Only to re-coalesce.

For all my fluid, unbreakable power and the numberless leagues of my extent, as great and mighty as I am, I am subject to an even greater force. I feel it pull me. This way and that, I know not whither. My depths are churned by its influence. I discover that my puissance is not unbiddable after all. It is not mine to wield as I will. It belongs to another. The Moon. I feel myself revolved by her stately revolutions. The surge that gives me motion comes all from her. Without her, I would be stagnant, the life within me stillborn.

For her, then, I will spread myself across the World. I will infiltrate foreign harbours. I will cascade over uncharted mountains. My rivulets will stream out into sodden ground, like a pack of hounds riven by conflicting trails.

I bear upon my buoyant back all the commerce of nations. Nothing can be conveyed from one place to another without my intercession. It starts with the very timber from which we build our oakfast ships. And all the manifold cargoes that are carried within their holds owe their transportation to me. The grain and ale we need for sustenance. Livestock and hides to a distant market. The bricks and slabs, the bronze bells and quarry slates that are the fabric of our towns. The wool we trade to Flemish weavers. The silks and other luxuries with which the East reciprocates our quenchless curiosity. Above all the wine, the casked and barrelled gallons of good sack and ruddy-twinkling burgundy.

I bear my agents out along my rivers and estuaries: the Cam, Isis, Medway, the many Avons, the Exe, the Ouse, the Trent, the Humber too; and now I stretch myself out into the Liffey, Shannon, Boyne and Blackwater.

But the greatest of them all is the Thames.

The boatmen wind from bank to bank of me, stitching a route along the length of me. Their passengers add to my retinue. Sea captains, mathematicians, alchemists, philosophers, poets, playwrights, conjurors of visions and projectors of prospects, the boldest adventurers of our age, and the most fearless, boundless minds. The men who will imagine our future into being. I summon them all to me, and bear them all on my irresistible tides. And she, the Moon, shines her benign nocturnal light upon our nightly enquiries.

The trade winds stir me. I hear the whispered hiss of a headlong keel and the boisterous crack of sails. I cannot sleep for their constant whip and clatter. Dark, fast-moving shapes block the sun's crystal light. My ships, my captains, taking my business out into the world, the full extent of it, furthering my cause ever farther. Rooting out new routes. Adventuring on my back and on my behalf. Adventuring! It lifts my restless, ever-expanding heart to hear their Hos! And Ahoys! And Halloos! I bear them up and bear them off. And bear them back safely (we pray) into home harbour, their hulls creaking with the strain of their prizes. These are the brave seizers of the day and all it contains. On my broad back there is much latitude, both topographic and moral. The Paradoxal Compass is much in evidence. It is a handy device for navigating through the niceties of predation. Some small part of everything they take comes back to me. I reward their rapacious roaming by steering bounty towards them. It is only right that I should receive a share of it.

I am the salt in their hair and the spray on their faces.

I carry, too, the dreams of our best men upon me.

I carry my brother, Sir Humphrey Gilbert, back across the Atlantic, in pursuit of his undying dream. I am in the conch shell that the Queen holds to her ear. I am the whispered promise of distant shores: America! America! In such wise I aid my brother's cause and speed his course.

I am Ocean. I am with him all the way. I bear him there. They are my rippling waves that wink him *bon voyage*. I send an escort of my porpoises to cheer him.

But I cannot save him from himself. It is beyond even my power. I try to guide him, in a brother's loving way, towards safety. But he trusts only to his own counsel, which time and tide will finally prove faulty. His fleet of discovery discovers dismal rewards: sickness, starvation, mutinous stirrings. His Newfoundland is found sorely wanting, a blasted northern desert, less hospitable to an Englishman than Munster's hostile swamps. One by one, his men waste and die. I must thank him for the gift of their diseased corpses, tossed overboard to feed the ravening fishes, a bloody jetsam of despair, devoured with merciful speed. He turns to Thomas More's Utopia for delivery rather than his charts.

I had tried to warn him, of the immensity of my extent, the violence of my tides, the unimaginable, shattering weight of me. Mountains of water moving with planetary momentum. Do not be deceived by my yielding nature when at rest. A puddle or a pitcher of me may be gentle things, the former easily forded with a spreading cloak, the latter securely contained and ever placid.

But an ocean of me?

It is beyond my power to restrain the crashing train of elemental rage that I drag in my wake. Again I must insist, I am subservient to another's force. And so all that sail upon me are prey to Her. There is no mercy manifest in the cold face of the Moon. Do what I may, I have not the might to save those She has already claimed.

How frail his frigate, the tiny storm-tossed *Squirrel*. Can he not see she is unequal to the crossing? The more so as she is over-burdened with his aggression: the weight of too many cannons, and countless pyramids of cannonballs, sitting her low in the water.

I try to warn him with light lashings across his face. He only laughs at them! So I flash flood his decks and drench his supplies.

He will not take heed. He will not turn back for safety, nor join the *Golden Hind* and abandon his battered *Squirrel*. His misplaced loyalty stirs me up to an even fiercer rage. He is faithful to a ship? To a battened hulk of wood? So many timbers tacked together? We give them names and deem them of feminine gender, but, by Christ, only a fool would take it this far!

Oh, Humphrey! How can I save you when you will not save yourself?

I am whipped up, drawn high into the night. I hang over the ship's swinging lantern, looking down upon him, still poring over his Utopia. I take time to note the bald patch on the top of his head. Strange I have never remarked it before.

The *Squirrel* plummets into the vacuum left by my uprising. She hits rock bottom with a shattering jolt. A breach in her hull is sprung on the port side. She lists. And takes on water – takes on me, my element – with unseemly, death-desiring haste. Now the mass of me that was suspended over the frigate's undoing bears down with all the weight of a toppled tower of Babel. I roar like Babel's tower too, with a clash of crushing destruction, mingled with the howls and screams of infinite voices: incomprehensible and uncomprehending.

Why do I not save him? Why do I not stay suspended over him, why not refuse to fall? For in falling do I seal his fate. Why am I so eager to rush in, to drag him down into my depths?

All that I do is in water's nature. I cannot fight my own nature.

His head smashes against a spinning beam as he sinks. His mouth opens as if to voice a quiet, considered protest. His last breath bubbles to the surface of me. His clenched hand unfurls, releasing the golden anchor that I gave him from the Queen. It bears the legend and the lie: *Tuemur sub sacra ancora.*

It sinks, as anchors do, even sacred ones intended to protect.

Oh, Humphrey, my brother. This is not defeat. I will not let this be defeat, not of your dream. Our dream. I will consume you and absorb you, and your dreams will become mine.

Do you not know that the only way to conquer the Ocean is to become the Ocean?

## *Whither?*

The letters patent that once were Humphrey's float and bob upon my lapping waves. I see others' hands reach out to snatch them. But no. They come to me.

The Queen herself commissions me to continue his work. She confides, whispering back now into my conch shell ear, he never did have good hap by sea. I cannot disagree. He was a better dreamer than a sailor. But I am Water, so named by her. I am Ocean. I *am* the sea. I swept into his dying dreams and now I bear them along, out into the world, towards its newest reaches.

Virginia! The greatest of her gifts to me, this name for the new land that I will found for her. A gift that will cost me dear. She does not see that it is her very benefaction that is the cause of my despised beggary. She gives me licence to plant a colony in her name. But not the funds to found it.

The sea captains and the mathematicians and the geographers and the astronomers continue to converge at Durham House, which is my house now, another of her gifts to me. From my high turret window, I watch them disembark and hasten up to the house through the garden gate. To a man, they are eager to be about our enterprise. There are alchemists among them too. But I feel myself to be the greatest alchemist of all. The materials of my Great Work are these very men. I mix them up and confine them in the pelican of my house. Warm them with the heat of conviviality and conference. And by my transforming influence, the sailors become mathematicians, and the mathematicians sailors.

One among them, young Thomas Hariot, exemplifies the complete virtues that I would inculcate in all my followers. Clad ever in black, Thomas is serious and learned, but his mind is as quick and all-encompassing as floodwater. Though he be modest in his manners and conduct, he is no timid scholar, never daring to glance up from his books, or venture out from behind his writing desk. Ofttimes, his eyes fix upon a distant point, as if seeking out a kindred blue. His pert and fine-wrought chin seeks the future like the bobbing needle of a compass.

And when those keen, questing eyes do meet mine, I seem to see his mind continually stretch and probe and reach out beyond itself. His intelligence strikes me as the very incarnation of Nature's infiltrating essence.

He is prodigiously well-read, in many languages. And yet not content is he to learn about the world from a mere library, not even if it be my own lofty, well-furnished study. He is oft to be found at the harbourside, gleaning jewels of knowledge from the rough discourse of homecoming sailors. I picture him now with an eye over his informant's shoulder, looking longingly at the ship from which the man has fresh disembarked. He has a scholar's mind, but an adventurer's heart.

And so the question we set ourselves to resolve is: *Whither?*

All who come to Durham House have their say, among them, Dr John Dee, the Duke of Northumberland, Francis Drake, Thomas Cavendish, the Richard Hakluyts, Arthur Barlow, Philip Amadas, John White, Adrian Gilbert, Christopher Marlowe, George Chapman, Ralph Lane, Sir Richard Grenville, Fulke Greville, and many more men than I may here name. Be assured that for as many men as there are, there are as many different opinions upon the matter.

For all his youth, it is Thomas whose arguments I find most pertinent and persuasive.

He holds up a chart that shows the vast extent of the Ocean – of me! – neatly circumscribed within a cartographer's lines. His finger plots a course across my Atlantic vastness to a point on the eastern seaboard of America, far south of Humphrey's preferred Newfoundland. 'Gentlemen, I propose we situate Virginia here.'

There is much head-shaking.

''Tis too close to the Spaniard's interests.' The objection comes from Ralph Lane, whom I would have govern the colony in my place, and who would therefore be called upon to contest the territory with the Spanish.

Patient Thomas is prepared for this. 'But there is a reason the Spanish have chosen to settle in the south. The warmer climes. The richer soils. To say nothing of the gold.'

We all, to a man, swallow hard, as if all it takes is the mere mention of gold to stir our pricks to a lusty stand.

Lane persists in his opposition: 'And we will pay for this gold with the lives of our men.'

Murmurs of concurrence grow into a restive rumble.

'Or we will make the Spaniard pay.' The intervention is my own. I speak with the sonorous weight of the Ocean, flexing my newfound might. I carry the room around.

And so I bear two scout vessels out to the Far West, the New West, the Unknown West, towards the southerly point we are agreed upon. With that small fleet I carry my Queen's large hopes for enrichment. The captains are Amadas and Barlow. And the pilot is, ah, who else would I choose but…:

'MAN THEY SHEETING GUNS, I cry! What? Say Capitano Rawlay. What they fucking arse? Air you a fuckarse cunting whoreson, you big Portingale cunt? I aim capitano of these sheep, no you, you hairy dayvil of a cunt. I geeve the ordairs, no you. I speet on his capitano of the sheep. Air you blind or air you stupeed, you English outsheeting of a weetch's twat? Man they sheeting guns, I say, or they Papist arsefuckers wheel get ay-way! Man they sheeting guns, shout Capitano Rawlay. He may smell like a whore's teats, but he is no fucking fool. Any man who say he is, I will cut off his fucking head and sheet my arse down his fucking neck hole. And I will laugh hard as I fucking do it, you scurvy cock scabs.'

Strange how it now heartens me to see the flashing gold of his earrings and to hear the strangled, mangled oaths spat out between his rotted teeth.

Thomas Hariot sails with them too. He is my proxy, my eyes, my ears. For the Queen will not permit me to go with them in person. She requires my presence at court. And in truth, I require it too. But I am with them in more than spirit, in my essence. I bear my brave adventurers along upon the heaving curve of my back.

To while away the long hours of the voyage, it pleases Simon Fernandez to educate Thomas in the particulars of his own history: the whores fucked, the whoreson dayvils killed, the bullets and the nooses dodged, the prizes taken, the ships sunk. It is a tale long in the telling, and with every new chapter the scholar's eyes hoist themselves a little wider, until the frail blue disc of each iris is entirely surrounded by white. Like a buoy afloat in an ocean of milk. The same Thomas, this, who dreams of one day mapping the face of the moon. And who, in the dreams within dreams, imagines himself sailing even there. Now he finds himself face to face with the greatest mystery of any that he might seek to understand: the mystery of another man's soul. It almost is beyond him, for all his great wit. The unknown frontier that he is bound for, that land of savages and wonders that is America, could not be more strange than all that is contained within Simon Fernandez. Thomas does not question that men have immortal souls. And so he fears greatly for the damnation of Simon Fernandez. If one tenth of the sinning that Fernandez boasts of is true he is destined surely for Hell. And the fires of that place seem to burn in his eyes already as if Satan has wasted no time in possessing that which is his by rights.

They smell the land before they see it, a sweet garden scent that wafts over the ever-shallowing sea. Thomas looks over the side to see the quicksilver flick and flurry of fish hastening away from the speeding hull. He beholds the first of many wonders: an ancient head projecting from the tawny carapace of a great sea turtle. The beast moves with unweighted alacrity, its lithe and supple limbs batting sunbeams in the shallows. He counts it as much a portent as a comet in the skies.

For many leagues the ocean bed is visible to him. Still no sight of land.

I race ahead of them to roar news of their approach along the eastern seaboard of America. My tidings crash and shatter upon the silted bank that shelters the true shore for nigh on seventy leagues of its extent. An immense natural breakwater, it was once a chain of elongated islands, which are now strung together by the accumulated sand dredged up from my ocean floor. I know, for I put in place each grain of grit, counting them as I did. Yes, I was complicit in my own taming. I always knew how precious this land would one day be to her who commands me. I knew I must provide a safe haven for those who would discover it on her behalf.

To Thomas's eye as he approaches it, the immeasurable length of this barrier must appear both daunting and dismaying. The first sight of his promised Utopia is a thin thread of sand-coloured scum upon the westward horizon, slowly solidifying into something that is barely land. He sees, stretching infinitely across his vision, a flat and dismal beach. There is simply too much of it, with too little variation of prospect. He suspects that it must be a screen. He prays that it may be. There is the sense of something hiding behind it, whether dangers or wonders or both. Though he dare not admit it to himself, his first sight of the New World is a disappointment. The relief he feels at having crossed the boundless fervour of the Atlantic is tainted by an apprehension that the prize may prove to be not worth the labour.

The sky is filled with silhouetted seabirds, wheeling and screeching in protest at this uninvited intrusion. Or is it in warning?

A man of science, Thomas discounts such superstitious qualms.

For his part, Fernandez falls unwontedly quiet, the curses dying on his lips, as he watches the unchanging shore pass by. I sense him listening out for subtle mutations in my ceaseless murmuring. His ringed nostrils twitch and quiver as he strains to catch the flavour of the breeze. For in it will be borne the harbingers of landfall.

At length the long bank dwindles to nothing and a fleeting opening appears. Fernandez celebrates by firing a gob of salty spittle across the bickering wind. 'Ahoy the cunt of the New World! Let us set to and fuck it, me lusty dogs!'

I carry his pronouncement down to cheer the fish-picked bones of my brother Humphrey.

I do my best to bear the two small barks of men into the long lagoon, but they are hampered by ineptitude and inebriation. Too soon have the sailors begun their celebrations.

Poor Thomas, I am sure, despairs to see the frustration of his hopes so close to their fruition. But the stern discipline of the two captains is enough to steer the barks back on course. They put this misadventure behind them. It is nothing more than the wonted disarray of seafaring. To restore their undoubted superiority, they fire off an arquebus into the air. The echoing boom of the piece is answered by the clack of wings and the panicked trumpeting of startled crane. Take that, New World.

Thomas gazes across the wide sound at the mouth of the estuary. He sees hills and vegetation, a more solid promise then of true reward. In the hills, there may be gold. The bursts of greenery confirm his faith that the land will prove a fertile plantation for what future colonists we install.

They drop anchor and fire off several more rounds of arquebus shot. It is not done merely to impose their presence on the new discovered world, nor to ward away their creeping fears. No, the arquebuses are discharged in the interests of science. Under Thomas's direction, they watch out for the plish of the lead as it hits the surface of the water and by that means get the measure of the vast lagoon. These my missionary men mark out distance in gunshot arcs.

A boat ferries a landing party to the nearest island. Thomas's heart pounds within him. His eager eyes drink in the strangeness of this New World. It is lit by a different sun, surely, to the one he has thus far known. How else could you explain the fierce clarity that claims each leaf of vegetation, each stone, each grain of sand.

As the keel of the boat scrapes the shoals, the men spring to their feet, each determined to be the first to set foot on the new land. And so it is a scrappy, splashing, joyous scramble, this first footfall, a race of fellow elbowing fellow out the way. Thomas takes his time, almost daunted by the long-deferred realisation of his dreams. Though it is more than dreams that brought him here, it is mathematics, astronomy, cartography, ships and money.

And it is I. I am the agent and the instrument of their arrival.

## Whispers

In the Queen's chamber at Whitehall, where now my audiences with her are held. Her Majesty lies abed, bolstered up on a mound of pillows. I hold the conch shell to her ear once more, for her to hear its distant hiss. It whispers tidings of the fertile land that abounds with wholesome corn, of gourds laden with pearls, and of peaceable naturals who will trade riches for trinkets.

'It will sustain a colony, Water?'

'Aye. The savages want for nothing. They have only to reach out and the fruits of the land fall into their open palms. 'Tis a veritable Golden Age, your Majesty.'

'You met with their king?'

She forgets that I was not there in person, for she would not let me go.

'Aye.'

'And is it true what I heard, that he goes before his people naked?'

She cocks her head as she tries to imagine the spectacle. Her lips purse out in something between amusement and censure.

'Aye, Majesty. Except that he had upon his head a broad plate of some unpolished metal, which was most assuredly gold.'

'Assuredly, Water?' She is sceptical. But I must bear her over her doubts, like straw flotsam borne over rocks by a raging torrent.

'Aye. Assuredly, undoubtedly, incontrovertibly. And if not...'

'If not, Water?' She likes not my 'if not'.

'We have chose the position of our colony most judiciously, Majesty. It is well placed for us to plunder the Spaniard's plate fleet, the route of which passes right close by the eastern seaboard of America. We are concealed and protected by the geography of the land, and may sail out from behind the outer banks with impunity.'

'Ah, the Spanish! You make too little of them, Water! You think they will be content to let their enemy settle upon this island of...'

'Roanoke, Majesty.'

She wrinkles her nose in disapproval.

'We saw no Spanish on the island, Majesty. This land is ours. We have established Virginia beyond contestation.'

'Your words are most persuasive, Water. Would that you could persuade the world to conform to your account of it.'

'I am no mere man of words, Majesty. As I believe I did prove to you in Smerwick. We are even now preparing our next voyage. We have the colonists ready to sail.'

'There must be gold there, Water. And I must have it.'

'You may count on me.'

'My enemies are all about me, Water. My cousin Mary conspires with traitors to kill me and finds no shortage of willing assassins. The Spanish are forever looking to attack our realm. According to Walsingham's intelligencers they are even now equipping an Armada to sail against us.'

The shadows stir, beyond the immediate glimmer of the clustered candles. I sense Walsingham bristling at the mention of his name.

'This land you have discovered, it is my best defence. When we have a source of wealth to equal the Spaniard's, only then may we rest easy.'

At the end of the audience, the Principal Secretary steps forward from the recess in which he has been waiting with a spider's patience and a spider's blackness. 'I wish you every success in your ventures, Ralegh.'

I remember the chill I felt when once he wished my brother God's speed. And in the intervening years, I have learnt the Principal Secretary is not a man to take at his word. His smile is but a thin thread of disguised malice in the gloom.

Rumours reach me that he is bankrupted by the necessity of maintaining the apparatus of his power, the web of intelligencers and assassins that he has cast across the shadows of the world.

He looks old to me. I detect some tremor about his person. I do not deem it to be a sign of hesitancy or any weakness. It is more likely the bursting out of a quaking rage that he has sought to suppress within him.

What do I care? I have the Queen's favour.

Now I am Sir Water to her. I feel the dub of princely sword upon my shifting shoulders; the proud floodtide of my accomplishments rises to its highest elevation yet. She appoints me Governor of Virginia, though she will not have me leave her Presence Chamber. I must govern in absentia. At any rate, I must secure our claim.

And so I send out more ships, laden with eager colonists, creaking at the seams with their dreams and hopes and projections. The desperation that drives them to this endeavour ticks away within the beams like the tap tap tapping of the deathwatch beetle.

My cousin Sir Richard Grenville commands the fleet. In his youth he was somewhat prone to duelling. The story goes that he ran through a gentleman with his sword and left him for dead. Who of us has not been involved in such scrapes?

You may take it that I have instructed him to be peaceful and conciliatory in all his dealings, both with any Spanish he may encounter and with the savages of the country. That said, I naturally give him licence to engage in what privateering exploits he may consider necessary en route.

With the company sail two German miners and a Bohemian Jew, an alchemist whose knowledge and understanding of minerals is unsurpassed. Even Dr Dee bows to Joachim Ganz as his master in this one field of science, if in no other. These are the men who will enable us to rape the virgin land of her riches. I am sanguine that she will reward us with both favour and fertility. I see before me always the glistening fecundity of her dark womb. The vision of it is so alive and present to me that I feel I may reach out and touch the precious veins therein.

I have put aboard an orchestra of players to charm the savages with English Music. We will have them swimming out to our boats to bathe in the sweet, enchanting sounds. What they will not surrender to us in return for more of this intoxicating physick! I have seen with my own eyes the civilising effect of music at court on Manteo and Wanchese, the two lusty savages my men brought back with them from the first expedition. Even Wanchese, who proved resistant to all attempts to teach him English was moved to evident emotion by a concert of the Queen's musicians. He looked about him in wonder, as if the air were filled with spirits.

## Fall

I am Water. I cannot be anything other than my nature.

And so when Simon Fernandez strands the Tyger on a sand bank and the hull is breached, I needs must rush in. It is my nature. I am Water. They are my men, it is my mission, but I cannot hold back my own floodtide as it drenches and wastes the fleet's entire stores. The ship that Simon pilots is the supply ship, alas.

The hopes and dreams of the colonists escape through the same breach.

I have sent with them Thomas Hariot, wise beyond his years, as well one John White, the painter. These two men – the one by his powers of scientific observance, the other by his skill as an artist – shall be my eyes. And the eyes of the world.

These are meticulous men, who between them measure and map the New World into which they all have been cast.

The colonists take heart and repair the Tyger. The friendly savages rally to their aid, swimming out as I envisioned to discover the source of the magical sounds drifting to them. In return for the gift of English Music, and a share of our wine, they willingly make up our losses with gifts of fruits and meats and fishes and grain. John White is captivated by their grace and manners and has them sit for him as he captures their likenesses upon the page. They are astonished to see how cleverly he depicts them, and credit him with supernatural powers, such things as paints, brushes and paper being hitherto not known to them.

As the days pass, our men are cheered, believing themselves to have found a very Eden.

But in this Eden, as in the original, there is a Fall.

Amongst the savages' abundant crops, tobacco grows, and they are prodigious imbibers of the smoke produced by burning that weed. John White sketches them at their pipes, which they are amenable to sharing with our men, as we have shared our wine with them.

The Englishmen cough, their eyes stream with tears. Some spit and vomit. Their whirligig minds spin with images. Their hearts hammer and trip. Their very bodies seem to loosen. Each draw upon the pipe takes them further from themselves. And further into an utterly new state of being. The nausea passes. Their eyes see more clearly. They hear every rustle of every leaf.

This is alchemy at work. By drinking in the savage smoke they are become New Men of the New World. But it is not the transformation I would have wished for them. Some strange new spirit of anger and suspicion has settled upon them.

I try to soothe them with a gentle rain. I try to quench the fires that now burn in them. My lapping on the shore serves as a soft susurration to ease their turbid spirits. I am their calling. But they do not heed me.

They heed only the call of the tobacco. Unmindful of their mission, they form new projects of their own. Banking on their fellow countrymen's quenchless thirst for novelty, they determine to carry it back to England and trade it for a profit. They grow wary of their gentle hosts and suspect them of all manner of evil intentions. Of how they will hoard the crop and deny them access to their reserves.

The echoes of these dark intimations are carried to us in the conch shell.

With every day that passes, my men prove themselves to be ever more unequal to the task of sustaining themselves. They are soldiers not farmers. Their increasing dependence on the native inhabitants, not merely for the tobacco they crave, leads them into beggary and worse.

A ragged flotilla is dispatched to sound the Sound. A party of sixty men all told in three mismatched boats: a pinnace hammered together *en voyage*, a ship's long boat and a simple Thames river boat.

The creaking, cobbled pinnace breasts the shallow waters aside and scrapes the sands, making slow progress. They put in at many villages, following the water as it nibbles at the land.

The fanfares of our trumpets, the thunder of our sackbuts and the reports of our inquiring arquebuses draw the curious savages to the shores. Our guide Manteo waves to them from the deck of the pinnace. They stand amazed to see one of their own among the white men.

John White is suffered to draw the chieftains and their wives and to map out their avenues and palisades and sketch their long houses and sleeping quarters. The men are fed and given pipes to drink the smoke thereof.

Among the villages they approach is one called Aquascogoc. The simple huts, viewed from the boats, are neatly laid out. But the villagers are unwelcoming. They refuse our men a landing. We will get no food or tobacco from them. What has happened to the boats full of fish, the baskets of coneys, and the gourds full of pearls with which once greeted us? They shout and jeer at us from the shore. Some of them turn their backs on us. Others swim out and reach into our boats, brazenly helping themselves to our possessions.

On the way to the next village, it is noticed that a silver drinking cup has gone missing. Now this cup is most precious to Sir Richard, as having come from one of the recently raided Spanish treasure ships.

Sir Richard orders swift retribution. The thieving magpies must be taught a lesson. In this at least, Sir Ralph Lane is in agreement with him. The only dissenting voices are those of Thomas and John White, who alone remember my strictures to treat the naturals with civility.

Our men, having drunk themselves into a righteous rage, return to shatter the peace of the unsuspecting village with gunshot and shouts. The simple mat huts, all arrayed in their neat rows are soon burnt to the ground. They do not stop there. They trample and burn the corn in the fields around the village. The smoke from all this burning is more intoxicating and enlivening than ever the smoke from the savages' pipes.

Soon enough the conch shell resounds with the agitated scratching of Sir Ralph Lane's quill. The smell of bitter bile wafts out in a smokey wisp.

Sweet Sir Water, one maid calls me. As I flood into her. And ebb from her.

The moan of my name upon her lips is like the rush of breakers upon the shore. The crash of them over rocks.

Is the Queen listening in her conch shell? The thought of it adds a piquant vigour to the ingress and egress of my tidal rhythms. She favours me as a goodly-framed and handsome man. A sturdy man of saucy wit and youthful energy. She must suspect the puissance of my pricking. I would have her know it. Have her know me. Utterly and entirely. But in the meantime…

Do I imagine that it is she, Her Majesty, who is the shore across which I break? It is never my intention to do so. But sometimes one's fancies take one unawares.

But she must be ever unattainable to me, as to all men. For she is the Moon. The Ocean's tides cannot crash upon the Moon, though she pulls him ever towards her.

In those moments, when I lose myself in the sweet oblivion of Eros, that is when I am most true to the name she has given me. When I am most Water. For I am a fish swimming, blindly at the bottom of the Ocean, with the weight of the Ocean pressing down on me, enclosing me. And I am also the Ocean in which I swim. I am every fleck of foam that swirls within me, riding and rising on my currents.

Within these moments is one moment: the pivot upon which all time is suspended. It is the moment of the tide's turning, when flood becomes ebb. The dying moment. When the ecstasy of consummation recedes, and the lap of a manageable grief washes over me, the small sweet sorrow that follows in the wake of pleasure's passing.

## The whiff of treasure

Sir Richard Grenville sails into harbour aboard a captive Spanish freighter. His pose as he waves from the deck is provokingly triumphant.

The dip and kick of the deck takes me aback as I step aboard. I had forgot how little I like the vertiginous roll of a ship, even one in its moorings. I find something withheld in Sir Richard's embrace and discern a complex reticence in his face too: a stubborn defiance that speaks of ills stored up. He puffs himself up, his smile a grimace of gritted teeth: 'Welcome aboard the *Santa Maria de San Vincente*! Flagship of the Spanish treasure fleet.'

The air is laden with the *Santa Maria*'s cargo. It smacks me in the face and stings my eyes to tears. My nostrils being somewhat phlegmatic with the change in the weather begin to stream with a gelatinous tide. The autumn chill is warmed to a fiery glow. I feel the itch of a sneeze building. It bursts out in a snotty explosion.

'Ginger?'

'Aye, and there is sugar in the hold too.'

'But no gold?'

'There is a fortune here, Ralegh. I reckon its worth at forty thousand ducats. Perchance even fifty thousand.'

'I grant you, it is some recompense for our pains.'

'What niggard's greeting is this!'

'I trust you left Lane and his Virginians in good order and good spirits?'

'The land abounds in many natural advantages. The savages of those parts are able to eke out a pleasant enough living. And so it should not be beyond the wit of an English Christian to do the same. However, I fear that our colonists and their governor are incapable of self-sufficiency. Rather than cultivate their own sustenance, they think only to replenish their supplies by means of my own speedy return.'

I do not like his complacency. Now is the time to remind him of his duty: 'Cousin, I beg to remind you that the fate of the Commonweal rests in the success of this distant colony. If you disappoint these men, you disappoint the Queen also. This colony of Virginia is like a tender shoot that we all must husband and nourish. If it takes root and flourishes, it will bear fruit that will enrich us all. You have a duty, as do we all, to safeguard its cultivation.'

'I need no lessons in duty from you, Ralegh. You may take it that I will make good on my promise to them. I will in due course return with the supplies upon which they rely. In the meantime, I trust that her share of the *Santa Maria de San Vincenti* will not disappoint Her Majesty?'

The haul is something. With it the Queen may begin to reap the rewards for her faith in me. I must hope that the profits from this prize alone will satisfy our investors and so vindicate the project. We may now attract more backers and finance more colonies along the eastern seaboard of America. Soon we will have a chain of harbour fortresses from which our adventurers may venture out and harvest at will the Spaniard's plate fleet.

Let the Spanish rape the land, and we will rape the Spanish.

'I grant you, the cargo of the *Santa Maria* is a rich enough prize, but hardly an unique one. The true prize I set you to attain was the establishment of a colony in America. Bring the Queen that, beyond dispute, and you will not lack for royal gratitude.'

'It is done, I tell you. I left Sir Ralph Lane building houses and fortifications. We have Englishmen established in America. Virginia is founded as we speak.'

Truly I am glad to hear it.

## Ripples

I carry the good tidings back to Whitehall, along with a casket of ginger for the Queen's kitchen, the spice's pungent scent sealed tightly from the wind's purloining.

My horse no sooner stabled, the journey's dust brushed from my clothes, my hair combed and my jewels fresh-burnished before a looking glass: all ready then for an audience with the Queen, when once again Sir Francis Walsingham steps forward from some shadowy recess to intercept me.

There is something new in the thread of his smile. A knot of knowing, taut with inherent power. 'You have come from meeting Sir Richard Grenville?'

I register no surprise at the quality or speed of his intelligence: 'I made no secret of my mission.'

'How did you find your cousin?'

'He is in good spirits, having captured a prize valued at forty thousand ducats.'

'Forty thousand, is it? My sources tell me that the true value is closer to a million ducats.'

'I had not heard that.'

'You are not seeking to dupe Her Majesty out of her due share by undervaluing your prize, I hope?'

'That is the value that my cousin has placed on it, not I.'

The blackness of him ripples. It is, I think, a shrug. Meant to signify: you, your cousin, little difference.

'It would not only be Her Majesty that you cheat. I have invested in your venture too, as you know. So too my son-in-law, Sir Philip Sidney. Do you seek to rob my family?'

'I say again, Sir Francis, I report only what Sir Richard has told me. I have no reason to doubt him. He is an honourable man.'

'Is he?'

'Do you know of anything that says he is not?'

'I have received certain letters. From Sir Ralph Lane. There is one among them addressed to you.'

'But it came to you?'

'It was entrusted to my agents for delivery.'

'You had agents on the voyage?'

I regret the question immediately. It shows me for an innocent gull. I see the satisfaction that it affords him in the kink of his smile.

'I have agents everywhere, sweet Sir Walter.'

Even there?

I must do my best to defend my cousin's interest, for in doing so I am defending my own: 'Regarding whatever Sir Ralph Lane may see fit to write, it should be remembered that he is himself a man of monstrous pride.'

'That is the very fault he lays against your cousin.'

'He bridles at his subordinate position and will brook no higher authority. One must be wary of placing too great credence in anything he says.'

'If one tenth of what he alleges is true, your cousin has a case to answer. It is a very catalogue of errors.'

Sir Francis stands on the threshold of a shadowed realm. He is ever oscillating between appearance and disappearance. It is unclear whether the shadows are pouring into him, and adding to his powers, or whether they seep from him, his swift, silent emissaries sent into the world. He holds within himself an infinite resource of darkness.

He slowly fades from my vision. His thin thread of a smile is the last of him to vanish.

R.N. MORRIS

## Have with you to Walsingham

I find the Queen at her virginals. Her fingers move with a relentless proficiency within the confines of the small keyboard.

The sound she produces somehow makes me think of a box of broken shells lightly rattled.

I am standing over her, and she is wearing a dress that pushes her breasts up towards me. They glow brilliant white. They are heavily powdered: a granular layer intercedes between my male eye and her female flesh. Somehow that makes it acceptable for me to stare at them. I feel sure that she wants me to look at them. Why else would she expose them in such a way? She wishes to remind me, and all the men who surround her and administer to her, that she is after all a woman. We are none of us permitted to possess her. Yet all are commanded to desire her. And through her our desire of all women must be mediated.

None may fall in love without her say-so. Certainly none of royal blood; so much is the Law. But now she has extended her right of veto to the whole of her court.

I watch the shimmering of her breasts as she works through the endless variations of the tune. The melody becomes ever more elaborate as it mutates. By the closing movement, I long nostalgically for a restatement of the theme at its simplest and boldest. The music fluctuates between the major and the minor key. I feel it in my heart as the old ebb and flow of my spirit. There is something undoubtedly humane at the core of this sound. Even taking account of the musician's somewhat mechanical performance, it cannot be repressed.

The end seems to take the Queen by surprise. Her fingers hover trembling over the keys as if bereft. She squints at the manuscript, as if willing more notes to appear.

Now is my moment: 'I have a gift for you.'

I hold out the casket of ginger. She turns in her seat at the virginals to regard it. 'A gift? From Water?'

'It is water-borne.'

'But you never bear me gifts, Water. Your refusal to give presents at New Year is notorious.'

'No gift can express the unbounded bounty of the love I bear your Majesty. Except perhaps the unicorn's horn I gave you once. Or America, which I have made my life's work to give you.'

The Queen frowns. 'You have never given me a unicorn's horn, Water. You may have dreamt you did, but you did not, and it was I who gave America to you, I think.'

She opens the casket and breathes in the hot blast of spiced air.

'Besides, can you be sure that our colony in America is secure? I like not the news that reaches me from there.'

'Ah, you have read Sir Ralph's letters, I think. You know how it is with these ambitious lieutenants. They are always quick to undermine their commanders.'

'I wish they wouldn't do it.'

'Whatever Sir Ralph alleges against my cousin, remember it is Sir Richard who has delivered you a true and great prize, the Spanish freighter now docked in Plymouth harbour.'

'What value do you place on it?'

'I would be surprised if it fell far short of an hundred and twenty thousand ducats.'

The Queen hands the casket of ginger to one of her ladies, one I have not seen before. She is neither the prettiest nor the plainest girl. She is respectful and discreet, but does not fawn. She knows when to bow her head and when to meet the eye. In short, she is not the least abashed, and refuses to indulge in the usual blushing coyness of young maids at court. As she takes the casket, her gaze is directed towards me. There is some challenge in it. And scepticism. It is as if she does not quite believe in me.

The Queen turns back to address the keyboard, reprising the piece she has just now played. Her fingers move with a more sprightly energy across the keys. She is enlivened by the prospect of booty, as I knew she would be.

'A pretty tune.'

''Tis one of Master William Byrd's compositions. An incorrigible recusant, I fear. You can hear it in his music. The elaborations are exceeding Popish.'

'And yet I like it.'

'As do I. Though I fear the Mary whom he extols is not the Mother of God, but my own troublesome cousin.' She says this with a regretful shake of her head. 'He meddles in matters it were better he kept out of. I had enough evidence against him to send him to the Tower, you know, along with the traitorous Throckmorton and the rest.'

The lady holding the ginger chooses that moment to bow out of the chamber. The Queen continues: 'But his music saved him. He is fortunate that his sovereign is both merciful and musical.'

I try to give voice as to why the music affects me so: 'It has progression. And purpose. One feels one's self transported and transformed by it, as if one were on a voyage. It takes one to a place from which one returns entirely changed.'

The Queen breaks off playing and looks up at me in what I judge to be approval. 'Not a voyage, Water. It is a pilgrimage. Have with you to Walsingham.'

Sir Francis is so much on my mind that I think the Queen is referring to her Principal Secretary. She sees my perplexity.

'The name of the tune. As I went to Walsingham, to the shrine with speed, I met with a jolly palmer in a pilgrim's weed.'

'I thought you were counselling me.'

'Mayhap I was. Make not an enemy of Walsingham, Water.'

This talk of Sir Francis Walsingham unnerves me. The hint that he dropped before, his sweet Sir Water, I see now that it is laden with danger for me. I would know whether he has said ought concerning me, and yet I dare not ask.

'If Sir Francis has made an enemy of me, there is little I can do about it.'

'Has he?'

'He seeks to set you against my cousin, which is very far from a friendly act.'

'I would say it is your cousin sets us against his self, if he would lie about the value of his prize to cheat us of our share. Do you advise him of that.'

I bow and take my leave purposefully. When the Queen bids, it is as well to give the impression that you are hastening to execute her wishes immediately.

As I leave the Queen's Private Chamber, I encounter the young lady in waiting to whom she handed the ginger.

Now that I have leisure to study the girl more closely, I cannot honestly say whether I am attracted to her or not. To be frank, her face has too much pride to it to be entirely appealing. What is both galling and arousing about all these aristocratic girls, is that they always hold themselves as if they were the world's greatest beauties, even the plain ones and those who are a little horsey about the features. Her face is piquing. The undoubted intelligence, undaunted frankness, and indifferent haughtiness of her eyes compels my attention. But an undying glitter of amusement softens and warms it all.

I bow deeply. 'You are newly arrived at Court, my lady? I do not think I have seen you before. I would surely have remembered.'

'Are you flattering me, Sir Walter? I do not like flattery.'

'I know all of Her Majesty's ladies in waiting. Naturally I would notice when their number is augmented.'

'Yes, I have heard it said that you take a keen interest in the ladies.'

I bow again in acknowledgement of her sally. 'As any true gentleman must.'

When I straighten from my bow, I find her unwavering and amused gaze waiting for me.

'I could not help but notice that you left the Queen's presence abruptly upon mention of Sir Francis Throckmorton.'

'The traitorous Throckmorton.'

'I believe Her Majesty chose that designation to distinguish him from the other, loyal Throckmortons.'

'He was my cousin. I am Elizabeth Throckmorton.'

'Ah… and your father is…?'

'Was. Sir Nicholas Throckmorton.'

'One of the loyal Throckmortons. More than that, one of the truest and best servants the Queen ever had.'

'I fear my traitorous cousin has spent all the stock of favour that my father laid by.'

'Not at all. The Queen has brought you to her presence to protect you, my dear. You may be assured of her goodwill and favour, I am sure. And, you must know, that which the Queen favours, I too favour.'

'I know nothing of the sort, Sir Walter.'

'I offer you my services, that is all.'

'In return for what, I wonder?'

'Your friendship?'

'Friendship cannot be bought, Sir Walter.'

'Cannot it be earned?'

'How do you propose to earn it?'

'By acts of friendship of my own.'

'I have always preferred acts to words.'

'I believe both may have their place. A word, at the right time, in the right ear, may have the force of an act. A man may be condemned, or pardoned, by a word. A life may hang upon a word.'

'You are alluding to my cousin's life?'

'No, to my own.'

'I do not understand you, sir.'

'I cannot say more, for I have not yet earned your friendship.'

'Do you mean rather, you do not know whether you can trust me?'

She is every bit as intelligent as I suspected her to be.

'There is something I would ask of you, my lady. And in return, I would have you ask anything of me.'

'So I must place a bond to secure your friendship?'

'Nay. You have already secured the bond of my friendship. It needs no payment. Whether you permit me or not, I am your friend.'

'If I consent to your asking this thing, it does not mean I promise to grant it.'

'I understand.'

'Very well. Ask it.'

'I would merely know whether, in your hearing, Sir Francis Walsingham has ever spoken of me to Her Majesty in such a way as to cause Her Majesty displeasure.'

'Have you done anything that may give him grounds to do so?'

'I fear that Sir Francis has conceived a great disliking for me.'

'That is most unaccountable.'

She meets my discomfiture with amusement.

'I cannot imagine what he may have to say against me. But he has dropped certain hints. He has found fault with my cousin.'

'As he did with mine.'

I qualify the mooted correspondence with a fluttering gesture of my hand. It is not quite the same. Her cousin was found a conspirator, condemned a traitor and executed a Catholic martyr.

'You may put your mind at rest, Sir Walter. I have only ever heard Sir Francis say good things of you.'

I place my hand upon her shoulder as if to steady myself. She is quite irrefutably solid, and for some reason this quality in her impresses me most of all. 'Thank you, Lady Elizabeth. I am gratified to hear it.'

There is an expression of surprise, though not outrage, in her slightly bulging eyes.

## Backwater

What do we hear in the conch shell now?

The cracking of the land in drought. The hungry rumbling of the stranded colonists' empty bellies. The angry mumblings of their native neighbours. No longer do they look upon our men as a prodigious wonder to be feted but more a bothersome burden they did not ask to bear.

We hear these sounds, but do not read them for what they are. They are crackles and rattles drowned in a whispered roar. Nor do we read how the savages come to equate the arrival of the white men in their villages with the consequent visitation of sickness and death. Familiarity breeds contempt, or so the proverb goes. On the island of Roanoke, familiarity turns the colonists from gods to men to accursed demons who drain the land of all its life. They are feared but not revered. As one fears a snake or scorpion. 'Tis a fear mingled with hate.

We hear the plash of oars as Sir Ralph leads a party of men and mastiffs away from the fort, to cast his net ever wider in the search for relief from his despair. (If only he had thought to include fishing nets in the equipage of the original expedition.) Winter has come. After a summer of drought, the land has got no easier to farm. And so he sets out to seek food, and to discover savages who have not yet turned against him. But more than anything he seeks the vindication of his mission, the one and only thing that will bring him the relief he longs for.

Gold.

The frail, pale sun flickers weakly through overhanging boughs. He has remembered why he is there, at last. It is to chase down gold. He lies dozing in the drifting tilt boat, wrapped up in his cloak beneath the gently flapping awning. He dreams of returning to England in a ship laden with bullion and ore.

He dreams of reaching his hand over the side of the boat and sifting gold out of the current between his fingers. His only strategy is to look for golden trappings on the bodies of those savages he encounters along the way. The more rings and plates that adorn their faces, the more hope he has of discovering a source. He has Thomas with him to communicate with the savages, but it is ever harder to make contact. Even Manteo can not induce them to speak out.

He has not heard the messages that have been sent ahead by Chief Wingina, who warns his neighbours to have no truck with the white men coming in boats.

The men who bring only disease and death.

They take whatever is offered to them: fish, corn, skins, coneys and deer. And when it is not offered will demand it. With only worthless trinkets to offer in return for the things they need to live.

These men who are incapable of fending for themselves. Who are more helpless than babes.

These men who will burn your houses and destroy your crops. What crops you have, after the worst drought that any can remember.

These men who are not men, but starving demons.

Sir Ralph Lane sits up in his boat and looks towards the river bank. He sees a soft glint flash and vanish in the dark foliage. The glint returns, then a kind of sparkling forest fire of glints ignites around it.

He beckons for Thomas, setting the boat rocking with his excitement: 'Did you see that, Hariot?'

'I did, sir.'

'It was gold, was it not? The naturals here are wearing gold about their persons.'

'I cannot be sure, sir.'

The river forks. Lane chooses the branch that seems to take them towards where the glints were seen. 'We're getting closer. I feel it.'

He does not hear the restive grumbling of his men, whom every oar stroke takes closer to starvation. The last scrap of cornbread that they brought with them was long ago consumed. They have not the corn to make more, nor is their cook versed in its making; for these loaves were baked for them by the women of Wingina's village. And, of course, they have no fishing nets.

It is left to Thomas to bring the matter to Sir Ralph Lane's attention: 'Sir, we are out of supplies.'

Sir Ralph frowns, as if this is more difficult of comprehension than any mathematical theorem that Thomas Hariot has ever tried to impart to him. Thomas, ever the teacher, sees he must put it more plainly: 'There is nothing left for the men to eat.'

'What says Manteo? Is there a village nearby to which we may look for succour?'

Their scout, once so eager to converse with the white men that he learnt their language, remains tight-lipped. He has no words in any language for them. His own language is lost to him, for his countrymen now look upon him as an outcast. He is dead to them. He has spent more time in the white men's company than any of them. And yet he has survived the white men's mysterious power to leave corpses in their wake. Whatever witchcraft the white men practice, he is corrupted by it now.

He feels a great weight inside him. His heart has become a stone. If he fell into the river, the stone would pull him down and drown him.

Sir Ralph Lane shakes his head impatiently at the savage's reticence.

*What is wrong with these people?*

The sleeping mastiffs prick their ears, as if they have heard his unvoiced question in their dreams. And then it comes. A chorus of high looping shrieks. The dogs sit up from their slumbers to bark indignantly at this rude disturbance. A cold shiver passes through the screen of trees nearest the river. Long thin shadows whip the air.

Thomas protects himself with his cloak, as if this hail of arrows is nothing more than a sudden squall out of a clear English sky.

The arrows clatter into the boats, or plunge into the waters like sleek swift herons. By some good fortune, not one of our party is harmed by this first volley, but they feel themselves to be very much sitting ducks.

'Return fire,' commands Sir Ralph.

For though they set out without fishing nets, they did not forget their muskets.

The crack and boom of the white man's weapons is enough to ward off the attack. The battle cry recedes, like the yap of a lap dog seen off by such beasts as the mastiffs in the boats. The dogs indeed bark lustily and proudly at the exultant clamour of the muskets. Some guard dogs these, who only raise the alarm after the danger has passed. Their excitement brings its own danger as they bound about in the boats, chasing the trailing echoes of the guns' discharges. The men shout at their stupidity, which does nothing to calm them.

The savages have given up their shrieking. The trees, their shivering. But still the dogs keep up their energetic barking, as if once they have started they cannot stop. The sound is deep and monotonous. They are barking at the echoes of their own barks. Their tone begins to wax quizzical, and then exasperated. The intervals between each bark increases. Until, at last, they are startled by the idea of silence. They prick their ears and begin a querulous whining.

Is it this that decides Sir Ralph? He gives the command sourly, for with it he gives up all hope of finding gold: 'Turn the boats about.'

(Behold the flash of wrath in the Queen's eyes as she hears the reverberation of defeat in her conch shell!)

The dogs settle back down in the boats, lulled by the resumption of movement. They care naught for the direction in which they travel.

The flow of the river speeds their retreat. 'Tis just as well, for the men have suddenly no energy remaining. They hoist their oars and lie back listlessly, taking their lead in this from Sir Ralph Lane. They follow him in their suspicions of Manteo also. Who else is there to blame for their hunger but their scout? At the very least, he has let them down. Possibly he has betrayed them.

Though he understands only a fraction of the complaints that are darkly mumbled, Manteo knows that he is the target of them.

Thomas is alert to the men's discontent, and understands well both its source and its most likely outlet. He fears their hunger may lead them into mutiny and murder. The sky darkens and breaks into a heavy downpour (of rain this time, not arrows). The drenching rouses their grumbles to a rabble's hue and cry. Thomas leans towards Sir Ralph and discreetly counsels: 'Sir, the men must eat. And soon.'

Sir Ralph's eye enlarges indignantly. 'Aye? You think? I need no Professor of Mathematics to point out what is plain for any fool to see. But if you have an idea how I may feed them, then I shall be truly grateful to you, Master Hariot.'

Thomas leans in further. And discloses his idea even more discreetly.

Now Sir Ralph's other eye enlarges to match the first.

But he gives the order. They put in and find shelter beneath the dense canopy of the forest. The men's tasks distract them from their malaise. The undergrowth is harvested for tinder. Branches are gathered. A fire soon blazes, though they have nothing yet to cook on it. The dogs circuit the campfire excitedly. They have learnt to associate the smell of burning wood with the prospect of scraps.

Thomas converses briefly with the man who serves as cook for the expedition. The fellow's head tilts sideways to an angle of astonishment. He blows out his cheeks but does not question his instructions. He is as hungry as the other men.

It is done quickly, expertly, as if this is something men have always done. Calling the dog over as if to pet it, or offer it the treat it craves. But instead of the caressing ruffle of the ears, a cold butchering knife at the animal's throat. The cook pushes it in hard and draws it through the taut sinews with a severing snap. The dog's startled whimper is short lived. Drowned out in a liquid gargle as it falls like a buckled trestle to ground. Its legs kick as if it is chasing one last rabbit. The floodtide of life drains from its wound, darkening the undergrowth.

The scent of blood draws the two other dogs to investigate. So trusting and starved are they that it does not occur to them that they may be next for the slaughter. It is beyond their canine ken to understand what has happened to their fellow. Indeed, all thought of their fellow has gone from their minds. They are overwhelmed by the pure proximity of meat. The smell of it gets into them. They are wild with it.

The men fear that the noise of the dogs will draw another attack. Blades flash to silence them. One dog's head is severed entirely from its body with the single deft sweep of an executioner's sword. It stumbles over its front paws to flop down, as if suddenly exhausted.

The men fall to, skinning and gutting. They fashion stakes upon which to spit the carcasses. Soon the crackle and savour of roasting meat fills the air. The men's spirits rally. Those who have never tasted dog are suddenly eager for the experience. The flood of salivation fills their mouths. They have an appetite for survival.

The first mouthfuls are torn away in ravening haste. But soon, as they feel the restorative gurgle of their filling guts, the men settle back to enjoy a civilised repast. Some pronounce the meat more flavoursome than beef. Some say it resembles mutton more. It is somewhat tough and would perhaps have benefited from hanging, say others again. But they pick the bones meticulously and lick every last greasy smudge from their fingers.

Manteo senses his reprieve in the dogs' destruction, but keeps his counsel. He catches the white chief's stare and flinches away from the danger in it. *You're next,* it seems to say. Indeed, if he did not know what a horror the white men have of eating human flesh, he might begin to fear it. But then, he never knew them to eat dog before this.

The men pay him little heed now. In the sating of their hunger, they have for the moment forgotten their suspicions. Thomas seeks to reassure him with a smile and a few words of encouragement in Algonkin. He persuades himself that Thomas at least still loves him.

When they begin to fill the air with dog meat farts, the order is given to return to the boats.

(Meanwhile, the Queen hands me back the conch shell, as if to say she has heard enough.)

## Ebbtide

I am struck by the smallness of her, and by how much of what seems to be her is in fact her dress. Her person is an edifice constructed around her. Every morning, her Ladies of the Bedchamber fuss about her, building up her presence out of layers of linen and silk. Underskirts, skirts and overskirts mushroom around her, built upon the hidden scaffold of farthingale and bolster. Cushioned puffs upon her shoulders swell out like the erupting sores of a pretty plague. Her hair is laid over pads to give it bulk. Her twig-like arms are eased into embroidered trunk sleeves, which are in turn encased in bloated puffballs of fine gauze. Such seeming strength she manifestly acquires, merely by the donning of a sleeve. Where necessary she is stitched into herself. Lines of gold braid, hung with spangles and pearls, radiate from her centre, deceiving the eye into extending her being beyond the limit of mere form. Even her face is enlarged upon, as a smooth, immovable crust of white lead paste is layered over her flawed and shocking skin. At last the immense lace disc of her starched ruff is fitted into place. She is obliged to hold her head stiffly to accommodate it, her movement now constrained by the trappings of her stately self.

When I concentrate on what I know to be her person, I see:

Her eyes, bleakly moist.

Her mouth, gaping a little.

That gape of her mouth is more revealing even than her eyes. It is almost a gasp, a silent gasp, as if she has just had news of the thing she most dreaded. Her own mortality.

We are in her private chamber. She is surrounded by the ladies who constructed her. They sit primly, no more able to move freely than she is. It goes without saying, that when the Queen shivers, they tactfully shiver too. As if they feel the same draught blow through the casement window, and it is not some inner thing passing through her bones that shakes her.

But if it is her women who create the husk of her, it is her men who breathe life into it.

I play my part, offering her the conch shell, that has long lain forgotten. She will not take it. There is no pleasant distraction to be found in its hiss now.

I hold it to my own ear. But can make no sense of the sounds that reach me through it.

I hear a chain of whispers, English cascading into Algonkin, passing back and forth between Sir Ralph and Wingina.

A cry, of: '*Christ, our Victory!*'

Then gunshot.

The choking gargles of the dying. The silence of the dead. The stunned aftermath of murder. A sudden stirring. More cries, garbled, incomprehensible. Footsteps, pounding, at a desperate pace.

The clarity of gunshot once more. The rattle of an Irish soldier's laughter: 'I hit him in the arse, the dirty lying savage.'

The first footsteps break into a stumbling stagger. Then stronger footsteps strike up in pursuit.

A final scream. The hushing *sssshhhh!* Of steel through flesh. A somewhat laborious hewing and hacking. The rip of parting bone and gristle.

The thud of something thrown onto the ground. It rolls a little and is still.

I feel a strangely personal sense of dread as I try to imagine what it is. Where is Thomas now, when I need him to be my eyes out there? Will he not gaze on this thing to ease my anguish? For the unimaginable is surely worse than any reality. Does he seek to spare me by not gazing upon it?

I close my eyes as the conch shell's hiss rises to a deafening roar: '*Ssssssssssssssssssssssssssssss…*'

I see only a seeping red. Then the red clears and I am looking up at Sir Ralph Lane. And I know that I am looking out from the severed head of Chief Wingina.

The hiss dissolves into silence. The seeping red returns. My mouth tastes of leather. I cannot explain it. My tongue lies in my mouth like a piece of burnt cinder. I cannot explain it. The taste of leather. The burnt cinder.

The brittle conch shell falls from my hand and shatters.

Our connection with the colony is broken. The bulwark that I promised the Queen lies too far distant to shield her from fears that are present and pressing.

The bleakness of her eyes appals me. It is unrelenting, as loneliness is unrelenting once it has been discovered in a heart. And I would give anything to close the small gape of her mouth, which gives her, in her unguarded moments, a look of startled imbecility. She remembers, of course, to seal her lips together in the Presence Chamber.

That she allows me – me alone! – to see her private fear, is an indication of how far I have progressed in her favour. I who was once forbidden by Sir Christopher Hatton admittance to her Private Chamber.

I suggest a ride out to Mortlake, to see the maps in Dr Dee's library.

The mouth closes. But only to ripple in a thin, wrinkled, old lady's pout. 'I know where America is. Unless it has moved since I last gazed at his maps?'

'No, it has not moved.'

'Well then, it is a long way to go to discover something that I already know.'

'He has new maps, I am informed.'

'Of the Moon?'

'Of the interior. They show the locations of a number of rich, reputed gold mines.'

'I would rather have a real gold mine than a reputed one.'

'These maps show us where to look.'

'Then look.'

'You will permit *me* to go to America?'

'I cannot spare your person. You know that. If you were to leave me…' The tremble in her voice is something new. Immediately I regret my peevish request, so laden with complaint. But she reciprocates with a prickly peeve of her own: 'If these new maps of Dr Dee's are so marvellous utilitarian, we wonder that you do not find some means to convey them out to those who may put them to good use. We may only look upon them. Sir Ralph may look *with* them.'

I always know when she is displeased with me. She pluralises, regally.

I dispatch a ship laden with supplies for the relief of the colonists, carrying also Dr Dee's new maps. I must advertise my faith in the maps, for did I not hold them out to her? I cannot now say: 'tis no matter whether the maps go or not. Though I do confess, the chief usefulness of the maps lies in their ability to engender enthusiasm for our enterprise, and to encourage hope for its success. Such things are not to be underestimated.

And for all I know, the maps may indeed point the way to endless seams of gold, as the Bible points the way to Heaven.

If they only succeed in enticing men across the Ocean, they will have served their purpose. For all that happens when they are there, they must look to their wits more than their maps.

But, ah, if only the Queen would permit me to go! I would show them how it is done. I would show them where to look. I would have gold out of that land… But no, I will not renew that old complaint.

Instead I urge my cousin, Sir Richard Grenville, to remember his duty to those he left behind. But the Queen, who is Moon to us all, has more pressing claims upon him. She reminds him of a duty that is more agreeable to him, as being more in keeping with his temperament. She urges him to harry Spanish interests where he can.

It is a cause in which my cousin wants for little encouragement. He is a fierce fellow. I have seen him bite down upon a glass and crunch its shards between his teeth until the blood runs from his mouth. Doubtless he is the very fellow to put the wind up the Spaniards. He is soon bound for Newfoundland, to wreak havoc among the enemy's fishing fleets. Each man does what he can to allay her fears.

That mouth, the small gape of her mouth. Its shape encompasses all the sorrow and the loneliness of her position.

They say she formed a horror of husbands from observing her father's dealings with her mother. But I, who have studied the forlorn gape of her mouth and the dewy gleam of her eyes, believe the explanation is both simpler and deeper than that. Her horror is not of husbands, but of what they may give her.

An heir.

An heir is the one thing that will ensure the stability of the Realm, and the continuation of her line. So say the men around her. Members of Parliament have even moved to present bills to that effect. But as a woman, she has always known that in so doing it might well kill her.

For even queens die in childbirth.

## Undertide

Dreams and rumours and tales for telling and retelling. I carry them all. Tales of treasure beyond imagining. They come newborn from the new West, tumbling out of the mouths of captive captains. Or if not tumbling, then, forsooth, they may be teased out. Do not think that I am advocating the application of pliers, or other such instruments of inducement. I have always found generous hospitality a more persuasive means of extracting information than even thumb screws. Commodious and pleasing apartments in a royal palace, affable company, diverting entertainments, flattery and free-flowing wine: all these together do effect more confessions than ever the Pope's Inquisitors have. For is it not the case that the man who believes himself a well-loved guest will willingly divulge more than he who knows himself to be under hostile interrogation?

I bear the wine that loosens tongues and bear too the men whose tongues it loosens. Men like Pedro Sarmiento de Gamboa. You may know all you need to know about him from his name. A proud conquistador, taken by my *Serpent* and my *Mary Sparke* off the Azores. His eyes are perpetually hooded against a remembered heat. Such a man does not take well to humiliation. I feel the Ocean's respect for a great navigator. It is honest, unfeigned respect. I may assume he respects me in return, though he is careful not to betray it, except to invite me to join his master's service.

'She will not last forever. There are men, even now, who are moving against her, with Philip's support. And when she is gone…?'

One must admire the arrogance of the Spaniard. He is my prisoner, but it is I who bow to him. He looks me square in the face and keeps his counsel. If there is somewhere else he would rather be, while I entertain him in the old castle of Windsor, he has the good grace not to show it.

It is from Sarmiento's lips I first hear mention of Manoa. We are in the apartment at Windsor that the Queen has put at his disposal, which I may say is more lavish and commodious than my own.

A minstrel plucks notes on a bandore with haphazard but not displeasing inventiveness, as if he is picking the music out of the air; discovering it, rather than reciting it. Attendants keep our cups well filled with wine from the Queen's cellar. There are plates of sweetmeats and nuts put out to delight our palates. Don Pedro settles back with a complacent air, as if all this is no more than he would expect. However, the smile on his lips has become more pronounced, I notice. He is a man capable of enjoyment, I think. Or rather, a man unable to resist it, once it is offered to him. He thaws before my eyes. The wine is wondrous warming in its effect.

I have spread a map out on the table between us. I draw a finger along the Megellan Straits, the great dog leg of water that cuts through the southern tip of the American continent, connecting the Atlantic with the Pacific Ocean. It was until recently the locus of Don Pedro's life.

He kinks an eyebrow half-inquisitively, as if to say, *What of it?*

'He who commands the Strait of Megellan, owns the world. All the riches of the Indies are his, as well as of the Americas.'

'Do you then concede the world to us?'

'There is no other way through. We looked for it. To circumnavigate the continent without the Strait of Megellan, one must press on south to round the tip of the land, as Drake did.'

He thumps the table at the mention of Drake's name: '*Draco!*'

'He is a cousin of mine, you know. A great navigator.'

'A great criminal. It pleases your Queen to send out these licensed bandits to harry and molest honest god-fearing sailors.'

'Indeed not! She never sends them out. They go out of their own accord. Those that do so unlawfully, you may be assured will feel the full weight of her law upon their return.'

'But not Draco. Never Draco. Draco is her *caballero.*'

'His activities are looked into by lawyers. If there is cause for reparation, reparation is made. It is the same with all our seafaring gentlemen.'

I signal to an attendant to replenish Don Pedro's cup.

'Her Majesty acknowledges there has been fault on our side. As I think your king must acknowledge certain far from legal acts undertaken by his agents. She wishes to put all that behind us. She hopes for a new era of friendship and peace to be inaugurated. God willing, you and I may be its ushers, Don Pedro.'

'It is fear that drives her to this position. Philip is not afraid. He has God on his side.'

He delivers these words with a mischievous suavity, a teasing twinkle in his eyes. And somehow the medium of a third language, Latin, in which we are obliged to converse, neutralises many of his remarks. Even a rebuff sounds elegant in Latin.

'You know why I wanted to meet you?'

'It was not to talk of God?'

'I wished to talk with you, as one sailor to another.'

'You want me to divulge my secrets?'

'I have been thinking over your earlier proposal…'

His eyebrows jump so sharply that the velvet hat moves atop his head.

I lean forward over the map, to lower my voice: 'I am a sailor. I go to sea for profit. It matters little to me which ports my ships set sail from.'

'Or what flag they sail under?'

I glance down at the map. 'We talked of the Straits of Megellan. It would be worth much to me if my ships were to be granted passage through it.'

He bows his head in consideration. His hooded eyes give nothing away.

I point out a small island at the mouth of the strait. 'This island in particular interests me. It is of great strategic importance. It guards the entrance of the only sea channel through from the Atlantic to the Pacific. And yet it has no name.'

Don Pedro peers down at where my finger points. After a moment, his shoulders begin to shake, and a rasping hiss escapes from his mouth. He runs a finger beneath his eye to catch the tears.

It is some time before he is able to regain his composure. But even then, the recollection of his hilarity comes over him and he must slap his thighs to beat it out of himself.

'My dear friend, that island has a name. It is called *The Painter's Wife's Island*.'

'The Painter's… *Wife*'s Island?'

'Just so. As the painter was drawing up this map, his wife begged him to put in an island for her. It was an easy thing for him to do. And it gave his wife much pleasure, I do not doubt.'

'But it is not there? In reality?'

'It is there in her imagination.'

'Will that not confuse the sailors who rely upon his map to navigate by?'

'Ah, but that is the great joy of exploration, my friend. It is the discovery of how the world as it really is compares to the world as we imagine it to be. You must know that, as a sailor.'

'But if I were to sail all the way across the Atlantic in search of this island, only to discover that it is a fanciful invention of the map painter, I might be justifiably aggrieved, do you not think?'

'If you do not find this island, you will certainly find some other one. But you are not looking for islands, I think. You are looking for gold. And you are looking for gold that has not yet been discovered. By its nature, you will not find it on any existing map. You will find it by following the whisper of a rumour caught upon a cross breeze.'

'I wager you will have heard such whispers while you were out there, Don Pedro?'

'It is fair to say I did.'

'And were you never tempted to chase them down?'

'I had my duty to attend to. My King had sent me to the Straits of Megellan for a reason. It was not to hunt chimaeras.'

'But if you had to put your money on one such rumour?'

'You wish me to tell you where to look for gold, Don Guattero?'

Now it is my turn to shrug.

'You have heard of Guiana? It is a mighty, rich and beautiful empire.'

Don Pedro locates the place upon a map. It sits upon the shoulder of the southern continent of America.

'There is a city in this land, which the naturals call Manoa. We Spanish call it El Dorado, for it is a great and golden city.'

'You have seen it?'

'Not I. Many have set off in search of El Dorado. Their expeditions invariably ended in death.'

'You are talking of Spaniards?'

'Eh? And what of it?'

I do not press the point, for fear of offending my guest and thereby inhibiting his confidences. But the failure of Papists to discover El Dorado should by no means discourage an honest English Protestant from seeking it out. I believe I know whom God would favour with success.

'We may take it that it is a difficult journey fraught with dangers.'

He narrows his eyes to study me: 'So would you follow Pedro de Urzúa, who set out in search of El Dorado while your Queen Mary was still alive and married to my King Philip? Be careful if you do. He was killed by one of his own officers, you know. A man by the name of Aguirre. This Aguirre also killed his next commander, and anyone who got in his way. The story goes he even killed his own daughter. To prevent her from being bedded by the naturals, he said.'

'What happened to him?'

'He was killed. They say his body was quartered and the various parts distributed about the land of Venezuela. I take it you have no desire to meet a similar fate yourself? Then perhaps you would be well advised to stay in Windsor. There is something about the quest that brings destruction and madness on those that undertake it.'

'Have you conversed with any men who have visited this city?'

'I have spoken with men who swear to have looked upon it with their own eyes.'

'Did any of these men give you good cause to trust in the rumour?'

'I knew them to be honest, sober men, if that is what you mean.'

'But proof. Did they not show you proof?'

'They had filled a chest with many finely wrought items of gold. Alas, the chest had been taken from them, stolen by your Draco, I do not doubt. It is a vast, wild and lawless land. If you go looking for your fortune there, you must take precautions that you do not lose it upon your return.'

'They described the items to you?'

He bows his head with persuasive serenity.

'And the city itself?'

'They had in their possession a drawing. It showed a walled city with many towers, and a raised citadel at the centre. It appeared as magnificent as any Christian capital.'

'And did they indicate to you the precise location of this city?'

He disregards the map I am holding out to him and talks the land into existence, his melodious words serving as signposts to the promised treasure:

'Barquasimeta… Cororo… Maracaiba… Truxillo…'

I see the towns and cities as he names them.

'Nuevo Reyno… Popayan…'

I smell the salt air of the harbours.

'Merida… Lagrita… Pamplona…'

I feel myself draw closer to Guiana with every place he names. He is casting a spell that transports me magically to that distant land of gold and riches.

'Marequita… Velez… Angostura… Timana… Tocaima…'

He is a greater conjuror than Dr Dee. And a greater alchemist too. For he needs no base metal to transmute to gold. He is able to produce it from the very air.

'Tunxa… Mozo, city of emeralds…'

The map falls from my hands, no longer needed. I am there! My hands plunge into the emeralds of which he speaks, merely a prelude to the gold of El Dorado.

'Until you come at last to Manoa, the great city of gold. The gold is so plentiful in the ground there, the rivers and streams so clogged with it, that even the common people go about decked in ornaments of gold plate. I am talking not of their princelings and chieftains. The meanest among them adorns his person with rings and baubles of the purest gold. As for their King, every day his womenfolk blow gold dust onto his naked person, which he then washes off by bathing in a great lake. If you only find this lake, you will sift from it enough gold to fill your Queen's coffers. You will have no need for mining tools or smelting apparatus. Take with you only a fine sieve. There are such great deposits of gold in the water that the naturals do not concern themselves with retrieving it.'

The image of Guiana conjured by Sarmiento's words begins to fade. To my eye, he shrinks within himself a little, as if the effort of speaking has robbed him of his vital strength.

'There is one man you should speak with if ever you go in search of the gold of Manoa. Don Antonio de Berrio. He is governor of the island of Trinidad, but he has made many journeys of discovery into the interior of Guiana. But hurry, my friend. Either he will find it before you, or he will die in the attempt, or he will be driven mad by his failure. Such is the hold that Manoa exercises. It destroys all who are not successful in finding it. And even those who are.'

His eyes narrow as he fixes me with a steady challenge. There is still strength in his gaze I see. And amusement too. Quite unexpectedly, a sly wink flicks across one eye, like the quick wash of surf over sand.

## Dreamtide

The Queen, her face, a white cake, the shape and luminescence of the moon. The surface of her is a thick impasto of powder. Her mouth, a small grey crater, like the shadow of a pockmark. It bubbles and pops as she speaks. The sound of her voice is a plectrum scraped the length of an overtightened lute string. She has no eyes. I am conscious of thinking this is wilful on her part.

I want her eyes to widen in wonder at the splendour and brilliance of me. But she refuses to have eyes. She is wilfully withholding her wonder.

'Say the names again, Water.'

I repeat the soothing recital: 'Barquasimeta, Cororo, Maracaiba...'

The dark concavity of her mouth pulses and twitches as attempts to form her lips into the shapes of the alien sounds. Drinking them in. So that they become part of her.

The powdered surface of her face erupts in a rash of lumps. Two of the lumps outgrow the rest and burst to form her eyes after all. They are emerald green. And now I see that the other lumps have become glinting green plague sores. I cannot help myself. I reach out and with my nails pick away at one of them. Its hard crystalline centre comes away. I hold it up to the light. It appears to an emerald stone. Or perhaps it is a large coloured crystal of sugar? I bite on it. My teeth fracture and crumble. I spit out the residue of them. But somehow manage to swallow the stone.

A streak of thick green liquor trails from the picked-out sore.

Now I work my nails into one of her newly-formed eyes, suddenly desirous to try that too between my teeth (or what's left of them). But the eye bursts under the pricking of my nails. More of the same green liquor dribbles out of her empty socket.

To distract the Queen from noticing that I have burst one of her eyes, I bring my list of names to a climax: 'El Dorado.'

She is like a child, held by the promise of my recital, enchanted by its music. 'The Golden One!'

I bow.

I notice that the liquor seeping over her face has begun to erode the powder, cutting through it in dark, treacly rivulets.

I am frightened to touch what's left of her face, in part because I dread the pure horror of it, but also because I fear that I will only ruin it further. The seeping liquor has licked away the powder in places to reveal the sleek, black beak of a parrot beneath.

As if in response to her new birdlike attribute, my mouth fills with a dry feathery texture. I am now afraid to speak, convinced that feathers instead of words will issue forth.

But no, not feathers, but an egg bursts forth from my mouth, to fall and crack upon the floor. We stand admiring its perfect golden yolk.

Eventually, the Queen steps on it and grinds it under her heel. I am unspeakably angered by this and throw myself at her in a rage. To my great surprise, I find there is no substance to her person. She appears to be an empty dress. I fall to the ground upon it. The cake of her face rolls away and addresses me from the corner of the room: 'Do you think I would give you Babington's estate now?'

I am rather shocked by her sudden broaching of this unspoken subject. 'I rather fear that Walsingham has his eye on it, your Majesty.'

'Have with you to Walsingham.'

With this last dull and senseless remark of the Queen's, the dream becomes at once unutterably tedious to me. I will myself awake.

There is a sleeping doxy snoring in the bed beside me. She lies with the curve of her back towards me. For one moment, I am persuaded it is the Queen herself. I lean over her to reassure myself that I have not inadvertently fucked the Queen. The wench feels my stirring and wakes. She pulls me to her.

I remember the egg yolk of the dream as I slide into her.

I close my eyes and wonder: *But what if this be the dream?*

## Lowtide

No dream this, the Queen inconsolable in her bed. I cannot even entice her out with the promise of hawking or hunting. And for once, a recitation of Sarmiento's wondrous-sounding far-flung places fails to lift her from her despond.

She weeps and rails, fears now turned to fiery rage, by the alchemy of Majesty. 'See what you have done, Walsingham!'

He bows his skullcap towards her, offering deference as his only defence.

'It is all your doing. That we are now called upon to put our cousin on trial for her life! To subject a crowned monarch to tribunals and testimonies! And what if they find her guilty? Will you have me sign her death warrant? My God! An absolute, divinely-ordained monarch… What precedent will this set?'

And so, it comes down to this. The bind has tightened around her. She can barely breathe, and thrashes in her bed to free herself.

Perhaps unwisely, Walsingham offers mitigation: 'She is deposed, your Majesty. She gave up her crown, fled from it.'

'And sought refuge with me, her cousin! Is this refuge?'

'She has plotted against you, Majesty.'

'Has she? How can you be sure, Walsingham? What if it were her secretaries behind these plots, not she? God's blood, I swear I know what it is to have a meddlesome secretary, who takes it upon himself to set in motion all manner of who knows what, without reference to his sovereign.'

Do I discern a flash of appeal in my direction from Walsingham? He wishes to embroil me, no doubt. Mayhap it would lessen his animosity against me were I to support him. But I am loath to be tarred with the same brush. I keep my counsel.

'We have the proof.'

'Proof! You think that makes it acceptable to chop off her head? You think her cousin the Duke of Guise will take it any less amiss because we have proof? Or her son, James, for that matter? In these matters, there is no proof, Walsingham. There is only policy. And they will take it that this is now our policy. Executing princes! Where will it end when once we begin executing princes? That is what they will say.'

'I would urge you to think of her not as a prince but as a traitor, your Majesty.'

At last she turns to me: 'Water, Water… my dear Water… can you not wash away this dark stain upon my conscience?'

She gestures insultingly towards Walsingham, as if he is the blot to be cleansed.

A slow bow provides me with a convenient interlude for the marshalling of my thoughts. 'If I may venture to suggest a solution, your Majesty?'

'You hear that, Walsingham? Water has a solution.'

Walsingham smiles. It is the means by which he compresses his hatred between his colourless lips.

'There is a fellow, a certain Wingfield.'

'Who is this Wingfield?'

'A nobody, your Majesty. A low fellow.'

'Why do you talk to us of low fellows?'

'Because sometimes, I fear, a prince may have need of the services of such a man. A man without means. Or name. Or conscience.'

'He has a name. His name is... What is his name again?'

'Wingfield, your Majesty. But it matters not. His name is immaterial. He could as easily be named Feathermeadow.'

'What of this Feathermeadow?'

'The last Duke of Northumberland... you remember what was said of him at the time of his death?'

'That he was a traitor?'

'I meant, of how he met his end? He stood accused of treason, but died before he could be tried.'

'The Duke of Northumberland took his own life. His cell was locked from within.'

'That is what some say, your Majesty. Others say…'

'I care not what these others say. His death is recorded as self-murder. That should satisfy us all.'

'A man such as Wingfield may have been employed. I do not say it was he. But a man such as him. It may have been Feathermeadow.'

'Do you know who it was, Walsingham? Was it Wingfield or Feathermeadow?'

'The Duke of Northumberland died by his own hand.'

'And in so doing he denied your Majesty the satisfaction of justice.'

'Tell me more of Wingmeadow, Wat.'

'Wingfield. He tried to kill me once. The Earl of Oxford sent him against me. All for a suit of clothes. By this you may have the measure of the man. He would take a life for a suit of clothes. For a suitable price, he could, I think, be persuaded to… well, let us merely say that he will ensure that your Majesty is never called upon to sign your Majesty's cousin's death warrant.'

It is wondrous to see the light of realisation dawn upon her face. I bask in the mixture of admiration and horror that Her Majesty turns on me: 'You would have me send an assassin against my cousin?'

Sir Francis misreads her voice. He thinks her appalled. She is in awe.

'Quite right, your Majesty. One simply cannot allow such conduct. If it were known…'

Here is the crux. It surprises me that Sir Francis needs me to point it out to him, of all men: 'It will never be known.'

'It will be suspected.'

'All manner of things are suspected.'

'No, no, Ralegh. You cannot simply… it is…'

'To me it is merely the most practical solution. A matter of expediency.'

'To order the murder of an anointed monarch?'

'It is not entirely without precedent. For did not Philip offer twenty five thousand crowns for the assassination of William Prince of Orange?'

'And so you advise that Her Majesty should model her conduct on that of her enemies?'

'There can be no question of the Queen ordering this. Perhaps Wingfield took it into his head to perform this act on his own account, in the hope of reward?'

'You talk as if it has already happened, Wat.'

'That is his way, your Majesty.' Walsingham means to insult me, but the Queen smiles affectionately. I think she loves this most in me: my ability to treat wishes as if they were deeds already done.

'This Wingfield is not the answer, your Majesty.'

'Cannot someone else be found? If not Merrywing, then someone who will do the deed for us out of love and obedience, not for pecuniary advantage. A man of fanatical Protestant faith, a great detester of Catholics. What of Sir Amyas Paulet? It is usually the gaoler who arranges these things, is it not? If Sir Amyas had any love for me…'

In truth, it is hard to imagine a more unlikely assassin than Paulet. He is a most sober and devout man, a very Puritan.

'You will write to him, Walsingham. You may remind him of the love and duty that he owes to us.'

Walsingham bows his head, in a grand display of meek obedience.

The Queen's eyes sparkle for me: 'We have made a decision concerning the traitor Babington's estates.'

Such is the power of a prince, to change the mood of a room with one startling announcement. We are all hanging on her words.

'It is our wish that they should go to Sir Walter Ralegh.'

Walsingham hides his disappointment with a deep, trembling bow.

## Woetide

I take a wherry, *Eastward ho!* I have found a new tailor, who has his shop on London Bridge.

I must endure the lifeless gaze of the severed heads that are arrayed atop the southern gate. I look for Anthony Babington, but in faith, being boiled in tar has given all the heads a somewhat similar appearance, so that it is hard to tell one dead traitor from the next. None of them do so much resemble the living men they used to be as they resemble each other. But, yes, I think I do recognise my unwilling benefactor. I do not shrink from meeting his eyes, or what is left of them. What has not been preserved by the tar has been pecked away by ravens, or eaten from within by worms. This ravaging has left him looking even more aghast than might be expected.

I sense Walsingham watching me through his black eyeless sockets. These are the traitors brought low by him. They are a warning to all men.

I cannot help but feel there is something personal in the message Walsingham means to send out. As if he put Babington there on purpose, knowing I have my tailor on the Bridge and would come to him today. He seems to say to me: '*Do not underestimate me yet, Ralegh.*'

The buildings along either side of the bridge seem to clamber up towards the rumour of light. Each overhanging storey is stacked carelessly on the one below, so that the topmost floors do almost touch. Some houses jut their arses out over the water, dribbling the detritus of their jakes directly into the river. It is a precarious, top-heavy edifice, such as is is built by a wanton boy rather than a Master Architect. It seems in danger of toppling over at any moment. The Thames rolls sluggishly through the arches beneath, caught in the snarl of the great stone starlings.

The traffic on the bridge moves slowly today; the thoroughfare is crowded with a beggarly rabble. There is famine everywhere in the country, and as always in times of need, the most needy are drawn to the City, as if it be some vast lodestone of Human Misery. But if the countryside has nothing to give them – neither labour nor grain – then the City has even less.

Those that still have some reserve of vital force about them stagger from one end of the bridge to the other, their hand out held for alms. A tide of woe and suffering. Their eyes are more blank than those of the traitors over the gates. Truly, they are dead on their feet. The rest lie unmoving on the ground, huddled around their empty bellies. The cobbles run with a filthy brown liquor.

Do not look too closely at those piles of rags trampled beneath the hooves of cart horses. At least such a death is speedy, unlike the lingering death of starvation.

The stink of all this is insufferable. And yet it behoves us all, even the highest of the land, to venture into the midst of such human ruin and breathe

the stench of unadulterated misery. There is a lesson here even more edifying than the array of heads above the gates.

Poverty provokes a man to do infamous deeds.

For that reason alone do I accept all the Queen's gifts to me. 'Tis my duty so to do. My duty too to exercise myself on my sovereign's behalf. I would not have my Queen or my country reduced to beggary. And the richer she is, the more liberal her gifts.

Behold the spectre of our Age: Starvation. And his wife, the crippled hag, Misery. And in their wake, their innumerable brood of sickly infants, Ague, Weakness, Disease, Despair, Thievery, Larceny, Murder, Prostitution, Beggary, Shame, aye and Wantonness too, as well Ignorance, Filth, Degradation...Too many, forsooth, to name each one.

It is no allegory, this. No masque for courtiers' delight. For yes, there is piquant pleasure in the pity that is stirred by the suffering of others. How we do delight to wallow in the luxury of our compassion.

Behold the driving force behind all human endeavour. The source of our questing natures. That which spurs us to action.

The repulsive degradation of such scenes is what compels us. We flee from Hunger and Poverty, as from our bitterest enemies. These are greater enemies of England's Common Weal than the King of Spain and the Pope put together. All the greater because they are enemies who will never be defeated. Does not the Bible teach us that our poor will always be with us? They are amongst us, destroying us from within, like a black festering canker deep inside the rotten core of our estate. Whatever external foes do threaten our Sovereign, they will always be aided and abetted by our own domestic armies of malcontents led by Hunger and Poverty. Albeit they are a weak and wasted force, but there is great power in their mere presence. It is the power to frighten and dismay. They inspire a horror tinged with indignation. Men begin to talk of Injustice. They look to hold those in authority to blame. They seek redress in foreign princes and traitorous religions.

Behold the desperation of the beggared poor. It is this that drives this great colonial project of mine. For will it not be to the good of all if we may transport such dangerous rabbles to far distant lands far better suited to support them? And if some perish on the way, it is all to the good.

Let us make sailors and planters of them, and ship them off to Virginia. And let us bring back in their place hulls creaking with gold and grain and glory. And if ever they do return, I am confident they will be wearing suits every bit as fine as the one I am about to have fitted.

It is a thing easily achieved in my imagination. The place, I confess, where all my best work is done.

## Bloodtide

We sent them out, the men and women, and, aye, the children too, as Richard Hakluyt advised.

We sent them out, with good John White their leader.

An artist with a generous eye, instead of soldier with a trigger-eager finger. He knows the land well, as is clear from his maps and landscapes. He knows the people too. All he wants to take from them are their likenesses and not their lives. His magnanimity shines forth in each quick brushstroke. He surprises us with their humanity. For all they seem so alien to us, with their tattooed faces and buckskin clouts, we acknowledge something of ourselves in them. To see the fierce shaven-headed savage sit across from his wife as they prepare their meal together; we recognise the love configured in the arrangement of their legs around the bowl of groundnuts. In some part of our souls, we even envy it. 'Tis clear that he looked upon them not merely with the cold discerning eye of a scientific observer, but with a lively, engaged curiosity that is driven by Christian love. And, I do believe, they loved him back for it. At the very least, they were at ease in his presence and suffered him to stand and sketch them as they went about their daily lives.

He is a father too. His daughter Elyoner sails with him, together with her husband Ananias Dare. She stands on the deck, back flexed to bear the burden of the future in her bulging belly. She watches the loading of their lives. The sturdy well-made tables and chairs, the bed frames and linen chests, all hoisted up and lowered into the hold. It is comforting to think that whatever else the future may hold for them, it will at least be furnished with these familiar objects.

There is scant wist in her gaze as she looks back at the land. She sees a pack of mange-ridden and starving dogs prowl the harbourside, sniffing out scraps and rats. When some stinking half-rotten bone is discovered, they snarl and bare their teeth for the privilege of choking on it.

She can have no regrets, sailing away from England's angry dogs to the silent, static paradise promised by her father's paintings. Elyoner has looked into the calm, gently inquisitive faces of the Secotans. She recognises Love when she sees it. And she sees it manifest in these homely scenes. Where there is Love there is Hope: Hope that she may bring them to an understanding of that greater Love. She will lead them to the way of the Lord, by her quiet, patient example. Her father vouches that the savages have the capacity for true Christian Faith, although he professes it is a matter of some regret to him that they may not return to that selfsame island of Roanoke to renew the bonds of friendship that he worked so hard to establish. He hints darkly at the reasons why not.

No matter. They will find a new site in a different distant bay, where they may begin anew.

She shapes her mouth to the saying of its name, feeling for it with her tongue against her teeth: 'Chesapeke.'

She tries to imagine what it will be like in this new land. Her father has said that they will be free there, his eyes alive with a strange mixture of anxiety and conviction, as if he must will himself to believe in his own word. She wills herself to believe it too. She tries to imagine the shape and flavour of the freedom he promises. She sees a spreading light over a broad, pleasant meadow, a fresh breeze wafting a perfumed air. But she feels it most keenly as an absence: a lifting of that oppressive weight which has born down upon them all, day after day, buckling their bodies into hunched and knotted wrecks.

In Chesapeke, they will be free to lift their heads. In Chesapeke, they will be able to look one another in the eyes. In Chesapeke, they may say aloud that which burns to be said, without fear of informants and intelligencers. In short, they will be free to worship in accordance with their conscience, without hinder or suspicion. Though first, of course, they must build the churches in which they will assemble. 'Tis as well that Ananias Dare is a bricklayer by trade. There is no shame in honest labour, and no thought that she has married beneath her station; Jesus was a carpenter, after all.

But aye, it will be a hard freedom, a hungry freedom, that her baby will be born into.

And they will have tribes of innocents eager for enlightenment. Veritable *tabulae rasae*. She will be the one to write God's word upon the blank tablets of their souls.

They will found a true Utopia, its streets mapped out according to the straight, unwavering principles of their beliefs. The bricks that build it, the bricks that Dare will lay for them, will be fired in the limekilns of their Faith. It will be a second Creation. And her child will be the first born in this reborn world.

But first she must endure the passage. What fears she has for the future are focused on the voyage. The ship is a flimsy, thrown-together thing. A mere act of will against the wild, destructive waves. The waves do not wish her well, she feels. The moment the cables are cast loose from their moorings, the first sickly flood rises in her gullet. She is sick enough these days, on account of her condition. It will be a rough crossing.

I bear them out upon my back, *The Lion*, the pinnace and the flyboat. Three ships a-sailing. The small fleet noses its way out of harbour, as all the broad cloth shipments, casks of wine, tin trades, and captured prizes come and go around them. The bobbing bustle of my enrichment.

She likes not the look of the sailors. They are surly and uncouth. If it were only that, she could bear it. But there is something else in their eyes, a kind of watchful, waiting malice. She has noticed that they never look directly at their passengers, the colonists, but only cast their veiled deceitful glances between themselves. As if they are looking out for a secret signal. Only she catches them sometimes eyeing the children at their play. She likes not the way they watch the children. *Must we be reliant on these wolves?* She wonders.

She forms the thought: *They will slit our throats as soon as look at us.*
She considers it just as well they do not look at her.

The only one who dares to is the pilot, who is as brazen and as bold as any man may be. For I have entrusted them to none other than my own erstwhile companion at sea, ship's master Simon Fernandez. Despite the unaccountable mishap of the last voyage, when he drove *The Tyger* onto a sand bank, I still maintain that there is no navigator in any prince's fleet who knows that coastline better than he. And now he sails in *The Lion*, not *The Tyger*, so we may hope for a lion's share of good fortune. I grant you he has a salty tongue in his head and that his manners are so far from being couth as to shame a heathen. But we do not hire our pilots for their manners.

In truth, he is unwontedly subdued on the voyage, mayhap chastened by the memory of his recent fault. In the main, he contents himself with licking his teeth and spitting. He keeps his magnificent talent for cursing to himself, except to pour dark, mumbling streams of invective into the ears of his closest lieutenants, who nod sagely as if they are Privy Councillors conferring on matters of state.

Elyoner says nothing of her fears, neither to her father nor her husband. She communes silently with her unborn child, sending soothing thoughts on the tides of their common blood.

How is't I can see all this? I can see even into her womb. I see her hopes grow toes and soft boned limbs in the blood-shadowed gloom of her belly. My all-seeing eyes have somehow entered into her veins. My vision flows with the flood of her inner sea.

I can taste her fears in the smack of my lips.

How is't? It is as if I am detached from myself and cast out into the world, to float, two plucked-out eyes bobbing on the tides of my own life.

How can it be that I am able to see the strange, unwonted look in Simon Fernandez's eyes? I detect an unfamiliar wariness about his demeanour. A constraint, I might almost say. It is as if his wings have been clipped. He comports himself as a man mindful of some weighty commission. A man of responsibility and duty.

This is not the Simon Fernandez I know.

He keeps his counsel and confides not in his captain, good John White, to whom he has sworn assistance.

I can only see. I cannot understand.

## Meta Incognita

Red.

Why is it I see only red?

My dear?

Where are you, my dear?

I cannot see you.

I hear your voice. I think it is your voice. I hear your weeping. I taste your salt tears. They moisten the cracked leather walls of my infinite mouth.

Who are you, my dear?

I mean to say, where are you… but also who…

So much I forget.

You carry me about, the remnant of me. I feel this. In your heart. Or mayhap in something more practical. You have a bag fashioned expressly for the purpose. A red bag. A red velvet bag. That must be it.

Your name is on the tip of my cracked tongue. The memory of your kiss is on my damaged lips.

Your kiss, my Bess.

That's right. You are Elizabeth. Yes, Bess. Not her. Not Good Queen Bess. No. Another.

Do not fear, Bess.

Do you doubt that I love you?

Perhaps there was a day when I did not. A day when I only wanted you. When my desire was more of a calculation than a surrender.

But now, in this wide red now, all I have is my love for you.

Something forms itself out of the red sea.

A face.

Piquing rather than beautiful. Though it is a face that believes itself beautiful. As with all these aristocratic girls.

Your face, my Bess.

I chose you. That is the thing. You were my ruin and I chose you.

Of that I am sure. That much I remember.

It is all that matters now. All that is left.

The memories crash over me, and then recede.

There are moments when the tide turns. Moments of seeming slackness, when the sea stands holding its crashing breath. But at the depths, a greater turmoil churns.

I always feel that turmoil, am always caught in the moment of the tide's turning.

It comes back to me. Crashes over me. The discovery of you. The hidden landing places of your body. The first touch. The hot cleaving. The unexpected riches.

I dissolve within you.

You carry me away.

I want to reach out to touch you. But I know not where you are, or where am I, or what is left to me with which to touch you.

All I am now is pink foam on a blood red tide.

I have passed the limit of my known world. I am in uncharted waters now. To see without seeing. To be without being.

The crash, the pulse, the flood, the tide.

The roar.

A strange roar.

To hear without hearing.

The taste of metal.

Yes, your body. I remember now. Let me dwell on that. Let me batten myself to it as a shipwrecked sailor to a cabin door.

Be my mooring.

Be the ocean bed into which I sink my anchor.

Be my landfall.

Be my Baffin Island, my Meta Incognita. My unknown limit.

She would not let me go to America. She cannot do without me, she says. And so I sent them off in my stead. Good John White and his planters. And denied the excitement of those discoveries by a jealous sovereign, I ventured off to encompass your territories. To prospect in your hills. To dig and delve in your abundant vale. To plumb your depths and mine your seams. To till your soil and plant my seed.

She may be my Moon, my Diana. You are my Continent. My America. My New World. I will never walk upon the Moon. I am content to map every contour of my Continent.

You are not within her gift, you never were. Indeed, you were the one thing she would deny me. We who were the recipients of her favour were to keep ourselves for her. That was the one condition of her gifts. We were to be her chaste lovers. Pure in heart and of intention.

It is a sign of how little she understands men.

We bind our lives together, make flotsam of ourselves. Now two shipwrecked sailors battened one to the other.

All must be secret. We are agents for a foreign power: for Love. You know there are intelligencers everywhere, all about the Court. The Queen has eyes and ears embroidered in her dress. And there are eyes and ears everywhere that you cannot see. And mouths that whisper.

We know this. For you have been my eyes and ears. And I have drunk the whispers from your lips.

I set you to spy for me – *remember*? We became intoxicated by secrecy. It is a most potent philtrum. Each secret shared is another thread that ties us to each other. And in surrendering a secret, we consent to yield power. We give a little of ourselves. In such an exchange of secrets, something flows between us, which feels much like love.

What's that, my dear?

You say the traffic was all one way? That I gave up no secrets to you?

Ah, but I gave you the greatest secret of all, I think. I gave you the secret of my frailty. I opened up the flimsy box that is my heart and showed you the rattling weighted fears that shelter there.

I let you see the ebb of me, as well the flood.

'Walsingham, Walsingham, tell me of Walsingham! What does he say to her Majesty? Speaks he ever of me to her?'

How much her good opinion means to me. How greatly I fear to lose it.

## Wind-whipped

Another face forms out of the red. Good John White. The red seeps into his eyes. They have been whipped and ground by salt wind and sadness.

A different wind whips at the window of my high room in Durham House, the vantage point from which I look out on the world. It hurls teeth against the rattling pane.

I confess I am surprised to see him back so soon. To see him back at all.

He produces a letter, signed by all and sundry, his proof that he did not abandon his colonists or his duty. Nor his daughter, for that matter.

'I did not want to be the one to return. They urged me to it.'

There is something dark here. It is written in his drawn, careworn and weather-blasted face. I bid him be seated and begin the unfolding of his dark tale.

'I take it very remiss, sir. Very remiss. After all that was agreed. In this very room. I must ask you, sir. Did you change your orders to that man?'

'What man is that, John?'

'I will not say his name, sir. The Portingale.'

'Simon Fernandez?'

He nods grimly. 'Did you change your orders to him?'

'Why no. I should think I did not. How so change my orders?'

'We were to go to Chesapeake Bay, sir. That was what was agreed. In this very room. You will remember, sir.'

'Indeed I do, John.'

'He took us to Roanoke, sir.'

'Aye, John. As we also agreed. To pick up the rump of soldiery left in the old colony.'

'No, sir. He put us ashore. He put us all ashore. Every last man, woman and child of us. Given all that we know of that place, it being such a very hostile and inimical place, I take it very remiss that he took us back there and left us there, sir. Without the means to sustain ourselves, for all our victuals were spent, or as good as. He had contrived to take on no fresh supplies on the voyage, not even water or salt. And it was too late for planting. He made sure of that, sir. I have left them, sir, in desperate straits. I have left them fearing for their lives. At their express request I have come back, sir. I would not have done it otherwise. I have come back to beg relief for them. We must prepare another fleet. We must hasten to their relief. There is no time to be lost, sir. Every moment we delay... why, I fear it may soon be too late, Sir Walter. I fear they will not last the Winter without fresh supplies.'

'But you know we cannot sail until the Spring, John. No captain will venture across the Atlantic now. I swear to you, I will spend the Winter making preparations, petitioning support. The Queen will not consent to see her colony fail. I know her Majesty's heart in this. She loves you for the sacrifices you have made. She will not abandon you. You are her children. She is like

159

the Mother Pelican. She will rip the flesh from her own breast with her beak to nourish you and yours.'

At my choice of analogy, John White's eyes grow wide and wild. He raves, distraught: 'I left her, I left my child! Abandoned!'

'Calm yourself, my friend. I remember your daughter, yes. Elyoner, is it not? But she has a husband now I think? Her husband will protect her now, I dare say. You need not torment yourself, John.'

'A baby girl was born to her. She and her husband christened the child Virginia.'

'This is glorious news, John. Her Majesty will be most happy to hear it. The future of our Colony is secure.'

'No! You do not understand. They are in Roanoke. I fear I will never see them alive again. We must make haste.'

'All will be done as quickly as it may be done. If we are to succeed, we must make careful preparations.'

'But your enemies move against you even now, Sir Walter. Every moment you delay allows them to steal a march on you.'

'My enemies?'

'He is not loyal to you. The Portingale. He serves another master. Mayhap he is loyal still to the Emperor. Was ever.'

'No. I cannot countenance it.'

'If not Philip, then some other. There was a dark design behind his deeds, of that I am convinced. He wished us dead. Did all he could to contrive it, without going so far as to slit our throats and slip our corpses overboard.'

'But why should he work to wreck his own mission?'

'Because his real mission was never to take us safely to our destination. His real mission was to destroy the colony. Your colony. You. It gives me no pleasure to say it, Sir Walter, but he was only ever bent on your destruction. The only question is, whom does he serve?'

One name inevitably comes into my head. You will know whose name it is, my Dear. I do not give it voice, lest I should add further to good John White's fears.

Simon Fernandez was ever Walsingham's man. Fernandez owes his life to Walsingham, who once reprieved him from the scaffold so that he may serve as pilot on my brother's voyage. I wondered then how it was that Sir Francis could demean himself so greatly as to extend the hand of friendship to a man like Fernandez.

Now I have my answer.

## Best hated

He arrives at Court with all the advantages that were never mine. I was only ever the nephew of her servant.

He is noble born. A first cousin to the Queen, somewhat removed. The ward of Lord Burghley. Stepson to the Earl of Leicester. And even Sir Francis Walsingham takes him under his darkly feathered wing, and pushes his own daughter, Philip Sidney's widow, on him. (What a dynasty would be created there!)

Verily, he is absurdly well-connected, is Robert Devereux, the second Earl of Essex.

They say he is handsome. I am no judge of that. Certainly he has red hair, upon which no doubt the Queen looks favourably. I see that she delights in his company, exults in his youthful disdain, adores his contempt. Manna from Heaven, his indifference.

To him she is no doubt a rather ridiculous old woman in a wig. He barely makes an effort to conceal his scorn, and in that he reminds me somewhat of Oxford. This is not wit! It is so crudely and gracelessly done, without any appreciation of her Majesty's great condescension. He takes her favour as his entitlement. Almost as if *she* must wait on *him*.

I am the one who delights her with debunking. I am the one she turns to for honesty and aperçus. I am the one whose wit is as sharp as his blade. We do not need another such at Court. I do not view him as my rival, but my pretender.

I'll grant he wears armour well, puffing his chest out and strutting like a general. Does this make him a soldier? I think not. He bears a medal that his stepfather gave him when he went with him to the Netherlands. I am not aware that he distinguished himself in any campaign while there.

And is this how the young men wear their beards now? He lets it fan out to the shape of a shovel. As if he has never seen the inside of a barber's shop. No doubt he thinks it makes him look even more the soldier on campaign. I find it a goading beard. I want very much to pluck it.

He makes me feel old. I am not old. It is unconscionable of him to make me feel so.

The Queen is not the only one to love him. The whole Court loves him. And they delight in their love for him. There is something personal and vindictive and I would say hateful in this love of theirs for him. That is to say, it is a message meant for me.

You are not he, they say.

You never were he.

You never can be he.

You are an aberration. You are a nothing. You are over.

He is loved. You are hated.

I confess, it rankles less with me than my enemies may think. The truth is I care little for other men's affections. It is only hers, my sovereign's, that I truly crave, and then only for what it brings to me. I am a trader in her affections. I convert them to my profit.

As for the others, the noble courtiers, the men who now trump and glorify this Essex, if they will hate me, then I will have them hate me to the full capacity of their hatred. I will excel at being hated.

I must ever be the best at everything.

Intelligence comes from all quarters of the Spaniard's gathering forces. The Pope and King Philip did not take well the news of Mary's execution.

I cannot stop the words from escaping my mouth: 'If only we had done as I advised.'

We are in the Presence Chamber, there to witness the Queen's bestowing of some little gift on Essex. Today it is a miniature portrait of herself. He looks down upon it with undisguised disdain. I want to slap the arrogant pup about the face, to bring the colour of shame to his cheeks.

I see that Sir Francis Walsingham likes not my remark. If I have a weakness, it is this: there are times when I act as if I wish to make myself detestable to men who have it in their power to harm me. But if it be true what good John White alleges, that Walsingham plotted the ruin of my colony, then there is no more harm he can do me. He has done it all. He has shattered my dreams absolutely and utterly. He has made a mockery of my ambition in the eyes of my sovereign.

He must know that I am not the man to take such hostility lying down. And if he does not know it, I must make him know it. I cannot be blamed if I do all that I can damage him in the eyes of my Queen.

In truth, Walsingham looks not so much a damaged man as a ravaged one. It is said that a canker eats away at him from within. I imagine the canker as a cluster of tiny black spiders. His skin is parchment pallid, except for around the eyes, where it is darkly shadowed. His eyes were always deep-set, but now they have sunk more deeply back into his head, as if they are retreating from the world they have spent so long watching.

I do not gloat in his physical decline but nor do I pity him. And it would be a mistake ever to underestimate him; even as his power wanes, he is preparing the ground for its continuation in another.

It is not Walsingham's way to answer criticisms directly. And so I am surprised, and even a little flattered, when he deigns to spend some of his diminishing energies in offering riposte to my sally: 'If memory serves, that advice of yours, which you are now in hindsight advocating to us, was that we should have had the Scottish Queen murdered by a secret assassin…'

This provokes a titter of amusement amongst those present.

Walsingham holds up a trembling hand to silence them. 'No, no, please! This is a serious matter. A most grave matter, in fact. To commission the assassination of an anointed monarch. How shall it be done? Who shall be trusted with such a terrible deed? I believe you proposed that we should find some desperate villain and induce him by the offer of a new suit of clothes…?'

'No, the suit of clothes was what Oxford paid to have someone kill *me*. No doubt the price for a Queen will be higher.'

'But you are still alive, are you not? Evidently, the very course of action that you are proposing failed!'

'I am a man, a soldier. I was able to thwart the plot. Mary was a woman. A sickly one, to boot. It would have been an easier task.'

'Easier? You think the murder of an anointed queen easier to organise than a brawl in an alleyway?'

'It could have been arranged. I know it.'

'No, you do not know it. You imagine it. For you, they are the same thing, but trust me on this, Ralegh, they are quite distinct activities of the mind.'

I do not like the ready concurrence that this easy, empty barb of his draws forth. It only goads Walsingham on to further attack: 'Do you really believe that an assassination, even if we could have kept secret the State's involvement, would have prevented the Spanish King from seeking revenge? Whom else would he have blamed for Mary's death but Elizabeth, under whose protection she was?'

At this mention of Her Majesty, it is natural that all should turn to her, to see how she takes the thrust of this debate, which pertains so closely to her person. I daresay I am not the only one disappointed to see that she is engrossed in whispering nothings over her miniature to Essex.

I want to provoke her into paying attention: 'I merely thought to save her Majesty trouble.'

'Do you think that the King of Spain would have been deterred in this his foul and noxious course by the extra-judicial murder of the Catholic bitch?'

Walsingham's intemperate language finally provokes the Queen to look up from her bowed tête-à-tête. She shakes her head at Walsingham. Whatever else Mary was, she was still a princess. But the Queen does not rebuke her Principal Secretary. She has described her own cousin in even more violent terms than this.

'He was already set on his great Enterprise against England on account of the many depredations he had suffered at the hands of your sea captains, Ralegh. If we had had the Scottish Queen murdered, as you recommended, his thirst for vengeance would have been all the greater! You would have achieved naught except the greater endangerment of the realm, not to mention Her Majesty's soul. Which brings us onto the most powerful objection that can be laid against your silly plan. The moral and the religious objection. I do not expect a man such as you, Ralegh, to be moved by such considerations, or even to understand them. You are worse, I would say, than a recusant, because you believe in nothing but your own ambition.'

I cannot let such dangerous accusations go unchallenged: 'Have I not fought against the Papist hordes? I soldiered in France on the side of the Huguenots. I delivered Ireland from an illegal invading army. Have my ships not taken the fight to the farthest Spanish territories? What was it if not my faith that had me fight for my religion?'

163

'Ambition? Cloaked in religion? But granted what you say is true, then how can you ever have urged such a course on Her Majesty? This is what the Catholics do, not us! Do I need to remind you of Gaspard de Coligny? I was in Paris, you know, on that St Bartholomew's Day.'

I am shocked to see tears run from Walsingham's eyes. I had not thought Walsingham was a man who could cry.

'He was there too. My son-in-law. Sidney. He understood. What an immeasurable loss he is to us.'

I seek to mollify him: 'Well, then, Sir Francis. You know the dangers. None better. Should we not fight fire with fire? You are not averse to secret measures, I think.'

He dabs the tears away with his cuff. A note of self-justification enters his voice, that quavers now as he speaks: 'Yes, I have employed secret means. I have sent out others to be my eyes and ears. I have watched and manoeuvred in the dark, to protect my Queen and my religion from a horror that I know only too well. I have gathered intelligence and buttressed it up around our state. In this case, the ends justify the means. But I would never advocate such a course as you proposed. It would make us little better than common criminals.'

And now he turns his two glistening eyes on me and stares deeply into me. He holds a finger up towards me. His frail trembling makes of it a wagging finger.

'You frighten me, Sir Walter. You frighten me more than the Spaniard because I trust you less. You have no respect for the Law. The religion that you claim to profess hardly touches you. You are a new kind of man. I tremble to leave my Queen in your care.'

The Queen once again looks up. She scowls at us, as if we are troublesome children: 'Have you two not yet finished your quarrel? Really, if you cannot comport yourselves amiably, we would rather you took yourselves elsewhere than in our presence. Walsingham, you do protest too much. You know that it would have been acceptable to us if a way had been found to shorten our cousin's life before it became necessary for us to sign her death warrant. She was manifestly a sickly woman. She could not walk without the support of her physician. It should not have been beyond the wit of her gaoler to make it seem a natural death. Why, we discussed such measures, did we not? Wat was not the only one to urge it. Leicester too. We looked into the ways and means most closely. If Sir Amyas Paulet had not proven himself too great a Puritan, the thing might well have been accomplished. And you would have rejoiced as much as anyone. You even wrote a letter steeling him to it, did you not?'

Walsingham's eyes blink weakly.

The Queen bestows a private smile on Essex, a more treasured gift than any miniature. I cannot but feel a pang of jealousy, for all that she has humiliated Walsingham and shown him for a hypocrite. That is proof enough that I am not entirely out of her favour. And yet I am beginning to know how Sir Christopher Hatton once felt.

I will not stoop to sending her silver sieves or buckets or whatever it was.

I will only deliver her instead a World. And I do not mean a silver globe. I shall yet win back her absolute and entire love.

R.N. MORRIS

## Hellburners

And now it appears. From the East. The gathering of all our fears. The low dark entity squat upon the horizon. At first it seems to be the surface refraction of some deep submarine Leviathan. The Spanish ships are packed so closely together we see them not as a sprawl of specks, but as one dense cluster of malice.

A giant, monstrous weapon of war rolling slowly towards us.

A vast cruel smile floating on the water.

The Armada holds its crescent formation admirably as it approaches. It is grimly fascinating for those of us upon the shore to watch. We needs must be patient as we powerlessly await our doom.

One thing follows upon another. All flows towards an end.

I at least have done all I can. All I was permitted to do.

It is for others now, for the Lord High Admiral, Baron Effingham, and for my cousin Drake, for them and their rope-muscled sailors and the pale gunners huddled around the cannon in the bellies of our ships and the raiders in the rigging. That said, it is well known that we have not enough ships and not enough soldiers to take on the Spanish fleet. Some three score vessels against one hundred and twenty. We must pray to God, in the fervent belief that He is no Papist.

It is powerful strange, this mixture of dread and devilment, the taste of fate in our mouths, as we wait for the onset of battle. To live inside a moment of true crisis, when disaster or deliverance may equally be the issue. I can smell the gun smoke before a single cannon is fired. The ghosts of men who are not dead yet call out to me, their voices whipped up by the wind. I see a wine red slick spread from the seams of the Spanish ships into the waters.

The end is foretold in the beginning.

Oakfast as ever was, our buoyant fleet bursts forth, at the head mine own Ark Royal gifted to the Queen, thrusting lustily towards the first engagement.

We watchers from the shore raise a rousing roar to urge on our fleet. There are those who from the comfort of court do seek to cavil and criticise the conduct of the Admiral at sea. I am not one of them, nor ever will be. I know what it is to be the commander in the field, who must take decisions on the hoof. (Albeit this is not a question of field and hoof, but the principle is the same.) That he keeps his distance and harries from afar, trusting to the superiority of his ships' manoeuvrability, is rather to his credit than not. Our ships will be the gadflies that goad the lumbering beast of the Spanish Armada. We will find ways to bite and pinch behind the armour.

I muster my men and have them race along the coast to keep pace with the shifting progress of the naval action. Hearts in our mouths. Sweat beneath our armour. It is like a battle in a dream. We charge but there is no enemy. The enemy is all at sea. We keep up our full-throated battle cry nonetheless.

The advantage is always with the fleet that has the wind on its side. But the wind is an unbiddable ally. One moment it is with us, the next with the enemy. Our swift and nimble ships are better fitted to run and ride the wind that the high and mighty Spanish galleons. We chip away at them. They scatter in disarray.

I am commanded to convey Her Majesty's orders to Effingham and so set foot upon the ship that was once my own.

As soon as I feel the sway and kick of the deck in my calves, the old familiar nausea swills in my belly. I feel a drum-skin tightness in my belly. It is drawn ever tighter and tighter, sending convulsive ripples upwards. If the drum should burst, I fear a great expulsion of matter. It is all I can do to swallow down my gorge. (The sailors' cry of *Heave!* That goes up as I board serves as a most unwelcome welcome.)

The greatest foe that each of us must conquer is the frailty of our own nature.

The Lord High Admiral greets me with an upward tilt of his pointed silver beard, a gesture designed to convey the great inconvenience I put him to, as well the little need he has for my intervention. I see fit to remind him of the nation's debt to me: 'She serves you well, I trust.'

I succeed in goading a querulous, inquisitive glance from him.

'The *Ark Ralegh.* I mean, *Royal.*'

He snaps out a begrudging acknowledgement, half smile, half snort: 'Aye, Ralegh. You may tell Her Majesty from me, that her money was well given for her.'

I do not disabuse him, but there was no question of any money given.

'I am commanded to inform you that she wishes you to drive home your advantage, to pursue the enemy all the way to Calais, and to destroy the Spanish fleet utterly before it is able to connect with the Duke of Parma's troops in Dunkirk.'

I see his eyes enlarge in indignation. 'Have I ever left my duty derelict? If not, then I beg you to discover to me, what cause Her Majesty may have to believe that I shall do so now?'

God preserve me from the quick affront of aristocrats. Sensing that he has even more rhetorical questions in reserve, I cut him short: 'Her Majesty is much beholden to you, my Lord. Please do not take it so amiss. She sends me not to hold you to account for any dereliction of duty. For indeed there is none that she knows of – how could there be? But rather she wishes only to spur you on to even greater glory. Know you that Her Majesty has nothing but the highest regard and esteem for you, Lord Admiral, and that all your efforts on her behalf are greatly appreciated. Forgive me if I have garbled her message in the conveying of it. Her Majesty's words are meant only to show how completely she trusts you. Her Majesty is confident that you will do what is ever in the best interests of Her Majesty and Her Realm.'

'Forgive me, I had thought that Her Majesty had relieved me of my command and was undertaking the direction of the campaign herself.'

I see I must waste further words and time in soothing his wounded pride. I swallow down a surge of seasick sourness: 'Far from it. She knows all that you intend. That you will not rest until the enemy is utterly destroyed. She merely wishes you to understand that she supports you in this. She stands four-square behind you.'

'I had rather she would stand the wages of my soldiers. Aye, and a decent meal would not go amiss either.'

'You cannot doubt her love for your men? You heard her speak at Tilbury?'

'Fine words, I'll grant you. All that heart and stomach of a king stuff. 'Twas well said. However, it will take more than fine words to destroy this enemy.'

'Imagine her, if you will, the Warrior Queen in full armour at the very prow of this vessel, her trident held out in front of her as you bear down upon the enemy ships. Her words are torched arrows sent to fire your martial spirit. Let her be the fire in your belly!'

Between the thought, the word, the deed, what a fine fiery thread is drawn! Not that I claim credit by my speech for the action that ensued and caused such havoc among the Spanish galleys. It was, no doubt, ever the Admiral's intention to set destruction loose into the wind.

To use three elements to keep the enemy from the fourth.

But I swear I do descry some igniting glint in his eye, a sharp quickening at my words, a crackling of the spirit.

He waits till midnight to release it. When it spreads like wildfire through the fleet.

'Tis a black, infinite midnight upon which the stars seem farther away than ever, as if they would distance themselves from the doings of men. The wind is less retiring. It has an inkling of what is afoot and is eager to inveigle itself into the commission of it.

Cries rise and crackle, like firecrackers thrown. Lanterns swing and dash, painting quick, bleary tails of purpose amid the blind confusion.

Five black hulks separate themselves from the English fleet. They loom and creak upon the sea of ink. The night is made darker by their presence. They are tarred and laden with the very stuff of night. Barrels of acrid pitch stacked amongst the dry kindling in the holds. These are dead ships, carcasses. They move with a wild, unpurposed veering. At times they are lost from sight all together and we can locate them only by the tense momentous shouts of the men who are charged with priming them. For they are ships no longer, but missiles.

The shouts from the water reach a frenzy of excitement. The five dark hulls reappear, in the gulf between our ships and the enemies. Their blackness now is haloed by a rich orange glow. A fierce St Elmo's fire plays along the decks and begins to lick at the masts.

We are upwind of them, but still can smell their ash-tainted drift. How much more pungent must it be to the Spanish sailors in their boats? Before they can raise the alarm and cut loose from their anchors, the wind, our ever eager ally, fans the floating flames into a fivefold frenzy.

We feel the roar in our throats before the thought forms to raise it.

And so we send our English Hell into the midst of the Spanish mass, turning their own Armada into a pyre for the damned.

Aye, God is no Papist, I swear.

Rather I do believe he is an Englishman.

## Politic

I catch your eye, my Dear. And I am startled by it. You seek me out, I see that. And await my regard. I am somewhat put to shame by you.

I feel a quickening in my heart, and a stiffening elsewhere, at the sight of you. I will confess that although I was always charmed by your looks, I had never considered you a great beauty. (You will agree there is nothing to be gained by flattery and false blandishments, not now, not any more; you are a sensible girl, I know you will agree.) It was the intelligence and character I detected in your gaze that attracted me most. But now I see that I had overlooked this in you. Is it conceit in me to imagine you have become beautiful on my behalf? That I have made you so?

Your lips are miraculous to me now. Profound mysteries that I must fathom and plumb.

And now I see there are things other than your lips that exist.

In your eyes, I see your deep and lively interest in me. The benignity of your gaze. The beam from your eye strikes me in the heart, sinks deep its hook and pulls me to you.

There is a promise in your eye. I do not just mean the promise of tender embraces to come, a renewal of our last pleasures, the secret bonds that chase away the tedium and chill of long nights.

Your look promises to reveal more than your body. You have news to tell me, I see it.

Her Majesty calls for Essex. *Where is he?* He is not there. No one knows where he is. She is out of sorts at his absence. She talks to me of him. Repeats his infantile inanities as if they were wit. Compliments his calves to me! How they tense when he dances the galliard, or mounts his horse. Relates the wearisome catalogue of his purported adventures in the field.

And I must applaud.

Does she forget how once I served her in Smerwick? How I delivered Ireland from the invader? And how more recently I laboured on her behalf, and at my own expense, to fortify the country against against the Spanish Armada.

I bow deep and beg my leave.

In the meantime, my Dear, I take solace in the Continent that is you.

Those lips, at last, I plumb the yielding jelly of those lips.

You are not coy.

We are reckless. Delight in taking risks.

I want to hurt her. I want her to know I love another.

I want to rub her face in it. In our love. In what it makes of us. I want to force her to watch at our bodies' transformations. How I am stiffened and steeled at the loins. And how you open yourself up to receive me. I want to confront her with our coupling. I want her to hear the wanton liquefaction as I enter you. I want her to smell the sweat upon our skins. The more than sweat.

The lubricious outpourings of your quim in anticipation of my ramrod's knocking. The fragrance of my seed. I want to take some of it in my fingers, after I have spilt it into your cunt, I want to probe the aftermath of our congress and gather the fruit of it, and then hold it to her nostrils and smear it on her face.

There is something about her that makes me want to do this. I cannot explain it.

And in the wake of our fervid coupling, I learn from you that which your eyes promised to tell me. It is news of my rival Essex: 'He is married!'

'Married?'

'Aye! He married in secret. Without the Queen's permission!'

'My God! Does she know of it yet?'

'She does.'

'And how does she like it?'

'Not at all. I have never seen her so… enraged. I thought she would burst the vessel at her temple.'

'But she calls for him? And extolls his virtues still?'

'She has forgiven him. But only after long exile from her presence. In time, she found that she could not bear to be without him and called him back to her.'

'Who was his bride?'

'Walsingham's daughter, Frances. Philip Sidney's widow.'

Your answer does not surprise me. The dynasty that her father worked for has come to be. Lord Burghley's ward married to Walsingham's daughter. I do not doubt that the enmity that Walsingham bore me will continue in him. There will be no love lost on either side.

Your lips work at the lobe of my ear, suckling it as a babe his mother's nipple. 'This is good for us, Wat.'

I pull away from your importuning. 'Good, how?'

'She found it in her heart to forgive Essex and his bride. She will forgive us too.'

'Forgive us? We do not need her forgiveness.'

Your frown awaits my meaning. I oblige: 'We are not married.'

'But when she finds out about us…'

'Why should she find out about us?'

'You did not see her rage, Wat. It frightened me.'

'You need not be frightened. She cannot do without me.'

'But what of me?'

I confess, your question startles me. The only answer I can think of is to seek out your lips once more.

In truth, I cannot believe that she does not know about us already. She knows it but will not acknowledge it. I want her to acknowledge it. Every part of it. I want her to acknowledge that you give me what she cannot.

Soon she will know it.

I allow myself to be seen slipping letters into your pockets.

We contrive to touch hands as we pass in the long gallery between Ceremony and Intimacy.

We meet in the palace gardens and, though we hide behind box hedges, we do not suppress our laughter or the other sounds of our pleasure.

You come to my chamber at night, stealing away from the Queen's slumbers. One of these nights you will be missed. One of these nights we will be found out. But for now the only certain witness of your coming is my servant William Pansfurthe. He will not easily forget the obligation that he owes to me. Once I did pay a fine to buy his freedom on a capital charge. I trust him not to betray us.

But if such things are not enough to draw the attention of my enemies' spies, soon your belly does. The fruit of our union grows within you.

And yes, I confess, it is at this point I deem it politic for me to absent myself from Court. It will be better if I am not there when the Queen discovers the full extent of your condition. Better for both of us, my dear. You must see that. For if I can contrive the means to perform for Her Majesty some great good, by striking hard at the heart of the Spanish King's interests for example, and delivering to her a greater prize than any yet known, how much more likely will she be to look indulgently upon our small and, it must be admitted, natural transgression?

She will rage. We must expect that. But she will soon move towards forgiveness, all the sooner for my absence. She will find she wants me by her side more than she wants to punish me.

And so I hasten to Chatham Docks to make preparations for the voyage that will be our deliverance. This time I must go with the fleet. It needs my personal intervention. I cannot trust the endeavour to lieutenants. I must seize the prize myself, and be the one to bring it back to her in person. Then, all will be forgiven.

Still you wait on her. And I cannot believe that she has not noticed your condition, though all the other ladies gossip of it behind their hands.

Your tears undo me. I feel me melt and flow into a pool of sadness.

The weight of your bowed head. I feel it in my heavy heart.

The tremble of your miraculous lips. I feel it flicker at my wrist, my pulse havocked by your piteous despair.

The kick of life within your proud belly. How can I not feel it?

We are like personages in a play. The Star-Crossed Lovers. I send another personage, the Faithful Servant (played by William), to fetch another, the Priest. We are married at midnight in my chambers. It is something Mr Kyd might pen and have performed upon the stage.

Come, lift your head. Wipe away your tears. Still your trembling lip. I shall not have you say that I abandon you.

What is good enough for Essex shall be good enough for me.

Come now, know this. I did not marry Alice Gould, the mother of my child in Ireland. But I marry you. I arm you with legitimacy, so that when the deed is discovered, she cannot charge you with a sin. I will be absent, but my name will be with you, to protect you and our child.

All will be well. I have spoken to your brother. Your brother has influence with Essex, and through him the Queen. He will buy her gifts to mollify her. And then I will return with the greatest gift of all. A New World. Or failing that, the pick of Philip's treasure fleet.

We must make a friend of Essex, though it grieves me to say it. He is our best hope. He will have sympathy for our plight, having suffered for a similar offence. Let us have him as godfather to our child. He will not refuse. I urge you to cultivate Robert Cecil too. He is a little twisted imp of a man, but his influence is large. So too his capacity for malice, if he chooses to set himself against us. However, his deformity may play into our favour. For it renders him friendless, and is the root and source of his bitterness. Therefore we must go out of our way to prove ourselves his especial friends. You may protest that there is too much calculation in this. I assure you, he is so starved of friends and allies that he will not suspect. I will write to him. These are the men to whom she looks now. We must count on them to protect us.

I go, my dear, but I will return and all will be well. All will be better than it ever has been.

### For what do I weep?

The wind is free. I place myself within it, lavished by the lick and spittle of the sea. The tug of kinship draws forth salt tears from my eyes. Little rivers in flow.

I stand on the deck of a ship racing away from England. Away from certain troubles to an uncertain future. I will always choose uncertainty over its opposite. Hope lives in uncertainty, whereas that which is certain is without hope: That which is certain is already dead.

This is the germ of a poem, I think. The long hours at sea will give me leisure to work on it.

*Desire attained is not desire…*

I believe I must always live inside a state of desire. I must always be desiring something. Desire attained is melancholy.

What if uncertain desire is an ache from which tears well? Even so, I will always choose it over certainty.

For what do I weep? I am where I want to be, in the midst of a desire, heading away from my troubles, towards uncertainty. I am in my element. At sea.

I have left my wife and newborn child but I do not weep for them. Like Peter thrice denying Christ, I have denied them. In my letter to Robert Cecil, I deemed it politic to deny my marriage. One day Bess will understand. One day she will even thank me. I have promised to bring back coral for the baby to cut his teeth on.

Do I weep for the lies I have told? I do not waste tears on them. I did what I had to do.

Every moment is a movement towards another moment. In each, we say and do what we need to in order to get from it to the next.

This is what it is to be a courtier. I have been at it too long to shed tears for such a life.

Do I weep to think of the rage I will provoke in my sovereign when she discovers my offence? For the grief I will cause her? My calculation is that the storms will quickly pass when she sees the prize that I am bound to bring back from this enterprise. She needs me by her more than she needs to punish me. Leicester is dead, Walsingham too; and now, my old rival for her favour, the giver of silver buckets, Sir Christopher Hatton, joins them in death. Only Burghley remains of her old guard. I think she is lonelier than I have ever seen her. Without me, she would be lonelier still.

Do I weep for her loneliness? I confess it stirs some pang of melancholy in me, but not enough to draw forth tears, for when it comes down to it, her loneliness is useful to me. It will be her loneliness that brings me back to her.

Her loneliness and her greed.

I weep because the wind whips at my eyes. That's all.

### Turn about

Above the canvas-crack of wind, a cry breaks out. *Ship ahoy!*

A swift pinnace skims the water, making purposely towards us. For one moment I think of giving chase. But we will never outrun her. We sit low in the water, burdened with an ocean's worth of provisions, both livestock and dead victual.

She is a lithe and nimble spright beside us.

As she draws closer I see the royal pennant fluttering from her masthead. I feel something shift inside me, the ballast of my soul as the keel of my being tilts.

Sir Martin Frobisher hails me from the pinnace deck. He looks as if he is about to spit, but then he ever does. The pinnace draws alongside. Our two vessels are tethered. We let down a rope ladder. Frobisher hauls himself aboard, with much grunting and straining. His face is dark with exertion and choler. He has always struck me as a man who wishes he was elsewhere, wherever he is.

His flattened northern vowels make wreckage of my name: 'The game is up, Rallee. You are to return to shore. I am to relieve you of your command. By order of the Queen.'

We are hardly out of harbour. I only smelled the whiff of freedom, had not the chance to taste it. And for once, the motion of the sea has sat easy on my stomach.

'My men will not serve you, Frobisher. They know your reputation. They signed up to follow me, not you.'

'You will defy Her Majesty, eh? That will not go well with you.'

'No, no! I am sworn obedience to Her Majesty.'

'Then go aboard the pinnace and be taken back to shore. I can take your fleet from here.'

'Her Majesty is misadvised. My enemies…'

'Your greatest enemy is yoursen, Rallee.'

'She will see. When I return with a hull laden with gold.'

'There is not enough gold in the world to buy you out of the trouble you'll be in if you do not return now.'

'I cannot answer for the men. They are West Country men. My men, not yours.'

'They are the Queen's men, I hope. Happen they will be loyal to her.'

'We will sail together! In joint command.'

'The Queen will not have it.'

'As far as the Spanish coast. And in that time I will endeavour to persuade the men to obey you.'

'They will obey me, with or without you. They know how it will sit with them if they do not.'

His mouth snaps into a grimace of disgust. He will not win them over with such faces.

'As far as Spain, Frobisher. Then I swear I will return to England and answer to my Queen.'

'What are you hoping for, Rallee? That you will pluck some great prize out of the sea between here and there?'

'Would that be such a bad thing? If I sail back to port in a Spanish carrack?'

Frobisher shakes his head doubtfully. 'I do not advise it, man. The Queen will take it most amiss if you defy her in this, as you have defied her in your marriage. The sooner you get yoursen back to shore, the better it will be for you. Put all your hope in her clemency.'

'You shall have a share of the prize, Frobisher. You may count on that.'

'Forsooth? I may count on a share of a prize that is not yet captured? I count myself very fortunate indeed.'

I call for the master to turn about. Frobisher looks more than ever like he will spit. More than ever like he wishes to be elsewhere.

### She takes

There was no raging.

She did not scream my name. Or hurl tokens of me back into my face.

She did not tear up my licences, nor consign their fragments to the fire. No gift that had already been granted was withdrawn. Not even Sherborne was to be withheld from me. A promise is a promise. She will be meticulous in upholding it.

There was none of this, that I know of.

For it is only that she will not see me. Yes, I am denied her presence. That is to be my punishment.

So what if I am to be confined to Durham House? She has set my own cousin to be my gaoler! I shall write verses of remonstration. I shall write letters to Robert Cecil. Not for nothing have I cultivated the cripple's friendship. It is time to reap the hard-won rewards of that uncongenial strategy. I shall let it be known by subtle hints that he should show the letters to Her Majesty.

*She gives, she takes, she wounds, she appeases.*

We only have to sit out the taking and the wounding.

We will get through this, my dear.

My dear?

Why do you not answer me?

Are you still hurting at my denial of our matrimony?

Your silence is absolute. It has stilled even the beating pulse in my ears. I hear nothing.

I see…

Only red.

Your absence is again filled with only red.

I know not up nor down nor any point of the compass. There is no land or sea.

Only red.

I cannot even blink the red away. There is nothing of me left to blink with.

She has taken all of me. And I thought she had taken nothing.

What's that I hear? Hammering at the door? Or is it the pulse returned to the vein behind my ear?

I call out for my servant:

'William! Will?'

The red clears and I see…

William's face before me at last, and there is something in his look that presages what is to come and explains all that has preceded. At once I see it was he who betrayed us. He only played the part of Faithful Servant at our wedding.

Is this how he pays me back for all that I have done for him?

Oh William, never let me see that face again. Let the red dissolve it in bloody oblivion.

At his back, the soldiers. She has sent soldiers. And he has led them to me.

Be brave, my dear.

I will write to Cecil. The little cripple is not to be trusted but I know how to handle him.

I will write verses of remonstration. This will end well yet.

## Menagerie

O, Damerei! Damerei!

My first-born, short-lived son.

What, pray, is your offence, unless it be your very existence?

For I am conveyed to the Tower to await Her Majesty's pleasure. And my wife and baby son are brought here too, to provide some solace for my captivity.

O, Damerei!

I am advised the Queen dislikes your name, it being too grand for the son of humble Walter Ralegh!

I cannot credit that Her Majesty has sunk to such a depth of rancour.

I am told it is because I did not go to her on bended knee craving her forgiveness. How could I? She banished me from her presence!

She knows I am not given to contrition. I consider it to be a sign of weakness. She would not have wanted weakness from me. She has Robert Cecil for that. So much for all the letters I wrote to him. So much for all my investment of affection in him.

There is nothing to be done. I will make the best of it. I will not mope and stare at walls, counting stones. I have been confined within worse prisons, after all. The Fleet is a noxious hole compared to this. But at least then I knew what my offence was. I was a wayward brawling youth. It was only right that I should be forced to kick my heels and cool for a while.

It is possible to be quite comfortable in the Tower. I might wish that we were held at some other time than the height of summer. The plague rages through London. We feel it closing in on us. Those who can, desert the city. Bess is anxious on the child's account. But there is nothing to be done, other than to make ourselves as comfortable as we can.

I make an apartment of my cell, with hanging tapestries and furniture. A little home for Damerei. I have my books brought to me. I am allowed servants.

My friends visit me on their way out of London. Yes, though my enemies have conspired to have me brought to this place, I still have friends. They assure me, with many earnest oaths, that they will move heaven and earth to have me out of here.

Good Thomas Hariot visits and brings with him one Laurence Keymis. This Keymis is another scholar, a fellow of Balliol college. He is made in the same mould as Thomas. If anything, he is more muscular and militant. He speaks of nothing else but venturing with me on a voyage to America. A slight strabismus in his left eye lends his face a distracted expression. It gives him the air of only half-attending to his collocutor, one part of his mind being focused on grand and distant schemes. In some wise it reminds me of the savage woman Egnock, whose casting gaze I once sought to catch on the harbour side in Bristol.

I gesture around me: 'First I must find a way to venture out of here.'

He shows me the Latin verses that he has written in my honour. They pertain to the injustice of my plight. It is his belief that when the Queen reads them, her heart will melt and she will order my release.

I advise him not to publish. Did not John Stubbe have his right hand chopped off for scribbling a naughty pamphlet against the Queen?

But I thank him for the sentiments. He is a good and earnest young man, whose intentions are worthy. I already detect in him a great love for me.

He will be of use to me one day, methinks.

I entertain any number of cousins and sea captains, among them Edward Denny, Thomas Cavendish, Sir John Hawkins and Sir Francis Drake. Even Henry Percy, the Earl of Northumberland is not ashamed to be seen in such salty company. We play cards and talk of happier times, those that have passed, but more especially, those that are yet to come. Our discourse is, however, tinged with melancholy when Northumberland brings us news of Dr Dee, who is returned from his travels in Poland. I am saddened to learn that things do not go well with the old alchemist. The Queen has turned her back on him too, it seems. And he was the man whose dream of Empire launched all our endeavours.

We fill the apartment with a tobacco fug. And fill the fug with our plans and projections. I share with my guests the litany of gold-dusted names: 'Barquasimeta... Cororo... Maracaiba... Truxillo...'

And the rest.

At the recital, I see the glitter in their eyes. There is talk of forming a company. Laurence Keymis outdoes them all in his eagerness: 'Take me with you! Where do I sign?'

'Ha! We have yet to draw up the papers. But what experience do you have of sailing, such as would qualify you for this mission?'

'I have read many accounts of great voyages, not least those collated by our friend Richard Hakluyt here.'

'Ah, so you have voyaged around a library or two!'

'I know the world cannot be understood from books alone. Which is why I am so earnest in my desire to accompany you. Please believe me, sir, when I say that it was for a mission such as this that I was born. My horoscope confirms it. Aquarius was ascendant at my birth. By which I take it to mean that water shall play a part of great significance in my destiny.'

'Aye, you are a great passer of water, no doubt.'

My jest is met with much merriment. Young Keymis takes it well and even turns it to his own advantage: 'But do not the alchemists use piss in the operation of the Great Work? That is to say they are able even to extract gold from it? So that one who is an excellent passer of water may yet be useful in the discovery of precious metals.'

'That is one for you, Northumberland. Is't true you fellows are nought but handlers of piss?'

The Wizard Earl shakes down his dark locks and turns a torpid eye on me. The languor of his reaction belies a sharp intellect. But he is cursed by a halting hesitancy of speech and needs must always be buying time for his *mots justes.* 'Aye, and it is the elixir of life too. For the whores that drink my p-p-p-piss do swear by its marvellous efficacy against the p-p-p-pox.'

His faltering delivery does much to magnify our enjoyment of his wit when finally it comes. There is never doubt that he will muster something to the point, even if he first must overcome Admiral Hawkins' hectoring encouragement: 'Spit it out!'

'That's what I t-t-t-tell them!'

He has us slapping our thighs in appreciation.

Too soon the fug clears and my friends are all dissipated with it. They return in dwindling numbers as the summer progresses. The hopes held out of my release dwindle too. Court is too preoccupied with its own salvation, while the plague tightens its hold on London. I find myself out of sight and out of mind.

Bess grows ever more morose and anxious. Her faithful brother continues to encourage us. Though if there were to be any hope of remission, I would not look to it from his efforts, but from the return of my fleet.

I walk the wall for exercise and am permitted to show my face to all who come to look at it.

But the pungent smell and lively gossiping of the river exercises the greatest draw upon me. I long to leap the stone curtain and dive into the river's babble. Let me be borne away in its incessant discourse! It whispers to me of my destiny, inspiring in me a nostalgia for places I have never visited except in dreams. It promises me a share in its own boundless freedom.

When the longing becomes unbearable, I turn to the animals of the Tower menagerie for solace. They are held in wooden cages within a semi-circular enclosure near the Lion Tower. I acknowledge fellowship with them, for we are all captive creatures. However strange they are – the striped zebra, the twin-humped camel, the long-necked giraffe, the tusked and trunked elephant, the horned rhinoceros – they are my brothers. They have been brought from the four corners of the world to this their prison, gifts for an indifferent sovereign.

I learn from the Yeomen of the Guard, in their bright-blazoned tunics, the names of all the lions. There is a Henry and an Edward and a Mary and even an Elizabeth. They have sad and sympathetic eyes. One imagines them shedding a tear for the prey they are obliged to rip apart. In that, they are unlike their royal namesakes.

They either sleep listlessly in the sun, or prowl the perimeter of their compound, looking for a point of egress that their minds have tricked them into believing in.

The heat mounts. In places, the Thames runs to a trickle. Fish flap and die in the mud. I watch the rats skitter out to feast on the carcasses. With the dwindling of the river I sense the vanishing of my hopes.

I endeavour to catch the dark and beautiful eye of the lioness Elizabeth. She steadfastly refuses to grant it, preferring instead to turn her back on me.

That which carries away the river carries away our Damerei too. Bess feels his loss sharply, to judge by the keening wail she gives vent to when she discovers his lifeless body. It is natural, she being his mother. But at least it is an end to her anxious fretting over him, and of his sufferings too. Through all his brief tenure of life, he never ceased to thrash and flail as if it were something he could not wait to shake off.

## Mother of God

I am borne along the river on a wherry. That which my heart has longed for is come to be: the water is Water's deliverance. I know that there are those who would criticise me for placing too great a store in the power of my wishes. To them I would say, you will never achieve anything if first you do not wish for it.

My thoughts outstrip the sluggish pace of my conveyance. I urge the river on: *Hurry, hurry! Take me away from the shadow of my captivity!*

The river whispers back: *Patience! Patience!*

The further I am borne, the less likely is it that I will return. It is true that I am leaving my wife and child behind in the Tower. To Bess, I say, *Fear not! By this one service, I shall secure your release too.*

I am hauled out of the wherry and put on a horse, to gallop westward. And my heart lightens at the thought of home. To be among my people. Ha! My good, unruly people. My cousins and countrymen. I knew I could rely upon them!

The fleet I sent out has returned. It brings with it a captive carrack, the *Madre de Dios*. She is quite the greatest prize ever to be hauled out of the Atlantic. And the irony of it is she is not a Spanish treasure ship. Taken off the Azores, she is a Portuguese vessel returning from the East Indies, by way of the Indian Ocean and Africa. What care we whether she is Spanish or Portingale, or whence she has come? She is ours now! All one thousand six hundred tons of her. And my own good ship *Roebuck* was instrumental in her capture.

In short, everything has turned out as I knew it would.

We catch the waft of her cargo blown to us on the West Wind. For she is laden with spices. Tons upon tons of precious seeds and dust. The invisible cloud brings tears to my eyes, overwhelming me with emotions as well as scents. I try to separate the strands of both. I detect pepper, cloves, cinnamon, cochineal, mace, nutmeg, benjamin… As to my emotions, their complexity is harder to unravel. I know not whether I am joyful or sad. Only that some great feeling leaps within me.

Each breath I take emboldens me.

The wind carries rumour of the other treasures in her hold. She is filled with every precious thing that the East has ever promised. Diamonds, silks, pearls, amber, ivory. The weightless desiccated seed pods of the poppy, the source of Paracelsus's famed panacea, come too late to soothe the pangs that Secretary Walsingham suffered.

On the road we pass a steady stream of merchants and adventurers drawn by the lure of the *Madre di Dios*. I see the same wild intoxication in all their eyes, bent on pillaging the *Madre*'s cargo. I must outrun them all if I am to make good on my promise to her Majesty.

For I am the especial man. The only one who is up to the task. Certainly little Robert Cecil has not the stature for it, though he was sent ahead to accomplish it. The mob have no truck with his truculence.

The closer we draw to the harbour, the denser the crowds grow. On the quayside, they cluster around the carrack, standing with eyes streaming and mouths agape to breathe in the hot air. They are dazed and seeming drugged.

I push against a wall of resisting backs.

In truth, I cannot entirely blame them, neither the looters nor the sailors who seek to profit from them. It is in man's nature to covet.

For all that, I would beat the rabble back with a staff if I could. They grin and chatter with an air of avid entitlement. They seem to assume that all are equally complicit in the gross criminality being committed.

I look up to see a sky pierced by the *Madre*'s masts. She is simply an immense vessel, towering over the ships around her, a mass of castles and decks and high-strung rigging. But broad in the beam too, and long. She still sits low in the water under the weight of what is left of her cargo. As it is lifted from her, I imagine her hull rising until she floats off into the air. It is my duty – and my destiny – to prevent this.

I catch sight of Robert Cecil, morosely looking on. His whining voice pipes up: ''Tis no use, Ralegh. They have no respect for authority. Even the Queen's seal does not deter them. I fear there will soon be nothing left for any of us. They have descended like locusts. The sailors connive in it, as you can see.'

I waste no time in arguing with him. I turn to the guards who escorted me from the Tower: 'I may count on you?'

They nod as one. Before this moment they were my captors; now they are my servants.

I prevail upon the guards to discharge their muskets into the air. The general clamour of the crowd is silenced and all heads turn towards us. The height of my person works to my natural advantage. I am a clear head taller than any other man there. Robert Cecil, the Queen's minister, comes only to my breast. The red and gold tunics of the guards surrounding me further impress the mob, already somewhat cowed by the disruptive reports of the firearms.

The looters begin to drift away. They are for the most part flighty opportunists, easily deterred. Shameless they may be, but they are not reckless.

As the crowd thins, someone calls out my name. There is a cheer. A different crowd, of sturdy and stalwart seafaring men, my people, gathers round me. I am mobbed for handshakes and patted and touched, as if for good luck. Another cry goes up and I find myself lifted upon shoulders and carried aboard the *Madre di Dios* in triumph.

I cannot resist a glance back at Robert Cecil. I see him shake his head in dubious, jealous wonder. For all that, he does not begrudge me a half-admiring smile.

## The ladder of years

And so now I stand in the centre of it.

I am in the very womb of the Mother of God. Utterly enveloped by an intoxicating dust cloud. The air feels combustible – nay, it is already on fire. My nostrils burn with each breath I take. I am dissolving in tears and sweat and snot. Like a mewling newborn babe once again, though it is more that I feel myself about to be reborn. Is this how it feels to pass from one existence to the next? From the life amniotic to the life mundane, for example? Or from the mundane to the eternal?

One of the sailors holds aloft a lantern. As he shows me the riches that have come from the East in the womb of the Mother of God, I show him the future rewards that will be his if he would only master his present greed. It is a hard argument for a simple sailor to grasp, for these are men of passion and appetite, and their grasping is seldom intellectual.

'Fear not, Sir Wat, we will not let them take you back to the Tower!'

And so it is the threat of my imprisonment that carries most weight with him!

The strange alchemy of the place works further magic on me. I blink away my tears. And in so doing it seems I blink away the years also. For when I ascend to the top deck I find I am no longer on the *Madre di Dios,* but on another ship entirely.

We are out on the open sea, sails bickering overhead in the snap of a brisk wind.

Bound for that city that the naturals call Manoa, which is known to the Spaniards as El Dorado.

A crew scurries around me, spitting salty oaths and phlegm. The air is pierced by the whistles of the master and the boatswain both. Each sharply nuanced note denotes a distinct command, which is well understood by the deckhands who heed them. There are hawsers to be hauled, ropes to be coiled, sails to be trimmed, boards to be caulked, yards to be raised upon their gliding parrels. Each man knows his part in the task at hand.

The sailor who just now swung the lantern is one among them. He has remained loyal to me through all the years that passed in the blinking of my eyes. His beard is fuller and longer, if a little greyer, than it was a moment since. So too the matted straggles of hair that peep out around his thrum cap. Yet his heaving arms retain their muscular vigour. They are dark sinewy knots, like the boughs of walnut trees suddenly animate.

I have never found it easy walking the decks of an ocean-going vessel, and prefer to stay coffined in my cabin. The swing and dip of the ship always plays havoc with my balance. I am left looking for my sea legs long after those around me have found theirs and no matter how many times I clear the contents of my stomach with a loud and lumpy hurrah, I am ever queasy.

Added to that, I feel a new discomfort as my foot goes down upon the boards. A fiery twinge shoots up in protest. I swear it was not there the last time I ventured shipboard. Yay, I feel me older in my bones. A wintry ache has set in. Shifts of pain dart around my joints as if some flighty little animal has the run of me, gnawing and nipping now at my wrist, now at my knuckle, now at my hip. I put it down to my time in the Tower.

I welcome these pangs as an eager soldier welcomes the onset of battle. I will take them on. I will defy them. I will vanquish them.

Even so, I sense a heavier stroke in the beating of my heart. I wear my mortality less lightly now.

But the bustling barefoot endeavour of a ship's crew is a sight to lift the spirits of any admiral.

It is strange to be thus liberated from her jealous thrall; but what do I do now that I am at last free of her? I venture forth to win back her love and my captivity.

Not even the Paradoxal Compass can navigate me out of that conundrum.

We are suspended on a disc of seething blue. I scan the encircling horizon for some disruption of its monotony but there is none. It is as hard to believe in the land we have sailed from as that to which we are bound. Both are equal fables now.

The only relief to the eye is offered by the straggling train of ships punctuating the middle distance in our wake. They breast the waves with an irrepressible jauntiness. Their sails surge like the puffed up chests of strutting pigeons. I am reminded too of the joyous porpoises that delight in keeping sailors company.

It was off the coast of Portugal that we lost sight of the *Gallego* which I had placed under the command of Laurence Keymis. I cannot quite shake off the notion that he has set his course to follow the gaze of his wayward eye.

I pray that he is not lost to me.

Baron Effingham's frigate *Lion's Whelp* we left in Plymouth. I could not waste a favourable wind just because she was not ready to sail with us. Likewise we were obliged to leave behind the four ships commanded by Captain Preston. I pray and trust and believe that we shall see them all again in due course.

To compensate me for this scattering of my intended fleet, I have garnered vessels along the way. Portingale carvels and fishing boats, as well a Flemish trader stocked with butts of sack. I know that such mean prizes, the mere fruit of picory, will fall a long way short of impressing my sovereign. But they serve to refresh and reward my crews. They are like cats, who chase and kill for amusement as much for appetite. The sight of the prizes behind us plumps them up with pride and is encouragement for the greater battles to come.

For we bear letters patent from Her Majesty granting us licence to annoy the Spanish King. Which is to say, we are licensed to spill Spanish blood. Should the Spanish learn the true purpose of our mission, I do not doubt they will engage to prevent us.

## The Black Lake

A vast expanse of black, desolate and stagnant, spreads before me. I reckon it to be two miles at least in its width. If it is land, nothing can grow here. If it is liquid, nothing can swim in it. It is a place of nothing.

The fresh air flees in horror from its sulphurous fumes, so that every breath now is a violent assault, an invisible fist punching out our lungs.

Islands of scaly crust float upon its surface, with veins of inky liquid standing between them. One may walk upon the hardened sections to peel off and harvest the layers of pitch. The floating plates sink and bob underfoot in a manner that brings to mind the shifts of a ship's deck. I feel my seasickness return in unwelcome waves. The native guides who have led us here make us to understand that the crust we step upon may at any time give way and the lake swallow us up entire. They seem to speak of it as a living thing. Or rather as a vast mouth belonging to a beast of immense size. I imagine it to be a sunken Leviathan. Its gaping maw open to drink in all the energy of the world.

From time to time it regurgitates the objects – and creatures – which it has previously consumed. But this regurgitation is wondrous slow. Everywhere I see the mysterious forms that are created by this process. It is impossible to say what the object bubbling up might be. But the protrusions and excrescences that disrupt the otherwise flat surface have a strange hold over me. They appear to have been shaped by a blind sculptor who has no conception of the true shape of things, but only a desperate yearning for form. Here and there I see what appear to be limbs reaching out skyward, as if they are the arms of men grasping for a handhold to pull them out. Elsewhere, our blind sculptor has been busy giving shape to the creatures of his half-crazed imagination. In their ponderous bulk, these remind me of etchings I have seen of beasts such as hippopotami, rhinoceroses and elephants. Or they are small whales petrified in the moment of breaching the surf.

Here and there, the lake bubbles with a viscous torpidity. It is with just such a liquid that I fancy the river Styx flows.

I would that Laurence Keymis was with us, or Henry Percy, the Earl of Northumberland, or my brother Adrian Gilbert. I fain would talk with them of philosophical matters. I wish to know more of that process in the great Alchemical Work philosophers call the Nigredo. It shortly precedes the discovery of the Philosopher's Stone. I have heard Laurence say that one cannot have the sublime transmutation without first knowing this bitter, foul descent into utter darkness.

I cannot help reflecting that the end point of our voyage, which is to say the discovery of the city Manoa, which the Spanish call El Dorado, is the equivalent to the end point of the Alchemical Work, the creation of gold from base matter. And so this moment, the discovery of the Black Lake in Trinidad, is the Nigredo of our voyage.

187

I follow a native guide out into the centre of the lake. We cannot proceed by walking in a straight line, but must pick out our route by stepping across the jet black channels where they are narrowest. At times, the crusted plates rock unsteadily beneath our tread. There is an art to timing our progress so that we each balance out the other's leaps and bounds. Sometimes we seem to double back on ourselves or are forced to flee the centre before we may approach it. It is as if we are walking through an invisible labyrinth, on a ground that we cannot wholly trust. I am ever conscious that the next step I take may be my last.

I close my eyes to envisage the utter blackness I will experience should I be swallowed. I imagine the thick noxious treacle flooding into my mouth and nostrils.

The plate I am standing on, from which I now find I cannot move, begins to quake.

My guide must have sensed my sudden paralysis. He looks back at me over his shoulder. He says something in a language I do not understand. His face is calm and unsurprised. His eyes are darker than the pitch that surrounds me.

He continues on his way. I follow him.

He comes to a stop in front of an open pool of glistening black liquid. We are at the very centre of the lake.

The liquid pitch possesses a strange quality. I discern that it is not black at all. A swarm of colours swim and swirl together: purple, green, red, blue, silver, aye and even gold. There are the inchoate makings of another world here. I am put in mind of the scrying stones, or crystals, used by John Dee.

As I behold that restless mirror, I become aware of a transformation taking place in its fundamental nature. My gaze is suddenly engulfed by the churning depths of the lake. I cannot say with any certainty that I have not fallen into the pool. Except that, as far as I can tell, I am still alive.

I am surrounded now entirely by the teeming colours, darkly intense, drawing their unearthly vibrancy from the unfathomed bottom of the immense well of pitch. Smooth rounded shapes, like drifting jelly fish, circle around me. They twitch and writhe.

On a sudden I recognise what these shapes resemble: the last throes of life spasming through the mounds of bodies at Smerwick. The colours take on a soft golden cast. As if the image that is presented to me is meant as consolation.

But the twitching of the bodies continues interminably. An equal, contrary assertion of the image's ugliness and horror.

At last the twitching slows to an even throb, in time with my heart. The golden cast mutates to a blood red. The shapes are no longer bodies, but pulsating ovoid forms. One of these eggs bursts, and a golden baby swims out. I recognise the child as my own daughter Alice Gould, when she was first born. She looks at me with her wide, trusting eyes and giggles. A golden bubble escapes from her mouth, contained in which is all the innocence and joy of her soul. I reach out towards my daughter, but my hands pass through her phantom body. As they do so, I feel an icy numbness. I see that the baby is longer golden, but blue. Nor is it Alice any more, but my poor dead son Damerei. The little corpse floats up above my head, out of my reach.

The formless shapes and many colours of the lake are swallowed up immediately in an infinite blackness. As if the sun has passed behind an immense edifice, whose shadow falls over everything.

## Caulking

We find the Trinidadian pitch excellent good, and far better suited to these southern climes than the pitch of Norway. It melts not in the hot sun. The shipwrights mix it with tallow and spread it with sheepskin mops. It is a paradox no doubt that by painting this Hellish paste onto our beams we secure our own Salvation.

The caulking completed, we head our small fleet north along the western coast of Trinidad towards Puerto de los Hispanioles. The name exercises a grim hold over us.

It is true that, regardless of the enmity of our two nations, there exists among the wider brotherhood of mariners a kindred sympathy that is evidenced whenever we sit down together across the table. It is then that we see the humanity in our enemy's eyes. We are all aware that we are Christians in a heathen land. There are times when the hand of friendship may accomplish more than the fist of aggression. Out here, where both sides are so far adrift from the official policies of our respective courts and councils, we must make up our own policy as we proceed.

We are not savages. We are civilised beings. I trust we are capable of conducting ourselves as such.

In the meantime, I daily look for the arrival of our other ships, for this is our assigned rendezvous. We would do well to proceed with caution until our forces are reunited.

Off Puerto de los Hispaniolos, we sight a small company of Spanish soldiers guarding the descent. And they us. In truth, it is my belief that we have been closely watched the whole extent of our coasting. On the flagship at least, we make no secret of our country of origin or our loyalty, with the red cross of Saint George aloft at the halyard, and trails of Tudor green bunting flapping in the breeze.

In response, the Spaniards raise the Saint George's Cross alongside the Cross of Burgundy. We take it as a sign of peace and drop anchor in the harbour.

I exchange a loaded glance with Jacob Whiddon, a seasoned grey-beard who has much experience of the Spanish in these parts. It was Whiddon, when captain of my privateer *Serpent*, who captured Pedro Sarmiento de Gamboa. It is only fitting that he is here with me now. I do not think he would wish to be anywhere else.

'You will go ashore and talk with them.'

'Aye, Admiral.'

'Let not be known our true intent.'

'You may be assured.'

There is history here, which weights his words with heavy irony. Last year I sent Captain Whiddon to these parts and he had dealings with the Spaniards. Their governor Don de Berrio, having led Captain Whiddon away on some pretext, promised safe passage to his men, allowing them to put ashore for water and foraging. Whereupon a company of Spanish troops did ambush them, slaughtering eight of their number.

'If any ask, say that we are bound only for the relief of those English I have already planted in Virginia.'

'Aye aye, Sir.'

'By all means have them come aboard. Let them know we will receive them hospitably. Show yourself to be their friend. Tell them we have new linens to trade. And wine, which we will gladly share with them. I would talk with them. I would have news of their Don de Berrio.'

Captain Whiddon bows assent.

## Discovery

We give them the run of our ship. They think it means that we have nothing to hide from them.

Our musicians play Moorish airs and sentimental tunes. The Spaniards weep. We put our arms around their shoulders. We fill their cups again. We join them in a toast to their mothers. To hear the word *Madre* bandied about so liberally, I cannot help thinking back to the great ship of plunder.

We are careful not to bring our own mothers into this. I fear that such fastidiousness will be our undoing. But the Spaniards are too deep in their cups to remark upon such nuances now.

I give them tokens to bear to their governor, Don de Berrio, a gold ring, symbolic of my goodwill and integrity. As well as a letter filled with my assurances. I place at his disposal what men or ammunition I have, to join with him in the pacification of the country. I have him to understand that we are conquerors of the Indies and that we are more than willing to make common cause with fellow Christians against the heathen tribes. I may even lead him to understand that I am one of those English gentlemen who have Catholic sympathies. In short, I say whatever it is necessary to say to win his trust.

I cut my teeth cozening my cousins in Middle Temple Hall, and before that in the taverns of La Rochelle, as Barnacle for a gang of conning soldiers. The stakes are higher now. We play for fortune and for life itself. But the game is still the same. 'Tis the game of conning dupes. The game I have been playing all my life, which some might call my career.

As well as the soldiers of the Spanish guard, but separately from them, we entertain some Indians of those parts. With these we drink tobacco and the strong liquor that they favour. We fill my cabin with thick clouds of pungent smoke.

I judge it politic not to let the Spaniards see the naturals, nor vice versa.

Amongst the Indians is a local cacique called Cantyman. By cacique, I mean he is a kind of princeling or chieftain of theirs. He holds himself with a noble bearing, as befits his standing. I warrant the Spaniards do not take kindly to his pride, being jealous of their own.

Cantyman speaks in a low rhythmic chant. From time to time he waits for our interpreter to translate his words for us. The interpreter is an Indian I brought with us from England, who now goes by the name of John Provost. It is curious that Cantyman fixes me with his gaze as John Provost speaks, as if to reassure himself that I am appreciating the full import of his words. He has news of Don de Berrio to impart, as well as valuable intelligence concerning the dispositions of Spanish defences. At the same time, I am transfixed by the dark flow of incomprehensible sounds that come directly from him. While he speaks, I cannot take my eyes from his mouth.

We learn that Don de Berrio has recently returned from another discovery of the interior of Guiana. He has a great determination to locate the city of

Manoa, or El Dorado as he would call it. Despite this, it continues to elude him. I grow more eager than ever to speak with him. According to Cantyman, Don de Berrio has now retired to the city he founded, San José, which lies ten miles inland from Puerto de los Hispaniolos.

Cantyman's voice drops to a barely audible whisper, and we strain to catch words we have no hope of understanding. We know, however, that he is telling us of something direful and dread. The interpreter lowers his voice to match Cantyman. He speaks of the cruelty and treachery of the Spaniard. Of how Don de Berrio has captured certain of Cantyman's fellow caciques and has tortured them by ordering hot fat to be dripped onto their naked skin.

It is clear that by his oppressive policies, Don de Berrio has destroyed all hope of friendship with the local populace and has in fact driven them into our hands. If I do but deal fairly and gently with them, I do not doubt I shall win their loyalty and support. I assure Cantyman of the enmity that exists between my own nation and that of the Spaniard. I tell him of the great love and sympathy that my Queen does bear towards his people. And how it is her earnest wish to deliver them from the yoke of Spanish oppression.

As to the strength of Spanish forces in the town of San José, Cantyman is able to reassure us that they are capable of being overcome, and that we may count on the aid of Indian fighters to achieve it. All that is required is that we act decisively and quickly, so as to secure the advantage of surprise.

Some discoveries cannot be made in the open light of day. The sky above Puerto de los Hispaniolos still bears the last luminescence of the dying day. A few smudges of charcoal clouds are smeared over a thin grey wash, encompassing the whole sky in sweeping trails. They seem to correspond to something in my soul. There is something benign about that sky that seems almost complicit. Its beauty is a great distraction from what we are about to do.

The last clatter of a flock of cranes returning to roost is all that disrupts the peace. And soon they are quiet too. All that we can hear is the water sighing in the harbour with a kind of listless inertia as it bears the chinking boats.

The whispering splash of oars as our landing boats breach the imminent night.

By the time we moor the boats, the moon is out. My Luna. I feel a yearning surge within me, upwards to her, the old familiar tidal pull.

The sky is inked in now. The night's infinite expanse evident in the depths upon depths of stars revealed.

Captain Calfield is the commander of the soldiery, a silhouette commanding shadows. Captain Whiddon is at his ear, whispering directions as to the arrangements of the harbour. Calfield nods tersely in acknowledgement, before translating the intelligence into a series of sharp arm movements.

It is done quickly, as well it were. There is just time enough to see the change in the quality of the Spaniards' surprise. First when we burst in on them, their eyes are lit with a sort of mild confusion, such as one experiences when one receives an unannounced visit from an important personage and hurries to button up one's doublet. Captain Whiddon says something to them in Spanish, which as far as I am able to judge pertains somewhat to their mothers. It is then that I think they take in the significance of a detail which cannot have escaped their notice: that we all have our blades already drawn. And so, that mild confusion changes in an instant to terrible understanding.

Some of them are already drunk, on wine that we sold them. They make as if to stagger to their feet. Captain Calfield and his men push them back.

There are cries, from them and us alike. You cannot put a man to the sword without yelling in his face. It cannot be done.

And so a discovery is made. That we were never their friends.

And another and another. That a man contains much blood. And may take a long tedious time dying.

I count nineteen dead in all.

## He is not surprised

Don de Berrio does me the honour of not being surprised.

It is as if each day begins with the sudden eruption of English voices, with cries of *Peace! Peace!* startling the cockerels.

He sees which way the land lies.

There is no discounting the appearance of one hundred English soldiers in his capital. Nor the presence among them of numerous sullen naturals, who eye him with a certain vengeful concentration. Cantyman's Indians are not cannibals, but they look for the moment that they could be persuaded to take up that evil practice.

He cannot be surprised by that. For here, chained together in the open, are the five famished and tortured caciques, their naked skins bursting with festering blisters from the dripping of hot bacon fat. Flies hover around their sores. Their manacled wrists and leg-ironed ankles are chafed raw by the rusted restraints.

But it is their Spanish guard who is dejected now, as we hold a good English blade to his throat.

Cantyman recites each one of the caciques' names as they are released, as if reaffirming their existence.

Wannawanare.

Carroaori.

Maquarima.

Tarroopana.

Aterima.

And as he says each name, he embraces the man.

He is all for killing Don de Berrio. Don de Berrio betrays no surprise at this, nor at my intercession on his behalf. He knows, as Cantyman does not, that the rules of engagement require us to spare the officers of rank among our enemies. (He knows too that, in return for their lives, we may expect a liberal ransom.)

By the same token, he is not surprised when I give the order for the guard's throat to be opened.

Don de Berrio registers no surprise, neither at those we kill, nor those we do not. He gives the impression that it is all the same to him.

San José is not so much a town as an encampment of shoddy wooden huts in a scrubby clearing. One hut is designated church. Another, the largest, serves as a Franciscan convent. More a triumph of nomenclature than a true town. But we live in a time of symbols. This rough camp serves as symbol of the Spanish hegemony in these parts. Just as its burning, after we have emptied it of anything of value, serves as the symbol of its end.

Again, Don de Berrio betrays no surprise. He merely wrinkles his nose at the acrid smoke, as if it is only the smell that he objects to.

This Don de Berrio is one of those lean, long-lived men. There is nothing but what is essential about him: His limbs are wiry, his cheekbones sharp, his skin, roasted to a deep nut-brown leather, his youth has long deserted him, but not his vigour. He shows no sign of being cowed by the prospect of mortality. He is every bit the soldier and the gentleman, and stands up to the world with a constant, upright valour. True, his gait is somewhat faltering and he is obliged from time to time to lean upon his lieutenant, Alvaro Jorge, but his eyes are fierce and piercing blue.

He directs their gaze towards me. We are in my cabin on the flagship, where I am determined to entertain him with all the civility that is due his rank.

He reminds me of his compatriot Pedro Sarmiento de Gamboa. And I cannot resist passing on to him the words the other conquistador once said: 'I was warned by one that knows you that you would be either dead or mad by the time I found you. Else you would have succeeded in locating that city of Manoa, which you call El Dorado. I congratulate you on being both alive and sane, and yet I can only presume you have failed in your search for the gold of El Dorado.'

'Have you come here to look for Manoa yourself?'

I engineer a shrug: 'I have heard the stories. Of Pedro de Urzúa and of his mutinous lieutenant Aguirre. If I have learnt one thing, it is the impossibility of ever finding this fabled city.'

Outrage flares in Don de Berrio's eyes. 'It is no fable! What of Juan Martínez? Did you not hear tell of him?'

I bow for Don de Berrio to continue.

'Juan Martínez was master of munitions for General Diego Ordas on his campaign into Guiana. There was an accident. The entire supply of gunpowder went up in smoke. Martínez was blamed. General Ordas sentenced him to death. He was set adrift alone in a canoe, which is to say, he was left for dead.'

'And?'

'He was rescued by Carib Indians.'

Don de Berrio widens his eyes, inviting me to fill in the significance of this detail for myself: 'They led him to Manoa?'

He gives a sharp, triumphant nod: 'He saw the place with his own eyes! And lived to tell the tale! I swear to you, it is no fable. Juan Martínez left detailed descriptions of its streets and buildings, from which it is possible to construct reliable maps. I have seen the deposition myself. It is a city of immense extent. It takes two whole days to cross from one side to the other.'

'Why then is it so hard to find it?'

'You do not know what it is to venture into that land. The rivers form a very labyrinth of water. The forests are impenetrable. The mountains disappear into the clouds. However you approach it, you will before too long lose your way entirely.'

'Why, Don Antonio! I had not thought to go looking for it before now; and if what you say is true, then I confess I should have no desire to make the essay. Besides, I have a more pressing mission than chasing chimeras. You will have heard of my colony in Roanoke. We are bound for there, to bring relief to those that remain.'

'I pray to God that you speak the truth, for your own sakes. The rivers that lead to the interior of Guiana are impassable to boats. Even the naturals are often grounded in their canoes. The way is long. Winter is at hand. The rivers will begin to swell, whereupon you will find it impossible to stem the current. Your boats will be washed away and smashed. You will find the Indians hostile and unwilling to trade with you.'

'There speaks a Spaniard! You will know that I have gone out of my way to show myself a friend to the local peoples. I have given them more gold than I have taken from them.'

'It will avail you naught. To them, you are a Christian. From Christians they expect only destruction and dispossession.'

'I have come as their liberator, not their oppressor.'

I see him lean back in his seat. He cocks his head to regard me closely. His eyes narrow in suspicion (but not surprise, never surprise): 'You are determined to enter Guiana, after all?'

He has caught me in a lie. No matter. He is my prisoner. I may use him as I wish. If I cannot deceive him into telling me what I would know, then I will not shrink from more direct and persuasive means.

'The land has been too long a virgin; The time is ripe to pierce its maidenhead.'

He shakes his head sadly. But he is not surprised.

### Forsooth

Don Berrio staggers like a drunken bear. His hands are bound behind his back. He must kick his feet in a high-stepping march as he is dragged through the crystal-rippled shallows. He must feel it as a gross insult, to hear the coarse laughter of the common English soldiery. He falls into the crashing surf and must be hauled to his feet by the halter around his neck. He is thoroughly drenched now. The weight of his clothes makes it even harder for him to go on. Even so, his spirit is not yet broken. I can still detect the conquistador's haughty snoop cocked at fate.

'Captain Calfield, have your men fire above his head. Try not to kill him. I would have him alive yet awhile.'

As the volley of musket fire is discharged, Don Berrio ducks his head in a most craven and pathetic manner. He stands not so tall now, methinks. The men are delighted to see him brought so low. In truth, it affords me little pleasure to subject the old hidalgo to this humiliation, but I had grown weary of treating him with civility. It had borne but little fruit.

We leave him sprawled on the sand like a strange weed-tangled sea creature that we have unexpectedly landed.

## The ebb tide and the flood

The day we burnt San José to the ground, we were at last reunited with the other ships of our small fleet, the *Gallego* and Captain Cross's bark.

It may be imagined how my heart leapt to see again my good friend Laurence Keymis. His bifurcate gaze swam wildly about him.

I had commissioned Captain Douglas to make trial of the Orinoco Delta, in order to scout the most propitious route for our discovery. It was the intelligence he reported back, concerning the depth of the approaches, that decided me to have the carpenters set to work on the *Gallego*. I knew that the shallow gulf would prove unnavigable to any true ocean-going craft, and yet her capacity was such that I was loath to leave her behind. She could hold as many as sixty men and their kit. The carpenters sawed away at her upper structures, throwing up clouds of wood dust, which settled to reveal a stunted and denuded relic. She sat higher in the water now, but with a slightly shamefaced air about her, like a newly shorn sheep. The proud galleon that she had once been was reduced to something like an oversized barge.

We put the discarded timbers to good use. With the help of the local people, we built a fort and claimed the island of Trinidad for our Queen. I had raised a pole to bear Her Majesty's arms. I do avow that when the Arawak Caribs of those parts gazed upon the Royal Virgin's portrait, they rejoiced to find themselves now under her protection. One of their number, to whom the Spanish had given the name Ferdinando, was pleased to come with us to act as guide for our voyage.

We set sail from Los Gallos Point at the south-westernmost tip of the island of Trinidad, a company of one hundred sundry gentlemen, soldiers, adventurers, labourers and oarsmen, as well as our surgeon Nicholas Mellechap, my cabin boy Hugh Goodwin, and one Christopher Fillis, a Negro and a very proper young man. Accompanying us were four Arawak canoes, in which were borne Ferdinando and his brothers and several of their wives. John Provost, our interpreter, travelled with the English company. The distance from there to the mainland coast is as great as that from Dover to Calais. We were obliged to cross this wide channel in our little boats and sawn-down *Gallego*, hoisting anchors at sunrise when the tide was just beginning its ebb. By the afternoon, we were riding the flood tide at its highest over the bar. The moon, my own dear Cynthia, was on our side, as I had hoped. It was a spring tide, as happens after a full moon, and so we were in no danger of beaching. But it was not all plain sailing. Once the tide had turned, the wind was against the incoming current. A great billow arose that churned the seas into a mighty ferment. The men were thrown one against the other. Water crashed in and spoiled the victuals, as well as drenching the suits we were in, the only suits we have. But we could see the coast before us now, the screen of trees at the land's edge, dark, impenetrable, unwelcoming.

We were at the mercy of the Trade Wind and the Spring Tide. It was wondrous to see the skill with which the Indians in their dug-out canoes rode the boisterous breaking waves and guided us to safe harbour sheltered in the curving lee of the land.

The land scraped against our hulls as we hauled the boats ashore. At last I felt the New World underfoot, kicking through the lapping shallows to reach it. The wet sand was soft and yielding, not quite land, but some liminal state between elements.

That first night came on quickly, as all nights do here. We raced to pitch camp, gathering firewood and clearing the ground. I felt the crossing's toll in my aching limbs and in the turmoil of my guts. A mighty quivering beset me that I could do nothing to suppress. I felt that the only way I might find relief from it would be to weep. It took all my powers of concentration not to do so. But I could not quell the shaking. Fortunately, the darkness concealed it from the others. And they were all too occupied in their tasks to pay me much notice. I was grateful for that. Had anyone addressed me, I know that I would have been unable to answer.

The following day we put to the river, making our entrance to the New World along a branch of the delta that was at its head as broad as the Thames at Woolwich. In this we followed Captain Whiddon's recommendation. A strong tidal current bore us speedily along, and in a few days we had covered a marvellous great distance. The densely screened banks rushed by. We pulled fruit down from the overhanging boughs and felt that it would not be long before we were walking the streets of Manoa, blinded by the flash of the gold croissants on the naturals who would welcome us there as their friends.

In the midst of such daydreams, we followed Ferdinando into a turning.

How long ago that was, is hard to say. We have been so long caught in this criss-crossing of rivers and streams, the watery labyrinth of which Don de Berrio forewarned. I hardly dare trust the tally of days that I tick off. Sometimes day and night are confused beneath the thick awning of leaves above us.

I sense the men's despondency grow apace with each turning that takes us nowhere. Or worse, back to a place that it seems we have been before. Even good Laurence Keymis, I fear, has begun to lose faith.

Myself, saving a miracle, I see no way out of here. I say nothing of my fears to anyone. I only sit in the prow of the pollarded *Gallego,* straining my eyes to penetrate the flickering vista ahead for sight of some variation that may signify our salvation. Straining my will to make it appear.

The Arawaks in their canoes are as lost as any of us. If my men were not so wearied and afeared, they would turn on them, but the Indians at least know where to look for turtle eggs, which is now all that is keeping us - and them - alive.

On a sudden I see the tail of something vanish round the bend ahead of us. A native canoe? I stand and urge my oarsmen on to greater exertion. They rally to my cries, though they have their backs to the prize we pursue. There are gentlemen now among the rowers, relieving those who are exhausted. All must play their part now.

The crudely dug-out trunk of a tree comes into view, shooting over the water, like an arrow in flight. It rocks precariously from side to side, as the three Indians rowing it lean their shoulders into each stroke. They show no sign of slacking their pace. We know that the Spaniards spread rumours about us English, that we are cannibals. That we will make captives of them, dispossess them of their land, eat their stores of food, rape their wives and daughters. That we will plunder their graves of gold.

In truth, it would not surprise me to discover that the fleeing Indians mistake us for Spaniards, who are themselves guilty of all that of which they accuse us.

We gain on the fleeing canoe. I have John Provost call out to them, assuring them of our goodwill, and above all informing them that we are not Spanish. This has the desired effect and they back paddle to hold their position in the water.

It is now that the dense screen of vegetation that borders the river shivers and divides. On both banks, lines of naked Indians step forward to reveal themselves. We have been watched all along, it seems.

I see that they bear bows, which are already charged with arrows. Poisoned, I presume. They do not yet aim them at us. But the presence of these arms is clearly meant as a warning. The dogs at their feet snarl with hostile intent.

I command my own soldiers to keep their hands away from their guns.

According to John Provost, these Indians are of the Ciawani Warao people, a grouping of the northern Tivitivas. They are said to be fiercely jealous of their independence and deliberately choose the most inaccessible places for their villages. Nevertheless, those in the canoe converse amiably enough with the Arawak Indians of our own party.

At my invitation, one of their number is helped aboard our barge, which we moor at the mouth of a creek.

He is an old man, somewhat bowed and short of stature with a deeply wrinkled face and a little pot belly. We show him the things we have brought to trade. The mirrors, goblets, and gold pieces. I have made it my policy not to fob the naturals off with worthless trinkets as the Spaniards do.

Those on the banks watch all the while in silence, holding their bows still drawn and ready to take aim. It is soon agreed that Ferdinando and one of his brothers shall go ashore to visit the village of their new friends, which we are told is some way along the creek. They are promised supplies of food, fresh water and Indian wine to bring back for our journey.

No sooner have they scrambled onto the bank than the Ciawanis lay hands upon them. There is some sudden change in the temper of the Ciawanis. A revelation of true intent. It is not just the dogs who snarl now.

Ferdinando and his brother increase their efforts to escape. First the brother succeeds in breaking free, and the commotion that ensues allows Ferdinando to escape too. Both men vanish into the bush. Urgent shouts from those who let them get away. They let slip the dogs and a party of men runs after them.

They will hunt the fugitives down like animals.

Those who did not give chase keep a watchful eye on us. They silently lift their bows and take aim.

The realisation strikes me: it all may end here. This is to be the pinnacle and summation of my career. All my hopes and ambitions. All my years of planning and projection. The careful schooling of my sea captains. The courting of courtiers for their backing and boosting. My slow, long, sideways approach to Her Majesty. My aching nostalgia for her presence. My desperate craving for rehabilitation. It will all end now.

Our bodies will never be found. The rump I left in Trinidad will wait until the onset of winter before concluding that we are lost. They will return to England in utter failure.

Captain Whiddon mutters darkly at my back: 'Only give the order. It will be a moment's work to wipe them out. Or at least, we will teach them to fear our firearms.'

'Wait.'

We can see nothing of the chase. But can only hear the barking of dogs and the cries of the running men within the forest. These sounds are widely dispersed, on either side of the creek. This, I think, bodes well for our two Indians. It is my hope that they have had the wit to separate.

On a sudden, their fellow Arawaks begin to shout excitedly, pointing to a dark shape moving through the water towards us. The surface of the river breaks and a man's head appears. He dives again and swims sleekly. He is like a serpent gliding. It is a matter of moments before Ferdinando's brother is hauling himself back into his canoe.

It is only now that I remember the old man who came aboard earlier. In truth my attention is drawn to him by a movement he makes to escape from our boat.

'Seize him!'

I call for John Provost.

'Make him to understand that his life will be forfeit unless Ferdinando is returned to us safely.'

The old man responds to John Provost's ultimatum with a long and agitated speech.

'Is no good, Guatterale. The Ciawani Warao do not respect their old. They will leave him to die. One less old man to feed.'

As if to prove the point, the Ciaweani in the canoe begin to row away, abandoning him to his fate. The old man remonstrates with them, but to no avail.

I draw my sword and hold it to his neck.

'We will cut off his head! Tell them that!'

John Provost passes on my message. The Ciawani there do not exactly laugh at the threat, but I have to confess they seem unduly troubled by it. Unlike the old man we have hold of.

At that point the sound of splashing draws our attention and we see Ferdinando plunging into the river, at a point downstream. His exhaustion shows in the untidiness of his strokes. To cover the final stretch of his escape, I order an arquebus to be discharged into the air.

At its startling report, the Ciawani on the bank vanish. We are left with the old man. I sheath my sword and push him away from me. He sprawls on his face in the bottom of the galley.

He seems as relieved as us to see the back of his fellows.

## Further discoveries

At our approach, clouds of wondrous birds burst into flight: the pink of a post-coital blush; the scarlet of a bloody droplet standing on pinpricked skin; the coral blue conceived in the marriage of Sky and Sea; the sundrunk yellow of a helianthus petal; the effulgent green of a midday midsummer meadow; such are the pigments in which their feathers are dipped. If it were a tapestry of silken threads, I could believe in it, but to see such fierce and fiery colours in Nature, blazoned on living wings, I must count it all a vision. They put the dun birds of England quite to shame.

We eat fruits that taste every bit as gorgeous as these colours strike our eyes, unless the flux deters us from such banquets. But the Indians of our party know well which plants to pick to cure all manner of diseases. It is a knowledge that I am most desirous to learn from them, a treasure even richer than the promised gold mayhap is hidden in the undergrowth, and may be plucked and gathered with little labour and less hazard.

With John Provost to translate for us, I and Laurence Keymis venture out on a foraging party with the old Tivitivian man. Before too long I have filled a bag with a mass of pungent cuttings, and a notebook with copious notes and drawings. The properties and descriptions of each specimen are carefully logged. Laurence approves of my method, which he admits to be *most scientific.* The old man waxes marvellous loquacious and I note down the sundry recipes that John Provost relates.

This leaf may be ground into a paste and applied to wounds to prevent them from festering.

The bark of this bush may be boiled to derive a gum into which the tip of an arrow may be dipped, rendering it fatally poisonous.

And here is the shrub from which may be derived the antidote.

These seeds, when dried and ground and mixed with the oil of the palm tree, have a soothing effect upon skin that has been burnt by the sun.

This grass, when stewed in boiling water, produces a marvellous purgative.

These berries, when eaten, will loosen the bowels.

The bark of this willow may be dried and ground and taken to relieve all manner of gripes and pains, whether in the head, the teeth, the sinews, bones and joints - but not in the belly, for which the unripe fruit of this tree must be eaten.

Forsooth, our old Indian knows more about the curative properties of flora than any English apothecary. And so, there are wonders here that I trust will be most gratefully received by the people of England, not least by their Queen, who suffers from many of the indispositions and infirmities that savage age inflicts.

By the time we return to the boats, my bag is bulging with specimens. I trust it will prove to be a most profitable foraging.

We reach a village of houses built high on wooden piles, and are welcomed with keen interest and amiable curiosity. It is more than humbling to realise the extent of my gratitude to these Indians. They are the answer to my prayers! How did it come to this? That I should come to be utterly reliant on a naked savage?

But I have always trusted to God. And I must trust that it is by God's divine will that we are now delivered from our present dangers. As we stride into the village, reviving at the odours of cooking, of fresh cassava bread and roasted deer, I begin to believe that I never truly did abandon hope, after all. How could I doubt my destiny? I must look upon these Indians as the instruments of God's Providence. Nothing happens that is outside God's will.

We join the Tivitivians in their rude banquet, crouched upon the beaten ground. Never has food tasted so good to me.

The cacique invites us to partake with them in the drinking of tobacco smoke.

The men of this village are prodigious drinkers of tobacco. There is a wild hunger to their imbibing. They do not so much drink the smoke as devour it. Their cheeks fill. Their eyes careen. The bowls of their pipes gurgle and whisper and an occult discourse begins.

I am told by John Provost that tobacco drinking is for them a form of religious communion. They believe that the smoke truly enters their souls and the two essences commingle. From what I witness, I believe it too. These men's faces speak of the surrender and swoon of some inner coitus.

At the height of their ecstasy, they rise from their haunches and prance around the fire. They screech like owls and flap their arms as if they are about to take flight.

It is startling, outlandish conduct. We English watch in stupefied amazement. But our first amazement is as nothing to that which grips us when we see them at last alight, their feet truly departing from the ground.

Lo, they rise and circle with the spiralling sparks from the fire! We are drawn by their example to rise to our feet ourselves. And somehow the power of the smoke has entered us too, though we are Christians to a man, and not followers of their heathen creed. Mayhap, if God has brought us to this place, as I earnestly believe, then He has brought us here for a purpose. It must be His will to become immanent within the smoke and so commune with us.

The smoke is alive. The Holy Ghost is in the smoke. I feel the smoke invade my blood. My blood becomes smoke, a swirling cloud of questing grey.

I feel myself rise and float and swirl and spiral. I drift exquisitely in a languorous dance with flaming motes, small planets of incandescence. My smoke, the smoke that I am become, mingles with the smoke of the fire and the smoke that the others have become. We are one in smoke, heathen and Christian alike.

Oh, and such visions are we afforded! Such discoveries we make!

I am a rolling billow of smoke chasing along one of the narrow streams of the labyrinth of rivers. The trees that crowd the banks lean over, as if in slow, petrified flight from the darkness at the forest heart. Monstrous shapes show in their half-drowned roots. As I pass, the roots come to life and writhe in a silent, vegetal agony.

I am spewed out onto a broad river. It is a raging torrent. The flood waters rise with unstoppable force and breathtaking speed. I see a foraging party ford a stream. They drag their feet through the plashing shallows. When they return, the same stream is up to their shoulders and they must lift their arms and the fruits of their foraging over their heads.

I feel something pull at the roiling particles of my smoky being.

It is the distant city of Manoa.

Deer come down to the river to drink. They lift their heads and flick their ears and sniff the breeze as I roll my way past them.

Above their antlers I see in the distance a ridge of mottled blue. The mountains of Guiana.

I feel myself drawing closer. On the right track at last. The proof comes when I discover an Indian basket abandoned in the bushes. I wheedle in between the wicker weave. Inside I find a Spanish gold refiner's necessaries: quicksilver, saltpetre and divers things for the trial of metals.

And there, at last I see it! The city of Manoa, which the Spanish call El Dorado! It flickers briefly before me. The smoke has revealed it to me. It is the will of God that I should find it.

My vision shows me that all I had heard tell about the city is true. It is founded on a mountain lake. The mountain pierces the clouds, and is at its summit a great triangular plateau, with the lake in its centre. When viewed from above, as I now am able to view it, it appears like a hull of a ship cutting through an ocean of cloud. The mountain is formed from pure crystal. When the sun strikes it, the light scatters into a rainbow fan.

Here is the lake in which the fabled king bathed to wash off the powdered gold that had been blown onto his oiled skin. The lake spills out into a mighty cataract of formidable extent, an immense ribbon of shimmering lace stretched out across one side of the mountain.

The cataract thunders into a broad river, which it strikes with the sound of a thousand church bells ringing. The mist it throws up sparkles with iridescent colours.

The deer bow their heads to drink the water once more. As if they would lap up the gold.

I see the gold seams in the very pebbles and rocks that lie along the shore. There for the picking! I send out wispy tendrils to curl around them. But the stones slip through my insubstantial grasp. I am freighted with woe and melancholy. Defeat saps my billowing course.

I start to feel the the smoke ebb from my soul.

The earth's tug and the return of corporeality.

A wave of nausea, far worse than anything I have ever experienced as a sailor, crashes through me. With it, grief at the smoke's departing. For God is leaving me.

I feel the last wisps of smoke disentangle from my soul. My quivering heart begins to quell. My limbs are suddenly returned to me. I hit the ground with a shocking jolt. A violent stream of liquid vomit shoots out from my mouth.

## The river gives, the river takes

Our negro, the very proper young fellow, dives into the river from his boat. His form and the dive he is executing achieve a unity of physical perfection. It is beyond admirable. It is breathtaking: a moment of wondrous privilege. His head disappears beneath the surface of the water and he glides away from us in a succession of strong, decisive strokes. We pale Englishmen who cower in the boats are quietly envious of him. But then we see the long dark shape approach him. We can do nothing to save him. (But would we if we could? I cannot say for sure. Such is the strange dark potency of envy.) His head breaks the water as his body is thrashed about by the great monster that has him in its jaws. His screams die in our ears just before he is dragged down into the darkening water. The foam that bubbles up is red flecked.

## A relic of a man

*Alas!* The land, the dream, the hope recedes.
And fair Guiana turns her back on me.
All told, a hold devoid of gold is all
I have to show for my adventurings.
That and the basket of refiner's tools.
A hollow hold indeed. We've ballast though!
Some rocks with yellow seams I gathered up
May yet unfold the tale of riches hid
Within the bounteous bosom of the land.
To while away the tedious hours at sea,
I school a native youth who sails with us.
I teach him English ways and words, so he
May speak of all the riches of his land
To those who'll come to wonder at his face.
His name is… hard to say. So *Harry* does.
I'll school the court in my discoveries,
Or else I shall be taken for a fool,
And th'only gold I have be counted fool's,
And all my company, a crew of fools.
Too cruel! Already do I rue the day
I first heard tell of El Dorado's wealth
And vowed to venture on this enterprise.
Was't all in vain? The river's winter spate
Did force us beaten back before we came
To rich Manoa, her golden hoard to claim.


*At last!* We land, in England. Back to skies
Of grey, and birds of dun, and hearts of lead.
My letters writ, are sent. And back comes no
Assent. The Queen will not relent. I'm told
If I had brought back gold, not mere report,
Her doors and then her arms would ope for me.
Meantime I see my son, my little Wat,
No longer little he, is grown somewhat.
He laughs now, as lusty little fingers grasp
The coral ring I brought for teething pangs.
And Bess, my Bess, so glad to have me back
She weeps, sweet tears of joyous disbelief,
For she had often thought me dead, it seems,
And given up all hope to see my face.
My face, my changèd face! The looking glass
Reveals a man much weathered, beggared, aged,
And withered. What a relic of a man!

## Cadiz!

I must show her, the one that doubts me most, that I can serve as well as dream. And so I ride twixt towns till I am saddle-sore, mustering a crew for the Queen's *Warsprite,* which is to be my command. I court the Court's most favoured man, the Earl of Essex, Robert Devereux, and join in common cause 'gainst common foe.

Together we will tweak again the beard that Drake once singed. We'll hit the Spaniard where it hurts: *Cadiz!*

The harbour is chocked with rich prizes. But ere our forces fight the Spanish foe, I must contend with Essex, whose pride threatens us far more than hostile shot. Our silken earl is all for Glory bound, forgetting profit also has a claim. But the council of command is barred to me. He would have us wreck our fleet in rash attack. I have me rowed among the fleet to stand and parlay with the captains. I find Essex surrounded by a crew done out in gaudy lace and feathered hats.

One bows and gives his name as John Donne, he says he knows me for a poet and a soldier. 'I read the story of your wondrous voyage, and conceived a great desire to meet with you.'

I nod. 'Well, now you have.'

Lord Essex is set on derring do, while I would caution more for derring don't. 'The merchant ships are ours to take like apples bobbing in a barrel. Therefore, let's not like fools engage in landing troops when we may pick our prize and steal away.'

Says Essex: 'The prize is Glory, aye, and Fame!'

Fie on his fame.

His thirst for fame is quenched when two score of our bravest men are drowned as the waves capsize their landing boats in a vain attempt to take the fortress.

And all the while the laden merchant men are there for the taking.

Come fall, ye heavy rain of deadly shot! Here is my breast and here my head held high. Come fall, if yet you dare, come fly at me.

*Alack! Alack! A fuck! A Christ! Alack!*

A crack that signals… God forsakes me now?

*God's blood!* My God! My God? Art thou still my God?

I've hit the deck. So then, is this the end? I cannot scream enough. The pain has made a ragged ruin of my leg.

I cannot look. The blessed smoke veils my wounds.

Hell's teeth have chewed my flesh. They gnaw my bones!

The smoke clears to show the aftermath.

The rigging blown apart. The shattered mast.

I dare not look what wreckage I've become.

My calf is ribboned by the blast. A thousand piercing shards have rent my skin. The deck's awash with crimsoned foam. *God's blood!*

Alas, 'tis mine, each salty lash of spray reminds me.

210

## Favour

She moves a little stiffly in her seat, as if her dignity pains her now. She is older, of course, but the Ladies of her Bedchamber are as skilled as ever they were in applying the mask that is her face. Her wig is as vibrant orange as it ever was.

I cannot look at her eyes. Not straightaway. I long to find forgiveness there but fear too much what I might see. I fear her fear above all else.

And so I keep my head bowed as I hobble to kneel before her. She holds her hand out. I press her Ring of State to my lips and close my eyes.

'We thought you dead. We heard report that you had sunk. In the harbour at Cadíz.'

'Fear not, Your Majesty. I am unsinkable. My death unthinkable.'

I can hold out no longer. I must read the message of her eyes.

The rigid mask of her face does not relent, but her eyes - I swear - smile at me. A little weakly, a little sorrowfully, and somewhat tearfully.

I am taken aback by this. I had not expected to see moisture there.

The coldness that I had ever ascribed to her, which my absence from her had magnified in my mind, I see no evidence of it now. Either my little jest has warmed her, or she was never so unpitying as I had reckoned her.

'Your leg… troubles you, we see.'

For all the welling throb of sympathy in her voice, I note she makes a point of retaining the regal plural as she addresses me. It is as if she is determined to hold something back. I am to apprehend that there are limits to the degree and extent of her forgiveness. (She will not receive my wife at Court, I know.)

I think I understand that well of emotion visible in her eyes, so too the stab and tremble in her voice. She is sorry for me, but more she is sorry for herself. I came to her a young man, with the world and a glorious future before me. Now I am a halting wreck.

So many dead. And a little bit of death has lodged itself in me.

She feels it closing in on her. The end.

She must be afraid. How can she not be?

She has called me back. Not because Robert Cecil petitioned her (as he assures me that he did). Nor am I recalled to reward me for my feats at Cadíz. Nor even to secure future prizes with which she may fortify her defences… no, she has called me back because I am the only one who can make her forget her fear. I am the one who makes her smile. I must not disappoint her in this.

'I shall not be dancing the galliard at the next Revels, Your Majesty.'

'You never were a great dancer, Water.'

Something like a dance trips through my heart. It feels like a galliard: fast, convoluted, skipping steps. By her use of her old nickname for me, she signals that I am forgiven. To the extent that I can be.

'Then 'tis no great loss, Majesty.'

She bows her head minutely in approval and gestures for me to rise to my feet. Then, with a great show of solicitude, she has a chair brought for me and placed by her side.

'You were always more for the sedentary pleasures. Cards and dice. Methinks I saw you at the gaming table oft enough.'

'Aye. I will own it.'

She smiles as a witticism occurs to her: 'Indeed you shall own it. All of it. As a sign of our favour, we grant you the monopoly on playing cards. It is the only one you lack, I think?'

I bow at her gracious teasing.

'It is most appropriate. No hand shall be played without some part of it passing through your hands. Cecil…'

She calls for Robert Cecil as once she called for his father.

He bobs forward on his cripple's gait and bows obeisantly. It is wondrous how quickly he can move when he is minded.

'You shall see to it.'

He bobs back to take his place again in a line of courtiers and ministers.

I do not like the nose twitching into a snarl and the curling lip I see on the face of the man at his right shoulder. Can that be, is it truly…?

Henry Howard, the Earl of Northampton?

He is much changed, by which I mean aged. As are we all, I dare say. To judge by his haggard face and crooked stance, the years have treated him less kindly than they have me. I allow the observation to afford me some satisfaction.

I recall his foul breath as he sniggered at Oxford's obscene reflections upon her Majesty's person.

But I will not allow Henry Howard's presence to take away from my triumph. What does it matter to me if he is here? All that signifies is that I am here. At last.

Therefore allow me to savour the moment, if you will.

Admittedly, there is no embrace. The only kiss is formal. And we both sense the coming of a nameless presence larger than us both. I once felt the chill of its shadow over me at Cadíz, as I shivered out my blood on the deck of the *Warsprite*. And now I find it stalks the corridors of Whitehall Palace, and looms large even in the Presence Chamber.

We both feel it. But we will not speak of it.

We will not speak of Death. Though I know that all those about her speak of little else. How can she not hear the deeply reverberating whispers?

And how can she not hear the frantic scratching of Robert Cecil's quill? The palace echoes with it.

The murmuring reaches fever pitch whenever any of the Scottish lords are present, most noticeably the Scottish king's ambassador, Lord Lennox. I do not like the way they gather and loiter, a brimming excitement evident in their feigned assumptions of gravity and respect. Even less do I like to see Henry Howard so thick with them. And is that a letter that he passes to Lennox? A letter for the Scottish king mayhap? I hate to think what scabrous lies are scribbled therein. And hate even more the bold vindictive glare he settles on me as the letter is taken.

*By Christ, she is not dead yet!*

Is this treason that I witness? He is so brazen about it that he makes no attempt to conceal the deed.

Lennox even has the temerity to sound me out. I give him short shrift, as you may imagine.

'I acknowledge only one Sovereign! I am so deeply in love with and in the debt of Gloriana, it would be treason to look for favour elsewhere.'

Afterwards I inform Robert Cecil of the exchange. He commends my fierce loyalty but thinks it better not to trouble Her Majesty: 'She will take it amiss that you were asked at all. And it would not do for her to think you begging thanks.'

I had meant to tell him also of what I espied pass between Henry Howard and Lord Lennox. But I think better of it. Henry Howard is Robert Cecil's ally, after all.

Although I do not entirely trust Robert Cecil, I find that I have warmed towards him of late. There are times when I almost do not think of him as a cripple. I had once thought him a cold and bitter creature. But lately I saw how hard he bore the death of his wife, when she was yet in her prime and their children young. Soon after that, his father died. Blow following upon blow, it seemed more than such a frail-framed man could bear. I saw him broken anew by each fresh grief. I could not fail to be roused to some measure of sympathy.

Mayhap he has manoeuvred against me, and I against him. But such manoeuvrings are part and parcel of the life of a courtier. They are as nothing to the restless motion of the human heart. Each beat reminds us that we are all brothers.

At the Queen's gracious command, I take me to Bath to take the cure. It amuses her (of course it does!) to think of Water being healed by water. The truth to tell, nothing has the power to restore me so much as the renewal of her favour and solicitude. But once I am immersed in the warm sulphurous waters of the spa, it is difficult to haul myself out. I feel that I might dissolve there. And if I were to, I would welcome it. My mind runs melancholy. I think of the spectre that looms over us. I hear the hushed talk of those who eagerly await her death echo in the ripples and drips of the bath house. My own wound is very much insistent too; it itches fearsomely as the curative minerals of the water infiltrate and cleanse it. I cannot help but think what might have become of me if the shot that shattered the mast had struck home a few yards lower and more to the right. In some ways, it would have been a release. To be thrown from the fray in a thousand bloody pieces. Sometimes I long for an end to it all, to the striving, and petitioning, and presenting, and manoeuvring. If only I could take me to Sherborne and let the world go hang.

But, no. It is not possible. Even the house I would retire to is only mine because it has been granted me by my sovereign. Should there come a day when her favour is no more, then I and mine may well be homeless. I must rouse me from the water and be about my life again.

Ah, but the pungent steam that rises from the bathing pool conceals one's farts marvellously.

## Blink

Riding the grounds at Sherborne. The horse's girth divides my legs painfully. I feel the saddle's punch in my bollocks and each jog of the horse sets off a fresh twinge in my damaged leg. I am too old for this. Too old for everything. Except playing Primero with Northumberland late into the night. (Needless to say, Her Majesty's most recent gift to me amuses my old friend: *You have gambled much, Ralegh. And now you have won the very prize of gaming itself!*)

I maintain a stately pace which mitigates the violence of the buffets, but prolongs the period of my suffering.

I rein the horse to a standstill in front of the house I had built on the site of the old hunting lodge. With the river behind, it affords a pleasing prospect to my eye. There is a perfect grace to it, a fitting balance. It is both as grand and as modest as it ought to be; as solid and as delicate; as refined and as robust. It fills its space with propriety and loveliness.

It stirs my heart.

A fleet of ships has gone into its construction. All sold off, one by one, until I have only the *Roebuck* left to my name. And I will sell that too, before too long, for I need more funds still. There is always need of funds.

My life has been a gamble. Lived by the throw of the dice or the turn of the cards. The tricks I learnt in La Rochelle have served me well. But one cannot cozen fate. I had hoped for much from Virginia. And won nothing. Had hoped for even more from Guiana. And lost all. Even from Cadíz, which went our way, I came back with naught but a ravaged leg to show for my labours.

But the game is not played out yet.

My son Wat appears around a towered corner of the house. He is riding a hobby horse. The toy is tied with ribbons that trail as he runs. An imagined crop whips the air behind him as his piping voice shouts stern commands to the invisible army at his back. It is an army, in fact, of one: Will Cecil, Robert Cecil's son, follows loyally. It is good to see young Will back on his feet, for he was sick when he came to stay with us. We thought - Bess and I - in truth it was Bess's suggestion - we thought the country air would do him good. And now that he has no mother, and his father is kept busy with the duties of his office, we thought - Bess thought - he might want for a mother's touch in his sickness. We offered - Bess offered - out of the goodness of her heart. I approved it. It was a good deed. I hoped it might be appreciated. But it is a good deed in itself, and I confess that I am heartily fond of the boy, in a way I could never be fond of his crippled father. And he likes me well enough, and will sit to hear my sailor's tales, those that are fit to tell. He would have me tell of the men without heads, whose faces are set within their breasts. Of the tribes of cannibals that I encountered, and of the fearsome female warriors, the Amazons, who live entirely without the company of men, except when they must choose a mate.

He loves Wat like a brother, and though he is two years the senior, is happy to be lorded over by my more wilful son. It is passing strange and a little shameful to confess, but in my heart I think I like Will better than I do Wat. But Wat is my blood. It matters not how much I like him. It is all for him, everything I do.

Once I was a boy their age. One blink and I am that boy again. The pain in my leg has gone. I run without faltering from the cob-built house along the scented path, past ruffled hens and sun-flecked pigs, towards the sea. Towards life, a future. This.

Blink. And I am back in the saddle, watching my son and his friend play in front of the house I have built.

The flaring light dies in the upper windows.

I feel once more my blasted leg and bollocks. What it is to be alive!

## All will be well

The words spill across a sheet of my best parchment. Black-ink broaching of a virgin field. Aye, it costs me dear to make my will, and will cost me more yet, to have a lawyer cast his eye over it. This constant questing and encroaching, converting what is other to ourselves. It is the way of all things, even to the end. My will neatly inked upon the world.

'Tis passing strange how strong and sudden the compulsion to see this through is. I cannot rest till I have set it all down. It is a settling of accounts, a promissory note from the dead to the living. And though I am not dead yet, I feel Death's presence near. A scavenging dog lurks beneath the table, its teeth sunk into my calf. I feel it dragging me down. Its mordant bite quickens my pen.

Death is a starving, snarling dog beneath my table.

We keep the dog at bay with our sundry scrawlings.

As I write, the grip of Death upon me lessens. I almost forget the wound that made a wreckage of my calf. A kind of peace comes over me. A serene certainty over the dispositions I make. There is no doubt in my mind. I hurry on to finish it.

I lay down my pen.

I sit back and look over my words. After the day's ride, my saddle and my house were foremost on my mind and I have disposed of them as might be imagined. The saddle goes to my brother-in-law, Arthur Throckmorton, in memory of his efforts on our behalf while we were incarcerated in the Tower. The house, of course, will go to Wat. This must be done quickly. This must be done before my death. I will have the lawyer draw up deeds transferring possession to my son forthwith.

Bess looks up from her needlework to rest her eyes. She arches her back against an ache. She catches me watching her and lifts the glove she is sewing for my approval, giving a smile that both craves and bestows reassurance. I feel the restraint in the smile I return. It is a mere kink at the corner of my mouth. I see it mirrored now in her sudden resignation as she resumes her task.

I look back down at the parchment. £500 from the sale of the *Roebuck* will go to my daughter in Ireland, born to me from the body of Alice Gould.

If I die now, all will be well.

The news comes, when finally it comes, in a flood of letters. My friends and enemies alike are falling over themselves to inform me. We all knew this day must come. But never thought this day would come.

Someone, Arthur I think it is, writes that they had to cut the ring of state from her finger with a tiny hacksaw. It leaves a fine line of gold trailings on her skin.

## Theobalds

A touchy bugger, this new king.

I cannot say I care for him overmuch. He is practically a dwarf who seems incapable of walking without leaning on the shoulder of some more strapping fellow. He has surrounded himself with such companions. His eyes caress them in a most arrant and disgusting manner. And they return the compliment by revering him as some kind of living god. There is much whispering. Much closeness of lips to ears. They seem ever only a heartbeat away from suckling on each other's ear lobes. So open is the mutual doting that one can only imagine what fondlings go on when they are ensconced together behind closed doors. For these are all fellows of the Royal Bedchamber. There is no shame about it. Just a sly, unnatural lasciviousness, as if they are impatient for the business of state to finish so they may begin their own private business. They say he takes great pleasure in the hunt. I do not doubt he finds it easier to sit in the saddle than walk upon his weakly legs. Except for the times he has been too lustily buggered by his favourites to sit anywhere comfortably.

The very stink of his depravity emanates from his stunted person. This is what it is to be an Absolute Monarch: one may place one's hands wherever one wishes. But this is a frayed and filthy Absolute Monarch, his quilted doublet coming apart at the seams, and spotted all over with the most dubious and unsavoury stains. The satin of his attire is dulled by a patina of slovenliness. I note, however, that he wears a necklace of diamonds, and that he has pinned another diamond in his hat. Like all princes, he has a fondness for glittering baubles, which is why all princes need men like me, to bring them the treasure that they crave.

I rode hard from Sherborne to Robert Cecil's house, Theobalds, to greet the King, by order of the Privy Council. It may be imagined what pains it cost me. However, I deemed it politic to comply. I needs must embrace this opportunity to impress upon him the value of my service and my loyalty.

I hope to God that he may prove himself worthy of both.

Our meeting does not begin well. He regards me with a sourness of expression that I cannot but take as an insult.

He does not like me because I was dear to the old Queen, he wants to signal his independence from her but in truth he owes everything to her. Mayhap that is why he secretly hates her, and why too he is bound to hate me.

But it is not given to us to fathom the workings of another man's mind. Least of all a man such as this Scottish king, who has presumed to set himself upon our country's throne.

I will not repeat the witless pun upon my name he attempted at our meeting. Indeed his wit is as feeble as his person.

Of course, I see the way the land lies. I know what it signifies that we are summoned to Theobalds. Such a big house for little Robert Cecil. His father built it. And now old Lord Burghley lies confined in an all together more narrow resting placed. Our friend Robert must rattle around in here like a pea in a drum. So now he fills it with the King's entourage, their savage accents clogging up the chambers and echoing in the corridors. If he is to be the English king it ill behoves him to surround himself with so many Scots.

But I will give Cecil his due. He has manoeuvred to place himself at the centre of the new King's court. Two crippled dwarves together, ruling over the whole and hale. I may only hope that he likes well the gift of gloves that my Bess made to him. But still I wonder what he wrote about me in those letters he scratched, what it was that prompted His Majesty to say he had heard rawly of me. There are others, I think, who have poisoned his mind against me. So be it. It is hard to imagine that there would ever be any love lost between us. Put simply, I am not his type.

Aye, it is galling to be the subject of such a sovereign. But subject I am. And will remain. Though it is intriguing to speculate what might have happened if the Queen had failed to incline her drowsy head to his accession as she lay propped up with cushions in her dying days. Her mind being so disordered, as we might expect it to be, she would have given the nod to anything. Had they proposed a monkey or mandrake, she would have assented.

Hence the remark that I let slip at our audience, to which he takes undue offence. I am but replying, and not without wit may I add, to an exceedingly provoking remark of his. What else am I to say when a foreign king expresses his willingness to have taken our country by force of arms, had it been necessary? Other than I wish to God it had been put to trial.

I see the colour flood into his cheeks. A royal flush.

Mayhap I spoke rashly, if not rawly (how I hate to justify the King's feeble quip). But I will not play the hypocrite. I have endured too much for our country's sake happily to see it ruled over by this odd prodigy.

He waves me away, as if I am nothing more than an annoying fly.

## Against attainder

How has it come to this? That I find myself once more inside this place of stone walls and iron bars; of thick oak doors slammed shut by turnkey gaolers; of the scratch and scuttle of small animals in blind corners; of waking in the darkest, coldest hours of an endless night, to shiver on a wooden pallet. To long for sleep, the sweet release of sleep, or something more than sleep; to still the buzzing gnats of thought that swarm inside my head; to sit upright and wonder what that strange inhuman sound is. Only to realise it is my own sobbing.

This place of footsteps and whispers, of whole days spent listening with ear to the door, the heavy dread of abandonment as the steps recede, the quickening of the pulse as they approach. A kind of numbness has descended on me. During the daylight hours at least. Exhaustion has its comforts.

Sometimes I must explain it to myself. Where I am and why. To wit: I am confined within a cell inside the Tower. And on a charge of High Treason.

There is no comfort in familiarity. I had no wish to renew my acquaintance with the lions of the menagerie. Though I note that one - the old lioness Elizabeth - is no more. The guards tell me that she died within days of the Queen.

My friends tell me - yes, I still have friends, and I thank God for them - Laurence Keymis most of all labours on my behalf… Laurence tells me that it is held against me that I did once transfer my property to Wat. They say the King sees it as proof of my guilt, that I did intend even then to commit treasonable acts against him, even before he had ascended to the throne. Knowing that if I were to be found guilty of treason, my estate would be forfeit, as once Babbington's was. That I began my plotting then, while Elizabeth was still alive. That in taking steps against attainder I took my first step against his Crown.

I am told the King believes this. I will give him this. He is deep. To plumb such unsuspected depths in me! Or do I detect the clever, crippled mind of Robert Cecil behind this? What hours Bess wasted in making that gift of gloves for him.

Do they presume to know what was in my heart when I had the deed drawn up? How can they say for certainty what I intended, when I do not know myself? I did it because… Because I am not a fool. Whatever else I may be accused of, I hope no one will ever say I am a fool. I foresaw my loss of favour, that much is true. Not clearly, but like the dim shadow of mortality that haunted the Queen's last days. I hoped against hope that the new king would favour me with his good graces, but I have seen the whirligig of fortune turn and turn again. It raises men up then pulls them down, oft times for no fault of their own.

I did not need to be a traitor to fear that I might be accused of treason. And by the turn-out of events, am I not vindicated?

It is held against me also what I said to Lennox once, that Gloriana was my Queen and I would serve no other, or some such words; but I spoke in temper. I did not like the way they clustered at her Court before she was even in her coffin. Like flies around a rotting fetid corpse. I did not want to see my Queen that way. I spoke in temper. And was I not, then, at that time, being tempted into treason against my still living monarch? Mayhap I was too sharp with Lennox, but can a man be hanged for the sharpness of his tongue?

And also held against me are the words I let slip to James when I welcomed him. It is said that my words had in them something more of menace than of duty. That he pondered and puzzled over my meaning and took it to be that I would have resisted him with arms. And what if that be so? We are in the realm of make-believe. He never did enter England at the head of an army. And I never did oppose him on the battlefield. Can a man be hanged for things that never were, deeds never done?

And now they say that Cobham has confessed! Confessed to what? Let Cobham confess, if he has crimes on his conscience, let him confess them.

They say that he has confessed and that my name is dragged into his confessions.

Damn Cobham with his loose tongue and addled brain!

He is author of all my misfortune.

He alleges that I did plot and conspire against the King. God's blood! What we talk about over cups and cards does not constitute a conspiracy! But he has made full confession, Laurence tells me. He flinches, as if I would strike him for the message that he bears.

He knows that I am given to striking out.

But no, I will not strike my true friends.

But if I could get my hands on Cobham, that would be another matter!

I do not doubt they only showed him the rack and it all came tumbling out. But to drag my name into it? Perhaps we had some fanciful speculative discussions over supper, as one may debate the existence of the soul of man, without, I hope, being found an atheist. I may have made certain remarks that were prefaced with words such as: *It would serve James right if you...* But that does not constitute incitement to sedition, I vouch. And what if we discussed the legitimacy of Arbella Stuart's claim to the throne of England? That is not to say that we meant to put her on it. Aye, I may have said words to the effect, *Give me a real Queen over this queenly King any day.* I cannot recall. But I do not expect to be hanged, drawn and quartered for a piece of wit.

I remember how Oxford did once speak of the Queen's person. Was that treason in him, or simply a bitter man's way of venting spleen? And I do not think we can be blamed for preferring the rule of a gentle, loving, gracious and - one might hope - grateful English Queen, to this grating, prating Scot.

Good Laurence is beside himself on my behalf: 'He claims that you plotted to petition the King of Spain for money. Six hundred thousand crowns!'

'Six hundred thousand crowns? The King of Spain does not have two halpennies to rub together! Where do they suppose he would get six hundred thousand pounds to give to two Englishmen?'

'Aye, it is madness. But that's what he says. That you and he would use the money to stir up sedition throughout the land. To raise armies. So as to place the King's cousin on the throne.'

'Arbella Stuart? I hardly know the lady.'

'It is beyond belief, Sir Walter. As if you would ever go begging to the Spanish King, who has always been your sworn enemy! That you would ally yourself with a Papist monarch!'

Good, Laurence… sweet, loyal, innocent Laurence.

I see it in his eye. The dawning of misery and fear. He has caught, perhaps, some clouding of my own expression. The shifting dart of my gaze away from his. His voice trembles as he asks: 'It is not so?'

'You need ask?'

Joyous relief floods into his expression. It was worth the lie to see the face.

'Cobham must retract his confession. You must go to him, Laurence. You must speak to him. I will tell you what to say.'

But Laurence only hangs his head and will not meet my eye. 'We cannot.'

He says, at length; 'It will not look well.'

### Unravelling

In the night, in the icy, empty hours of the night, I lie shivering on my comfortless pallet.

To see everything that I had worked so hard to win, slipping away from me. My life unravelling.

In truth, I was often drunk when I sat down with Cobham. To that I will confess. And there is a kind of careless anger that comes on a man when he is drunk and in despair. A kind of reckless energy.

I may have let slip a careless word or two. That may have been taken the wrong way by that addled Lord.

Perhaps I was guilty of…

But no. It did not happen. It cannot be allowed to have happened. There were no witnesses.

Perhaps I might have said, as I saw him off in the boat that bore him to his meeting with the Spanish Ambassador, *If the King of England won't favour us, then perhaps the King of Spain will!*

I cannot recall.

If I cannot recall it, I did not say it.

Besides, there were no witnesses to that. I am sure of it.

Cobham must wipe the slate clean with one final retraction, is all. Or I'll be damned.

My poor Laurence. I hear they threatened you with the rack.

I hear you told them what I had said, how I had urged you to talk to Cobham on my behalf.

I hear too how gleefully they leapt on that, taking it as proof of my treasonable guilt.

I do not blame you. I do not count it as betrayal.

To threaten a gentle scholar with the rack! Barbarous! Monstrous! Are we Spaniards now?

This is not how Englishmen behave.

They tortured you, did they, these Puritan gentlemen? In the eye of the Law it is torture, to show a man the rack. I feel sure the court will not look kindly on it. It will sway them to our cause.

Unless…

Unless the King approved it.

If that be so, it were better I had died at Cadiz.

It were better I had been eaten by lagartos in Guiana. Or cannibals. Or drowned at sea. Or that we had never found our way out of the maze of rivers.

If the King approved your torture, Laurence, I am done for.

## The nighttime of the night

There is plague in the city. The church bells toll incessantly. It is rumoured that two thousand died last week. There have been three deaths in the Tower even.

My own father visits me every night. Whether he is a ghost or a dream, I cannot say. I feel that I am awake when I see him, but I do not know how that can be. Have I lost the ability to distinguish between the living and the dead?

He appears to me wearing the priest's cope which he stole from St Sidwell's church when he was once imprisoned there. If it be a dream, this would be the point at which I should awake, knowing it to be absurdly false and impossible. For the cope was cut up and the cloth from it used to make a canopy for my father's best bed. A cope into a canopy. It can no more be in one piece than he can still be alive.

Yet here he is. And here it is too, whole and entire. Upon his back.

But why would my father, who was the most vehement anti-Papist, choose to appear attired in the vestment of a Romish priest?

I think he means to shame me. For his face assumes an expression of sorrowful rebuke.

I want to cry out: *Injustice!*

But am no more able to speak than he is. Though his eyes are marvellous eloquent.

They make me want to protest: *I did not take the Pope's coin!*

He lifts his chin, defiantly. As if to say, that is not the matter at issue and you know it, son.

*I never intended it!*

And now he narrows his eyes to regard me. 'Tis an old-fashioned parental look.

*I do not lie!*

He shakes his head in stern dismay. He is not having any of it.

*I hoped to tease him out. To tease them all out.*

He pulls aside the cope and jabs at his chest with the fingers of one hand. It is like a mummer's show. A pantomime of stabbing himself through the heart.

And now to make his meaning clear, he forms his hand into a grip, as if he is holding an invisible knife. He mimes plunging the knife into his heart. And when he is done, he mimes the wrenching out of the blade and holds his flattened palm out to me, as if he is offering me the invisible knife.

I hear a baby crying. It can only be my son, Damerei, who died in this place. He is calling out to me to join him.

My father, by his gesture, beckons me too.

There is an hour that is the nighttime of the night. What I mean is this: that in its utter blackness, it is to the night what the night is to the day. It is the witching hour of the witching hour, when even witches fear to go abroad and do the Devil's work. It is the hour when ghosts appear to us and bring their prospectuses of death for us to study.

I probe between my ribs with the ball of my thumb. I am looking for a soft yielding spot where I might plunge the point of a blade. It will have to be a long narrow blade, methinks. To slip between the ribs and reach the heart. I have always found it wondrous easy to envision the future, and by envisioning, will it into being. This faculty in me has oft times made me impatient for the dragging hours to pass, so that I may race to the moment that I have imagined. Never more so than now. I cannot wait for dawn, for my keeper to come, so that I may procure the knife I need.

I feel a lifting somewhat of my oppression. I am always more at ease when I have formed a plan, into which I may invest my energies. And it is my particular skill that I am able to rally others to my cause.

I must think what I will say to him. Mayhap, I could ask Laurence Keymis for it but he is too solicitous and will suspect. I cannot ask anyone who loves me.

The keeper has but one tooth remaining to him. It is an estimable tooth, a great tooth even. A tooth that protrudes proudly from the middle of his upper jaw to snag upon his lower lip. He seems to think it a tooth for flaunting. Wherever he goes, he always leads with his tooth. One has the impression that this is a champion of teeth. That it has vanquished all other teeth that dared to venture into his mouth. And now alone possesses the field.

It must be said, it lends a somewhat imbecilic look to his face.

'Here.' I hold out a half crown. He regards it with wonder that quickly turns to suspicion. Methinks he has never beheld such a fortune.

He is not so rash as to approach the coin.

I explain: 'There is something I would have you procure for me. This is to pay for it, and any surplus, you may keep.'

'Procure?'

In truth, he is proving more suspicious than such an evident simpleton has a right to be. Why in God's name does he choose to latch upon that word? He gives it a most indecent imputation. His mouth forms a leer, which the snag tooth does little to enhance.

'I need a knife, a long bladed knife… I find it is the most suitable implement for stirring wine. A long bladed knife. You must be sure that the blade is long and fine. A poniard will do it.'

He shakes his head dubiously. 'I cannot bring ye a weapon, Sir Walter.'

'Not a weapon. 'Tis an implement. One might even call it a utensil. For stirring my wine.'

'You cannot manage with your finger?'

'I think not. It is too much to ask a gentleman to stir his wine with his finger.'

'Must you stir your wine at all, I wonder?'

'I would like to. I have always stirred it. And oft have used a knife. I have one for the purpose but I know not what has happened to it.'

The keeper looks dubious. 'I shall have to ask Sir John.'

'There is no need to trouble the Lieutenant of the Tower with this. It is a trivial matter. Sir John will not thank you for troubling him.'

'No matter. I shall have to ask him.'

'Do you require more money, is that it?'

'No amount of money will induce me to procure for you a dangerous weapon.'

'I have no wish to attack you. You do not suspect me of that?'

'Oh, no, Sir Walter. I have no fear of that! I know you. You are a good man. A great hero. You have done great things for this country. I do not like to see you brought so low. 'Tis not right. But what I fear… I cannot tell you what I fear.'

I see that I will get nowhere with him.

I pocket the half crown. ''Tis not important. Let's say no more about it. And, please, there is no need to mention this to anyone. There's a good fellow.'

He nods uncertainly. That great heroic tooth bites down savagely on his lip.

Later, he brings me my dinner. As always, there is a knife there for cutting meat. The blade is somewhat broader than I had hoped. And weak and flimsy too. Certainly, it could not be used to overpower another man. But for what I have in mind, I think it will do well enough.

I must act quickly.

I probe beneath my linen and find a suitable spot against which to position the blunt tip of the blade. The knife must be held so that the width of the blade is aligned with the direction of my ribs. It is too broad to penetrate sufficiently if the blade is held across the ribs.

It proves harder than I had imagined to manage this. For as I push the blade in, at the first throb of pain, I cannot but release the pressure on the knife. Oh, for the long-bladed knife I had envisioned!

It is easy enough to hold the knife. And I begin to rock on the balls of my feet with keen alacrity. I have great hope that I will be able to go through with it. But no! Each time I try to throw myself down, the blind instinct for survival catches me. I hold out my arms to balance myself.

If I do not act soon, my opportunity will be gone. There is, I realise, only one way to accomplish this. I must close my eyes, so that I do not see what I am about.

First I open my doublet and pull apart the linen shirt beneath. Now I extend my arm in front of me, with the blade of the knife angled back. It is now that I close my eyes.

Yes, in closing my eyes, I make it possible. All I must do is summon my will, and direct my will, towards the accomplishing of my purpose.

A mighty shudder passes through me. A great release of tension and energy. The shudder has a voice. The shudder is a scream that fills my cell and echoes between its cold walls.

This cry is the summoning of my will.

The surging of my last great effort.

It is the cry to deafen and drown out the small rebel part of me that wants to live.

It is the cry that rages against the injustice of an ungrateful Prince.

It is the cry of a pain that can be borne no more. And of a new pain that must be endured before release can come.

It is the last sound I will ever make.

It is the cry that brings the keeper running.

Alas, the blade snaps in the blow. I am cut. I bleed. But it is no mortal wound.

The broken knife is wrested from me.

Before too long my cell is filled with fussing notables. The Lieutenant of the Tower, Sir John Peyton, rushes in. He is followed at some hobbling distance by Robert Cecil. Should I be flattered by their concern? They help me to sit down and send for a doctor.

'This will not do. This will not do at all, Ralegh!' says Cecil.

I see that I am some kind of prize to them. They want a trial of me. I nearly robbed them of it.

Cecil halts at the door as he is leaving and shakes his head at me, as if I am some recalcitrant grammar schoolboy and he my schoolmaster. 'I gave you my friendship.'

He raises an eyebrow sceptically at my protestation. 'You gave me nothing, Ralegh. You looked down on me. You sought to flatter me and control me. You thought, the little cripple will be eating out of my hand if I but condescend to show him a few crumbs of attention.'

'No... I... I came to respect you.'

'You sound surprised. You are always surprised, Ralegh. That is your trouble. For all that you are capable of imagining and envisioning... such a great poet and prospector as you are... you simply cannot conceive what it must be like to walk four paces in my bolstered shoes.'

He is gone, upon his shuffling, limping way.

## So fickle is the vulgar crowd

'You shall be led from hence to the place whence you came, there to remain until the day of execution. And from thence you shall be drawn on a hurdle through the open streets to the place of execution, there to be hanged and cut down alive, and your body shall be opened, your heart and bowels plucked out, and your privy members cut off and thrown into the fire before your eyes. Then your head to be stricken off from your body and your body shall be divided into four quarters, to be disposed of at the King's pleasure. And God have mercy on your soul.'

It is passing strange to hear such words addressed to you. A kind of numbness descends upon you. There is no argument can be offered to such words. I had no argument. The time for arguments had passed.

And so, is this how I am come to this? This blow about to fall? This terrible anticipation of nothingness? This glimpse of only red? Of the universe blotted out by infernal red?

Is it the red silk of my judges that blinds me?

But no, not yet. Not yet this.

I am not come to this, yet.

The ugly crowd cheers as I am led away, forgetful of how once they did cheer me as their champion. I am spat upon and pelted. I am called *traitor, devil, atheist.* And, for good measure, *bugger.*

Though I had lately and earnestly sought to end my life, that crisis in me has now passed. I want to live now. I will do anything to live.

I will write letters, craven letters in which I crave pardon, plead for my life, beg for mercy. Swear loyalty, faithful servant to the noblest prince.

I consign it all to paper with the frantic scratching of my pen. This was what it was all for, I do not doubt. The whole show. The whole trial. To draw those letters out from me.

I write to Bess too. The letter from a dead man to his widow. I write as one surprised by death. Most sorry. Most sorry. My love. God knows. Most sorry I am. Most sorry. All my great determinations come to this. Most sorry.

I urge her to remarry.

And pray to God.

I prepare my soul for Death. With a gallows joke or two.

As always is my way, I put some considerable effort into envisioning the precise moment of my decapitation. I think about the axe blade cutting through my neck. How it will deal differently with the soft flesh, the gristly sinews, and the crunching bones. How my veins will start and spread. I have a wonderfully clear vision of the blood spurting from the severed stump. I see my head roll across the boards of the scaffold.

It is painless to imagine it.

When the pardon comes, and I am told that I mon live after all, it almost is a disappointment.

To owe my reprieve to such a prince. To have begged for it.

And the price I had paid for it - to swear to *him* my loyalty.

He robs me of more than he gives me.

But that small rebellious voice in me that ever clamours for life, that part of me, acquiesces. More, rejoices.

## The companion of my captivity

I take her face in my hands and draw her to the bed. I know in my heart that I must win her again. Or that I must prove myself still equal to her love. If she is to be here with me, the companion of my captivity, then it must be willingly done. Not out of pity for all that I have lost, nor out of loyalty to all that I once was - no, it must be out of love for the man that I still am.

It is not a formula that I put to her. We do not speak of these things. I only take her face in my hands and draw her to the bed.

I taste her lips and probe her mouth with my tongue. My heart flutters like the heart of a virgin. If she would refuse me, stay with me only for duty and form, then I am lost. More lost than ever.

She eases herself back on the bed and aids me in the unbuttoning of our daytime selves.

I am taken aback by the rigour and urgency of my desire for her.

She is all the world to me now, the whole world given human form, and like the world she may come and go as she pleases. You cannot possess the world, only detain a small part of it for a moment. And so I would detain her. If I can. If she consents.

She is my freedom too. All that is left of it. As I travel the short dark distance into her, I am carried away utterly from this imprisoned present. I am taken into the world. I close my eyes. The rocking of our bed becomes the pitch and yaw of a seaborne ship.

Then again, the scent of her hair is my home. So that I am taken away from myself and brought back to myself. Such it is to love.

The softness of her body is my comfort. And yet, and yet… she remains eternally mysterious and other to me.

Every night, I must win her again. I must detain the world one more night.

That first night when we were left alone, Wat sleeping on rugs in the next room, we made a brother for him…

I have reacquainted myself with the animals of the menagerie. I am given free range of the Tower gardens, where I gather herbs for the brews and pottages that it is my pleasure to concoct in my cell. I still have some of the specimens I gathered in Guiana and have perfected the recipe for a Balsam which is efficacious against a great many maladies.

I am even permitted to walk the walls. At certain hours, a crowd assembles in the expectation of seeing me. I do not like to disappoint. And so I wave to them and they cheer me.

I find myself in the interesting position of possessing a certain celebrity. Those who once hated me, or feared or envied me, are content that I am now defeated and contained. They leave me well alone. (Either that, or they are dead themselves.) But there are many others who seek me out. The younger generation come to me, for they would know what life was like under the old Queen. It is gratifying to discover that there are many with whom our current

King's reign rankles somewhat, though they would never go so far as to engage in rebellion or conspiracy. Instead, they would fain look back upon the golden age of Gloriana, whose champion they recognise in me. Wondrous to relate, foremost amongst these younger visitors, is the King's own son, young Prince Henry, who is often in my company.

The Prince is everything his father is not: strong in his person, handsome, sober in his habits, wise beyond his years, modest and moderate in his authority. He hates his father's court of favourites, not least of them, Robert Carr.

I have great hopes for Henry, and from him. I can hope for nothing from his father, only further disappointment. The final blow: James is minded now to deprive my wife and sons of Sherborne, which he intends to give to Carr. He even refused an audience with Bess, when she would beseech him to reconsider. So that she was forced to go unbidden to Hampton Court and wait for him so that she may throw herself upon his mercy. All to no avail.

And I am powerless to act, except that I may show my love for Henry and his mother. And hope, through them, to influence the King.

It is on the Prince's behalf that I have undertook my latest enterprise, which is nothing less than to tell the history of the world until this present day. I have the leisure for it, being here confined.

He looks up to me. I would even say he loves me, for he has upon several occasions had the courage to stand up to his father on my behalf. And he was much moved by my relating of his father's intentions regarding Sherborne, and of his hateful treatment of Bess.

Of my own imprisonment, he said: 'No king but my father would keep such a bird in a cage.'

All the while, my friends are active on my behalf. Not least among them, the Prince's mother, Queen Anna, who appreciates more than any all that I do for her son. She expresses herself marvellous pleased with the action of my Balsam, in which if I could only produce more, I would have a means of enrichment more certain than any foreign adventure.

Good Laurence busies himself too. I see the old familiar gleam in his eye. Lit by the sun of a distant land. He is aglow with thoughts of Guiana once more. There is a plan afoot; and I am the man, the only man, to bring it about. I feel the familiar floodtide surge of blood within. My old heart skips like a wooing gallant at the dancing master's. Sagging sinews tauten anew as they fill with strength and vigour.

I watch the Thames flow by my prison wall, and dare to hope that I may soon be in my element once more. One final throw of Fortune's dice awaits.

Letters are written. Petitions drawn up. We have increasing cause for hope. We receive the news of Robert Cecil's death as the lifting of one more barrier. Though he was small in stature, he bore a grudge the size of the planet. It was this, I think, more than the King's antipathy, that has kept me confined so long. The King has not the fixity of purpose to bear a grudge so long.

## Tidings

Yes, I am Water once more.

And it is fitting that he, the Prince, is wont to swim so often in my element. Even on a cold November morn, he stretches out his lithe and strenuous arms. He plunges his face fearlessly beneath the icy surface, his muscular legs kick. (So unlike his father is he!) He forms his hands into sharp blades with which he scythes and delves and churns the murky waters of the Thames. His body flexes and ripples with a smooth and wondrous flow. If he were painted silver you would think he were some large and marvellous fish. He blows his cheeks out as he holds his breath, then lets loose a stream of dancing bubbles. His body twists and turns, exploring every dimension, with restless freedom.

I bear him up. I, Water. He entrusts himself to me utterly.

Perhaps it is a dream but I think that I am there with him as he swims. And that his fondness for swimming - it is his preferred exercise - is somehow a deliberate compliment to me. A reminder of the old Queen's name for me. The name that told the world not just who I was, but what I was for.

Water. The conduit for wealth, conquest, empire, peace, and fame.

But in my depths I also bear unsuspected dangers.

As the Prince swims in the turbid, turd-silted Thames, other creatures shift their loathsome limbs to be about their business. They swim not in sport or leisure, but in the urgent struggle to exist. Anything that comes into their view is either prey or predator, and they must attack. And so some filthy river rat, scrawny and half-starved, seeing the Prince's sleek form glide past, is heedless of his beauty and his royal grace. Unmoved by the quick, easy motion of his parts.

It bites him.

The Prince, if he is conscious of the bite at all, feels it as a quick, sharp pricking of his skin. He thinks nothing of it. Swims effortlessly away from the source of his sudden pain. It is one more irksome pang in a world that ceaselessly pecks and gnaws at us, even at princes.

In the days that follow, the sore festers and swells. The Prince falls into a fever. He takes to his bed. The royal doctors cluster round him. They stroke their beards, and shake their heads, and cluck like hens. And make trial of every remedy known to them.

The Prince does not improve.

I miss him. I miss his visits, his princely presence in my cell. And when I ask for news of how he fares, my keeper only shakes his head.

One afternoon, I am more surprised than you may imagine to receive a visit from Sir William Waad, now the Lieutenant of the Tower.

'The Queen would have some of your Balsam, Ralegh.'

'I trust Her Majesty is not unwell?'

'It is for the Prince.'

A heartbeat's worth of silence before: 'And so I am their last and only hope?'

'Do you seek to turn the Prince's disease to your own advantage, Ralegh?'

'I do not. You misunderstand. No one loves the Prince more than I.'

'You had better hope that he does not die after taking your Balsam then.'

I retrieve a phial of my cure from its shelf. 'It has no efficacy if poison has been administered.'

'I shall pass on to His Majesty the King your vile insinuation.'

Without a further word he takes the Balsam from me and leaves me to my cell.

That evening Laurence comes with the tidings I most dread. I see from his face how it is. He shakes his head. 'He revived when he partook of the Balsam. He sat up and spoke. Lucidly, as he had not been able to for several days. There was great hope. Even the King spoke your name warmly. But alas… within an hour he succumbed again to the fever. More deeply than before.'

'Do they blame me?'

'They are most grateful to you, I think. The Queen especially. For those last few lucid words. The Prince was able to pray. His soul is with God. He is at peace. It is thanks to you. I am sure that is how they will see it.'

'But is he really dead?'

Laurence bows his head in sorrowful confirmation.

### Further tidings

Bess hands me a letter from my own son, Wat, whom we have sent to Paris for his education.

*Derest farther,*

*We ar havvin a merie tim off it hear. I like Master Jonson verry mutch. He is a moast exelent tewter and guvner. He has tort me meny exselent lesens, too wit.: howe to tel if yure doxy be poxy; howe to telle if your drabs have crabs; howe to tell if youre wenchis be Frenchies. In truth, moast of them arre. Last nite, at my biddinge, he didde drink so much sack that he was enable to wok, or een stande, let alon tok. He wos so ataunt and ded drunk that he knewe not where he was. Yu may be shur there were no lessens laste nit; exepting that I did teech him a leson. I pusht him thru the stretes of Paris in a weellbarowe that I precyurde fo the purpess. I got it of a costermonger's lad. It wos a mery jape. I cryed out too the Cathlicks to com se thiss fine exsampelle of a Croosafix. Thiss morning Master Jonson did not ris from his bed till after noon. Nor wer ther enny lessens tooday on ackownt off his exeding melincollie. Beinge determind to mak gud yuse of my tim, I hav writtin yu this leter. Yure dyootifull sonne, Wat. R.*

Bess only laughs at my despairing groan.

Does he not know how greatly his conduct wounds me? To create a public scandal in a foreign city! Does he not understand? News of this will get back to court. His name is my name too. If he brings himself into disrepute, he damages me too. Everything is in the balance for me now. Though I have lost my greatest advocate in Prince Henry, still, the Queen is much exercised for our cause. She begins to persuade the King that he has need of my unique abilities and knowledge.

As for Ben Jonson, I did not employ him to tutor my son in carousing and blasphemy.

Bess chides me for my severity. 'Was I never young?' She asks.

I will admit to being so young but never, I think, so stupid.

### And yet more tidings

For all his manifold and manifest faults, this King has one great virtue: he is in exceeding debt. And every day, as is the nature of debt, his indebtedness increases.

I remember how he appeared to me when I first saw him. The grubby, frayed tunic and the gleaming diamonds. No truer portrait of a Prince has ever been depicted. He ever wants for ever bigger, brighter diamonds.

How is it that I count this quality of his a virtue, when most consider it a failing? Because a Prince who is in debt will always look for ways out of his debt. He will look to men like me, in other words. Especially a Prince with whom it rankles to go cap in hand begging to his Parliament. That is not how an Absolute Monarch comports himself. He need not beg with me, but only command.

But how can I help him? I who am a prisoner in the Tower? Well, not by remaining a prisoner in the Tower, that is clear enough.

It is not too much to hope. For the world is turned topsy-turvy. Henry Howard is dead, and better still, is posthumously disgraced. It has been discovered that he has long been in the pay of the Spanish King. He and Robert Cecil both. The very thing that they alleged against me, my accusers are now found guilty of. Howard is found to be a murderer too, at the very least an accomplice in murder. The poisonous uncle of a poisonous niece. A poisonous clan, the lot of them. For yes, it is by poison that they killed their victim. Which leads another old adversary of mine, the Attorney General Sir Edward Coke, to go so far as to accuse Howard of Prince Henry's murder. For it is now accepted that there must have been poison administered there, after all.

Did I not say?

And Robert Carr, the King's late favourite, and usurper of my Sherborne home, is mixed up in the same toxic conspiracy, and loses all, including Sherborne.

Aye, topsy-turvy does not come close to it.

There is a movement building. A tendency inclining towards me. Many who kept silent all these long years are suddenly not afraid to speak out on my behalf. Queen Anna ever petitions her husband. Though he is not a King who inspires much affection in his subjects, he would like to think himself popular. So vain and self-deceiving is he, he would do the popular thing if it costs him nothing, and by it he may profit. The King will show himself a greater hearted man than any. He will pardon me. That is the rumour now.

Thirteen long years I dreamed and wished and willed for this moment to come about. It has been the greatest labour of my life, to shape my future in my mind.

In the end, it has all come about through no doing of mine. The world has simply changed around me. All I had to do was stay alive long enough to see it happen. It is passing strange. We seek to be the agents of our own destiny, only to find the future wash up at our feet.

I pace the two rooms of my prison apartment. From time to time, I am allowed to take the air and exercise. I pick herbs from the Tower allotment. Greet the lions in the menagerie. The furthest I may venture from my cell is to stand upon the Tower walls and look out on the river rushing by. No matter. I draw the world to me, as if I were the lodestone of men's attention. My visitors, both loyal friends and curious strangers, bring me tidings from every corner. The courtly intrigues, the global shifts of power, who wages war, who sues for peace.

They are like the messengers in a play, who bring the actors news that turns the drama all about. Noises off. Catastrophes too large to fit upon the stage. Battles, slaughter, miracles and magic. A forest moving. I hear Mr Shakespeare put such a thing in his Scottish play, writ especially for the King's pleasure.

Laurence is a frequent visitor. He spreads out the charts and maps for us to pore over. My gaze skits over the inky lines and wriggles, scanning desperately for a feature or a name that I recognise. I find that I have lost my bearings utterly. It is so long since I was there. For one dread and fantastical moment, I cannot even remember the name of the place that for so long preoccupied me. I must approach it through the old incantation, my finger hovering over the page, as I recite: 'Barquasimeta... Cororo... Maracaiba... Truxillo... Nuevo Reyno... Popayan... Merida... Lagrita... Pamplona... Marequita... Velez... Angostura... Timana... Tocaima... Tunxa... Mozo, City of Emeralds...'

My finger falls upon a strange beast-shaped scribble, like a many-legged insect crawling across the map. 'Until you come at last to... to... to... Mmmm...'

'Manoa?'

'Aye, that's it. Manoa. El Dorado as the Spanish call it.'

Laurence frowns doubtfully. 'But, Sir Walter, you know the King will not tolerate talk of El Dorado. He has called it a myth. He does not want for myths. He wants for gold.'

'And I shall bring him gold. There are rich mines here. Here, where the Caroni River merges with the Orinoco.'

'San Thomé?'

'Why else would the Spanish build a fortress there, unless they had something valuable to defend? Mines, I tell you.'

'The Spanish will not give them up without a fight.'

'I am not afraid of a little skirmish.'

'The King is most insistent that there shall be no engagement with the Spanish.'

'I know. He has a new favourite. The Spanish Ambassador. The world has turned topsy-turvy indeed. A Sarmiento, they tell me. I knew a Sarmiento once. Pedro Sarmiento de Gamboa. He was my guest.'

'He was your prisoner. It is said the Ambassador bears you a deep grudge on his cousin's behalf.'

'Nonsense. Don Pedro was content to enjoy my hospitality. He was even happy to share with me the location of… of…'

I click my fingers to summon the name. But it does not come.

'Let me see. How does it go? Barquasimeta… Cororo… Maracaiba…'

'Manoa.'

'That's right. Manoa. El Dorado as the Spanish call it. I treated him well, Don Pedro. We parted on the most amicable terms.'

'I have heard that the negotiations concerning Prince Charles's betrothal to the Infanta are at a delicate stage. And His Majesty is anxious that we should not do anything to jeopardise the promise of a rich dowry for his son.'

I shake my head. Here's a pretty paradox to consider: England's greatest turncoat is her King. He courts our enemy's friendship for his coin.

My finger falls again, upon a point halfway up the Orinoco. 'Mark it. With an X.'

Laurence does as he is bid.

'Now write the words next the X.'

'The words?'

'Aye. *Gold Mine.* Or you may write *Rich Gold Mine.* Or *Gold Mine Here.* I will leave the exact words to you.'

'There is a gold mine there?'

'There is now, my friend. Or there will be, as soon as you have writ the words. The King wants a mine? Then we must give him one. Once he sees this map, with these words on it, he will release me.'

'But if the words are not true?'

'They are true. If we make them true.'

He does not concur as heartily as I might wish, but gives only a somewhat guarded wince. 'I shall write *G.M..*'

'*G.M.?*'

'Aye, Sir. It may stand for Gold Mine. But… if no mine be yet found it may as easily stand for something else.'

'What else?'

Laurence rolls his quill between thumb and forefinger thoughtfully: 'Gold… *Mentioned?*'

I must slap my thigh at his wit: 'That's cunning. I like that.'

'It is not intended to be cunning, Sir Walter. I mean it only as a precaution. You would not have me commit a fraud?'

'If it lies more easily with your conscience to mark it thus, I do commend it. In any event, see that this map gets to His Majesty. Be sure that he understands perfectly the meaning of your G.M.. I warrant that it means a pardon for that notorious old scoundrel Walter Ralegh!'

Laurence cannot help but smile, even if ruefully. 'I fear His Majesty has made it eminently clear that there can be no question of a pardon, Sir Walter. This is to be only a conditional release. You shall still be under sentence of law. You shall still be a convicted traitor. A condemned man on reprieve. You will have a keeper with you at all times. Your friends will have to pledge your good conduct.'

''Twas the same when Elizabeth released me in order to secure her share of the *Madre de Dios*. I need only fulfil my promise to my Sovereign and the full pardon will follow.'

'Is not this promise somewhat harder to fulfil than that last? Then there was a ship, laden with treasure. In port already.'

'As here is a mine with gold, *here!*, upon the map. See! The very spot is marked with an X! We have no need of El Dorado. We have an X upon a map!'

I fear that Laurence is exhausted. He holds his face in both his hands and sighs.

R.N. MORRIS

**Brave new world**

I do not recognise the London into which I am released.

There are streets now where there were not streets before. And some that were before are no more, or are so transformed that I cannot recognise them.

I cannot even find my former London residence, Durham House. I stand on the Strand and look towards where I know it to be. The view is utterly taken over by the long monotonous facade of the New Exchange, which I am told was all Robert Cecil's doing. I do not contest that it is very striking and modern, and that it obliterates everything that stands behind it. The message of this modern architecture is that all must obey the unbending will of the Master Architect. It is Absolutism in bricks and mortar.

My astonishment is met with equal astonishment in those who pass me by. I am pointed out to children, who cannot take their eyes off me.

'You know who that is, don't you? Old Sir Walter Ralegh.'

'What is he wearing?'

'That was the fashion once.'

'He looks as if he's seen a ghost.'

'No. He *is* the ghost.'

Very droll. It's just taking me a while to get my bearings is all.

Court is barred to me. For I remain a convicted criminal, as Laurence predicted. I have a fellow dog my steps. They say he is my keeper. I think of giving him the slip, for he is rather a dull-witted knave. (I would not mind if he were good company.) Everywhere I go I must explain his presence. I oft times make a jest of it, saying that he is my tailor, or my guardian angel, but he will insist on correcting me. It is most humiliating. As I am sure was always James's intent.

What do they think I will do? Run off? On these legs!

He will not even sit down at the gaming table with me, being something of a Puritan. Mind you, I cannot take the same pleasure in the cards as I once did. No one plays Primero any more. And I will not take a hand in Maw, even if it is the King's favourite. They say it is a Scottish game, but this is just to flatter him. All the Irish devils in Munster used to play it.

I feel as if I have been dropped into a foreign city. One whose inhabitants speak a language that I do not understand. Words coined in the period of my confinement trip easily from their tongues. When I say that I once saw a man eaten by a lagarto, I am corrected (by my son Wat, needless to say): 'You mean an alligator?'

I grip my fist and raise my hand to box his ears. But no, I will save that privilege for a more fitting occasion. I do not doubt that there will be one.

Everyone talks about plays I have not seen. And so I hie to the new Globe Theatre for a performance of Mr Shakespeare's Tempest. I am told that there is matter in it that may interest me. (My puritanical keeper waits at the door for me, and takes a pledge of coin against my return. My finances being what they are, I cannot afford to forgo it.)

The play I find a most novel and startling spectacle. Poetical and dramatical both. Unaccountably, I find that I am in places moved to tears by it. I swear that there is nothing in the performance or the plot to provoke such emotion, it being rather a fantastical entertainment. It is simply, I think, that it is here that I feel most keenly all that I have missed during my long years of imprisonment.

I find my keeper waiting for me with a sour expression. He greets me by turning his back on me, without a word. I am glad of his silence. I do not wish to hear his grating voice and carping sentiments after the music of the play. He wears the style of hat favoured by those of his sect, and is hot and red-faced beneath it. In the clamouring rush away from the theatre, the hat is separated from his head and trampled. Whether it is by accident or not, I cannot say. For sure, its loss provokes a burst of raucous laughter from a group of young wits who press around us. The youths remind me of Wat, but he is not among them. At any rate, my keeper looks at me as if I am to blame.

Miranda's words from the play come back to me: 'O, brave new world, that has such people in't.'

He looks at me as if I am a madman.

## Destiny

I hie to Deptford to see my *Destiny* take shape. She is to be our flagship.

I think I love the smell and clamour of a shipyard even more than I do a harbour, and certainly more than a ship at sea.

What one sees and hears and smells at the shipyard is nothing other than the fabrication of a reality out of a dream. For we are closer to the conception of an ambition rather than its fulfilment. Dream, wish, intention, will. It is here where these things are planed and hewn and coaxed together. The dovetail joint. The driven-in dowel. The abutting of strakes. Thus are the pieces of a dream fitted together. With mallet blows and sawtoothed ratchet. The swish and scratch of sanded paper. The clack of wood against wood. Here the sounds of the men are muted, for their minds are fixed on their labour. From time to time, a snatch of whistled melody loops joyously upwards in celebration of a job well done. The air is scented with sawdust, paint and flaxseed oil. Honest, uncomplicated odours that look only to the future. They are the smells of a world new-made. True, there is also the acrid stench of melting pitch for caulking, but even that, in its fierce, fire-forged pungency, has something pure and perfect and cleansing about it.

A ship in a busy port is only one among so many. Her neighbours may tower over her. Certainly, at sea she will be dwarfed by the vastness of the ocean, her precarious frailty suddenly, shockingly apparent. Whereas here, raised on stocks in a shipyard, with the full extent of her hull evident, she is singularly, magnificently, splendidly enormous. A looming citadel of the sea. We have to crane our necks to take in all of her greatness.

Master Phineas Pett, the famed shipwright himself, comes to greet me with a courteous bow. He is an impressive individual, with a gaze as true and straight as the lines of his industry. He is dressed as a gentleman. With a silver silk tarboosh upon his head, he has about him more the air of a visionary or an alchemist than an artisan, as if he conjures up his ships, rather than hammers them into being. His face is fine-featured, with an intelligent and amused expression at all times. His hands appear rather delicate. He is not a burly man, far from it. I had been told that he is a graduate of Cambridge University. Now that I meet him in person, I can believe it. You might take him for some kind of artist.

'It is a great honour, Sir Walter.'

He gestures to the ship. 'Your *Destiny*. How do you like her?'

'She is very fine. When will she be ready for sailing?'

'Another week should see us finished here.'

My heart throbs at the imminence of it. I had not expected it so soon. 'A week? That is not long.'

'Usually my clients are happy that I am able to deliver their commissions so promptly. My motto is Fast Ships, Quickly Built.'

'Ah yes. Everyone must have a motto. I trust they are well built too?'

'Well enough to earn me a royal appointment.'

'I fear there is much to arrange before we are in a position to sail.'

'No matter. Take as long as you need. Your *Destiny* will await you. You may take her when you are ready.'

'I am grateful to you, Mr Pett.'

'There is just one matter outstanding, Sir Walter. I will not be able to hand over the ship to you until the balance of your account is settled in full.'

'You understand the nature of my enterprise?'

'I think I do. Even so, I must insist.'

'Do you have any conception of the wealth that I will bring back from Guiana?'

'There is a rumour, Sir, that you intend to turn pirate. That you will never return to these shores. That it is your intent to petition the French court for refuge. That you will commence a career of brigandeering out of French ports. It is the talk of all the shipyards and chandleries hereabouts.'

'Is it, by God? I can assure you there is no truth in it.'

'Even so. I must insist on full payment of your account before you sail. I think you will find that I am not alone in this.'

This is a low blow indeed. I know not how these rumours are disseminated. Evidently there is no shortage of unscrupulous individuals who feel entitled to spread baseless lies about matters of which they can have no knowledge. They speculate on what I may or may not do if this or that circumstance should come about. But in no case is it evidence of my intention to do any such thing. It is true that I have had discussions with certain gentlemen connected to the French court. Many people from many lands are eager to meet with the celebrated Walter Ralegh. The King has so constrained my mission with his needless conditions and limitations that I am obliged to seek elsewhere for aid in its execution. He forbids me from engaging with the Spanish forces at San Thomé. Very well. I trust that he has not similarly forbid the entire fleet of French corsairs. In the course of such discussions, certain delicate positions must be negotiated. The sharing out of the gold we will find, or any other booty that may be liberated by our enterprise. If certain of the French gentlemen see fit to make unsolicited offers regarding what I might do if our actions fail to meet with favour from my Sovereign, what am I expected to do? Stuff his mouth with wax? My days of such high jinks are over, I think.

Perhaps I did not refuse such overtures with all the vehemence that I might. Perhaps I may even have appeared to go along with them. This is the nature of diplomacy. It is a necessary stratagem to secure the assurances that I wanted. For all these tittle-tattlers know, the King himself may have approved my policy. I am not saying that he did, but it is very likely that he would, had he known about it. He wants the gold, after all. Mr Pett need not trouble himself. Everything will pass off to the satisfaction of all, and the gold that I will deliver to James will be sufficient for him to forgive the means of its getting. He has proven himself to be a great over-looker of wrongs in the past, provided the price be right. We have only to look at his mother's execution.

I place my hand on Mr Pett's shoulder and meet his steady gaze with its equal. For all his brimming mirth, I can tell that he is a man who puts great store by a steady gaze. He laughs at the world because he believes he has seen straight through it. I must not waver in my assurances: 'You shall have it.'

I look up at the looming hulk of the *Destiny*. Not a single blot or barnacle tarnishes her perfection. Every line is straight, every edge sharp, every surface pristine. She is all potential, an empty vessel indeed.

She stands like the sounding box of some giant instrument, waiting to be plucked.

## Wild weather

I turn my head to puke into a bucket and shift my bones to shit into the same bucket. There is no question of making it to the shitting hole at the bow of the ship. The flux is upon me.

The cabin swims around me. I must trust that we are making good progress. From time to time, Laurence looks in on me. He mops my brow with a vinegary rag. He offers to administer a spoonful of my Balsam. But I must shake my head. I cannot even keep fresh water down.

My tongue is like a weight of leather in my mouth. My lips are stuck together with the dried crust of my last vomiting.

Somehow I am able to part my lips and shift my tongue. 'Canaries yet?'

'Not yet, sir. Alas. The wind is against us. We have been blown back into Plymouth harbour. We must await the tide again.'

I cough up a spoonful of green bile and close my eyes. I hear Laurence haul away my bucket of filthy slops. He cannot suppress the groans of disgust that the task necessarily provokes. But he is so good that he waits until he believes me asleep before giving vent to them.

Dreams. You do not want to know the dreams I have. But the relief I feel at waking from them is short-lived. For always I awake to a cabin that spins and swims around me. I cry out for Laurence, but my voice is too feeble to be heard above the beating of the drummer boy.

But Laurence must know that I need him. For he always looks in on me.

He props me up and mops my brow and squeezes a few drops of water into my mouth. It is all I can take.

'Canaries yet?'

'Alas, no. We set out once more but the winds were against us again. The master will have us put in at Falmouth.'

Falmouth! I felt sure we should be in the Canaries by now.

'How fares the crew? I like not the crew.'

''Tis true, they are a vicious and recalcitrant rabble.'

'Put them ashore.'

'Put them ashore?'

'We will fare better without them.'

'We cannot fare at all without a crew, Sir Walter.'

'Consult with Wat. And the master. As to whom we may keep.'

'If that is your wish.'

The effort of this consultation wears me out. I sink back onto my couch. I hear the clink and slop of the pail as Laurence takes it for emptying.

I dream we are buffeted by a violent storm.

I open my eyes to discover it is no dream. How much later it is I cannot say. The cabin is rocking more violently than ever. A wind howls through the timbers. I hear the lash of rain against the cabin. I grip my couch for fear of being tipped from it. My clothes are drenched as if I have been out in the wild weather.

I call out for Laurence but he cannot hear me over the rage of the storm. I close my eyes once more to wait for it to pass.

It is calm when Laurence looks in on me again. Truth be told, I feel a little better in myself. I am able to sit up without his help.

'We were hit by a storm.'

'I know. I felt it.'

'The Master is hopeful that he will be able to reach safe haven at Cork.'

'Good Christ! How long have we been at sea?'

'It is nearly two months, sir.'

'Good Christ! We have lost the best part of the summer.'

'We have not been blessed with the weather, I fear.'

'Cursed. One of James's witches cursed us.'

'The King has no witches that I know of, sir. He rather is against witches.'

'But he believes in their power. Otherwise he would not take the trouble to warn against them.'

Laurence acknowledges the truth of this with a bow.

'And what will we do in Cork, pray?'

'We must put ashore to take on fresh supplies.'

'Have we eaten up all our stock in getting to Ireland?'

He ventures a smile: 'You seem better in and of yourself, sir.'

'Aye, mayhap I am.'

'Shall I fetch you a little something to eat?'

'Is there anything left?'

'I'm sure I can find you a sweet prune to suck on.'

'Laurence, how does Wat fare? As captain.'

There is a faltering beat before: 'Well. Quite well. He does you proud.'

'He does not seek to ween too boastfully over the Master?'

'Not at all, sir.'

'And the crew? And the other officers? They like him well enough? They respect him, is what I mean.'

'I have no doubt of it.'

'It will be the making of him, this, Laurence.'

'Assuredly so.'

'If he could find the time to visit me, so that we may consult together.'

'He has been much occupied with his duties, sir. But I am sure, now that the storm is passed…'

We are quiet together for a moment.

'Cork, eh? I had thought I had done with Ireland.'

## Oranges in sand

Red, still red. The red is thickening now. I feel it closing in on me. It touches my eyes (which I find I can no longer close). It seeks to infiltrate everything that it touches. This is in its nature. In the nature of all things. I feel it contaminating me.

It is getting harder to summon the moments out of the red. As if whatever memories remain to me now do not wish to be summoned. It is a blessing then, the red? I have no choice but to live my life. Must I be forced to live it again? Perhaps I choose instead to submerge it all in red.

And those moments that I am able to summon. It is harder than ever to understand them.

Something happened. Something that made my world turn red.

Bess? Bess? Can you tell me? Are you there, Bess?

What happened to me?

I remember Wat coming to my cabin. He brings prunes for me to try. No doubt he has been sent by Laurence. But he sits with me for a while. I feel my strength return. He talks a little wildly. I think he has been conversing with some of the gentlemen volunteers. I have not the strength to box his ears. I wait for him to talk himself out.

'You are to remind the men, before we land, of the rules. Our mission depends on it. Discipline. That is the key.'

'It is all very well having rules, father. But the men are somewhat restless. I would not antagonise them. I think if we give them their head in little things, they will be all the more compliant when it matters most.'

'No! You must insist on obedience in all things. There is to be no carnal enjoyment of any woman, be she Christian, or heathen. Upon pain of death. Do you understand?'

'That rule in particular they do not like.'

'You are the Captain. You must see to it that they obey you.'

'Aye, I am the Captain. You're right. And they must obey me. But...' He shakes his head. Thinks better of whatever he was about to say.

Let the red shroud all that passed in Ireland. Too many reminders everywhere I look of all that I have lost. I once had lands there. A vast estate. A castle even. Let the red swallow them up.

There is something clean and uncomplicated about the red. More and more, I feel at peace when I am submerged in it. More and more, I feel it is where I belong.

And yet there is a nameless formless anguish hidden within it. And the deeper I go into the red, the more I am consumed by that anguish.

We reach the Canaries, at last. There is some unpleasantness in Lancerota. A brawl or skirmish or some such trouble with the Spanish. Three of our men are killed. We cannot get to the bottom of it. I suspect them of some provocative action. No doubt a Signorina was involved. Or some unwarranted insult. To Wat, I storm: 'This is what happens when my rules are ignored!'

We beat a hasty retreat to Gomera.

I am recovered from my first indisposition, and am able to step ashore without assistance. But others of our company have now fallen sick in their turn. After the unpleasantness in Lancerota, the men are somewhat contrite and conduct themselves in Gomera entirely as I would have them. Not only is there no recurrence of hostility, but baskets of miraculous fruit appear on the quayside for us to stow.

'You see, Wat! The fruits of discretion.'

There are oranges as large as cannon balls, and gleaming, sun-laden lemons, their tips as pert and proud as a whore's nipples. A mound of the plumpest grapes gives off a sweet, ripe smell. There are ruby pomegranates too - indeed, we think them more treasured than rubies! - and the most intensely delicious figs. And what a joyous sound is the clucking of hens as they are loaded aboard!

It is all the gift of the governor's wife. She is a very courteous and gentle lady, whose sympathy to our plight is in part due to her English maternity.

We cover the fruit in sand to preserve it. It has the most marvellous property for drawing moisture. The drier you can keep the fruit, the slower it is to rot. And so we bury the oranges, in full expectation of their resurrection.

And now, at last, we broach the Atlantic. The wind is set fair. But it cannot blow away a putrid stench that I begin to detect. It is not the fruit. It is the men. We are but days out of Gomera when it begins. The flux rages through them. They drop like flies. And soon the decks are filled with huge filthy black flies swarming around the first of the dead.

Weakened from my first sickness, I too fall prey to the fever. And so I take to my cabin again. Liquid shit leaks from my arse before I make it to my bed.

Please, come red, and swallow up that sad and suffering time.

Among those we lose, John Talbot, my secretary. He who stayed with me through all my years of captivity. He begged to be taken with me on my next adventure. I wish I had refused him. Still, it was he who begged me.

Red, swallow it! The terrible unending misery of a sea journey. We are beset by storms. Veritable hurricanoes. I hear iron nails flung against my cabin door. Shrieking devils scratch at the timbers with their claws, straining to prise them apart. The hull protests with a deep creaking and cracking groan. I will give Phineas Pett his due. There are times when I am convinced the ship is about to break up. I picture the beams flying apart as if they suddenly cannot stand their fellows' company. Hungry Ocean consumes them with unseemly eagerness.

Thanks be to God, and Phineas Pett, that it has not happened yet.

And to Bess, whose tireless harrying of her wealthy relatives helped pay the shipwright's bill. We may have scrimped on such things as cordage and supplies, but I am thankful now that we found the means to commission a sturdy vessel. All those benefit dinners where I was brought out to entertain the curious like a monkey in a skull cap - I do not regret a single one of them now. Not even those where I was forced to endure Wat's disorderly conduct.

Thanks be, we have ridden out all storms so far. But there will be more storms. And they will be worse than the last. You may imagine how we are buffeted about, with only a skeleton crew to trim our tattered sails, and barely enough spare rope to stitch together replacement rigging for that we have lost to rot and weather.

The moment comes when you pray to God to end it. To send a thunderbolt, if He will, to strike the main mast and turn the ship into a blazing furnace. Or that we will strike rocks in the dark night and shatter into a thousand pieces. Or that a wave as high as a mountain will crash down on us and bear us to the bottom of the Ocean.

But of course, you do not mean it. You offer up these prayers only as a means to avert the very thing you pray for. For you know that God never grants a sinner's prayers. It is a way of tricking God. If that be blasphemy, then very well, I am a blasphemer after all.

In my defence, I will say that God knows what is truly in our hearts. He does not fall for our tricks. He only pretends to.

And I am quite utterly sick and know not what I am praying for any more. My prayer becomes only this: 'Please God... Please God... Please God...'

I burn. Hell has not fire like this. It is unending torment.

It is only the juice of resurrected oranges that can quench me.

## Journal

My journal of the voyage. I have it here to hand.

It is strange. Passing strange. Each page of the journal that I turn is red. Only red.

### Return

I am carried ashore on the shoulders of my men. They lower me to the ground with trembling care. My feet sink into the sand of the bay. My calves quake prodigiously. I fear for a moment that I will faint. Or that the flux will come upon me again. A chair is brought for me.

I recognise some of those who come to greet me. The lines of their facial tattoos cross-hatched with wrinkles that deepen as they smile. Such smiles. Here is the real gold of this country, the love and honour of her people. I ask after some of the caciques who entertained me on my last trip. They are either dead or too old and distant to make the journey.

At the head of our welcoming party I spy that Harry who sailed back with us before. He has forgotten well nigh all the English that I taught him, except for my name which he cries out in aspirate delight: 'H-woté H-rolé!'

A cacique now of his own village, he brings me gifts of tender tidbits to tempt my poorly palate. I have not strength enough, nor teeth, to crunch the pistachios, but the roasted mullet melts easily on my tongue.

I beckon Wat and point him out to Harry. 'This is my son. Walter Ralegh son. You understand?'

Harry looks Wat up and down approvingly. 'H-woté H-rolé son!' He nods and smiles and laughs. As do we all.

Without warning, a great weight of exhaustion descends on me. I find myself thinking of my cabin. I cannot say that it has been either a comfortable or happy place in which to be confined. But there is a couch in it. And more than anything, I want to lie down.

I summon one last burst of energy to confer with Laurence. 'I shall not be coming with you.'

'Sir, this is most…'

'No, it's for the best. I'm too weak. I'll slow you down. I'll wait aboard the *Destiny* for your return. Laurence, I want you to lead the expedition. You are in overall command of the landing force. These are my orders.'

'I, sir? But I'm no soldier, I'm a mere bookish fellow…'

'That's why I am putting you in command. For your wisdom. Wat is altogether too rash and intemperate. You must watch him like a hawk. Stay his hand if he ever seems likely to… well, you know how he is. Avoid the Spanish at all costs.'

'What if they would not avoid us?'

'Do not approach San Thomé. We'll find our own mine easily enough. You have the map. There is a spot marked with an X and the letters G.M., for Gold Mine.'

'I know, Sir Walter. I marked it so myself. Do you not remember?'

I know not why he frowns so confusedly then.

'Don't let the men sleep on the ground. You understand? There are snakes and scorpions on the ground. They must show you everything they would eat before they taste it. Especially fruit. If you don't know what it is, or cannot vouch that it will not give them the flux, or send them blind, they are not to put it near their lips. And you know my prohibition regarding women. If any of them goes with a woman, I give you the authority to kill him.'

'I wish you were coming with us, Sir Walter. I would feel more confident if you were.'

I look closely into his face, hoping by my look to instil in him the courage that he wants. It is this look, more than anything, that robs me of my own last vestiges of strength.

I have no more words for him. Only the mute trembling of my lips caused by the involuntary convulsion of my jaw.

## Nigredo

I sleep through the heat of the day. My dreams are much populated with the shades of the dead. I do not take it for an ill omen. It is simply that I am old. When one is old one has as many acquaintances among the dead as the living. And it is natural that one should dream of one's acquaintances.

In one such dream, Wat appears unaccountably with Sir Francis Walsingham, Queen Elizabeth, the Earl of Essex, that negro who was devoured by an alligator, and my late secretary, John Talbot. Wat's presence angers me beyond reason. I rail at him: 'No! You do not belong with them! Must I box your ears here too?'

Though I do not know where *here* is.

My couch now smells of all my fevered hours spent on it. All these dark and morbid dreams have soaked into it. So that it is almost an abhorrent thing to me, and yet it is the only place afforded to me for relief and release.

The waiting is long and strains my nerves most horribly.

I have the ship sail north to Trinidad, so that I might revisit the Black Lake of pitch. Only now I must be carried to it on a litter.

I want to bring about that part of the Alchemical Operation that precedes the transmutation from dross to precious metal: the Nigredo. The Alchemist must go deep into himself, and in so doing, he causes the utter annihilation of his being. His soul is burnt to cinders and ash, rendered a black stinking residue in the bottom of a pelican vessel. From this, the Gold of transformation will be created.

I understand the theory of it, but not how it is to be accomplished in practice.

I sit on my litter at the edge of the Black Lake. It is as if I am waiting for some sign. At last it comes. All at once the surface of the pitch lake ignites. A soft red glow covers it.

Red. All becomes red. Black no more.

I must have dozed off. The next I know I am back in my cabin. I know not how I was conveyed there.

I have a letter in my hands. Who gave me the letter, I cannot say. It is written in Laurence's hand.

## Will it console you?

Must I read that cursed letter again? Will the blessed red not swallow it forever? Will the paper not grow red, as if a pool of blood has seeped into its fibres? And the ink too. As if the pen that wrote it was dipped in a well of blood.

'Tis naught but a farrago of lies and excuses and mealy-mouthed extenuations.

He seeks to console me! Do not even attempt such a thing! Not you! Not for this loss.

*We buried him with full honours. He lies a hero in a hero's grave...*

Do I want to read such words?

Come, red! Consume them.

*Fearless he led the charge against the Spanish...*

He dares to write such words to me?

*We have routed the Spanish forces entirely and now have possession of San Thomé...*

San Thomé! Did I not expressly forbid them to approach the Spanish whatsoever? And now he boasts that they have possession of their fortress!

Oh, Bess, my Bess! How shall I write to you of this? Will it console you to know that we now have possession of San Thomé, and that your son lies a hero in a hero's grave, and that he died a hero's death?

## Undone

All is dark. I know not whether it is noon nor midnight.

He has returned now. I cannot bear to look at him. I sense his scattered gaze swoop about my cabin, in a frantic search for some scrap of justification. But there is none. There never can be any.

He hangs his head in shame. I will not look at him. But I know without looking that he hangs his head. I hear it in his voice. The angle of his shame constricts his throat. The words emerge, half-choked in despair. I have no sympathy for his despair. I hate his despair. I have my own to contend with. And he is the author of it all.

Red, red… come now and devour him!

I will not look at him. Not even now.

Needless to say, he found no gold. Other than tobacco. I can smell the heady waft of tobacco coming from the hold.

He speaks of certain documents that he thinks will be of interest to me.

'What do I want with documents?'

'They show that the Spanish knew of our coming. They were forewarned. Every detail of our expedition had been discovered to them. Someone had betrayed us…'

'None of this matters.'

'I… I… I…'

'You were to have stayed his hand.'

He cannot justify himself. And so he seeks to turn the blame on the one whom he failed: 'H-h-he… H-he cried out as he led the charge against the fort. Against San Thomé. He cried out…'

'He was not the commander. You were.'

'I could not… control him. And I rather had the impression that you must have… that you… *there is no other mine than this*… That was his cry. The meaning of that I took to be that you approved his action.'

'You have undone me, Mister.'

'I have prepared a letter… to be sent back to the King. It will, I think, justify our action. His Majesty will see, he will have to see, that we did not invite this calamity. The Spanish provoked us. They attacked us. We were obliged to defend ourselves. And, as every general knows, the best form of defence is attack. The King will look with compassion on your loss… He will not blame you. If you would look it over and give it your seal of approval…'

'I will have nothing to do with your poxy letter. You must look to yourself now.'

'I understand. Yes. Quite right. I know what I must do.'

I do not look at him. The sight of him is utterly hateful to me. He has the effrontery to live!

He knows what he must do? Very well. Let him do it. It is nothing to me.

I lie but cannot sleep upon my couch. The spittle dribbles from my mouth and seeps into the stuffing, to join the dreams that have already soaked into it. The boat rocks with a gentle cradling motion. The lap of the water against the hull cries out: *Pity! Pity! Pity!*

A strange dead calm settles on the boat. Until it is ripped apart by the single thunderous crack of gunshot. There are shouts. And the rapid hammer of running feet. A man screams out in violent agony.

I know from which quarter the noises come. And am unmoved.

The door to my cabin bursts open.

'It is Mr Keymis. He has… he is… no more.'

I nod. And the nodding of my head somehow comforts me.

In truth, I care not whether he is alive or dead. It makes no difference to me. His death will not bring Wat back. But at least I will not be called upon to hear his voice again. Even had he not done this, I never was going to look at him again. He was dead to me the moment I received his accursed letter.

No, I do not wish to see him.

So how is it that I see him?

He lies upon his back, pooled in red. The hilt of a dagger projects from his chest. It seems it was not the gunshot that killed him, after all. He bungled that first attempt as he bungled his mission. In the end, he chose to thrust the point of a long-bladed weapon between two ribs. Has he made of his death some kind of message to me? He seeks to elicit my sympathy by reminding me of my own attempt at self-murder, my own darkest nighttime of the night until this moment?

A circle of red seeps outwards from the point where the hilt meets his body, staining his linen. And so he managed the deed more successfully than I did. But then, he is a man of Science. He would know precisely where to position the tip of the blade and how to drive it in.

At last I face his eyes. His gaze is as divergent in death as it ever was. One eye looking back over his ruined life. The other vainly seeking out the hereafter.

### The wings of a man's life

I am told the King does not look with favour on my return. I am told he rather wishes I had stayed out there to die. It confounds him that I am still alive. If I am honest, it confounds me too.

It confounds him more that I am come back. I am a great embarrassment to him. He has promised my head to his Spanish friend, Señor Don Sarmiento. Imagine! He will hand me over to the little Spaniard so that I may be taken to Madrid to be hanged. He rages that he will make good on the promise too. But he knows that it will not play well with the general populace. Even the Privy Council are up in arms against it.

It is somewhat gratifying to see that the public love me now. They have turned their hatred upon Don Sarmiento. In truth, he is an easy man to hate, and when he moves to killing English children in the street, whether accident or not, he does not make himself any more beloved. They hate him too for the arrogant demands he makes of James, and hate James for his craven submission.

Aye, I could have fled. I could have turned pirate as it was bruited that I would. I could have gone to France. The French would have welcomed me.

Assuredly I would have given anything to spare myself the rigours of that return voyage. For I fell sick again with the flux. Sicker than ever I was on the outward voyage. 'Tis a wonder that I had anything left to shit out. I thought I should have died this time. I prayed for it.

As if that weren't enough, the crew mutinied. Scurvy ungrateful scum that they were. I can still hear their mewling plaints. So, they would turn pirate on me, would they? *Why must we go back?* they clamour and whine. *We may make our fortune out on the open wave.* And they complain about the rigging. Tired of mending and making do. By Christ, I wish that I had bought in more rope after all, so that I might hang the lot of them.

No, I do not think the King appreciates all that I went through in order to come back here and give an account of myself. But what else could I have done? I would not have abandoned Bess to her grief. Nor could I have borne it myself alone. I needed to see her. And if she urged me to it, then I would go to France. But only if she urged it.

A man is trapped in his own life. I wished for wings to take flight above my life. But my life is a trap. A trap that has sprung. There is no escape now. I do not have wings. And even if I did, birds may still be trapped in birdlime.

What was it Humphrey once said? The wings of a man's life are plumed with death.

### I am cheered

The world sees things in simple terms. It loves and hates with bold and monolithic passions.

A man must be a hero or a traitor, a villain or a saint. A Jesus or a Judas.

But the truth is, a man may be all these things. Aye, and all at once, in the very same moment.

The people call him Judas now. The man the King sent to arrest me. Sir Lewis Stukeley. Sir Judas Stukeley, they call him.

I see him now. He comes to me out of the red. He is distraught. His hair unkempt. His beard matted. Eyes stark staring. He raves like any Bedlamite. And craves my forgiveness. Does he not know that I have already forgiven him? I forgave him before he even betrayed me. He could no more escape the trap of his life than I could mine.

I forgive him now. Here in this place, whither he has led me with his Judas kiss.

A man may have nothing left to live for, but still be not prepared to die. Or he may well be prepared to die, and yet find that he cannot quite relinquish life.

It is a cold day, but I must not be seen to shiver. My enemies will put it down to fear, not cold. I drank a cup of sack to keep the chill at bay. Dignity, dignity... it is all that is left to me. The time for pleas has passed. All my arguments have fallen on deaf ears. I am accused of infamous and detested deeds. There will be no reprieve. I will not go into the judicial aspect of it. There is no time for that.

But what a crowd has turned out to see me die! It cheers my heart to see - and hear - them. Yes even on such a sad and solemn day as this, I am cheered. I must speak to them. I must find words. I must make myself heard above their roars.

A group of lords call out from a balcony that they cannot hear me. They will come down, for they do not want to miss my speech. I wait for them. They come onto the scaffold to shake my hand one by one. It is most considerate of them. Most heartening and gratifying. I thank them for it.

I must think of my son, Carew. For his sake, I must not die a coward's death. Though I can hardly stand from the pain of my swollen side, I must hold myself upright as I address the crowd.

There is much to say. I do not need to draw my speech out with filibustering. There is enough pertinent matter to keep me here until the end.

I make a point of forgiving them all. I even forgive Sir Lewis Stukeley. Let them not call him Judas on my account.

The axeman is very patient. But I must not keep him waiting any longer.

I lay my head upon a cold, hard cushion. And close my eyes to rest.

### Red

Red, red. I see only red. For an instant. For a lifetime. For a time beyond a lifetime. For I cannot say how long. There is only red.

The red begins to clear. Slowly. Quickly. All at once. Never. I cannot say how. It begins to clear.

I cannot say anything. My tongue is turned to the thick immutable leather of a saddle. Or has someone stuffed my mouth with wax, paying me back for the tricks I once played on my enemies?

To my brother-in-law Arthur Throckmorton I leave my best saddle.

Visions appear in amongst the clearing, fading, drifting red.

Moments. Floating free. I seek to tether them together, to make some sense of them. In vain.

I look for you, my dear. But you're not there. I see only...

An acorn.

An acorn hurtling into oak.

R.N. MORRIS

## ACKNOWLEDGEMENTS

This book would not exist without the encouragement of Michael Jacob and Daniela de Gregorio. They urged me to write it. And when it was written, their enthusiasm did not wane. Thank you, Mike and Dani.

Thanks also to Richard Foreman of Sharpe Books; my agent, Christopher Sinclair-Stevenson; and my wife, Rachel Yarham.

Most of all, thank you for reading my book. If you've enjoyed it, please consider leaving a review somewhere. To find out about my other books, visit my website, rogernmorris.co.uk, where you can also learn about the research that went into this book and sign up to my newsletter. I'm on twitter as @rnmorris. Feel free to email me at contact@rogernmorris – I love to hear from readers.

Printed in Great Britain
by Amazon

60160481R00153